THE OWL ALWAYS HUNTS AT NIGHT

Also by Samuel Bjork

I'm Travelling Alone

THE OWL ALWAYS HUNTS AT NIGHT

Samuel Bjork

Translated from the Norwegian by Charlotte Barslund

Doubleday

LONDON · TORONTO · SYDNEY · AUCKLAND · JOHANNESBURG

TRANSWORLD PUBLISHERS
61–63 Uxbridge Road, London W5 5SA
www.transworldbooks.co.uk

Transworld is part of the Penguin Random House group of companies
whose addresses can be found at global.penguinrandomhouse.com

First published in Great Britain in 2016 by Doubleday
an imprint of Transworld Publishers
Hardback edition published in 2017
Originally published in Norway as *Uglen*
Published by agreement with Ahlander Agency

A CIP catalogue record for this book
is available from the British Library.

ISBNs 9780857522528 (hb)
9780857522535 (tpb)

Typeset in 11/14pt Sabon by Thomson Digital Pvt Ltd, Noida, Delhi.
Printed and bound by Clays Ltd, Bungay, Suffolk.

Penguin Random House is committed to a sustainable
future for our business, our readers and our planet. This book
is made from Forest Stewardship Council® certified paper.

1 3 5 7 9 10 8 6 4 2

One Friday in the spring of 1972, as the vicar of Sandefjord was locking up his church for the day, he received an unexpected visit that made him keep his office open a little longer.

He had never seen the young woman before, but he recognized the young man. He was the eldest son of one of the most respected men in the town, a shipping magnate who was not only one of the richest men in Norway but also a staunch supporter of the church, a man whose generosity had, among other things, made it possible ten years ago to commission the huge altarpiece in roughly carved mahogany which depicted seventeen scenes from the life of Jesus Christ, an altarpiece of which the vicar was extremely proud.

The young couple had a special request. They wished to get married, but they wanted the vicar to perform the ceremony with no one else present. That in itself was not unusual, but the reason behind their request was so peculiar that at first the vicar thought it had to be a joke. Then again, he knew the shipping magnate well, knew how religious and conservative the old man was, and began to realize that the couple were indeed serious. The shipping magnate had been in poor health recently, and rumour had it that he was on his deathbed. The young man now sitting in front of him would soon inherit a huge fortune; his father, however, had attached one condition to his son's inheritance: no outside blood could be mixed with the family's. The woman his heir chose to marry must under no circumstances have children from previous relationships. And herein lay the problem. The young woman with whom the son of the shipping magnate was deeply in love did have children from an earlier marriage. A little girl aged two and a boy aged four. The children would be hidden away, and the vicar could then quietly marry the couple so that the bride would appear to comply with the shipping magnate's demand, and no one would be tempted to try to discover the truth. Was that possible?

This was the plan the couple had come up with: the young man had a distant relative in Australia. She had promised to look after the children until the shipping magnate died. A year, maybe two, and then the children would be brought back to Norway. You never knew, the shipping magnate might reach the pearly gates sooner than expected. What did the vicar think? Could he find room in his heart to help them in their hour of need?

The vicar pretended to ponder their request, but the truth was he had already made up his mind. The envelope the young man had discreetly placed on the desk was fat, and why not help the young lovers? After all, the old shipping magnate's demand was utterly unreasonable, wasn't it? The vicar agreed to wed the couple, and the following week, in a small ceremony held in a closed church in front of the magnificent altarpiece, they were married.

Less than a year later, in January 1973, the vicar received another visit; this time, the young woman came on her own. She was clearly distressed and told him she did not know where else to turn. The old shipping magnate had died, but something was wrong. She had not heard a word about her children. She had been promised pictures, letters, but nothing had arrived, not a single word, and she was starting to doubt if this relative in Australia even existed. The woman also confided in him that the man she had married had not turned out to be what she thought he was. They were no longer on speaking terms, nor did they share a bed; he had secrets, dark secrets, things she could not make herself say out loud; she could hardly bear even thinking about them. Could the vicar help? The vicar calmed her down, assured her that of course he would help her, that he would think things over, and he asked her to return in a few days.

The next morning the young woman was found dead, slumped over the wheel in her car in a deep ravine close to the shipping family's luxurious home on Vesterøya, outside the centre of Sandefjord.

The newspapers hinted that the woman had been intoxicated while driving, and the police did indeed treat her death as a tragic accident.

After assisting the family with the funeral arrangements, the vicar decided to pay the young shipping magnate a visit. He explained, as was the truth, that the young woman had sought him out the day before the accident. That she had been anxious about her children. That something, well, that something did not add up. The young shipping magnate listened and nodded. Explained that, sadly, his wife had been very sick recently. On medication. Drinking excessively. After all, the vicar himself had seen the tragic outcome. Then the young shipping magnate wrote a figure on a piece of paper which he slid across the desk. Surely this town was too small for the vicar? Would he not be better off serving the Lord in a different location, possibly nearer the capital? The vicar rose from the chair, and that was the last time he ever saw the young and powerful shipping magnate.

A few weeks later he packed his suitcase.

He never set foot in Sandefjord again.

The little girl lay as still as she could on the sofa under the blanket while she waited for the other children to fall asleep. She had made up her mind. She would do it tonight. She would be scared no longer. Wait no longer. She was seven years old and very grown up. She would leave once it started to get dark. She had not swallowed tonight's sleeping pill. Just pushed it under her tongue, where she had kept it when she showed Aunt Julia what a good girl she had been.

'Show me.'

Tongue out.

'Good girl. Next.'

Her brother had been doing it for a long time. Ever since the time they had locked him in the beaten-earth cellar. Every night he would hide the pill under his tongue without swallowing it.

'Show me.'

Tongue out.

'Good boy. Next.'

Three weeks in the dark for refusing to say sorry. All the children knew that he had done nothing wrong, but the grown-ups had put him in the cellar all the same. Since that time he had changed. Every night he would slip the pill under his tongue without swallowing it and, as her own pill started to take effect and she grew sleepy, she would see his shadow tiptoe out of the room and disappear.

The little girl waited until she could hear that the other children were asleep before she sneaked out of the house. It was winter now and still warm, though the twilight had settled softly between the trees. The little girl walked barefoot across the yard, keeping to the shadows until she was hidden by the trees. Having made sure that she had not been spotted, she had run along the track between the big trees down towards the gate that bore the wording 'Trespassers will be prosecuted.' This was where she had decided to start her search.

She had heard her brother and one of the other boys whisper about this. An old, ramshackle shed, a small, forgotten cabin on the far side of the estate, but she had never seen it herself. They were woken up at six o'clock in the morning every day and went to bed at nine o'clock every night. Always the exact same routine, no variations, with only two fifteen-minute breaks from lessons, homework, yoga, laundry and all the chores that had to be done. The little girl smiled at the sound of the crickets, and she felt the soft grass tickle her feet as she veered from the path and moved cautiously along the fence towards the place which she, in her mind's eye, had decided must be the likely location of the cabin. For some reason, she was not scared. She felt almost light; the terror would not set in until later; right now she felt happy, free as a bird, all alone with her thoughts in the beautiful forest which smelt so good. She smiled broadly and trailed her fingers over a plant that looked like a star; it was almost like being in one of the dreams she often had when the pills they were given were not very strong. She ducked under a branch and did not even jump when she heard rustling in the bushes a short distance away. Perhaps a koala bear had ventured down from the trees. She giggled to herself and wondered what it would be like to pat one. She knew that they had sharp claws, and that they were not cuddly at all, but she tried to imagine what it must feel like, anyway, the fluffy, warm fur between her fingers, the soft nose tickling her neck. She had almost forgotten why she had come outside, then suddenly remembered and stopped in her tracks when the wall of the cabin came into view only a short distance ahead of her. The little girl tilted her head and studied the grey wooden boards. So it was true. There was a place in the forest. A place where you could hide. Be on your own. She crept cautiously closer to the hut and felt a delightful tingling under her skin as she approached the door.

The little girl did not know that the sight which awaited her would change her for ever, that it would haunt her every single night for years to come: under the blanket on the hard sofa, on the plane crossing the globe after the police discovered the crying children, under the duvet in the soft bed in a new country, where the sounds were different. She knew nothing about this as she reached out her hand towards the wooden handle and slowly opened the creaking door.

It was dark inside. It took a few seconds before her eyes allowed her to see properly, but there was no doubt. At first just an outline, then everything came into focus; he was inside.

Her brother.

He wore no clothes. He was completely naked. Completely naked, and yet his body was covered by . . . feathers? He was curled up in a corner, a birdlike, crooked creature from another world, with something in his mouth. A small animal. A mouse? Her brother was covered in feathers and held a dead mouse between his teeth.

This was the image that would change her life. Her brother turned slowly and looked at her, his eyes filled with wonder, as if they did not know who she was. The light fell through the filthy window across his feather-clad hand, which was moving gradually through the air. His mouth turned into a grin over glistening white teeth as he took the mouse out of his mouth, locked his dead eyes on to hers and said: 'I'm the owl.'

ONE

Chapter 1

2012

Tom Petterson, a botanist, took the camera bag from his car and paused to enjoy the view across the calm fjord before heading up to the woods. It was early October and the cool Saturday sunshine bathed the landscape around him in a pretty glow, soft rays falling across red and yellow leaves which would soon be shed to make way for winter.

Tom Petterson loved his job. Especially when he was able to work outdoors. He had been hired by Oslo and Akershus County to register findings of Dracocephalum, or dragonhead as it was also known, a plant threatened by extinction but which grew in the woodlands around Oslo Fjord. He had received a fresh tip-off via his blog, and that was his task for today: log the number and exact location of newly discovered specimens of this very rare plant.

Dragonhead grew to a height of ten to fifteen centimetres and had blue, dark blue or purple flowers which would wither in the autumn, leaving behind a cluster of brown seeds reminiscent of a cereal grass. The plant was not only rare; it was also home to the even rarer dragonhead sap beetle, a tiny metallic-blue beetle which fed only on these flowers. The miracles of nature, Tom Petterson thought, and could not help smiling as he left the path and followed the route which an observant amateur biologist had sent him. Sometimes – he never said it out loud, because he had been brought up to believe that there was absolutely no God, his parents had been insistent on that, but even so – he could not help

13

marvelling at it: the wonder of creation. The delicate relationship between all things, from the smallest to the biggest. Birds flying south every autumn to nest, vast distances to the same place every year. The leaves changing colour every autumn, turning the trees and the ground into a living work of art. No, he would never say it out loud, but the thought would often cross his mind.

He turned right between two tall spruces and followed a brook up towards the location where the plants were supposed to be, smiling to himself again.

He crossed the brook and came to a complete standstill when he heard rustling in the shrub in front of him. Petterson raised his camera ready to shoot. A badger? Was that what he had heard? This shy animal was nowhere near as common as people thought. A good picture of a badger would be great for his blog, and it would make a nice story, some dragonheads and a badger, the perfect Saturday trip. He followed the noise and soon found himself in a small clearing, but was disappointed not to see any animals.

But there was something in the middle of the clearing.

A naked body.

A girl.

A teenager?

Tom Petterson was so shocked that he dropped his camera and didn't notice it falling into the heather.

There was a dead girl in the clearing.

Feathers?

Dear Lord.

There was a naked teenage girl in the forest.

Surrounded by feathers.

A white lily in her mouth.

Tom Petterson spun around, stumbled through the dense vegetation, found the path, ran as fast as he could back down to his car and called the police.

Chapter 2

Homicide investigator Holger Munch was sitting in his car outside his former home in Røa, deeply regretting having agreed to come over. He had lived in the white house with his then wife, Marianne, until ten years ago, and he had not been inside since. The fat investigator lit a cigarette and rolled down the window of the car. He had had his annual health check a few days ago, and the doctor had recommended, yet again, that he cut down on fatty food and quit smoking, but the fifty-four-year-old police officer had absolutely no intention of doing so, especially not the latter. Holger Munch needed cigarettes in order to think, and thinking was what he enjoyed more than anything.

Holger Munch loved chess, crossword puzzles, maths conundrums – anything that stimulated his brain cells. He would often sit in front of his laptop, chatting to friends about chess games, or solving brainteasers. Just now he had received an email from his friend Juri, a professor from Minsk he had met online some years ago.

There is a metal pole in a lake. Half the pole is in the seabed. A third of it is under water. Eight metres of the pole protrudes above the water. What's the total length of the pole? Best wishes, J.

Munch pondered the answer and was about to reply to the email when he was interrupted by his mobile ringing. He checked the display. Mikkelson. His boss at Oslo Police's headquarters in Grønland. Munch let the mobile ring for a few seconds; he considered taking the call but ultimately decided to ignore it. He pressed the red button and returned the mobile to his pocket. Family time now. That was the mistake he had made a decade ago. He had not spent enough time with his family. He had worked round the clock and, even when he was at home, his mind had been on other things. Because of that he now found himself outside the house where Marianne now lived with another man.

Holger Munch scratched his beard and looked up in the rear-view mirror at the big, pink present with golden ribbons on the back seat. It was his granddaughter Marion's birthday. The six-year-old apple of his eye. The real reason he had agreed to drive up to Røa, although he had sworn never to set foot in the house ever again. Munch took a deep drag on his cigarette and realized he was rubbing his finger where his wedding ring used to be. He had worn it for ten years after the break-up, unable to make himself take it off. Marianne. She had been the love of his life. He had imagined that they would always be together, and he had not gone on a single date since the divorce. He had had opportunities. It had never felt right. But he had done it now, removed his wedding ring. It was in the bathroom cabinet at home. He had not been able to throw it away.

Holger Munch heaved a sigh, took another drag on his cigarette and had another quick look at the pink present. He had probably gone overboard – again. His daughter, Miriam, constantly reproached him for spoiling little Marion, giving her anything she wanted. He had bought her a present which he knew Miriam would disapprove of, but it was something his granddaughter had set her heart on. A Barbie doll with a massive Barbie house and her own Barbie car. He could already hear the lecture. About spoilt children. About the female body and role models and unattainable ideals, but for Christ's sake, it was only a doll. What harm could it do if it was what the little girl wanted?

His mobile rang again; Mikkelson for the second time, and again Munch pressed the red button. When his mobile rang a third time, he was tempted to pick up, because the caller was Mia Krüger. He was extremely fond of his younger colleague, yet still he did not take the call. He had to put his family first. He would call her back later. Perhaps they could have a cup of tea at Justisen sometime tonight? Talking to Mia after the family reunion would probably do him good. He had not spoken to her for ages, and he only now realized how much he missed her.

Six months ago he had gone to bring Mia back from an island off the coast of Trøndelag. She had isolated herself from the world, had no telephone; he had had to fly all the way up to Værnes, rent a car and get the local police to sail him to the island to find her. He had brought with him a case file. It had persuaded her to return with him to the capital.

Holger Munch prided himself on the strength of his team, but Mia Krüger was unique. He had hired her while she was at the police college, still in her early twenties, after a tip-off from the head, an old colleague. Holger Munch had met her in a café, an informal meeting away from police headquarters. Mia Krüger. A young woman in a white jumper and tight black trousers, with long, dark hair almost like an American Indian, with the brightest blue eyes he had ever seen. Intelligent, self-assured and poised. He had been taken with her at once. She appeared to have guessed that he was there to test her, and yet she had answered his questions politely, with a glint in her eye: *do you think I'm dumb or something?*

Mia Krüger had lost her twin sister, Sigrid, many years ago. They had found her dead from a heroin overdose in a basement in Tøyen. Mia had blamed Sigrid's boyfriend for her death and, during a routine search of a campervan by Lake Tryvann some years later, they had happened to bump into him, now with another victim by his side. Mia Krüger had killed the boyfriend with two shots to the chest, a crime of passion. Holger Munch had witnessed the shooting and knew that it could be justified as self-defence on Mia's part, but, as a result of backing her, he had been transferred out of the city as punishment and Mia had been hospitalized. After two years in the sticks, Munch had finally been reinstated as head of the investigative unit in Mariboesgate in Oslo. Munch in turn had reinstated Mia. However, after that first case back on the job, Mikkelson still had concerns. He'd suspended Mia for a second time, with orders not to set foot inside the building until she had seen a psychologist who was willing to declare her fit for duty.

Munch rejected yet another call from his boss in Grønland and continued to look at himself in the mirror. What was he really doing here? It had been ten years.

You're an idiot, Holger Munch. Mia's not the only one who should be seeing a therapist.

Munch sighed again and got out of the car. It had grown colder outside. Summer was definitely over, autumn, too, it would appear, though October had barely begun. He pulled his duffel coat across his stomach, took out his mobile and replied to Juri: *48 metres ;) HM*

He finished his cigarette, picked up the extravagant present from the back of the car, took two deep breaths and slowly made his way up the gravel path.

Chapter 3

The lips of the man with the thin moustache were moving, but Mia Krüger could not be bothered to listen to him. His words failed to reach her ears. She missed the seagulls. The smell of the sea as the waves crashed against the rocks. The silence. Yet again she wondered why she was putting herself through this. Seeing a therapist. Talking about herself. What good would that do? She took another lozenge from her pocket and regretted for the umpteenth time ever agreeing to therapy in the first place. She should have quit on the spot.

Unstable and unfit for duty.

Bloody Mikkelson. He didn't know which way was up; he'd never worked a case, he'd only got the job because he knew how to suck up to politicians.

Mia sighed and tried to work out what the man behind the desk had said; she was clearly meant to respond, but she had not heard his question.

'What do you think?' she said, as she remembered the waiting room filled with magazines whose covers made no sense to her. 'Mindfulness and wellness'. 'Easy ways to fitness'.

'The pills?' the therapist said, possibly for the third time, as he leaned back in his chair and took off his glasses.

It was a sign of intimacy. A signal that she was safe here. Mia sighed and placed the lozenge on her tongue. He really had no clue as to who he was dealing with, did he? Ever since she was a little girl, she had been able to look inside people's heads. It was the reason she was missing the seagulls. No evil to be found in them. Only nature. Waves crashing against rocks. The sound of silence and nothing else.

'Good,' Mia said, hoping it was the right answer.

'So you've stopped taking them?' the therapist said, and put on his glasses.

'Haven't been taking them for weeks.'

'And the drinking?'

'Haven't touched a drop for ages,' Mia said, lying again.

She looked at the clock above his head, at the hands, moving far too slowly, telling her she was doomed to stay here a while longer. She loathed Mikkelson. And this psychologist. But she couldn't blame him. He was only trying to help. And he was said to be one of the good ones. Mattias Wang. She had been incredibly lucky; she had picked a name from the Internet after agreeing to give therapy a try. No way was she going to see one of the people available through the police force. Patient confidentiality at police HQ? Not likely, not for her, not for Mia Krüger.

'I guess we ought to talk about Sigrid?'

Mia had dropped her guard slightly, but now the armour was back on. No matter how nice and empathetic he was, Mia was not here to talk about her feelings. She was here to get back to work. Have the required sessions with a psychologist. Get the piece of paper she needed. *She seems in good health, conversations are meaningful, she is working on her issues. I recommend that she is reinstated to full duties with immediate effect.*

She smiled to herself, and in her mind she gave Mikkelson the finger.

Unfit for duty.

Screw you, had been her first thought, but after five weeks alone in the new flat she had bought in Bislett, surrounded by removal crates she did not have the energy to open, trapped in a body still screaming for the pills she had drugged it with for so long, she had backed down. She had lost everyone she loved. Sigrid. Her mother. Her father. Her grandmother. The only person missing from the cemetery outside Åsgårdstrand was her. All she had wanted was to leave this world. Say goodbye to all this misery. But then Mia had begun to realize that she had grown fond of her colleagues. Being back at work after her solitary existence on the island had made her believe that it might be possible, that life might be worthwhile after all. At least, she was prepared to give it a go. For a while. Her colleagues were fine people. Good people. People she actually cared about.

Munch. Curry. Kim. Anette. Ludvig Grønlie. Gabriel Mørk.

'Sigrid,' the man behind the desk prompted her.

'Yes?' Mia said, as her thoughts wandered back to the girl she had seen leave the consulting room who had had the appointment before her, probably fifteen years separating them, but equally shameful: *that's right, me too. I'm not normal, either.*

'We need to, don't we?'

Sigrid Krüger
Sister, friend and daughter.
Born 11 November 1979. Died 18 April 2002.
Much loved. Deeply missed.

The therapist took off his glasses again, and leaned back in his chair once more.

'We ought to talk about her soon, don't you think?'

Mia zipped up her leather jacket and pointed to the clock on the wall.

'Definitely.' She nodded and gave a small smile. 'But it'll have to wait until next time.'

Mattias Wang looked almost disappointed when he realized the hands of the clock were telling him that the appointment was over.

'Yes, of course,' he said, putting down his pen on the notepad on the desk in front of him. 'Same time next week?'

'OK.'

'Because it's important that . . .' he started, but Mia was already gone.

Chapter 4

Holger Munch felt irritable but also relieved when he entered his former marital home. Irritation at having agreed to this, celebrating Marion's birthday here. Relief because he had dreaded being surrounded by old memories; he could not have known how he would react, but the house he was inside now bore little resemblance to the one he remembered. They had renovated. Knocked down walls. Painted them in different colours. To his surprise, Munch found his old home very attractive and, the more he looked around, the calmer he grew. Nor could he see any signs of Rolf, the teacher from Hurum. Perhaps the afternoon would not be so bad after all?

Marianne had met him in the doorway with the same facial expression as on every other occasion they were forced to spend time together, be it confirmations, birthdays or funerals, with a polite and pleasant *hello*. No hugging or signs of affection, but nor had there been any signs of bitterness, disappointment or hatred in her eyes, which had certainly characterized the early days of their divorce. Just a measured yet pleasant smile: *Welcome, Holger. Why don't you take a seat in the living room? I'm just decorating Marion's cake – six candles. Can you believe she's growing up so fast?*

Munch hung up his duffel coat in the hallway and was about to carry the present into the living room when he heard a high-pitched squeal followed by eager little footsteps coming down the stairs.

'Grandad!'

Marion raced towards him and gave him a big hug.

22

'Is that for me?' the little girl exclaimed, her eyes widening as she gawped at the present.

'Happy birthday.' Munch smiled and stroked his granddaughter's hair. 'So what's it like to be six years old?'

'Not very different, actually, it's almost like yesterday when I was five.' Marion smiled precociously, never once taking her eyes off the present. 'Can I open it now, Grandad, right now? Oh, please may I?'

'We should probably wait until we've sung "Happy Birthday",' said Miriam, who had also come down from the first floor.

His daughter came over to Munch and hugged him.

'I'm glad you could come, Dad. How are you?'

'I'm well,' Munch said, helping her carry the big present into the living room, to a table that held several presents already.

'Oh, they're all for me! Please, please can we open them soon . . .' the little girl pleaded; it was clear she felt she had already been made to wait far too long.

Munch looked at his daughter, who returned his smile. The warmth in her eyes did him good. After the divorce, their relationship had been far from easy, but the hatred his daughter had felt for him all those years was slowly fading.

Ten years. A frosty relationship between father and daughter. Because of the divorce. Because he had been working too hard. And yet, oddly, it was his job that had brought them closer to each other again, almost as if there were some kind of justice in the world. A major case less than six months ago, possibly the most serious his unit had ever investigated, in which Miriam and Marion had been directly involved. The five-year-old girl had been abducted; Munch had feared that it would only widen the gap between them, that his daughter would hold him accountable for this, as with everything else, but the opposite had happened. Miriam had not blamed him once; she was only grateful that the unit had solved the case. A new-found respect. He thought he could see it in her eyes, the way she looked at him. It was different now; she finally understood how important his job was. They had had therapy, both of them, Miriam and Marion, with a skilled police psychologist, to help them process the terrible events, but, luckily, they did not appear to have left deep scars in the little girl. Too young to understand how badly things could have ended, perhaps. Yes, there had been some broken nights, Marion crying after waking from distressing nightmares, but they had quickly passed. It had been worse for her mother, of course, and Miriam had continued with the sessions on her own for a while. Perhaps she still went, he was not sure; they were not so close that she told him absolutely everything, but at least they were heading in that direction. One step at a time.

'Where is Johannes?' Munch asked when they had sat down on the sofa.

'Oh, he was on duty and they called from Ullevål Hospital, so he had to go in. He'll try to get back if he can. It's not easy when you're an important person, you know,' his daughter said with a wink.

Munch reciprocated her wink with a friendly smile.

'The cake is ready,' Marianne announced, entering the living room with a smile on her lips.

Holger Munch watched her furtively. He did not want to stare, but neither was he able to take his eyes off her completely. She made eye contact with him for a moment, and Munch was overcome by the desire to drag her to the kitchen and hold her tight, just like the old days, but he managed to restrain himself. Marion, who also had trouble controlling herself, though for different reasons, provided a welcome distraction.

'Please let me open one? Presents are more important than some silly song.'

'We have to sing "Happy Birthday" and blow out the candles on the cake first, you know that,' Marianne said, stroking her granddaughter's hair. 'Besides, we need to wait until everyone is here, so we can all see the nice things you'll be getting.'

Marianne, Miriam, Marion and him. Holger Munch could not have wished for a better setting for a more pleasant afternoon. However, his ex-wife's words, saying they needed to wait for *everyone*, was like a line from a play, a cue for someone to make an entrance. The front door duly opened, and there was Rolf, the teacher from Hurum, holding a huge bouquet of flowers in his hands and grinning from ear to ear.

'Hi, Rolf,' Marion chirped. She raced to the door and threw her arms around him.

Munch felt a pang of jealousy as he saw his granddaughter's small arms embrace the man he absolutely loathed. He prized the little girl more than anything in the world but, as far as she was concerned, it had always been like this: Grandad on his own. Grannie and Rolf together.

'Look how many presents I've got!'

She dragged Rolf into the living room so that he could admire the display.

'How nice,' he said, stroking her hair.

'Are they also for me?' Marion smiled, pointing to the big bouquet of flowers in his hand.

'No, they're for Grannie,' Rolf said, looking over his shoulder at a blushing Marianne, who was watching them from the doorway.

Munch saw the way his ex-wife looked at Rolf. And it was all over. The good feeling. Playing happy families. He stood up to shake Rolf's hand and watched as the man he despised gave his ex-wife the extravagant flowers and kissed her cheek.

Thankfully, Marion came to his rescue for the second time. Her face now red with excitement, she refused to wait any longer.

'Oh, please can we get that singing over with?' the little girl implored them.

They sang hurriedly. Marion was not paying attention, in any case. She blew out the candles on her cake and attacked her presents.

Less than thirty minutes later the little girl was done, and was sitting quite exhausted in front of her spoils. The Barbie doll had been a big hit. Marion had flung her arms around Munch's neck and, though he had expected a reproachful look from Miriam because he had ignored her wishes – again – it never came. His daughter had merely smiled, almost as a thank-you, and made him feel that everything was all right.

There was one awkward moment after the presents had been opened. Marianne and Rolf were sitting on the sofa on the other side of the coffee table, and there was pressure to engage in conversation, which none of them really wanted. Luckily, Munch was saved by his mobile. It was Mikkelson and, for once, his timing was perfect. Munch made his excuses and went outside, lit a much-needed cigarette and took the call.

'Yes?'

'Have you stopped answering your phone?' an irritable voice grunted on the other end.

'Family time,' Munch replied.

'How nice,' Mikkelson quipped. 'However, I'm afraid I'll have to wreck your family time. I need you.'

'What has happened?' Munch asked, curious.

'A 233. Teenage girl,' Mikkelson continued, less acerbic now.

'Where?' Munch said.

'On the outskirts of Hurum. A botanist found her earlier today.'

Munch took a deep drag on his cigarette. He could hear little Marion laugh on the other side of the door. Someone was chasing her around the house, probably that idiot who had usurped him. Munch shook his head irritably. Celebrate Marion's birthday in his former marital house – what had he been thinking?

'I need you to go there at once.' Mikkelson said.

'OK, I'm on my way,' Munch said, ringing off.

He discarded his cigarette and was about to go back inside when the door opened and Miriam appeared.

'Is everything all right, Dad?' his daughter asked, looking at him with a frown.

'What? Oh yes . . . It's just . . . work.'

'OK,' Miriam said. 'I thought I would just—'

'What, Miriam?' Munch said impatiently, but then checked himself and patted her shoulder affectionately.

'Prepare you for the big announcement,' his daughter said, avoiding eye contact.

'What announcement?'

'They're getting married,' Miriam said swiftly, still evading him.

'Who?'

'Mum and Rolf. I tried telling her that now might not be the best time to announce it, but, well . . .'

Miriam was looking at him now, clearly worried.

'So are you coming inside?'

'I've got a case,' Munch said abruptly, not knowing what else to say.

Getting married? The afternoon had started out with such promise, and he had, well, what had he really been hoping for? He got annoyed with himself. What was he thinking? There clearly was no fool like an old fool. But now he had something else to focus on.

'So you're off?' Miriam said.

'Yes.' Munch nodded.

'Hang on, I'll go and get your coat,' Miriam said, and returned with his duffel coat shortly afterwards.

'You'll have to pass on my congratulations,' Munch mumbled, and made a beeline for his car.

'Call me, won't you? I want to talk to you about something, it's important to me. When it's convenient for you, promise?' Miriam called out after him.

'Of course, Miriam. I'll call,' Munch said, before he jogged down the gravel path, quickly got into his black Audi and started the engine.

Chapter 5

It was barely five o'clock in the afternoon and yet it was nearly pitch black when Holger Munch reached the police cordons on the far side of Hurumlandet. He pressed his ID card against the windscreen and was quickly waved on by a young officer, who looked a little embarrassed at having stopped him.

Munch parked his car on the verge a few hundred metres inside the cordons and stepped out into the cold autumn air. He lit a cigarette and tightened his duffel coat around him.

'Munch?'

'Yes?'

'I'm Olsen. I'm the head of operations.'

Munch shook the glove-clad hand belonging to a tall, broad, middle-aged police officer he did not recognize.

'Status update, please?'

'The victim was found approximately six hundred metres from the road, in a north-north-westerly direction from here,' Olsen said, pointing through the dark forest.

'Who is up there now?'

'Forensics. Pathology. One of yours . . . Kolstad, is it?'

'Kolsø.'

Munch opened the boot of the Audi, took out his wellingtons and was about to put them on when his mobile rang.

'Munch?'

'It's Kim. Are you here?'

'Yes, I'm down by the road. Where are you?'

'I'm up by the tent. Vik has finished and is getting impatient, but I've told them not to move her until you get here. I'll come down to meet you.'

'Great. What does it look like?'

'We won't be getting much sleep for a while. This is one sick bastard.'

'What do you mean?' Munch said, as a sudden, uneasy feeling crept over him.

Holger Munch had nearly thirty years' experience as a homicide investigator under his belt; by now, he had seen most things. He could usually keep a professional distance from the scenes he encountered and, if the statement had been made by anyone other than Kim Kolsø, he would not have worried. Had it been Mia, who allowed herself to get emotionally caught up in every single case, or Curry, who was up and down like a yoyo all the time, he would have brushed it off, but Kim? This did not bode well.

'Do you want me to tell you, or see for yourself?' Kolsø went on.

'Give me a brief summary,' Munch said, sticking a finger into his ear as a patrol car from the crime scene suddenly turned on its siren and passed close by him.

'Are you still there?' he heard Kolsø say.

'Yes, yes. Please repeat what you just said.'

'Teenage girl; sixteen or seventeen, we think,' Kolsø continued. 'Naked. It looks like a kind of, how can I put it . . . ritual? Feathers all around her. And candles . . .'

Munch stuck the finger back into his ear when yet another patrol car followed its predecessor, with flashing blue lights.

'. . . arranged as a kind of symbol . . .'

Kolsø's voice cut out once more. Munch glared at Olsen, who was talking on his mobile while gesturing towards something that was happening near the cordons.

'I can't hear you,' Munch said.

'Some kind of pentagram formation,' Kolsø went on.

'What?'

'Naked teenage girl. Her body twisted into a strange position. Her eyes are wide open. Feathers all over the place . . .'

More static.

'I've lost you!' Munch shouted, sticking his finger into his ear once more.

'. . . a flower.'

'What?'

'Someone stuck a flower in her mouth.'

'A what?'

'You're breaking up,' Kim crackled. 'I'm coming to get you.'

'OK, I'm by the—' Munch shouted into his mobile, but Kolsø had already rung off.

Munch shook his head and took another deep drag on his cigarette as Olsen came up to him again.

'A couple of nosy reporters got a little too close at first, but I think we've finally managed to cordon off the whole area now.'

'Good.' Munch nodded. 'Have you started door-to-door inquiries? The houses up there?'

'Yes.' Olsen nodded in turn.

'Anyone seen anything?'

'Not that I've been told.'

'Right, make sure to include the camping site further up the road. I imagine it's closed down for the winter season, but the caravans are still there. You never know, we might be lucky.'

Olsen nodded again, and disappeared.

Munch put on his wellingtons and found a woolly hat in his coat pocket. He chucked aside the cigarette and lit a fresh one with raw, cold fingers which were barely able to flick the lighter. Good God, surely it had been summer just the other day? It was only late afternoon, and already it was as cold and dark as a winter's night.

Kim came towards him, appearing in between the trees, his face in darkness behind a large torch.

'Are you ready for this?'

Ready for this?

'Stay close behind me. The path is a trip hazard.'

Munch nodded, and followed his colleague towards the path which led up through the woods.

Chapter 6

Miriam Munch was standing outside the flat in Møllergata, wondering whether or not to ring the bell.

Julie's flat. Julie was an old friend who had texted Miriam repeatedly to say that she absolutely had to come. Years ago the two of them had been close; rebellious teenagers, they would hang out at Blitz and volunteer for Amnesty International, believing there was a point in protesting against oppression. That seemed like a lifetime ago now. A different era. Another life. Miriam sighed as her finger slowly approached the doorbell, but she pulled it back and continued to procrastinate. Marion was with Grannie and Rolf. A sleepover. She had insisted on spending the weekend after her birthday there. Johannes was working as usual, their flat was empty and not terribly tempting, but even so she could not make herself ring the bell. It was not as if she had not been to a party since having Marion, for heaven's sake. No, she did have a social life; it was something else that stopped her. She looked down at her shoes and suddenly thought she looked ridiculous. Wearing a frock and pretty shoes. She could not remember the last time she had dressed up like this. She had spent over an hour in front of the mirror at home, trying on different outfits, put on make-up, changed her mind, changed her clothes, removed her make-up, sat down on the sofa, turned on the TV, looking for anything that could make her relax, but she had found nothing. So she had turned off the TV again, reapplied her make-up, had another session in front of the mirror in various outfits, and now here she was. As nervous as a teenage girl, butterflies in her tummy for the first time in ages.

What do you think you're doing?

She shook her head, despairing at herself. *She was happy, wasn't she?* She had repeated this sentence many times in her head these last weeks. *You're happy, Miriam.* You have Johannes. You have Marion. You have the life you wanted. And yet she could not help it – thinking thoughts she should not. She had tried, but they refused to go away. At night, her head on the pillow, just before she went to sleep. In the morning, from the moment she woke up. In front of the mirror in the bathroom when she cleaned her teeth. When she took Marion to school, waving goodbye from behind the large, cast-iron gate. The same thoughts over and over again, and this image in her head. A face. All the time the same face.

No, this won't do.

She had made up her mind.

No further.

She took a deep breath and had started walking quickly down the stairs when the door behind her opened and Julie appeared.

'Miriam? Where do you think you're going?'

Julie had had quite a lot to drink already; she waved a full glass of red wine in one hand and laughed out loud.

'I saw you from the window but thought you might have got lost. Come in.'

Julie raised her glass in a toast and beckoned Miriam up the stairs again.

'I got the wrong floor,' Miriam lied as she walked slowly up the steps to hug her friend.

'Darling,' Julie giggled, and kissed her cheek. 'In you come, in you come.'

Julie – who had once known everything about her – dragged Miriam inside the flat and kicked the door shut behind them.

'No need for you to take off your shoes. Come on, you have to meet everyone.'

Reluctantly, Miriam let herself be ushered into the living room, which was crammed with guests. There were people sitting on the windowsills, sofas and armrests, and on the floor; the small flat was packed to the rafters. The smell of tobacco and illegal substances wafted heavily across the room, across bottles and glasses in all shapes and sizes. A young man with a green Mohican had hijacked the sound system and was playing The Ramones so loud the walls were shaking, and Julie was forced to shout at the top of her voice to get everyone's attention, something Miriam could have done without.

'Oi, Kyrre,' Julie whistled. 'Turn that wannabe punk rock off.'

Miriam said nothing; she suddenly felt overdressed and completely exposed as she stood hand in hand with her friend in the doorway.

'Everyone, hello!' Julie shouted as the boy with the Mohican reluctantly turned down the volume. 'This is my dear old friend, Miriam. She has joined the ranks of the upper classes now, so do try to behave like human beings rather than plebs tonight, will you?'

She laughed uproariously at her own joke and raised her red-wine glass in a toast.

'Wait, everyone, I haven't finished. Miriam is the daughter of a police officer. Yes, you heard right. Her father is the super-detective himself, Holger Munch, so if you don't want the Drug Squad crashing this party, then keep your weed out of sight. Geir, I'm talking to you.'

She pointed her glass in the direction of a young man with dreadlocks and an Icelandic sweater who was slumped on the windowsill with a big joint between his lips and a blissful smile on his face.

'Right, you can turn it up again.' Julie smiled to the young man with the Mohican. 'But if you're going to play punk rock, then please pick something decent.'

Miriam wished more than anything that the ground would open up and swallow her but, luckily, no one seemed to care about what Julie had said. Two seconds later the music was back on and people were bent over their drinks as if nothing had happened, while Julie dragged Miriam through the living room and into the kitchen, where she poured her a brimming glass from a carton of red wine on the kitchen counter.

'I'm so thrilled that you could come,' her friend said, giving her another long hug. 'I'm a little tipsy, sorry.'

'That's quite all right.' Miriam smiled, looking cautiously around the kitchen.

He had not been in the living room, nor was he here. Perhaps she had worried unduly. A party. It was just a party. A party with people her own age, acting like teenagers. That was all it was. Nothing more. She had been to enough formal dinners with Johannes's doctor friends. Spent enough time discussing cars and country cottages, brands of silverware and china. She was wearing the wrong clothes but, apart from that, it was like the old days. Just a party. Nothing else. No harm done.

'Is that true?'

Miriam turned to the spot where Julie had just been standing, but she found someone else in Julie's place.

'Is that true?' the young man in front of her said again with a cautious smile.

'Is what true?' Miriam asked, glancing around the kitchen a second time.

'That Holger Munch is your father? The police officer? He's a homicide investigator, isn't he?'

Miriam felt a certain irritation at the question. She had heard it many times, had dealt with it ever since she was a child – *her daddy is a policeman, we can't tell Miriam anything* – but when she met the eyes of the young man who had asked the question, she realized that he meant well, no hidden agenda. She was no longer eight years old and alone in the school playground. The young man wore a white shirt and round glasses, he had kind eyes and was merely expressing an interest, no ulterior motive.

'Yes, he's my father,' Miriam said, sensing for the first time in a long while that it was actually OK to say so.

'Cool,' the young man with the round glasses said, and sipped his drink, looking as if he wanted to say something more, but found nothing.

'Yes, it is cool,' Miriam said, raising her gaze over the rim of her glass of red wine once more.

'And what do you do?' the young man said.

'What do you mean?' Miriam said, a little defensively. She regretted it immediately.

The lad was shy and a little awkward. He was just trying to make conversation; he might even be trying to hit on her, something he quite clearly did not have much experience of or talent for. She was almost starting to feel sorry for him as he stood there, clutching his drink, hoping that tonight might be his lucky night. He seemed just as out of place as her, his white shirt tucked into pressed trousers and shoes which almost looked like shiny, expensive Italian shoes but which were not, only a cheap copy. She shook her head at herself, ashamed at the last observation. Years ago, she would have been one of the people sitting on the windowsill with a joint between her lips; these days, she could spot the difference between a pair of genuine Scarosso shoes and fakes.

'I'm a mum,' she said kindly. 'I used to study journalism, and I think I might go back, but right now I'm just a full-time mum.'

'Oh, right,' the lad with the round glasses said, looking slightly disappointed.

Miriam Munch was a pretty girl, never short of interested parties or offers. *I have a six-year-old daughter*, however, was usually enough to make them slink away with their tail between their legs. Never mind that she also had a boyfriend.

'And what do you do?' she asked, still kindly, but the air seemed to have gone out of his balloon now and the young man was already looking for someone else.

'He's brilliant at designing posters, aren't you, Jacob?'

And suddenly there he was.

'Jacob, this is Miriam; Miriam, this is my friend Jacob. I see the two of you have already met, how nice.'

He winked at her and smiled.

'Oh, so she's the one you've . . .' the lad with the round glasses said; he seemed a little embarrassed and all at once very keen to get away.

'I think I need another one,' Jacob mumbled, pointing to his drink before he disappeared.

'She's the one? As in . . .?' Miriam smiled.

'Oh, you know,' he said, laughing softly. 'Nice dress, by the way. Good to see that somebody here has style.'

'Thank you,' Miriam said with a small curtsy.

'So?' he said.

'What about it?' she asked.

'Don't you think it's getting a bit crowded here?'

'Far too crowded.' She giggled.

'I've heard they serve quite a decent margarita down at Internasjonalen.' He smiled.

'I never thought I would ever say this' – Miriam laughed – 'but right now I could really do with some tequila.'

'Then that's what we're going to do.' He winked at her, put his drink down on the kitchen counter and calmly led the way through the noisy crowd.

Chapter 7

Investigator Jon Larsen, known as Curry to his friends, tried to get into his flat but struggled to fit the key into the keyhole.

He had promised his fiancée to stop so many times. They had been saving up for over a year. Two thousand kroner every month; Fiji was her dream destination. Three weeks in paradise. Drink exotic cocktails with parasols. Swim with colourful fish in azure seas. Time off from a job she did not really enjoy; only now he had gone and ruined it again.

Curry muttered curses under his breath and eventually managed to get the tiny key inserted into the barely visible keyhole, letting himself into the flat as quietly as he could. He tried hanging up his jacket but missed the peg and stood swaying in the hallway, wondering whether to head for the bedroom or to exile himself to the sofa immediately. It was where he ended up sleeping when he came home in this state, pissed out of his mind, incapable of explaining himself, having squandered their savings. Yet another poker game. A big loss – again. He had had good cards all night but had then gone all in with a straight, only to be met by a flush; the winner grinned at him across the table as his chips found a new owner. He had no choice but to get drunk, surely she could see that?

Shit.

He leaned against the wall, managed to kick off his shoes, staggered into the living room and steered himself in the direction of the sofa.

Fiji, that was her idea, but why did they have to fly halfway round the world for a drink? They could do that at home. Curry stumbled across the living-room floor before crashing his muscular body on to

38

the white Ikea sofa. He put his head on one of the scatter cushions and tried to pull a blanket over himself, only getting it as far as his knees, then was woken up by the sound of his mobile, without realizing that he had even been asleep.

'Hello?'

It was daylight outside.

'Are you awake?' Munch said.

'Awake?' Curry mumbled, unable to lift his head from the cushion.

Munch sounded stressed and bad-tempered. 'We're calling everyone in, can you be here for a team briefing in an hour?'

'On a Sunday?' Curry yawned.

'Are you in a fit state for that?' Munch asked him.

'I'm . . .' Curry tried.

He had been dribbling in his sleep. His cheek was wet. He struggled to get the words down from his brain and out through his mouth.

'The office in one hour?'

'Sure,' Curry mumbled, and managed to half sit up on the sofa before his body sent him a brutal reminder of last night and forced him to lie down again.

'I just need to . . . talk to Sunniva . . . cancel our Sunday walk . . . We were heading up to the hills for a bit of fresh air, but that . . .'

Curry peered anxiously around the living room through eyes he could not open fully for his fiancée, who seemed not to be at home.

'I'm sorry to disturb your romantic plans, but I need you to come in,' Munch said, without sounding at all apologetic.

'What . . . what happened?'

'Not on the phone. One hour, OK?'

'Yes, of course, I'll be there, I just need to—' But Munch had already rung off.

Curry staggered to the kitchen, found three painkillers, which he washed down with almost a litre of water. Stumbled into the shower, where he stood until the hot water ran out.

Once he reached 13 Mariboesgate, he was about to enter the code to the front door when Anette Goli arrived. Curry liked Anette. She was a fairly quiet person, never drew much attention to herself, but she was a gifted lawyer, always straight and no-nonsense. Some people felt that Mikkelson favoured her because she sucked up to him, but he had never seen any evidence of that.

'Morning,' Anette said, stepping in front of him into the lift.

'Yep,' Curry mumbled.

The whisky-and-cigar voice, he could hear it now, and he coughed to clear his throat.

'Late night?' Anette asked, flashing him a droll smile.

'No . . . why?'

'You stink,' Anette said.

'A few drinks, that's all,' Curry muttered, and felt last night return with a vengeance as the slightly wobbly lift started to make its way up to the second floor.

'So, what's up?' he said, attempting a smile.

'Teenage girl found in Hurum,' was all Anette said.

'I see. Any . . . leads?' Curry tried, as the lift reached the second floor.

Anette looked at him with a frown, then shook her head lightly and walked in front of him into the office.

Curry took that as a sign that he was better off keeping his mouth shut today. He walked into the kitchen, where he poured himself a large coffee, which he tried not to spill on his way to the incident room.

He nodded briefly to everyone in the team: Kim Kolsø, Ludvig Grønlie, Gabriel Mørk, the new woman Munch had hired recently – now, what was her name again? Something starting with Y? Short, blonde hair, pretty in her own way, although her clothes were a little too boyish for his taste. Ylva, that was it. Curry found a seat at the back of the room and carefully put his coffee cup on the table in front of him.

Munch had already taken up position by the lectern and was holding the remote control to the projector in his hand. His brow was furrowed and he was not smiling, as he usually did during team briefings.

'Ludvig, lights off, please,' he said curtly, pressing the button in his hand.

A photograph appeared on the overhead screen behind him. Curry jumped when he saw it. The alcohol shakes. They hit him hard now, and he regretted coming to work. He should have lied. Said he was ill. Stayed on the sofa. The sweat started pouring under his shirt; his hands were trembling, he could not control his fingers. Curry clung to his coffee cup, hoping that no one had noticed.

'Yesterday, at 12.40, the body of a young girl was found in the woods on the far side of Hurumlandet,' Munch said. 'Some way beyond the path leading to a place called Haraldsfjellet. The body was discovered by Tom Petterson, a forty-six-year-old botanist who works at the University of Oslo. Petterson had gone there to photograph some plants and stumbled across the girl by accident.'

Curry had seen a lot in his lifetime and thought he must be immune by now, but this was completely different, and his hangover did not help. The naked girl. She looked terrified. Her eyes were wide open. Her body was twisted into an impossible position – a shape really – one arm pointing upwards, the other sticking out strangely from her side.

Munch clicked again. Another picture appeared.

'According to the pathologist, the girl was strangled, possibly at the location where she was found, and posed the way we found her after death. We will look more closely at the details later, but at this stage it's worth noting this . . .'

Munch clicked more quickly now, and a series of pictures appeared on the screen behind him.

'Feathers.'

Another picture.

'Candles.'

Another picture.

'A wig.'

Another picture.

'The posing of her arms.'

Another picture.

'This tattoo. It's a horse's head with the letters A and F below it.'

Curry tried to drink some coffee but was unable to swallow and spat it back into the cup as discreetly as he could. He was struggling to keep up with the briefing. His eyes were swimming, and he was overcome by desperate craving for fresh air. He had still been drunk when Munch called. It was the reason he had managed to make his way to the office without collapsing completely, but now it hit him like an avalanche, and he had to steel himself in order not to flop across the table. Hooch? Had he been drinking hooch? A vague image appeared in his mind, a lift in a block of flats up by . . . Østerås, was it? Some guy with a moustache, women in high heels wearing much too heavy perfume, and a big jug of alcohol on the table. Christ, no wonder he felt like crap. And where was Sunniva? Had she already worked out the truth? Had she gone to stay with her mother again, for good this time?

'And last, but not least, this.'

Munch's voice sounded very far away.

Another picture.

'The flower in her mouth. Her eyes wide with fear.'

'Bloody psycho,' Kim Kolsø hissed behind him.

Curry was unable to hold it back for much longer. All of yesterday wanted up and out of his body. He looked around desperately for the door; he wanted to run outside, but his legs refused to obey him. So he stayed where he was and took deep breaths while continuing to cling to the cup.

'The preliminary pathology report,' Munch continued, taking no notice of the reactions across the room, 'shows a series of peculiarities which we'll also look at individually, but, for now, there's this.'

New pictures. Curry was unable to look at any of them.

'One final picture. Grazing to her knees and elbows. The palms of her hands are heavily blistered. In addition, the girl is strangely thin. Emaciated, in fact, as you can see – practically anorexic – and we think this might be the reason.'

Munch left the last picture on the screen while he flicked through some papers in front of him.

'According to the pathologist, the only substance found in her stomach was pellets.'

'What?'

Now there were more reactions across the room.

'Animal feed?' Ludvig Grønlie asked.

'Yes,' Munch nodded.

'But Jesus Christ . . .'

'Pellets?'

'How is that possible . . .?'

'I don't get it?' said Ylva, the new girl. She looked genuinely confused.

'There's nothing in her stomach that resembles normal food,' Munch said. 'Like I said, this is just the preliminary report. Vik has promised me more tomorrow, so we'll just have to wait for that. Meanwhile . . .'

Munch looked as if he were about to say something, but he was interrupted by his mobile ringing. He checked the display and decided to take the call.

'Hello, Rikard. Did you get my message?' he said.

Rikard Mikkelson. Curry had never heard Munch address their boss by his first name before. He saw that many of the others also exchanged looks and shrugged their shoulders in blank incomprehension.

Munch stuck a cigarette in his mouth and pointed to the balcony to indicate that they could all take a break.

Chapter 8

Mia Krüger was kneeling on the floor in her flat, a line of pill jars in front of her, looking for a reason not to open the lids.

She had paced up and down the empty flat all night, spent hours going back and forth, her arms hugging her cold body, before finally passing out on the mattress in front of the window.

There, she had dreamt happily. About Sigrid. A recurring dream. Her twin sister in a white dress, running through a yellow wheat field, smiling, waving.

Come, Mia, come.

And it had been so soothing. It had made her so calm. So warm. Made her feel that life really was worth living after all. But then she had woken up. To the sound of the city. The noise of reality. To this overwhelming darkness, and now she could not remember why she had agreed to try living. Because she had made up her mind, hadn't she? Out at the house by the sea. On that lonely island, Hitra. To leave this world behind. She had decided a long time ago – did she really have to go through all this again?

Come, Mia, come.

Yes.

At least try?

No.

Come, Mia, come.

Mia was so cold her whole body was trembling. She tightened the duvet around her and reached a thin, white arm towards one of the jars. Tried reading the label, but was unable to see it properly. She had not turned on the light. She couldn't be sure she had paid the electricity bill.

She got up to get a drink.

I don't drink.

She had been good, put all the bottles away, in an attempt at living, being healthy and virtuous; hidden them at the bottom of the laundry basket.

I just hide bottles among filthy clothes I hope to wash, in a washing machine I haven't even connected, in a flat, in a city, in a world I don't want to be a part of.

She caught sight of her reflection in the bathroom mirror and remembered seeing herself some months earlier in one in her house out on Hitra.

Back then, she had barely had the guts to look herself in the eye, but she did so now, staring at herself, a kind of ghost, deep inside the mirror.

Sparkling, blue Norwegian eyes. Long, dark hair cascading over skinny, white shoulders. The scar by her left eye. A three-centimetre cut, a scar that would never disappear. The tiny butterfly she had had tattooed just above her knicker line on her hip after a night of youthful stupidity in Prague. She stroked the small silver bracelet on her right wrist. They had been given one each at their confirmation, her and Sigrid. A child's bracelet with charms, a heart, an anchor, and a letter. M on hers. S on Sigrid's. That evening when the party was over and the guests had gone home they had been sitting in their shared bedroom in Åsgårdstrand when Sigrid had suddenly suggested that they swap.

You take mine, and I'll have yours?

Mia had never taken the silver bracelet off.

Mia Moonbeam.

Her grandmother's pet name for her.

You're very special, did you know that? The other children are fine, but you know things, Mia, don't you? You see the things that other people overlook.

Granny had not been her biological grandmother, yet she had loved her as if she were her own. Sigrid and Mia. Mia and Sigrid. Two gorgeous twins adopted by a middle-aged couple, Eva and

Kyrre Krüger, when their birth mother, who was too young, did not want to, could not look after them.

Mum. Dad. Granny. Sigrid.

Four graves in the same cemetery; all that was missing was hers. Mia poked her arm through the pile of dirty laundry, retrieved a bottle and carried it, still shivering in her underwear, back to the mattress on the floor in front of the line of pill jars.

See a therapist?

Screw that.

She had tried, hadn't she?

Mattias Wang. With his wispy moustache and in the smartest part of Oslo, kind and good, clever and committed, educated and trained to within an inch of his life, and yet he knew absolutely nothing.

'*Do you know what I think, Mia?*'

Mia twisted the cap off the bottle. '*No?*' And raised the bottle to her lips.

'*I think it's your job that's making you ill.*'

She felt the warmth spread down her throat.

'*What do you mean?*'

The feeling took her close to the dream. To Sigrid.

'*You're not like other police officers.*'

Mia took a swig of the bottle and felt the warmth disperse through her body.

'*How is that?*'

She could barely feel the cold now.

'*You care too much. I think it's killing you.*'

Mia tightened the duvet around her, anyway. It felt comforting and soothing.

'*Why, Mattias?*'

Five jars of white pills.

'*All the evil. Everything you have to see. Everything you have to feel. For other people, it's just a job. For you, it's, well, I don't know . . . As if it's happening to you, as if you're the victim of all these cruelties – or do you think I'm being too dramatic?*'

Mia raised the bottle to her mouth again.

'I think you're wrong.'

Five lids to open.

'Obviously, we haven't had many sessions – I can't claim to know you, or know anything at all – but that was my – how can I put it? – my first impression of who you are.'

This time, Mia let the bottle rest against her lips for a long time.

'Shall we carry on next week?'

No.

'I think we can find a way out, don't you, Mia?'

No.

Mia Krüger put down the bottle and calmly stroked the little silver bracelet around her wrist.

No. I don't think so.

And she carefully started unscrewing the lids on the pill jars standing on the cold linoleum floor.

Chapter 9

Holger Munch was in a foul mood as he sat behind the wheel of his black Audi, driving towards Bislett. He stopped for a red light at Ullevålsveien and watched a smiling young couple push a pram across the junction in front of him. He lit a cigarette and shook his head. How had this happened? That had been him not so long ago. Marianne and him. With Miriam in the pram. And why could he not get it out of his head, her getting married again? Surely he had better things to think about. A seventeen-year-old girl. Murdered and left naked in the woods. On a bed of feathers. A flower in her mouth. And he had sucked up to Mikkelson; it was quite possible he was mostly annoyed about that. But from the moment he had stepped inside the white tent in the forest and seen the girl lying there, he had known what he had to do. *He needed Mia Krüger back*. He had a great team, he did, the best investigators in the country, but there was no one like her.

A horn beeping behind him snapped him out of his reverie. The light was green, and the young couple had gone. Munch put the car in gear and turned off down towards Bislett Stadium. Getting married? What on earth was the point of that?

He had just parked the car and was about to get out when his mobile rang.

'Munch?'

'It's Ludvig.'

'Yes?'

'I think we have identified her.'

'Already?'

'I think so.'

48

Munch had told Ludvig Grønlie and his new assistant, Ylva, to check the missing-persons lists.

'Good work. So who is she?'

'We still need to have it confirmed, but I'm fairly sure it's her. Camilla Green. Reported missing three months ago. The description matches – height, eye colour, the tattoo – but something's not quite right.'

'What do you mean?'

'This is why it took some time,' Grønlie continued.

Munch smiled to himself and lit a cigarette. Some time. It was less than two hours since he'd made the request. He felt almost guilty for insisting to Mikkelson that he must have Mia back. He was already in charge of the country's very best investigators.

'Go on?' Munch said, getting out of the car.

'Camilla Green,' Grønlie continued, and it sounded as if he was reading aloud from his screen. 'Born 13 April 1995. Green eyes. Shoulder-length, dark-blonde hair. 1.68 metres tall. Weighs about seventy kilos. Parents dead. Reported missing by Helene Eriksen, she's the manager of a place called Hurumlandet Nurseries.'

'Seventy kilos?' Munch said, taking the case file from his car before locking it. 'Then it can't be her, can it? The girl we found was skinny, don't forget—'

'I know,' Grønlie interrupted him. 'But I've got a picture, and it's definitely her. Camilla Green. Everything else matches. The tattoo and everything.'

'OK, and when did you say she was reported missing?'

'The nineteenth of July. But this is the strange thing, and it explains why it took some time to find her in the register.'

'What is?'

'The woman who reported her missing, Helene Eriksen, must have reported her – er, what's the term, "not missing"? – only a few days later.'

'You mean, she was found?'

Grønlie disappeared for a few seconds, as if he was checking his screen again.

'No, not found. The report was merely withdrawn.'

'But that makes no sense,' Munch said, glancing up at Mia's flat.

Both windows were dark. He had tried calling her, but she had not answered her phone, which was why he had made the decision to drive up to see her.

'. . . but she isn't picking up,' Grønlie said.

'Who?'

'Helene Eriksen. There's a number listed here, but she isn't answering her phone.'

'OK,' Munch said, crossing the street. 'Did you say Camilla's parents were dead? Surely somebody must have been responsible for her? What else do we know about her?'

'That's all I've got for now,' Grønlie replied. 'Only this place, Hurumlandet Nurseries.'

'Which is?'

Munch went up to the entrance and studied the array of doorbells, though he knew it was pointless; Mia would not want people to know where she lived. He took a few steps back and looked up at the windows again. Funny, really. They did not live all that far from each other – his flat in Theresesgate was only a few minutes away – and yet he had never visited Mia at home. Well, it was not funny; more sad, really. He chucked his cigarette stub on the ground, lit another one, and felt guilty again. Ever since Mikkelson had suspended her, they had met up only a few times. Brief, almost superficial meetings at Justisen. Mia had seemed distant, monosyllabic. No wonder, after everything she had been through. A few telephone calls. A few cups of tea. Perhaps he should have done more for her. Been a better boss. And friend. But Mia was like that. She valued her privacy, hated intrusion, and so he had left her alone.

'We haven't found out a great deal yet, but it looks like it's a kind of home for troubled teenagers,' Grønlie went on.

They have a website, but it's a bit—'

'1990s,' Ylva piped up in the background.

'Needs updating,' Grønlie said.

'But it *is* a gardening business?'

'Yes,' Grønlie said. 'As far as we can gather. A place for young people who, well, have problems. They go there to work. That's pretty much all I know for now, that's all I've got.'

'Great,' Munch said. 'Keep trying – what's her name?'

'Helene Eriksen.'

'OK, keep trying until she picks up. And see what else you can find on Camilla Green.'

'We're already on it,' Grønlie said.

'Fine,' Munch said, and rang off.

He tried Mia's number again, but there was still no reply. He stood for a moment, wondering whether to try all the bells without names by them to see if he might chance upon the right person, but caught a lucky break when the door suddenly opened. A young woman in tight, colourful exercise clothes appeared, and Munch just had time to discard his cigarette and slip through the door before it closed again.

It was the second floor, this much he knew. They had walked home from Justisen once, and she had pointed it out.

That's where I live. My new home.

She had been drunk and spoken sarcastically.

Home.

She had not sounded as if she had meant it. Munch was wheezing as he took the stairs up to the second floor. Fortunately, there were only two flats. One had a sign on the door: 'Gunnar and Vibeke live here'. There was nothing on the other door.

Munch unbuttoned his duffel coat, pressed the doorbell twice and waited.

Chapter 10

Miriam Munch had woken up in a strange flat. Not in a strange bed, no. She had not done that; he had been a gentleman, he had not even suggested it. He had fetched a duvet and made up a bed on the sofa in the charming little flat, which looked nothing like her own.

A completely different life, a life that looked like the one she had lived before she got pregnant; a freer life, somehow. Her and Johannes's newly bought flat in Frogner had Italian floor tiles and downlighters in the bathroom. A fridge that could make ice cubes, and a special drawer to keep vegetables fresher for longer. A dishwasher with a digital display. They had electric radiators they could remote-control through their phones, so they could come home to the perfect temperature. A new car – Miriam did not even know what make it was, but it apparently had all the things you are supposed to have these days: GPS, four-wheel drive, airbags front and rear, DVD screens, sunroof and ski box. This flat represented something completely different. Old posters stuck to the walls with Sellotape. A record player in one corner. Clothes everywhere. She could feel a draught from the window as she sat up on the sofa; it was so cold in here that she tightened the duvet around her. She reached for the cigarettes on the coffee table.

October in Oslo. Winter was coming and, normally, she would have turned up the thermostat in the kitchen, which controlled the temperature throughout the flat, so Marion would be warm when she appeared bleary-eyed from her bedroom and sat down at the kitchen table to eat her breakfast, and Miriam's guilty conscience returned. She wasn't a good person, was she? Going to a party. And then to come back here afterwards, sitting up all night on a stranger's sofa, drinking red wine, talking for hours about things she could barely remember ever telling anyone before. About her dad. The divorce. How she had really felt about it. About Johannes. The sneaking suspicion that she had picked him to get away, to rebel, to have a child while she was very young with a man who was the complete opposite of her father.

Miriam lit a cigarette, fumbled for her phone in her handbag on the table, but there was nothing from Johannes. No: *I miss you.* No: *Where are you?* Just a message from her mother: *Is it all right if Marion stays another night? She would like us to take her to school tomorrow.*

Miriam texted a reply: *OK, Mum, sure, give her a kiss from me.* She put down the mobile, stayed huddled under the duvet and studied the posters again.

Animal freedom is our freedom.

Stop Løken Farm.

A poster of a farm in Mysen. A place in Norway where people made money buying unwanted animals, keeping them in cages before selling them for testing abroad.

It was how they had met.

Ziggy.

Miriam felt riddled with guilt again, and yet she could not make up her mind whether to get up, get dressed, take a taxi home to Frogner, greet Johannes when he returned from his shift at the hospital, like a good girlfriend, a good mum, the person she ought to be, or whether to pull the duvet over herself in this tiny but vibrant flat which reminded her strongly of the life she had once led.

Stop Løken Farm.

She had been at the Animal Protection League shelter on Mosseveien, because she felt she ought to do something with her life. Something other than just being a mum. Tove and Kari, two decent women with no other ambition than to care for cats no one wanted. Feed them. Cuddle them. Make sure they knew they mattered. It was simple, but it had been enough for her.

And suddenly he had been there.

*

They had almost turned into giggling teenagers, Tove and Kari, the first time he came, blushing as if some celebrity were visiting them. And to begin with, Miriam could not see why he was any different from the other volunteers.

But she could see it now.

Damn.

Miriam reached for another cigarette, and had just lit it as the bedroom door opened.

'Hi.'

'Hi,' Miriam said.

'Did you get any sleep?'

He rubbed his eyes, walked softly across the floor, and sat down in the chair opposite her, wrapping the duvet he had brought with him more tightly around himself.

'Not much, a little,' Miriam blushed.

'Good,' he smiled, reaching out for a cigarette from the packet on the table.

Ziggy lit the cigarette and tilted his head slightly to one side, studied her over the glowing tip with his fine, smiling eyes, then he opened his mouth and came straight to the point.

'What do you think we should do, Miriam? About this?'

Suddenly, she felt a little queasy. She stayed where she was, studying her cigarette without seeing anything. She had thought that this intoxicating feeling of sitting up a whole night with someone who made her feel like herself would pass.

'I need coffee. Do you want some?'

Please.

'I think I'd better leave.'

I want to stay here all day.

'I understand.' Ziggy smiled. 'I just didn't think I could let you leave without breakfast but, obviously, it's your choice.'

Please stop talking, or I won't be able to go.

'No, I should probably be going.'

'Of course. You must do what's right for you.'

And when she had got dressed and was outside the flat, Miriam Munch realized she had a problem.

She had fallen in love.
It was more than just a crush.
What if I don't contact him again?
She hailed a cab and tried to hold on to this thought all the way home.
It'll pass.
She put her keys down on the console table by the front door, undressed as she walked to the bedroom, slipped under the duvet and was asleep almost before her head touched the pillow.

Chapter 11

Holger Munch had rung the bell again, knocked a couple of times and was about to leave, when the door finally opened and Mia appeared.

'What time do you call this?'

Mia flashed him a wry smile and let him into the flat.

'Four o'clock on a Sunday afternoon?' Munch said.

He took off his shoes and looked in vain for a peg for his coat, so he put it on the floor and followed her into the living room.

'Sorry about the mess,' Mia said. 'I haven't got round to unpacking yet. Can I get you something? A cup of tea? I take it you're still not drinking alcohol?'

Munch looked for an undertone in the last sentence, a hint that it had been too long, that he should have visited her sooner, but he could find none.

'I was just about to have a shower. Do you mind waiting?'

'No, of course not,' Munch said.

'Good. I'll be two minutes.'

Mia disappeared into the bathroom, while Munch stayed in the middle of the living room, not knowing quite what to do with himself. *Haven't got round to unpacking* was an understatement. The place reminded him of his old flat in Hønefoss. He had never unpacked either, never had the motivation to turn the bedsit into a home, and this flat was the same. There was a mattress on the floor under the window with a duvet and a pillow. Stacks of cardboard boxes were dumped about the place. Some looked as if an attempt had been made to open them, before they were closed again. The walls were bare, and there was hardly any furniture.

It looked as if Mia had made an effort at some point. There were Ikea boxes here and there, a white chair partly assembled, the legs still on the floor next to the instructions, a small table she had at least managed to put together. Munch sat down heavily on a low couch, put the case file on the table. He did not like what he saw here.

She looked extremely ill. Again. Almost as bad as on Hitra. He had shuddered at the sight of her then, and he got the same feeling now. Mia, normally strong, brimming with energy and clear-eyed, reduced to a ghostly version of herself. There was a half-empty bottle of Armagnac and a glass on the floor next to the mattress; three empty pizza boxes were stacked in a corner. Munch felt guilty again. He should have visited her sooner. She looked dreadful. The last time they had met, that evening down at Justisen, she had seemed more cheerful, harbouring some kind of hope that things would work out, but now her eyes looked just like they had out on Hitra. Absent. Lifeless.

Munch got up and fetched his cigarettes from his duffel coat in the hallway.

'Can I smoke inside or shall I go out on the balcony?' he called out towards the bathroom, but she had turned on the shower and there was no reply, so he opted for the balcony. He stood outside, freezing, as he watched the last of the daylight disappear, and Bislett Stadium and the rest of the city descend into mute darkness.

A sick bastard.

Munch allowed himself a minute to process it all.

Not in front of the team. Never. Professional. Measured. Calm. Resourceful. It was why he was the boss, he never let the others see what the cases did to him, but he could feel it creeping up on him now; the memory of what he had seen in Hurum disturbed him greatly. They had had many cases. And Munch always felt compassion for the victim, the family; he felt the extreme tragedy that hit people who lost a loved one, but most of them had a rational explanation. Random arguments with unhappy outcomes. Scores being settled among the city's criminal gangs. Jealousy. Sometimes the cases he worked had an element of humanity. Saying that a killing could be human did not make it acceptable, but in his profession – and he never said it out loud, but he often thought it – he was always relieved when there was, ultimately, an explanation he could understand.

Not this time.

This was not human.

Munch fetched his duffel coat from the corridor, went back outside on the balcony and lit another cigarette. He saw Mia slip out of the bathroom wrapped in a towel and disappear towards one of the bedrooms, presumably to a wardrobe, or a box of clothes; he felt a little uneasy again, about everything, the whole situation. Not so long ago, she had chosen to leave reality behind. Hide away, all alone on an island in the sea. And he had brought her back. They had used her because they needed her, and then they had tossed her aside, leaving her unsupported. No, not them. It was Mikkelson who had left her high and dry. The department. The system. Not him. Had it been up to Holger Munch, Mia Krüger would have stayed on doing whatever the hell she wanted, as long as she carried on working with him.

'If you're going to leave the door open, you might as well be smoking inside.'

Mia appeared from one of the bedrooms, smiling, wearing tight black trousers, a white roll-neck jumper and a towel wrapped around her head, which she removed and used to start drying her hair.

'Oh, right, sorry.' Munch smiled. He hadn't thought about it; his mind had been on other things.

He chucked the cigarette into the street below him and went inside, closing the balcony door behind him this time.

'If I were still working as an investigator,' Mia smiled, sitting down on the mattress below the window, 'I would have deduced that if Holger Munch happened to drop by on a Sunday afternoon with a file full of photographs, it meant that something horrendous had occurred in the outside world, that the department was desperate, and that I might be needed back at work?'

Munch sank back into the sofa.

'Unofficially. And it'll cost you,' he said.

'So you want me to grovel, is that it?'

Again Munch searched for an undertone in her voice, but again he failed to find it. She seemed relieved, happy, almost. The dead eyes that had met him in the doorway had regained a little life, and she appeared to welcome his visit.

'So, what have we got?' she said, dropping the towel on to the floor.

'Do you want to see for yourself, or do you want my take on it?'

'I have a choice?' Mia said, taking the file from the table.

Munch saw her eyes change as she opened it and started arranging the pictures on the floor in front of her.

'We found her yesterday morning,' Munch began. 'On the far side of Hurumlandet. A few hundred metres into the woods. A hiker – no, some kind of biologist, a botanist, out photographing plants – came across her, found her like this, in the middle of—'

'A ritual,' Mia said. She sounded distant.

Munch sat quietly as Mia placed the last pictures on the floor.

'Seems like it. But . . .'

'What?' Mia said, without looking up.

'Do you want me to be quiet, or do you want . . .?' Munch said, with a sudden feeling that he was intruding.

'Yes, no, sorry. Carry on, please,' Mia mumbled, opening the Armagnac bottle on the floor and filling a filthy glass to the brim.

'At the moment, as you said, it looks like a ritual,' Munch continued. 'The wig. The feathers. The candles. The posing of her arms.'

'A pentagram,' Mia said, raising the glass to her lips.

'Yes, that was what Ylva said.'

'Ylva?'

'Kyrre was reassigned,' Munch said. 'And Ylva had just graduated from the police college, so . . .'

'Like me?' Mia smiled, shifting her gaze to the pictures once more.

'No, because you never finished, did you?' Munch said kindly.

'You didn't give me a chance! So what's the deal?'

'With Ylva?'

'No, with me,' Mia said, holding up a picture from the floor.

'What do you mean?'

'With Mikkelson. What's the deal this time? Wait, let me guess: I'm back – if I agree to continue seeing the psychologist?'

'Yep,' Munch said, shifting in the chair.

'You can smoke in here. There's an ashtray somewhere – in one of the kitchen cupboards over there, I think.' Mia pointed. She still hadn't taken her eyes off the pictures.

'Camilla Green,' Munch said, once he had lit his cigarette. 'Aged seventeen. Reported missing three months ago from some kind of institution for troubled teenagers. The preliminary autopsy report shows that her stomach contained animal feed.'

'What?' Mia said, looking up at him.

'Pellets.'

'Christ.' Mia turned her gaze back to the photographs.

She took a big swig of the Armagnac. Her eyes were distant now. He had seen this so many times before. She was no longer here.

When his mobile rang and he went out on the balcony to answer it, she did not even notice.

'Yes? Munch speaking.'

'It's Ludvig. We got her.'

'Who?'

'Helene Eriksen. The woman who reported the girl missing. She's coming in.'

'I'm on my way,' Munch said swiftly, and rang off.

When he returned to the living room, Mia had already refilled her glass.

'So?' he asked.

'So what?' Mia said, looking up at him with glazed eyes.

'What do you think?'

'I'll be in the office tomorrow. For now, I want to be alone with these.'

'OK,' Munch said. 'Are you sure you'll be all right? Do you want me to – well, get you some food or something?'

Mia waved him away, her eyes already back on the pictures.

'Then I'll see you tomorrow.'

Chapter 12

A forty-year-old woman in a short, red puffa jacket was standing under a streetlight by Bislett Stadium, watching a fat man in a beige duffel coat leave the block of flats. He lit a cigarette and looked as if he was pondering something before getting into a black Audi and driving off.

'What are we waiting for?'

The young lad next to her, twenty years her junior, glanced around warily, pulling his beanie further down over his ears.

'I'm freezing.'

'Be quiet,' the woman said, sticking a hand into her pocket to check that it was still there.

The bracelet.

'How hard can it be?' the young lad said, and lit a roll-up dangling from the corner of his mouth with trembling fingers. 'I thought you said she was going to give us money?'

The woman in the red jacket regretted bringing him along; after all, they did not know each other well. This was something she should have done on her own, something she ought to have done a long time ago.

She tightened the jacket around her and continued to look up at the second-floor flat. There was a faint light up there, so she must be home, and yet something did not feel right.

'I need a hit,' the lad said with a light cough.

'Be quiet,' the woman said again, because now she could feel it, too.

The craving for the needle that would make her misery disappear, that would give her the warmth she wanted.

'Show me,' he said, holding out his hand.

'Show you what?'

'The bracelet. I thought you said she would pay us for it?'

She looked up at the flat again and showed the boy what was in her pocket.

'That thing?' The boy sounded incredulous as he held up the bracelet to the light from the street lamp.

'How can that be worth anything? Looks like tat to me, something a kid would wear. Shit. We could have robbed a kiosk or something, a 7-Eleven, in and out in five minutes; what are we going to make from this? Come on, have you gone mental?'

The woman snatched back the bracelet and slipped it into her jacket pocket.

A silver bracelet, a heart, an anchor, and a letter. M.

'Sentimental value,' she said quietly, the craving hitting her with full force now.

'Eh?'

The young lad glanced around nervously and took another drag on his roll-up.

'Sod it, let's do a 7. Or see if Leffe will give us some. He owes me a favour. I'm sure he'll give us a fix, and he lives nearby – how about it? Fuck it, that bracelet isn't even worth a fiver – what's the point of that? I'm not hanging around here.'

The woman in the red jacket looked up as a door opened and the dark-haired girl appeared on the balcony. She had a drink in one hand. She stayed there for a little while; she seemed to be peering into the city darkness, then she went back inside, closing the door behind her.

Mia Krüger.

She should have done this a long time ago.

A long, long time ago.

'Oh, come on,' the young lad said, almost pleading now, tossing aside his cigarette butt. 'Let's get the hell out of here, all right? I'm bloody freezing.'

'Shut up. It's not just about the money.'

'It isn't?' the boy said.

'No.'

'But for fuck's sake, you said that—'

'We used to be friends,' the woman interrupted him, irritated now. *She should have come alone.*

'Friends? Who? You and that woman up there?'

'Shut up, will you?'

'If you're friends, why don't you just ask her for money? Christ, Cisse, this is ridiculous! Why are we standing out here?'

'No, not her. Sigrid.'

'Who is Sigrid?'

'Her sister.'

The boy fetched a nearly empty tobacco pouch from his pocket and tried making another roll-up with the crumbs that remained, his eyes darting frantically.

'Bloody hell, Cisse, I wasn't kidding, I can't wait any longer, I need something now. Don't you?'

'I was there,' the woman in the red jacket said, without taking her eyes off the shadow in the flat above them.

'Where?'

'I saw him.'

'What do you mean?'

'I saw him kill her.'

He grew quiet now. Stopped with the thin roll-up between his lips and the lighter in front of it without lighting up.

'Christ, Cisse, you're freaking me out. Killed who?'

Sigrid.

She could feel it coming back.

She should have come a long time ago.

She was there.

'For fuck's sake, Cisse, I just wanna get high. I thought you said we were going to get some cash?'

'What?'

'I know Leffe will give us credit. It's not far. Come on. This is a total waste of time.'

The forty-year-old woman carefully curled her fingers around the small silver bracelet in her pocket once more, feeling it between her fingers as the light in the flat above them suddenly went out and only darkness was left.

'Come on.'

'Do you think you could shut up for a moment?'

'Fuck you, Cisse! Are you coming, or what?'

'You're sure Leffe will give us credit?'

'Of course, he owes me. This is useless. Let's go.'

She threw a final glance up at the dark windows of the flat.

And followed the twitchy young man down towards Pilestredet.

TWO

Chapter 13

Gabriel Mørk stopped in front of the newspaper stand outside the kiosk on the corner of Mariboesgate and thought back to the very first time he had come here, six months ago, worried about starting his job with the police. Back then, the young hacker had had no real police experience – in fact, no job experience at all. The police had got his name from MI6. He had solved an extremely difficult code which the British security service had uploaded on the Internet: *can you crack it?* It had turned out to be a recruitment campaign, and he was informed that his solution was correct, but in order to get the job he had to be a British citizen. Gabriel had promptly forgotten all about it until, one day, he got a call from Holger Munch. How could he turn down a proper job with a baby on the way? His girlfriend would never have forgiven him.

Gabriel found his card and swiped himself inside the yellow building. A teenage girl. Found naked in the woods in Hurum. He shuddered at the thought of the pictures he had seen. They had not had a case like this since the little girls who had been found hanged from the trees, and he had almost thrown up then. His first thought was that he had made a big mistake taking this job, but, luckily, they had solved the case.

And he had contributed.

Afterwards Munch had called him into his office and thanked him, said, 'We couldn't have done it without you, Gabriel.' And he had felt proud; part of something important.

Gabriel held up his card to the lift panel and was about to press the button for the second floor when he heard a familiar voice behind him.

'Wait for me.'

Gabriel turned around and was both surprised and delighted when he saw Mia running towards him.

'Thanks,' she panted as the lift doors closed.

Mia Krüger.

'Are you back?' Gabriel said, aware that he was blushing a little, but hoping that she would not notice.

'So it would seem. I should have told them to go to hell, shouldn't I?'

'Possibly,' Gabriel smiled.

'Have you got hold of the records?'

'Eh?'

'Her phone records? The victim?'

'No,' Gabriel said. 'Things like that take time, but it's in progress. Red tape and so on – you know what it's like.'

'Why don't you just hack their system and get it yourself?'

'Munch likes doing things by the book.' Gabriel smiled, a little embarrassed.

Mia laughed.

She walked in front of him down the corridor, ran her card through the reader, held open the door for him and closed it behind them, just as Munch appeared.

'I thought we said eleven? Eleven means eleven, not quarter past,' Munch barked, and disappeared into the office.

'He's in a foul mood at the moment,' Gabriel said, somewhat apologetically.

'Clearly,' Mia said, but she did not look as if it bothered her all that much.

'Eleven means eleven. Seriously, people, let's show some professionalism, shall we? Where are we? Where is everyone?' Munch was now shouting from the incident room, his voice growling and deep like a bear someone had roused from hibernation.

Mia Krüger.

Gabriel was glad that she was back.

Chapter 14

'OK,' Munch said, having taken up his usual spot in front of the overhead screen.

Gabriel Mørk saw everyone's face light up as Mia entered the incident room.

'Moonbeam,' Ludvig Grønlie called out, and got up to hug her.

Anette Goli also rose in order to shake Mia's hand, while Kim Kolsø grinned and gave her a thumbs-up from his chair.

'OK,' Munch said again. 'As you can see, Mia is back, and we are all really pleased about that. And if you're wondering who to thank, then you're looking at him. And just so you know it: this is the first and last time I suck up to Mikkelson but, in my opinion, it was worth it.'

Munch allowed himself a small smile as he turned on the projector.

'Where is Curry?' he suddenly said. 'Kim? Ludvig?'

Munch looked around the room but was met only with shaking heads.

'Haven't heard anything,' Kim said.

'OK,' Munch said, clicking a button.

A picture appeared on the screen. The dead girl, but alive now, smiling faintly at the camera in something that could be a school photo.

'Last night we had it confirmed that the girl we found in Hurum is seventeen-year-old Camilla Green. Born in 1995. Grew up in care. Her mother died when she was little, in a car crash. Her father is French, his name is—'

'Laurent Clementz,' Ludvig Grønlie interjected.

'Yes, thank you, Ludvig.'

'So far we haven't managed to contact him,' Munch continued, 'and, according to Helene Eriksen, Camilla Green had very little contact with him. She used to visit him in France during the summer holidays when she was younger, but she was looked after by social services in Norway.'

'Sorry, who is Helene?' asked Gabriel.

'Yes, of course. It has been a long night, and I'm sorry that not everyone has been updated about recent developments.'

He cleared his throat and drank some of the Farris mineral water on the table in front of him.

'Helene Eriksen . . .'

Munch looked across to Grønlie.

'We don't have a picture of her, do we?'

Ludvig Grønlie shook his head.

'OK, Camilla Green grew up in foster care with several different families, but she never seemed to settle with any of them.'

Munch quickly flicked through his notes. 'I think we have a list of four addresses here, all of which she ran away from, before she came to Hurumlandet Nurseries at the age of fifteen.'

Munch seemed to expect questions, and he held up his hand towards the team.

He strangled a yawn; he did not look as if he had had much sleep.

'Helene Eriksen,' Ylva prompted him.

Gabriel could see Ylva watching Mia Krüger furtively, and he recognized the feeling. He, too, had experienced it when he started working here. The sense of awe at being in the same room as Mia Krüger, not wanting to say or do the wrong thing.

'Yes, thank you,' Munch went on. 'Yesterday, we met with Helene, the manager of Hurumlandet Nurseries, the woman who reported Camilla Green missing three months ago. Ludvig and I accompanied her to the Institute of Forensic Medicine, and she confirmed that the girl we found is Camilla.'

At this point, Munch stopped and looked across to Grønlie again. 'How was she on the way back?'

Ludvig sighed and shook his head. 'Not good. She was in shock.'

'And someone met her at the nurseries, someone who could look after her?'

Ludvig nodded again. 'A guy called Paulus. Her assistant.'

'Good,' Munch said, flicking through his notes again.

Silence descended now, and Munch clicked the button again. This time, a photograph from the crime scene appeared, one they had seen earlier, Camilla lying on the heather, naked, in the strange pose, with the white flower in her mouth.

'This Paulus . . .?' Munch went on, glancing in the direction of Grønlie again.

'No, we don't have a picture yet.'

'OK, anyway, Paulus appears to have been a former resident at Hurumlandet Nurseries, and now, as far as we can gather, he seems to be Helene's right-hand man; it was he who sent us lists of residents, employees, teachers and everyone else with a link to the place. Ludvig, over to you?'

'OK,' Ludvig said, checking the papers on the table in front of him. 'Hurumlandet Nurseries is a place for troubled teenagers. It was set up by Helene Eriksen in the autumn of 1999, and is privately owned but receives government support. The centre also works with mental-health services and the eating-disorder clinics at Ullevål and Dikemark hospitals. I've made a few calls, and no one has anything but good things to say about the place. It would appear that children and young people who have failed to settle elsewhere really benefit from a stay at Hurumlandet Nurseries. Some have lived there for several years.'

He leafed through his papers again.

'Yes, as you know, it's early days yet, but everyone I've spoken to praises the place, and Helene Eriksen in particular. She seems to have become a substitute mother for these young people. I'll carry on digging, but so far I haven't come across any red flags.'

'Great, Ludvig, thank you. Uh . . .'

'My turn?' Kim Kolsø said with a wry smile.

'Yes, great, Kim.' Munch nodded.

'We've had officers at the crime scene ever since we found her,' Kim said. 'Knocked on doors, gone through the area with a fine-toothed comb, but, as far as forensic evidence goes, we have found little. The area is popular with hikers, so we can forget about footprints, unless we test the shoes of half the locals. The lack of much else is something I personally find a little odd, but we're still on it. We've requested back-up from Svelvik, Røyken and Sande, and we'll keep looking until we find something, because there has to be something useful out there. We're talking about a huge area, so it will take some time, but we've started and we won't stop until we're done. Of course, we do have some forensic evidence, but you've already seen it. The feathers, the candles, the flower in her mouth – a lily, I believe. And then we have a witness.'

He swiped his iPad.

'A woman called Olga Lund, a pensioner, who lives on the road that leads to the path near where we found the victim, thought she saw a white van with a sticker on the side driving past, as she put it, just after the early-evening news, and coming back the same way, again as she put it, just before the eleven o'clock bulletin.'

The team smiled at this. They could easily imagine the old lady, her sense of time measured by her TV schedule.

'A sticker?' Mia said. It was the first time she had opened her mouth.

'Yes, that's what she said.'

'A logo?'

'I think that must have been what she meant.'

'Nothing about what kind of logo?'

Kim scrolled down his iPad again. 'There's nothing written down here. I got the report from another officer, but I thought that I would drive up and talk to her myself.'

'Great, Kim, thank you. Gabriel?'

Gabriel Mørk had been lost in a world of his own and was startled when he heard his name spoken.

'Yes?'

'Telephone records?'

'They've been requested, and are on their way.' Gabriel nodded.

'Good.'

Gabriel looked across to Mia Krüger, who winked at him.

'OK,' Munch said. 'Mia?'

Mia rose and stepped up in front of the screen. Munch gave her the remote control and sat down on a chair beside the lectern. Mia swept her long, dark hair behind her ear before clearing her throat and clicking to bring up the first picture.

'I haven't had much time to study them, I only got these yesterday.' She smiled, a tad apologetically.

'But there are several things which I believe are vital for us.'

Everyone in the room was silent now as Mia turned to face the screen.

'There can be no doubt that this was planned, and that it had been planned for a long time. The first thing that struck me was that the crime scene is very contrived. Wouldn't you agree?'

Mia clicked through a few pictures without waiting for the team to reply.

'The wig. The feathers. The candles placed around her. The fact that she's naked. The way her arms have been arranged. The flower in her mouth. A ritual. The first thing to cross my mind was an offering. A sacrifice.'

Mia took a step towards the screen and pointed out various sections of the picture.

'The way the candles are arranged. This five-sided shape. The pentagram. It prompts immediate speculation, because it's a well-known symbol, the gateway to, well, darkness, the devil. I'm not drawing any definitive conclusions now, but I've no doubt that we're dealing with a person, or group of people, who are into that. The occult. Satanism.'

Mia looked across the room now to see if there were any questions, but everyone continued to sit completely still.

'Do you understand what I mean?'

Some nodded faintly, but no one spoke up yet.

'As I'm aware, there were no signs of sexual assault, is that right?'

Mia looked across to Munch, who nodded.

'OK,' Mia said, clicking through a sequence of new pictures.

'The virgin,' Mia continued, stopping at a close-up of the victim. 'That's what all these rituals are about, isn't it?'

Still no one said anything.

'I'm not saying that Camilla Green was a virgin, not many seventeen-year-old girls are these days, but the fact that she wasn't sexually assaulted, the fact that she was placed here, among these symbols, naked, and *pure*, if you will, that's important.'

Mia reached out for Munch's mineral-water bottle and took a swig, lost in her own thoughts.

'Mia?' Munch coughed softly.

'What?'

Mia looked at him.

'Yes. Sorry.' She pressed the button again and another picture appeared.

'Like I said,' Mia went on, 'I haven't had much time to look at these photos, so this is just surface.'

Mia raised her head again and smiled cautiously across the room. There was the odd nod here and there. Gabriel Mørk knew that, like him, everyone felt that familiar tingle of expectation. Mia would lead them through this. To the killer.

'So someone posed her. Naked. Exposed her. A seventeen-year-old girl. Camilla Green. And so my next thought . . .'

She paused, but not so long that Munch had to rouse her.

'Is it so that we would find her? Or to display her somehow? That's an important question.' Mia looked across to Munch.

'Absolutely.' He coughed.

'Then we have the – let's call it, the more physical evidence,' Mia continued.

She clicked a few more times, until she found the picture they had started with.

'Camilla Green was a healthy, normal girl. She had her problems, that's true, a foster child, living in a kind of home . . .?'

'Hurumlandet Nurseries,' Munch interjected.

'But look . . .'

Fresh pictures.

'When she went missing, Camilla's weight was normal. But when she was found, she looked like this.'

Gabriel almost could not bear to look.

'Thin. Starved. With bruises and cuts to her knees.'

Mia kept clicking. 'Her elbows . . .' And on. '. . . to her calloused palms. She disappeared three months ago. A healthy teenager. Then she reappears like this. She was kept prisoner.'

Gabriel lowered his gaze now; he could not bear to look at the picture on the screen. A prisoner? He could feel he was not the only team member who struggled to process this development.

'Any questions?' Mia continued.

It took a while before anyone spoke.

'I've been wondering about . . . the animal feed?' Ylva ventured cautiously.

'Precisely,' Mia said. 'An animal.'

'What do you mean?'

She glanced across the room. 'An animal, don't you think, Kim?'

'I don't know what to think, Mia.' Kim spoke in a low voice.

'She was treated as if she were an animal,' Mia explained, taking another gulp from the bottle on the table in front of her.

'But why . . .?'

It was the new girl again, Ylva, still ashen.

'That, I don't know.' Mia shrugged. 'Like I said, I only got these pictures yesterday. These are just initial thoughts.'

Mia looked to Munch, who indicated that she could sit down again.

'OK, great,' he said as Mia went back to her chair.

There was a long silence in the room.

The others had seen Mia in action before and knew what she could do, but Ylva still looked baffled by what had just happened.

Munch rose and stepped up in front of the screen again. 'OK, yes, good.' Their boss scratched his beard. 'Time for a cigarette, don't you think?' he said, and clapped his hands. 'A quick fag, that's all, before we carry on. It's looking promising.'

No one in the room said anything, but Gabriel could see a smile form at the corner of Kim Kolsø's mouth: Munch was the only member of the team who smoked, so these breaks were purely for his benefit.

Munch put on his coat and disappeared out on to the balcony while everyone else stayed behind.

'Promising?' Kim Kolsø was puzzled. 'What has got into him today?'

Mia shrugged again.

'It . . .' Ludvig Grønlie began, but shut his mouth as quickly as he had opened it.

'What, Ludvig?' Kim asked, but Grønlie seemed reluctant to answer.

'Perhaps Munch should tell us himself,' Ludvig muttered.

'What?' Mia asked, now curious.

Ludvig hesitated, then he pulled out a piece of paper from the file in front of him and shoved it across to her.

'We got the lists an hour ago.'

'What lists?'

'Of the residents and employees at Hurumlandet Nurseries.'

'Oh, shit,' Mia mumbled, her eyes scanning the paper in front of her.

'Why, what's wrong?' Kim Kolsø said.

'Rolf Lycke,' Mia mumbled.

'Who on earth is Rolf Lycke?' Kim said, taking the paper from her.

'Marianne's boyfriend.'

'Marianne who?'

'Marianne Munch,' Ludvig said quietly.

'His ex-wife?' Kim sounded surprised.

'Yep.' Ludvig Grønlie nodded. 'Marianne Munch's boyfriend. Rolf Lycke. He teaches out there.'

'Oh, shit,' Kim said.

'Exactly,' Grønlie muttered, slipping the list back into the file as Munch returned from the balcony.

Chapter 15

Isabella Jung was standing in front of the mirror in her room, feeling terribly nervous. She had not felt like this before. It was odd, really. When her therapist had recommended this place several months ago, she had reacted as she always did – *whatever, I don't care* – but now everything was different.

She had been in and out of care homes her entire life. She wanted to be in Fredrikstad with her dad, but he was not well enough, so that was not an option. Not according to social services. She did not mind that he drank a bit and that he was often out. Surely she could cook her own food? Surely she could pack her own schoolbag and make her way to the bus stop? But no, she had had to go and live with her mum up north.

Her mum.

Isabella shuddered at the thought.

She swore softly to herself. That witch was not a proper mum. Couldn't they see that? Mums were supposed to care about their kids. Say nice things. Praise them. Not complain all the time. Criticize her. Tell her she was ugly. That she was useless. That she would never amount to anything. No matter how well she did at school, how many nice comments she got from the teachers, how nicely she tidied her room. First one home, then another, until she had run away at thirteen. Hitchhiked. Made it all the way back. She was not bothered that her dad had been drink-driving and ended up in jail. She could look after herself. But no. Social services had taken her away again, and this time she had ended up at an eating-disorder unit in Oslo, because she had stopped eating.

After that time, she had decided they could all go to hell.

Whatever.

I don't care.

But she had heard rumours among the other girls at the unit. That it was nice out there. At Hurumlandet Nurseries. That it was not like the other places. So when the therapist had suggested it, she had agreed, reluctantly, and now she was standing in front of the mirror, surprised how much she wanted this meeting to go well so that she could stay.

Isabella Jung wondered whether she should have put on different make-up, worn nicer clothes, a blouse or something; maybe she should not have worn the hoodie and the ripped jeans, even though she knew that Helene never cared about such things.

On first arriving here she had not been so positive. They had rules here. Lessons were compulsory. There was the big dormitory where the girls lived, a smaller dormitory for boys, three large greenhouses and a number of outbuildings, some tool sheds, and a garage for the cars. Helene had given Isabella a tour of the place on her first day and shown her the map with the boundaries marked on it. *Yeah, right – as if anyone could tell her where she could or couldn't go.* Everyone had to wake up at seven, breakfast was at eight, then it was either working in the greenhouses or lessons until lunch, depending on what day of the week it was, then more chores until dinner, which was at six o'clock, then leisure time until lights out at eleven. No one was allowed to leave the area, unless they had jobs such as delivering flowers to customers. And there was no Internet or TV all day, only between eight and ten in the evening. There was also a phone ban. No one got their mobiles until after dinner, and they had to be handed back before bedtime. On that first day, she had thought, *I'm not going to last long here*, but she had been surprised.

Within a matter of days, she had found a kind of peace. There was no nagging. No criticism. Everyone here seemed to be just fine. It was all down to Helene. Helene was not like the other grown-ups. *I know what's best for you.* Helene was not like that at all. *I want to stay here.*

For the first time in a long while, Isabella had felt, well, almost happy. At the many homes where she had stayed before, no one had cared about what she did. She could get up late in the morning. Stay up for as long as she wanted to at night. Spend hours on the Internet watching TV, chatting; at one point she had spent so many hours in front of the screen that her eyes had started to flicker. She would never have believed that she would enjoy getting up at the crack of dawn – seven o'clock, who does that? – only to work all day. But she loved it.

Isabella decided not to dress up after all; she left on her usual jeans and hoodie, took a last look in the mirror and left her room. It was not until she had closed the door behind her that she noticed the flower on the floor. A white lily. Why was there a white lily in front of her door? She picked it up and studied it for a moment, and then she saw the note on her door.

I like you.

Isabella Jung glanced quickly up and down the corridor, and she felt her cheeks grow hot.

Someone had stood out here, too scared to knock, just left the flower, the note and crept away again.

I like you.

There was a drawing of something underneath. A kind of signature. Whoever had left the flower had been so shy that they had not dared write their name but had drawn something instead. At first she could not make out what it was. A bird? A bird with big eyes – an owl, perhaps? Isabella sniffed the flower, then she quickly glanced around again, aware that her heart was beating a little faster.

Someone likes me?

A secret admirer?

Isabella Jung returned to her room, and put the flower and the note carefully under her pillow before she went back outside, with a spring in her step.

She had barely left the girls' dormitory before she realized that something was amiss.

She saw Cecilie, one of the girls out here she liked the best; she had tears in her eyes and her arms were wrapped around another girl Isabella didn't know so well.

'What's wrong?'

'Haven't you heard?' Cecilie could hardly talk.

'No, what is it? Tell me.'

'They've found Camilla.'

'Camilla Green?'

Cecilie nodded.

'She's dead. Someone killed her. They found her in the forest.'

'Oh my God,' Isabella stuttered.

'Helene wants us all to come to the classroom now,' Cecilie sobbed.

'But . . .? How . . .?'

They were interrupted by Paulus, who called out to them from the other side of the yard.

'Helene is waiting for you, girls. Are you coming?'

At the sight of the boy with the dark curls and the unusually bright blue eyes, Isabella's heart beat faster. He sounded unbearably sad.

Chapter 16

It was six o'clock and darkness already lay heavily across the capital when Munch and Mia drove to Hurumlandet Nurseries in the black Audi. Had it been up to Mia, they would have left much earlier, right after the briefing meeting.

Helene Eriksen had to inform everyone first, that was the reason for the delay. Break the tragic news to everyone who knew Camilla Green before the police came blundering in. It explained why it was just the two of them going there now – 'so they don't have hordes of us trampling around at the same time', as he had put it. And this Mia did agree with. A group of teenagers with a troubled past – it was not unthinkable that some of them also had a tricky relationship with the police. Sending a fleet of police cars with flashing lights could do more harm than good when it came to getting the information they needed. But Mia was uneasy. She had a feeling that she had missed something. In the pictures. She could not put her finger on what it was.

Too impatient.

Maybe that was her problem. Munch was much steadier, much calmer; though he had acted oddly today, but that wasn't so surprising given what she knew about the staff list.

She took a lozenge from a packet in her jacket pocket, and opened the window as Munch lit another cigarette and joined the E18. It had been dark since five o'clock, a dense, overpowering darkness, and Mia hated it. This time of the year. The cold. Being smothered by a black blanket; as if the world was not inhuman enough already, now they had to live without light for months. It came back to her again, the warmth from her dream about Sigrid in the field, but she pushed it away, shuddering at the thought that, less than twenty-four hours ago, she had opened and swallowed the contents of the first jar.

He had saved her again. A twist of fate. If Munch had not knocked on the door when he did, she would no longer be here. She had stuck two fingers down her throat and vomited the pills up again. Mia felt a little ashamed now. She had promised herself to try, and then she had given up so soon.

Mia leaned forwards to turn the heating up to max and mulled it over for a while, but there was no way out, no point in pretending that she did not know.

'So, when were you going to tell me?'

'Tell you what?' Munch said.

'Oh, come on, Holger. I saw the list, we all did. How exactly do you think this is going to play out?'

'What?' Munch said again, although she could tell from looking at him that he knew what she meant.

'Rolf,' Mia said. 'Rolf is a teacher out there.'

Munch looked as if he was about to light yet another cigarette, but he stopped himself and continued to stare through the windscreen.

'It means you shouldn't be working on this case. You know that, don't you? If Mikkelson finds out, he'll take you off the investigation. Holger, what were you thinking? You're personally involved, you're compromised, and you don't say a word to the rest of the team, and—'

'OK, OK.'

He interrupted her with a wave of his hand and continued to stare out of the windscreen for a while before he said anything: 'They're getting married,' he said, not looking at her.

'Who?'

'Marianne and Rolf.'

Mia shook her head. 'What the hell does that have to do with anything?'

Munch fell silent again.

'Oh, come on, Holger, you're better than this.' Mia sighed.

'Than what?'

'Do I have to spell it out?'

'Do you have to spell *what* out?'

Munch looked truly irritated now. He pulled out and overtook an articulated lorry before returning to the inside lane, then he reached for the cigarettes on the dashboard and lit one.

'Holger,' Mia sighed. 'I don't have to be a therapist to know what you're thinking, but this is absurd.'

'What is?' Munch said, although again he looked as if he knew perfectly well what she was about to say.

'That if Rolf Lycke by some fluke turns out to be a suspect in this case, then Marianne will dump him, leaving the way open for you. I mean, seriously, Holger? Straight out of a Hollywood film with a bad script and a happy ending. This isn't like you.'

She smiled tenderly at him now and was relieved when he eventually returned her smile.

'Sometimes you can be a real pain, did you know that?'

'Yes, yes, I know. But somebody had to tell you.'

Munch shook his head as if to confirm his own naivety.

'He brought her a huge bunch of flowers,' he said with a small sigh.

'I'm sorry to hear that,' Mia said. 'But then again, it's been ten years.'

'I know, Mia.'

'So what do we do?'

'About what?'

'About the fact that he works there? That you should not really be working on the case?'

Munch pressed the accelerator and overtook another lorry before letting out another small sigh and saying, 'We'll eliminate him as quickly as possible.'

'That should work.' Mia nodded. 'He obviously didn't do it.'

'Obviously.'

'So let's get that confirmed and cross him off the list.'

'Exactly,' Munch said.

'That should do it, shouldn't it?'

'Definitely.'

'Problem solved.' Mia nodded again.

'It wasn't even a problem to begin with.'

'Quite.' Mia smiled.

'Where the hell is Curry?' Munch said as they reached Asker and found the exit to road 167.

He clearly wanted to change the topic, and Mia was happy to indulge him. She knew that he still carried a torch for Marianne, but that he would take it so badly, after ten years, had surprised her, and she felt for him.

'No idea,' Mia replied. 'He's not answering his phone.'

'He'd better get himself back to work soon. He knows how pushed we are,' Munch grunted over the steering wheel.

'I know, but, like I said, I can't get hold of him. I left a message with Sunniva yesterday, but she isn't answering her phone either.'

'We can't afford to lose another one,' Munch muttered grimly.

'What do you mean?'

'Haven't you heard?'

'Heard what?'

Munch looked at her.

'Kim.'

'What about Kim?'

'He might be leaving us,' Munch said with a sigh.

'Oh?' Mia was taken aback. 'Why?'

'He has requested a transfer to Hønefoss.'

'Kim? Move to the countryside?' Mia laughed. 'Why on earth would he want to do that?'

'I think he's getting married,' Munch grumbled. 'Seems very fashionable these days.'

'Getting married? Who to?'

'Do you remember that teacher who lived out there? And the two brothers?'

'Of course,' Mia said. 'The ones who found the little girl in the tree?'

Munch nodded.

'Emilie Isaksen. She and Kim are an item, a couple, and I believe they hope to adopt the two boys.'

'But that's great.' Mia smiled.

Munch laughed mirthlessly. 'Yes, yes, I suppose so, for them, but not for us, is it? I can't imagine how we'll manage without Kim, and if that moron Curry can't be bothered to turn up for work . . .'

'You'll find a skilled replacement. You're good at that.'

'He won't be allowed to quit until this case is over. I've made that perfectly clear,' Munch grunted.

'So what do you think?' Mia said, as the front beams caught the sign ahead of them.

Hurumlandet Nurseries. 500 m.

'About this case?' Munch said.

'Yes.' Mia nodded.

'Just between us?'

'Yes.'

'I have a really bad feeling. I recognize something about it. Do you know what I mean?'

'Darkness,' Mia said quietly.

Munch nodded softly, turned off the main road and drove down a tree-lined avenue towards the glow from the greenhouses further ahead.

Chapter 17

The air in Helene Eriksen's small office was thick with grief. Mia was grateful to Munch for giving the manager and the other residents time to digest the sad news. The tall woman sitting in front of them was so distraught she was almost incapable of stringing a sentence together.

'First, I would like to thank you for seeing us at such short notice.' Munch cleared his throat and unbuttoned his coat. 'And then, of course, for your help last night. I understand that this has come as a shock to you, and I'm sorry that we now have to trouble you with questions you might consider irrelevant in the light of the tragedy that has occurred. For us, it is obviously important to start the investigation as quickly as possible, and I know that it won't bring Camilla back, that it can't cancel out the grief you all now feel, but whoever did this must be found.'

'Yes, of course.' Helene Eriksen gave a slight nod.

It was clear to Mia that this woman was in charge here. Even the way she sat at her desk showed authority.

'Good.' Holger nodded. 'We've already had lists of all staff and clients out here from your assistant . . .'

'Paulus.'

'Yes, Paulus. Thank you.' Munch smiled. 'What we also need is more detailed information about the patients—'

'Residents,' Helene Eriksen corrected.

'Yes, of course, sorry. More details about, well, the residents here. Right now, we only have their names, but we also need access to medical records, case histories, more details about who they are, what they've been through, why they ended up out here, if you know what I mean?'

Helene Eriksen looked as if she was debating this for a moment, but at length she nodded.

She's protecting her girls.

Mia Krüger felt a growing respect for the woman.

'Good.' Munch smiled and flicked through his notepad. 'So, let's just get this out of the way. You reported Camilla missing on 19 July, but a few days later you contacted us and retracted the report. Why?'

'I feel like an idiot now, of course I do. But Camilla has always been like that. I mean . . . she *was* like that.'

Helene Eriksen sat very still for a moment, and Mia could see her struggle at having to talk about Camilla Green in the past tense.

'What was she like?' Munch said, coming to her rescue.

'Unstable.'

'In what way was she unstable?' Munch said kindly, to help her back on track.

'No, not unstable. I'm sorry, that's not the right word. Special. Camilla was special,' Helene Eriksen continued. 'She hated rules and authority. She would often run away, but she always came back when she was ready. Everything had to be on her terms, that was just the way she was, if you know what I'm saying?'

'I do.' Munch nodded. 'So, she was reported missing, but then . . .?'

'The rules here are quite strict,' Helene Eriksen said. 'Some people like it, others don't, but it's just the way it is, it's how we live here. In order to get something you have to give something, you understand?'

Helene gave them a faint smile.

'So . . . she . . .?' Munch said.

'Camilla failed to turn up for the late shift on 18 July, and she wasn't in her room when we checked the following morning, and then I reported her missing.'

'And the reason you withdrew the report was?'

'A few days later she sent me a text message.'

'What did it say?' Munch asked.

Helene Eriksen sighed and shook her head. 'That we shouldn't look for her. That she was fine. That she had gone to France to see her father.'

'And you believed her?' Mia spoke now, realizing immediately that she might have come across as rather brusque. 'I mean . . . was there anything about the message which made you suspect that something might be wrong?'

Helene Eriksen looked to Munch now, wavering for a moment. 'No, I . . .'

'No one is accusing you of anything. That goes without saying,' Munch said.

'Perhaps I should have known,' Helene Eriksen said, shifting her gaze to the desk in front of her. 'But she tended to be a little . . .'

'Unstable?' Munch said.

'No, no . . . Like I said, I used the wrong word . . . wilful,' the blonde woman said, looking up at them again. '"Wilful" is better. Camilla didn't like people telling her what to do.'

'So the message felt genuine?' Mia said.

'Yes.'

'Do you have any idea who might have done this?' Mia went on.

'No, absolutely not,' Helene Eriksen stammered, looking towards Munch again.

'None of the residents here, or the staff, no one with a traumatic background? Someone who has had such a difficult childhood that they might take pleasure in posing Camilla on a bed of feathers and putting a flower in her mouth?'

'No . . . I mean, how would I be able to . . .?' She had a frightened expression in her eyes now.

'No gut reaction?' Mia pushed on, ignoring the look Munch was giving her.

Helene Eriksen fell silent for a moment and glanced swiftly at Munch before fixing her gaze on the desk again.

'No,' she said softly, then raised her head and looked up at them. 'No, of course not.'

Munch glared at Mia again, and looked as if he was about to say something when they were interrupted by a knock on the door and a curly-haired young man popped his head in.

'Helene, we need to—'

The young man stopped halfway through the sentence when he realized that Helene Eriksen was not alone.

'Oh, I'm sorry, I . . .'

'That's quite all right, Paulus.' Helene Eriksen smiled. 'What is it?'

'Some of the girls, they . . . well, I didn't know that . . .' the young man began, taking another look at Mia and Holger.

'Can we do it later?'

'Yes, of course we can, but . . .'

'We can wait.' Munch nodded. 'It's not a problem.'

The young man in the doorway looked at Helene, and glanced anxiously at Mia and Munch again before turning his attention back to his boss.

'It would be good if . . . well, now would be good. If that's all right?'

'Are you sure you don't mind?' Helene Eriksen said, looking at both Mia and Munch.

'Of course not,' Munch said. 'We have all the time in the world.'

'Great, thank you.' She smiled and rose from her chair. 'I won't be long.'

There was the sound of the door closing behind her, and suddenly they were alone in the small office.

Munch looked at Mia and shook his head.

'What?' Mia said with a shrug.

'Don't you think you were a little harsh?' Munch said.

'She knows something.'

'What do you mean?'

'I'm sorry about that. Where were we?' Helene Eriksen said as she came through the door and sat down in her chair again.

'Patient records?' Munch said, a little embarrassed.

'Residents,' Helene Eriksen corrected him again.

'Yes, of course, sorry,' Munch said. 'When do you think we can access them?'

'I just need to talk to our lawyer first,' Helene Eriksen said. 'Just to make sure that we're doing everything right, that we don't reveal any information we shouldn't.' She smiled at them, her eyes brighter now.

'Good.' Munch nodded, flashing Mia a short, sharp look before scratching his beard and turning to the next page in his notepad.

Chapter 18

Gabriel Mørk sat in front of the monitors in his office in Mariboesgate feeling quietly pleased with himself. The young hacker had nothing but respect for Holger Munch but, as always, something had been missed during the briefing. Age. Perhaps that explained it. Munch would turn fifty-five soon, which did not make him a relic, but, at times, their boss forgot that they were living in a different age to when he first joined the force.

A seventeen-year-old girl, Camilla Green, found dead in Hurumlandet with a flower in her mouth, and no one had thought to mention social media. Gabriel had wanted to raise his hand and suggest it but had decided against doing so. Munch had been in a weird mood and Gabriel had felt that it was not the best time to lecture his boss on the modern world.

He was better off checking it out for himself, and perhaps he'd earn some praise in the process. Gabriel took a swig from the Coke can beside his keyboard and popped a fresh piece of chewing gum into his mouth. Gabriel had found several Facebook accounts under the name Camilla Green, but none of them belonged to the girl in the pictures they had seen. There was a girl from South Carolina in a bikini, an elderly woman from Florida with a picture of her cat, someone from Sweden, a girl from Hungary, but not one of them was *the* Camilla Green he was looking for. Strange, really, he thought to begin with, strange that she was not on Facebook, but then he had started playing with her name and, after trying several different combinations, he had finally found her.

cgreen

A Facebook account, and one on Instagram. That was all. He flicked through the Instagram pictures once again, trying to reconnect with his inner police officer, analyse what he had discovered. Because something was odd. He had noticed that immediately. There were very few postings. Very few status updates on Facebook. Not all that many pictures on Instagram. Unusual for a seventeen-year-old girl. Some selfies; 'Bored', was the caption under a picture which Camilla had posted of what he presumed to be her bedroom at Hurumlandet Nurseries; 'Am riding Whirlwind tomorrow!' below a picture of her smiling and with her thumb up, in the same bed, with the same background. Several pictures of horses. A few likes. A few comments: 'Happy birthday!' 'Miss you, babe!' But apart from that, there was very little content, and that was what had caught Gabriel's eye, right until he scrolled down to see the dates the accounts were opened.

30 June.

The accounts were recent. Both opened on the same date. The thirtieth of June. Just three weeks before she disappeared.

Gabriel took another swig of his Coke and tried to think like Munch. Had she really only just joined social media? Or had Camilla Green deleted her old accounts and created new ones three weeks before she disappeared? Why?

Gabriel reviewed the pictures again. He was startled by a sudden knock on the door, then Mia Krüger popped her head round.

'Are you busy? Have I caught you in the act?'

'What?' Gabriel was confused.

'Secrets?' Mia smiled.

'What?'

'You're not watching porn, are you?'

'Oh, yes, totally.' Gabriel nodded vigorously. 'I'm looking for pictures for Curry.'

'Of course you are.' Mia laughed as she unzipped her jacket. 'So what does he want this time?'

'Asian babes in Norwegian national costumes riding camels,' Gabriel said, feeling the heat in his face starting to subside.

Mia laughed. 'He's capable of most things, isn't he?'

'Yeah, probably,' Gabriel said, a little flustered as Mia looked him right in the eye.

'So have you found her?'

Mia nodded at the pictures on the screen.

'Yes,' Gabriel said.

'Munch is not exactly an Internet whizz, is he?'

'No.' He smiled.

'Just as well that we have you.' Mia smiled, too, and punched his shoulder lightly.

'Indeed,' Gabriel mumbled, hoping the colour would not flare up in his cheeks again.

'So what have we got?' Mia said, looking at the screen again.

'One Facebook and one Instagram account.' Gabriel brought up the two Internet pages so she could look at them side by side.

'I can't boast of much expertise myself,' Mia said. 'So, what are we looking at?'

'New accounts.' Gabriel cleared his throat.

'Oh?' Mia's eyes widened for a moment. 'How new?'

'Three weeks before she disappeared.'

'You're kidding me?'

'Nope.'

'And what does that mean? I mean, to you, who's into this?'

'Into the Internet, you mean?'

Gabriel was starting to relax. The warmth in his cheeks had stayed away.

'Well, I'm not a teenage girl on social media, so I wouldn't know. Can she not just be new to the whole thing?'

Gabriel made a face. 'Not likely.'

'OK. How about if someone deletes their accounts and opens new ones? Why would they do that, in your opinion?'

'There could be several reasons. It could be a coincidence, I guess. It doesn't *have* to mean anything,' Gabriel went on. 'You might have Facebook friends you can't be bothered to keep in touch with, but it's awkward to unfriend them, because then you would have to explain yourself, so it's simpler to create a new profile.'

Mia raised her eyebrows and gave a light shrug.

'But, most of the time, it means that something has happened.'

'Like what?'

'Could be anything. You've broken up with your boyfriend and you don't want him to know about the people you're hanging out with now, say.'

'"Hang out with"?' Mia smiled. 'Is that what you do?'

'What do you mean?'

'Hang out with each other? Is that what people do on the Internet?'

Mia's question belonged to someone Munch's age. But Gabriel knew that she did not participate in social media. She was in the public eye. She valued her privacy. Years ago, there used to be Mia Krüger fan pages on Facebook.

'Yes, when we're not looking for Asian babes in Norwegian national costume.' Gabriel laughed.

Mia smiled, without taking her eyes off the screen. 'Horses?' she said, indicating one of the pictures.

'Yes, it looks as if she was into horse-riding.'

'Whirlwind,' Mia said quietly, pointing to the Facebook message.

'Yes, got to be a horse, don't you think?'

'Very likely. Unless it's a camel.'

Gabriel smiled and felt the heat return to his cheeks.

Mia got up, but remained in front of the monitors for a moment, as if pondering something. 'OK.' She nodded after a while. 'Are you coming, or what?'

'Where?'

'We've received her things from the Nurseries. They back up what you have here.'

'What do you mean?'

'Horses. I think that's where we should start.'

Mia paused in front of the monitors again, but her mind appeared to be elsewhere.

'So, are you coming?' she said, after a pause.

'Sure.' Gabriel nodded, and followed her down the corridor to the incident room.

Chapter 19

Skunk found himself in a dilemma he had never had to consider before.

The young hacker pulled his beanie further down over his coarse, black hair with the fat, white stripe down the middle that had given rise to his nickname and crossed the street in order to stay in the shadows.

Under normal circumstances, the thought of going to the police would never even have crossed his mind. Out of the question. It went without saying. In his world, helping the authorities was a mortal sin. But now? After the film he had seen last night? He did not see that he had any other choice.

Shit.

He pulled up his hood, lit a cigarette and chose a route different from the one he usually took, on the rare occasions he left his house. Skunk did not spend much time outdoors. He saw no reason for it. He had everything he needed in his basement in Tøyen. His very own bunker. Where no one could find him. But he needed to clear his head now.

That poor girl.

Why hadn't he listened to his gut? Kept away from that server. He had a nose for these things, a kind of sixth sense about where to go and what to stay the hell away from when he was online; it had warned him again this time, but he had not listened. The temptation had been too great. What he had found, the film he had seen.

Christ.

Skunk took another drag on his cigarette, turned around quickly and started walking back the same way he had just come.

He despaired at his own behaviour. Paranoid? It was not like him. In almost ten years as a hacker he had never been scared. Not once. He had always been in control. Never left behind any traces. He was no amateur. He muttered curses under his breath, chucked the cigarette, crossed the street again, and chose his route home at random, constantly looking over his shoulder.

Skunk could feel the anarchist inside him starting to resurface as he reached Tøyen Park. His conscience never troubled him about doing what he did. He saw it almost as his duty. He was no Robin Hood, he kept all the money for himself, but the people he stole from were so corrupt that they got exactly what they deserved. His business concept was as simple as it was brilliant. He would pick a company he did not like, discover a security weakness in its servers and collect information about dishonest transactions, which most businesses were involved in – corruption, bribery, breaches of environmental legislation, anything – and then make them pay.

Skunk shook his head. If the people of Norway knew what they were up to, these big, popular companies whose services they used, whose products were in every shop and whose owners were regarded as pillars of the community – if the public knew how these companies really made their money, how they had grown as rich as they had – then people might have rebelled.

It was never difficult. He never encountered problems. Every time he found something, and he pretty much always did, he would send an anonymous email with his discoveries and ask for money in order not to go public with it. Virtual blackmail. Of idiots who deserved it. And they were always willing to pay. They always had skeletons in their closets. Always. Skunk's conscience was absolutely clear.

But this was different.

This film.

This was not just a company making an illegal payment to an old Soviet state to get the monopoly to sell its product to the communications market. Or a transfer to an African leader who had already squandered millions of development aid on his own personal consumption, or quid pro quos, permits to drill an oilfield, the sale of weapons, landmines or ammunition.

It was not one of those.

It was . . .

Shit.

Skunk lit another cigarette in an attempt to clear his head. There was always Gabriel Mørk.

They had started out together years ago and, at first, it had just been a bit of fun. In front of the computers in their bedrooms, Electron and Phoenix, from an age when there was hardly any Internet and computers had a storage capacity of only 10MB, with processors the size of calculators, and yet the two of them had hacked everything – NASA, CIA – but back then it had been just a game; they had got a kick out of it, he and Gabriel, every time they had managed to break into a system that was said to be impenetrable, until one day, Gabriel had switched camps.

That was why they had drifted apart. Gabriel thought they should use their skills for good, not to destroy, not to create chaos, and they had had a massive row the last time they saw each other, over a beer at Teddy's Soft Bar. They had not spoken since. The last he had heard was that Gabriel had started working for the police.

Shit, shit, shit.

Skunk took a fresh drag on his cigarette and made up his mind.

It had to be.

Gabriel Mørk. There was no other way. Skunk tossed the cigarette, checked over his shoulder again and made his way home to his bunker.

Chapter 20

Mia Krüger summoned the waiter, ordered a Guinness and a Jägermeister and waited for him to leave before she opened the file in front of her.

She was in the venerable old pub at the bottom of Hegdehaugsveien where she had started seeking solace when her flat, which was only a few minutes away, grew too lonely and cold.

She had found a table she liked, in the far corner, where she could hide, be alone with her thoughts, while at the same time feeling there was life around her. Mia had always liked this place. As a student, she had spent a great deal of time here. There were booths with red leather seats and white tablecloths. Waiters in white shirts with bow-ties. A varied clientele, everything from businessmen in suits to shabby-looking artists and writers. You could hide here but, more importantly, it was one of the few venues in Oslo that did not play music. Mia preferred the silence, the muted voices over clattering glasses, to the constant intrusion of noise from loudspeakers.

She took a big gulp of her beer and stared at the first photograph. A naked girl. Posed in a pentagram of candles. On a bed of feathers. Wearing a blonde wig. With a flower in her mouth. Mia drained her beer, felt the alcohol kick in, ordered another round and took a pen and notepad from her bag.

Three months.
Skinny. Grazes and blisters.
Animal feed in her stomach.
Went missing three months before she was found.

The voices around her slowly faded away while she disappeared more and more deeply into her thoughts.

That had to be it.

Someone had kept her prisoner.

Here. In Norway. While ordinary people got up in the morning, said goodbye to their loved ones, went to work, chatted over lunch, picked up their kids from nursery, had dinner, did the housework, watched the news, went to bed, turned off their bedside lamp in the expectation of another, ordinary day, seventeen-year-old Camilla Green had been trapped somewhere, almost starved to death, terrified, alone.

Mia Krüger took a swig of her second Guinness, pressed her lips shut and tried her best not to let herself be taken back to the place she had been less than twenty-four hours ago. This evil. This darkness.

Come, Mia, come.

No.

Come, Mia.

No, not now.

But we can be together!

No, Sigrid, I have to . . .

'Another round?'

Mia Krüger was roused by the waiter standing in front of her.

'Huh?'

'Another round?' The old waiter with the bow-tie nodded at the empty glasses in front of her.

'Yes, please,' Mia said, and managed to produce a small smile.

The waiter nodded politely, returned with two fresh drinks and disappeared back into the room.

Sod it.

Mia put the file back into her bag and drained the shot glass with trembling fingers.

Crap.

Perhaps she had lost it. Her talent. Her ability to see things other people could not. The reason Munch had picked her out from the police college, before she had even finished her training. Perhaps the therapist had been right.

I think it's your job that's making you ill.

You care too much.

I think it might kill you.

Mia lay the pen on her notepad and put on her jacket. She nodded to the bouncer and stepped outside for a bit of fresh air. She found a chair and watched two drunk businessmen smoke while they discussed a deal they had made during the day.

He dresses her up.

She had tried to push it aside, yet now it crept up on her again.

He dresses her up. A blonde wig. A flower in her mouth. He makes her look nice. He gets her ready. Camilla. She is naked. The virgin. He needs her for something. Something we can't see.

Mia walked unsteadily past the bouncers, back to her table, and put pen to paper again.

He?

Or was there more than one?

Her mobile vibrated on the table in front of her, the display said 'Holger', but she just let it ring.

Mia took a sip of her beer and thought more deeply. The wig. *Why this particular wig?* Camilla was not exactly blonde. Was that why? Blonde? She had to be blonde, because . . . ? Seventeen years old. Young. Scandinavian. Blonde. Thin? Had he starved her because he wanted her to be thinner? Was that why she had been imprisoned? Because she had to look like this? Exactly like this? The pen raced across the sheet now, as the room around her disappeared. *She has to look like this. The wig. Blonde and skinny. She is not herself. She is not meant to be herself. It's not Camilla, lying there. It is someone else. Who is lying there? Who are you?*

Mia drained her glass, almost without noticing it, then continued to scribble on the paper.

A present.

The candles and the feathers.

They are the wrapping.

The flower.
She is presented to someone as a gift.
'More?'

A baffled Mia looked up from her notes, not quite sure where she was. She had been close to something, something deep inside, but reality had called her back.

'Another round?' the waiter asked.

'Yes.' Mia nodded quickly, trying to get back to the place she had been, but the feeling was gone. There were only drunk people with their beer glasses in the booths now, and she became aware of just how much alcohol she had consumed; she was barely able to read the display on her mobile.

Holger Munch.

He had called her six times.

And sent her a text message.

Where are you? Call.

She found his number and tried to pull herself together as she heard the ring tone far, far away. Mia could not put her finger on it, but there was something about Munch which made her feel guilty. For drinking so much. For being depressed. For wanting to disappear. He had had high hopes of her, perhaps that was the reason. She could vividly recall their first meeting. He had tried to make out that she would be *incredibly* lucky to be offered a place with the newly created investigation unit he would be heading, but during the entire interview it had become so blatantly obvious that he wanted her at any cost that she had not felt uncomfortable or nervous. He was good like that, Holger. That was why she was so fond of him. He loathed talking about his feelings, and yet he was almost transparent. Or he was to her. *Come, Mia, come.*

The waiter returned with another round as she heard her boss's deep voice on the other end.

'Yes?' Munch grunted.

'Yes?'

'Yes, what?'

'You called me,' Mia retorted, hoping she sounded relatively sober.

'Right,' Munch replied. He sounded as if he was busy doing something else, as if it had slipped his mind that he had called her earlier. 'We've had two phone calls from the press, some hours ago, one from *Dagbladet*, the other from *VG*,' he said, concentrating now. 'The cat is out of the bag, if I can put it like that. They will be printing pictures from the crime scene tomorrow. They might already be available online.'

'From the crime scene?' Mia was surprised. 'How did they get hold of them?'

'Beats me,' Munch growled. 'But there's not a lot we can do about it, so we just have to deal with it. I've spoken to Anette, and she will take it up with Grønland tomorrow morning. We will hold a press conference at nine o'clock, and we'll just have to take it from there. But . . .' Munch fell silent again, as if pondering what to say next.

'But what?'

'We've got it under control, but it's important that . . .' Munch cleared his throat.

'What is?'

Another silence followed.

'You need to keep a low profile,' Munch then said hurriedly, as if it was something he had dreaded telling her.

'What do you mean?' Mia asked.

'We need to keep you on the outside.'

'Outside, how?'

'You're not officially back at work, so, well, you know how these things work; with your reputation, if the newspapers find out that you're working on the case, while you're still suspended, then . . .'

Mia could feel herself getting irritated. She reached for her beer and took a long swig.

'Are you still there?' Munch asked feebly.

'Yes, I'm here,' Mia said abruptly. 'Has Mikkelson been after you?'

'Well, yes, but . . .'

Munch seemed uncomfortable about the whole situation, and Mia saw no point in giving him a hard time. It was not his fault. She knew that if Munch had been in charge, then he would have done anything for her.

'Relax, Holger,' she said, and managed to calm herself down. 'I can be invisible, if you need me to be. No problem.'

'Thank you,' he said, sounding relieved.

Why would she want to talk to the papers, anyway? They had persecuted her for weeks back when she shot Markus Skog, Sigrid's boyfriend. She had not been able to leave her flat and, eventually, she had been forced to hide in a hotel in another part of Oslo. No, definitely not. She had absolutely no problem keeping a low profile.

'No problem. Don't worry about it, Holger. So, online tonight, and on the front pages tomorrow morning?'

'Sounds like it,' Munch said, happy that she was changing the topic.

'But they're not going to show pictures of the body, are they?'

'No, no. They're a bunch of morons but, occasionally, they have some kind of moral code, oddly enough.'

'So what will they publish?'

'Just the crime scene.'

'Pictures from the location where the body was found?'

'I don't know the details, but I'm guessing they have the pentagram, the candles, the feathers from where she was lying. Bloody vultures. Ludvig is trying to figure out how they got them. And speaking of . . .'

Mia took another swig of her beer as she saw a familiar face appear at the door. A compact bulldog of a man with a shaved head was arguing with one of the bouncers, who clearly had no intention of letting him in.

'Ludvig has information about the feathers.'

'What?' Mia said, getting up.

'The feathers from the crime scene,' Munch continued. 'They're owl feathers.'

'An owl? All the feathers?'

'Yes, apparently. Not that I know how they can tell them apart, but—'

'We'll have to do this tomorrow,' Mia interrupted him. 'Something has come up my end, OK?'

'What? Yes, OK. Team briefing at ten o'clock.'

'Sure thing.'

'Great, and thanks for, well, you know,' Munch mumbled.

'No problem,' Mia rounded off, now on her way to the squabble by the door.

'Mia.' Curry grinned and held out his arms to her when he spotted her.

'He's not coming in.'

'I'm not pissed, you moron,' Curry slurred, freeing himself from the massive bouncer's grip on his arm.

'It's fine,' Mia said. 'He's coming with me. Just let me get my things.'

'Mia, tell him!' Curry said, tripping over his own feet and crashing to the floor.

'He's banned. We don't want to see him here again,' the bouncer said sternly when Mia returned to the door with her bag.

'How can I be banned? I haven't even been inside yet. And I'm not drunk. You should see me when I *am* drunk . . .'

'Come on, Curry,' Mia said, and flashed the bouncer an apologetic smile as she ushered her colleague out of the pub.

THREE

Chapter 21

The man with the white bicycle helmet did not like leaving the house, but he had no choice today, because there was nothing left in the fridge. He had hoped that the food would last longer, the groceries he had bought the last time he went shopping; he could not quite remember when, but it was some time ago. Possibly last Tuesday, or was it in April? No, April, he was quite sure of that; April followed March, and March was a long time ago. In March the bin men had come to collect everything he had put in the green container by the outhouse. No, not in March, on Tuesdays, they emptied the bins on Tuesdays, when he would usually hide in the bathroom, so he was sure about that. Not in March. On Tuesdays, he would hide in the bathroom so they would not come to the house to ask if they could borrow his telephone or use his lavatory, because they had done that once. And the bin man with the gloves had peed on the edge of the toilet seat and laughed at him for wearing his bicycle helmet inside, and ever since then he had hidden himself in the bathroom every time they came.

Every Tuesday. In March. No, not only March, every month. October. It was October now. He had turned the page on his calendar some days ago. Yes, he had, he remembered that. Going from September to October. September had had a picture of a seagull. And now the seagull was no longer there; instead, there was a fox. Quite a cunning fox, with a tail that was white at the tip, and it had winked at him as he sat at the kitchen table eating the last tin of tuna. It had made him realize that the fridge was empty and that, although he did not want to, he would soon have to cycle down to the shop again, and hope that they would not laugh at him, like they usually did.

Furtively. That was how they did it. Not when he was in there, no, never then; at times they would even pretend to be friendly. The young woman with the chewing gum, and the other woman who was behind the till, when he showed them the list he had written of the things he needed, they pretended to be kind to him then. Walked around with him and helped him put things in the basket, crispbread and tins of mackerel in tomato sauce and pork chops; they would not laugh then. Nor when it was time to pay either, even when he was unable to make the money in his wallet match the number on the till. Not then either – they would pretend to be nice and help him count – but afterwards. When he had left the shop and pretended to have cycled home but was really watching from behind the bottle bank, or from behind the van, which said 'Hurumlandet Supermarket', then they would laugh at him, laugh out loud while slapping their knees, because he always wore his bicycle helmet. It took twenty-four minutes to cycle each way, if the road was not too slippery, as it was today, and he realized that he was dreading it more than usual as he unlocked his bicycle and pushed it carefully down to the main road.

It took nearly thirty-five minutes today. It was that icy. October, no longer September, but still it was almost winter. Perhaps it was all his fault? He had worried about this recently, that it might be his fault that it was so cold. The sky was heating up, he had read about it; the ice around the North Pole and the South Pole would melt unless you sorted your rubbish properly. Usually, he was very careful about it – food waste in the food-waste container, plastics in the plastic container; he never mixed cardboard or paper with the other rubbish, and always compressed milk cartons and cans before he threw them out – but he had been ill some weeks ago. His head had been aching, and he had had feverish dreams in the middle of the day, and it had made him forget all about recycling; he had just chucked everything into the same bin and, when he realized his mistake, it had been too late. He had eaten nothing for four days, in the hope that it would make up for his mistake, but he had started passing out and been forced to eat something in the end. When he had woken up the next day, there had been ice in the yard outside, and ever since then he had been sweating profusely, and he had hidden himself behind the kitchen curtains every time he saw light down on the road, scared that they had realized what he had done. That they were coming to get him. But, fortunately, none of the cars had turned off and driven up towards the house. They hardly ever did. He rarely had any visitors. Just the bin men on Tuesdays.

He attached the front wheel to the bicycle stand with one lock and looped the chain, which he had carried in his rucksack, around the rear wheel. He spent a few minutes checking that both locks were secure before he started the long walk towards the door. He never went straight inside; no, he had tried that once, and it had gone horribly wrong, his mind had been on other things, and he had just opened the door and stepped right into the shop, and no, that had ended badly. There had been wolves inside, huge, grey wolves with big eyes and slavering jaws, and he had been so scared that he had knocked over a stand with sunglasses and, on his way out, he had run right into the door, then an ambulance had turned up and they had laughed at him again, all the nurses and the doctors who had stitched his face with a needle and thread, and after that time he had learned that it was best to be careful. So now he always approached in a small arc, swinging past the glass doors so that he could take a look inside, then a quick glance at the advertisements, because it was OK to pretend to be looking at today's promotions, you didn't look stupid. Barbecue sausages for 19.90 kroner. Three packets of nappies for the price of two. No wolves today. The man with the white bicycle helmet heaved a sigh of relief, yet still he waited several minutes and had another look inside to be sure before he plucked up the courage and walked the last, heavy steps up towards the door to the supermarket.

As always, a bell rang out above him, but this time he was prepared, so he was not scared. He picked up a basket from the stack, took out his shopping list from his pocket and moved as quickly as he could up and down the aisles. Milk. Yes. Eggs. Yes. Salmon fillets. Yes. He was starting to feel better now: the things on his list were easy to put into the basket today; none of them refused, like they did sometimes. Bananas. Yes. Potatoes. Yes. Chicken. Yes. He began to smile: today was his lucky day; look how well it was all going. He liked chicken, but it would not always go into the basket, sometimes he had to eat just potatoes, but today nothing was difficult at all. The chicken came of its own accord today. Perhaps it was not his fault, after all, that winter had come so early? He smiled to himself, put the last items on the list into his basket and walked proudly up to the till.

The young woman put down a magazine and blew a big, pink bubble, and she did not look at him as if he were an idiot, no; in fact, she smiled faintly. He could feel his heart beat a little faster under his puffa jacket as he started putting his groceries on the conveyor belt. She had probably realized it, too. That today was his lucky day. That it was not his fault, this business about the weather.

'Do you want a bag?' the young woman said when she had scanned all the items.

'No, thank you.' He smiled contentedly, and was just about to put his shopping into his rucksack when he saw them.

On the stand nearest the till.

The newspapers.

Oh no.

'Cash or card?'

He stood rooted to the spot, unable to move.

On both front pages.

The photograph.

How could they have . . .?

'Excuse me? How would you like to pay?'

'The chicken came of its own accord,' he muttered, not taking his eyes off the photograph on the front of the newspapers.

'What are you talking about?' the girl said.

'The chicken.'

'Yes?' The girl sounded hesitant now.

'It came of its own accord. It doesn't always.'

'No, OK . . .' the girl behind the till said. 'So will you be paying by card or cash?'

'No, I have a rucksack.'

'Rucksack?'

'I don't need a bag.

'No, OK . . . But . . . How are you going to pay for your shopping?'

'It's not my fault.'

'What do you mean?'

'I didn't kill the cat.'

'The cat?'

The expression in the girl's eyes had changed.

'I didn't kill the dog either.'

'The dog? Yes, OK . . . Will you be paying by card or . . .?'

A wolf was approaching. A fat wolf with glasses. From another door at the back of the supermarket. The wolf was getting closer and closer to him, and all the man in the white bicycle helmet wanted to do was run out of the shop, but his feet were no longer working; they seemed glued to the floor. He closed his eyes and stuffed his fingers into his ears; today was Tuesday, and it was probably better to hide in the bathroom, especially in March, when the bin men came – no, not March, October, the fox had said so.

'Hello, Jim, is that you?'

Jim opened his eyes and saw that it was not a wolf after all. It was the nice man. The nice man with the beard who owned the shop.

'The chicken wanted to get into the basket,' he insisted as the nice man with the beard looked across to the girl behind the till, who just shrugged.

'Is there a problem with the payment?'

The girl with the chewing gum pressed her finger against her temple and shook her head, but the nice man with the beard looked at her sternly so she quickly lowered it.

'Come on, Jim, let's pack up your shopping,' said the nice man who owned the shop, and helped him get his things into the rucksack.

'I didn't kill the dog,' Jim said, and shook his head vigorously.

'I'm quite sure you didn't,' the nice man with the beard said, walking him to the doors, and they opened easily now, almost automatically.

'Don't worry about paying me today, Jim. We can do that some other time, OK?'

The nice man smiled and did not laugh, showing his teeth, even when Jim struggled with one of the bicycle locks.

'You know that I'd be happy to deliver your shopping, don't you? You only have to call, and I'll come to your house.'

'It's very important to do things for yourself.'

'Yes, of course it is. And you're doing really well, Jim. But if you need anything, you just call, OK?'

'The tip of the fox's tail is white, that's why it's October,' he said, before stepping hard on the pedals and cycling home: a new record this time, less than twenty-two minutes, even though it was terribly, terribly slippery, especially in the middle of the road.

Chapter 22

Curry woke up to a beeping sound and reached for the alarm clock on his bedside table to make it stop. His fingers found the button and the sound disappeared. He drifted back to sleep with a smile on his face, hugging the duvet around him and rolling towards Sunniva to feel the heat from her body. He loved lying like this. These short moments, brief minutes where they would act as if neither of them had to go to work. When they turned off the alarm, pretending it was a day off to be spent as they wished, do exactly what they wanted: no demands, no bosses, just the two of them under the duvet. Her warm, soft skin against his as she buried her nose at the base of his neck and snuggled up to him, as if she wanted him to take care of her. Curry smiled and pulled her closer. Sunniva. He had known it from the very first moment he saw her. That she was the one for him. With her long, red hair and pretty smile; the woman always got her morning coffee at the same place he did every day, he on his way to the police college, she a nurse on her way to work.

Curry opened his eyes and saw a pile of cardboard boxes in a flat that was not his own, and reality slowly began to dawn on him. He had been asleep, fully dressed, on a sofa, not at home, no, definitely not at home; she had changed the lock, she must have done, because his key no longer fitted. The beeping sound came back. Curry slowly got up from the sofa and, still half asleep, followed the sound out into the hallway until he found a man on the other side of the door to Mia's flat.

'Mia Krüger?' the man with the thin moustache said, checking a piece of paper in his hand.

'Does it look like it?' Curry mumbled, realizing he was still drunk.

A two-day bender. After she had told him she had had enough. Sunniva.

'Eh, yes, no,' the man said, looking around now, clearly taken aback by the sight he had stumbled upon.

Screw you, Jon. And this time I bloody mean it. I've had it up to here. All the money? All our money? Do you know how hard I've worked for that? Do you?

'Do I look like my name is Mia Krüger?'

He could smell himself now, and hoped that this man had not noticed.

'I can come back later,' said the man, who was wearing a boiler suit; he looked almost apologetic now. 'But there's mould in the basement . . .'

'What?' Curry said. He was struggling to stay upright; the narrow passage was moving under his feet.

'Only this is the last flat,' the short man outside the door said. 'The housing co-operative has . . .'

'OK.' Curry nodded, grabbing the wall for support as the floor underneath his feet started undulating.

A little later, he was outside Bislett Stadium, now also wearing his shoes and coat; he had given the man in the boiler suit the key to the flat, told him to just pop it through the letterbox. He searched his pockets until he found a box of snuff and stuffed a lump behind his upper lip as he flagged down a cab that was driving slowly down Bislettgata.

The lift at work felt oppressive. He had taken it a million times, but today was different. It was like being inside a tin can; he was relieved when the doors opened and let him out.

'Hello?'

Curry slowly wove his way through the office, but it was quiet. He went to the kitchen, fetched himself a cup of coffee from the pot, slowly made his way to the incident room.

'Hello?'

'Hi, so you decided to come in after all?' Ylva had suddenly appeared in front of him in the corridor.

'What do you mean, "after all"?' Curry smiled, took a sip of his coffee, tried to appear sober.

'Mia said you were ill, that you wouldn't be coming in, that was all,' she said, continuing in front of him down the corridor.

'Yes, I have a bit of a cold,' Curry said, and coughed. 'But I had to come in. I couldn't bear being at home, you know what it's like. How are things here? Anything happened?'

He followed Ylva down to her desk, making sure to keep a safe distance so that she would not detect his bad body odour.

Bollocks.

He took out his mobile from his pocket: nothing, not a word from Sunniva, although he had called her a million times and left just as many messages.

Come on. Surely we can talk about this?

Why won't you pick up the phone?

Call me?

Call me, OK? When you can?

I miss you.

Call me, please?

'Anette took part in a press conference this morning at nine o'clock, and Munch gave a team briefing at ten. Has Mia brought you up to speed, or do you want me to?'

Ylva smiled and straightened her glasses, then went over to the computer by the window.

'No, no,' Curry said, and took another sip of his coffee. 'I'm totally up to speed, obviously, but where are all the others?'

'Would you like the short version of the morning meeting? Although you're totally up to speed, obviously?'

Curry smiled and nodded back. She was not so bad after all, the newcomer. He followed her into the incident room.

'So, how far had you got?' Ylva said, pointing to the big board by the window. 'Do you know about Anders Finstad?'

'Eh?' Curry said.

Ylva scratched her head and turned to him. 'Why don't I just start from the beginning?'

'Thank you.' Curry nodded and took a seat.

'What's the last thing you know?' Ylva asked him.

'Naked girl. Found strangled in the woods with a flower in her mouth.'

'Camilla Green,' Ylva said.

'We've identified her?'

'Yes,' Ylva continued; they both knew he should have known this. 'Camilla Green, aged seventeen, living at some kind of halfway home for teenagers, children in care. Do you want the details, or . . . ?'

'No, no, just make it quick.' Curry smiled.

'OK,' Ylva said, turning to the board again. 'So, Camilla Green. Reported missing from this place called Hurumlandet Nurseries three months ago, but then they withdrew the report because they were told that she was fine and not to look for her.'

'Told how?' Curry asked, feeling the detective inside him starting to stir.

'A text message,' she said, taking a piece of paper from the board and placing it in front of him.

'Her telephone records?'

'Yes.' Ylva nodded. 'Gabriel got them from Telenor yesterday, but the strange thing is, and this is something Munch, Kim and Mia have been discussing all day, that the message was sent from the Nurseries.'

'What do you mean?' Curry asked, surprised.

'Gabriel should really be explaining this to you, but he said something about – mobile towers?'

'Go on?'

'Camilla disappeared, and they reported her missing,' Ylva continued. 'But then they got a text from her, saying she was OK and that they should stop looking for her.'

'And that message was sent from that place? Hurumlandet Nurseries?' Curry was intrigued.

'Yep.' Ylva nodded.

He got up and walked closer to the board with all the pictures.

'So . . . you mentioned a name. Do we have a suspect already?'

'Anders Finstad.' Ylva placed her finger on a black-and-white picture of a middle-aged man in a riding helmet in front of something that had to be stables.

'And who is this?'

'The tattoo?'

'What tattoo?' Curry asked, starting to feel a bit stupid now.

A two-day piss-up, drinks in both hands, wallowing in self-pity, while a madman was on the loose. They had made extensive progress, and he had contributed sod all.

'The initials AF – do you see them?'

'Yes,' Curry said, following her finger on the picture.

'And the horse's head?'

'Aha?'

'He's Anders Finstad,' Ylva said. 'Camilla loved horses. Finstad runs a riding school, not far from the Nurseries, where she lived.'

'And?'

'We found him in our files: sixty-six years old. Previously reported for assault. Encouraged two girls at the riding school to strip from the waist up in front of one of the horses so that he could take pictures of them. The girls were twelve and fourteen years old.'

'Holy shit . . .'

'I know.' Ylva nodded.

'So? What happened?'

'The report didn't lead to anything. Clever lawyer, lack of evidence – what do I know? – but, anyway, they're focusing on Anders Finstad now. Camilla belonged to his riding school. She was a skilled rider, too, as far as I can gather. Might have been a contender for the junior national show-jumping team.'

'Wow.'

Ylva nodded. 'Mia has gone there now. The rest of the team are out at Hurumlandet Nurseries.'

'Any cars left in the basement?' Curry asked.

'I don't know,' Ylva said, leading the way out into the corridor. 'Do you want me to put you down as being on duty, or are you off sick?'

'I thought it was Grønlie's job to log that?'

'Nope.' Ylva sighed. 'Does the newcomer always get all the crap jobs?'

'You'll have to take it up with Anette.' Curry winked, found a set of car keys in the cupboard, left the empty coffee cup in the kitchen and took the lift down to the basement.

Chapter 23

Munch was quickly let through the cordons outside the entrance to Hurumlandet Nurseries and, as the press photographers' flashlights struck his car, he was extremely pleased that he had chosen to send Mia to the riding school.

He shook his head and glanced up at the rear-view mirror as he drove up the avenue leading to the Nurseries. Helene Eriksen had called him early that morning, and she had not exaggerated: 'The place has been invaded by the press, like a swarm of locusts, they get in everywhere. The girls are scared. What do we do?'

Munch smiled to himself as he parked in front of the main building and got out of the black Audi. He was starting to like Helene Eriksen. Locusts. He could not have put it better himself.

Munch lit a cigarette as Kim Kolsø came down the steps of the big white house.

'What a circus,' Kim said, nodding towards the bottom of the avenue.

'Seems we have it under control,' Munch said. 'How does it look?'

'Good.' Kim nodded, looking about him quickly. 'We have been given two classrooms and an office. It's a bit primitive, but we have managed to get started. Grønlie seems chuffed to be out of the office, the Jensen Twins are here, I've put up the lists like you asked me to; you and I will interview the more important ones.'

Munch had requested assistance from police headquarters at Grønland, and Mikkelson had allocated them two officers from Kripos, the national crime agency, both called Jensen, and better known as the Jensen Twins. They would not have been Munch's first choice, but they needed more manpower, so it was better than nothing.

'Curry is on his way. He can work with them,' Munch informed him, taking a deep drag on his cigarette in order to hide his irritation.

'Really? I thought Mia said he was ill?'

'He seems to have recovered.'

'Good,' Kim said, walking in front of his boss up the steps and into the improvised interview room.

'So who is first?' Munch asked when he had taken off his coat and rubbed his hands warm.

It was still cold outside. Munch thought about Mia. Munch hated the cold and the darkness but knew that his young colleague suffered much more from them. It was as if the darkness took hold of her mind and did not release its grip until springtime. He put Mia out of his mind and looked at the name at the top of the list Kolsø had put in front of him.

'Benedikte Riis?' he said, looking quizzically towards his colleague. 'I thought we had agreed that you and I would take this Paulus first?'

Kim gave a light, apologetic shrug. 'Grønlie took him.'

'Why?'

'He insisted. Paulus was standing outside when we arrived,' Kim said. 'Didn't seem like he had got a lot of sleep: "I guess you'll want to talk to me first, given who I am? I would like to be interviewed first."'

'I see,' Munch grunted. '"*Who I am*"? What did he mean by that?'

'I guess he thinks we've seen his rap sheet.'

'Minor stuff, wasn't it?' Munch was a little surprised.

'Yes, indeed. Possession of a bit of cannabis, breaking into a shop, crashing a stolen car, all when he was a juvenile. He might have done other things we don't know about. He was certainly feeling guilty about something.'

'OK,' Munch said, flicking through the papers in front of him. 'And who is Benedikte Riis?'

'The last person to see Camilla Green alive. Says she has important information. I believe Helene Eriksen has tried to get it out of her, but she refuses to open her mouth unless she can speak to a police officer.'

'Is that right?' Munch said, raising his eyebrows. 'OK, let's get her in.'

Chapter 24

Anders Finstad was waiting on the steps when Mia Krüger pulled up outside Hurum Equestrian Centre. From the outside, it looked very much like the Nurseries. A long avenue with majestic birches flanked by frost-covered fields leading to what seemed to be a beautifully maintained estate. An impressive main house, a gravel yard, a very pretty red-brick building which would appear to be the stables. Mia Krüger got out of her car; she had a really good feeling about the place. True, there was no open sea, and yet it was like being at Hitra. There was calm out here.

'Hello,' he said, walking quickly down to meet her. 'Anders Finstad.'

'Mia Krüger,' Mia responded, shaking his cold hand. He had clearly been outside for a while.

'Yes, I know who you are.' He nodded, smiling faintly. 'Under different circumstances, I would have said that I'm honoured by your visit.'

'Ah.' Mia smiled, trying to determine whether this was an attempt to charm her, to make her more favourably disposed to him, but she could see no signs of it. Her first impression of Finstad was similar to her feelings about the place he owned: he was a man who cared about his appearance without it in any way seeming excessive.

'What a tragedy,' Anders Finstad said, once he had shown her into what Mia took to be the living room. He gestured to a chair, and smiled again cautiously.

'May I offer you something or should we . . .?'

'Get right to it?' Mia smiled and hung her leather jacket on the back of the chair.

'Yes . . .' Finstad said, looking as though that was the answer he had been expecting and hoping for.

He pulled out a chair opposite her, sat down and stared at the white tablecloth, then seemed to brace himself, though Mia had yet to ask any questions.

'I realized it, of course,' he said, looking up at her tentatively.

'What did you realize?'

'That you would think it was me.'

'Who told you we think it's you?'

'You don't?' Finstad looked surprised.

Mia could not help but feel a little sorry for the polite, well-dressed man sitting in front of her. He had dark rims under his eyes, and his hands were fidgeting on the table in front of him. It was clear that recent events had affected him deeply.

'Right now, we don't think anything. We're keeping an open mind,' Mia said. 'But, of course, you knew Camilla. She was a student here—'

'Oh, no.' Anders Finstad said.

'No what?'

'Not a student, no. I wouldn't call her that.'

'What do you mean?'

'Camilla was . . .' Finstad leaned slightly back in his chair, as if trying to find the right words.

'What was she?'

'Special,' he said after a while. 'She was nobody's student, if I may put it like that.'

'Please explain.'

'You couldn't tell Camilla what to do. She was very headstrong, very strong-willed.'

'So she wasn't your student, here at the riding school?'

'What? Oh, yes, on paper, but you could not tell Camilla what to do. Fine girl. Absolutely. I realized it the first time Helene brought her. Has that ever happened to you? That you meet people who, well, who are more charismatic than others, who have a kind of, well . . .?'

Finstad didn't seem able to find the words and continued to fix his gaze on the white tablecloth.

'You liked her?' Mia asked.

'What? Yes, everyone liked Camilla.'

'Including you?'

'Oh, yes.'

'Were you very fond of her?'

'Oh, yes,' Finstad said again, then suddenly realized where Mia was heading with her line of questioning.

'Oh, no, no, not like that . . .'

Finstad continued to sit very still; he seemed to be expecting the next question.

'September 2011.'

'Yes.'

'You know what I'm talking about?'

'Of course.' Finstad nodded, still without looking at her.

'Two girls, your students, aged twelve and fourteen.'

'I know . . .'

'The photographs of them naked from the waist up in front of a horse?'

Finstad raised his hands from the table and covered his face. 'I'm not proud of it . . .' he said hesitantly.

'But you did it?'

'We all make mistakes, don't we?'

He looked at her now, and Mia's pity suddenly turned into disgust.

'"Make mistakes"? So you think it's acceptable to take pictures of naked little girls, is that what you're saying?'

'What?' Finstad said, shocked.

'You went out to the stables. You took your camera. You used the power you have over innocent girls to make them pose naked for you. That is somehow forgivable, is that what you're saying?'

For the first time, Mia could feel last night's alcohol rush to her head. Bloody Curry. He had kept her awake half the night.

Talking about Sunniva. His gambling. It was not the first time, and it was probably not going to be the last. Finally, she had made up a bed for him on the sofa and dragged her mattress into one of the bedrooms, where she had tried to get some sleep. She had not had the heart to wake him when the alarm clock went off. The lack of sleep was starting to take its toll now; it made her angry and irritable, less professional than she ought to be.

'You're a paedophile, and you're making excuses for it, is that how I'm supposed to see it?'

'What?' Finstad was mystified.

'You heard me.'

'What? God, no,' Finstad said. 'You don't have all the papers?'

Mia had not got the full file from Munch, but she did not tell Finstad that. 'You took pictures of two girls naked in front of a horse, that's what we have.'

'No, no, no!' Finstad exclaimed. 'You don't have all the documents from that dreadful case? But you must have!'

She had taken pills as well. In order to be able to sleep. Sitting up with Curry half the night. Three hours until the briefing. She had swallowed some in the bathroom and passed out almost without any recollection of her head hitting the pillow.

'So what is it that you're not proud of?' Mia cleared her throat, and pulled herself together.

'Of course I wasn't proud. I cheated on her. My ex-wife,' Finstad said, looking at her now, puzzled. 'Doesn't your file tell you that?'

Mia cleared her throat again. She could feel herself starting to lose patience with Munch. He had sent her out here without all the relevant information.

'Of course,' Mia lied, 'but I had to check.'

'That it was her revenge?' Finstad said.

'Yes,' Mia said.

'That my wife made it all up? To get her own back? Because I cheated on her? That she admitted it later? That the investigation was called off?'

'Yes, yes, we know, but I had to ask.'

'Yes, yes, of course.'

'I'm sorry,' Mia said, and she meant it.

'Don't mention it,' the well-dressed man said, offering her a small smile now. 'But I regret it. I behaved badly. I'm not really like that, but . . .'

'It's none of my business,' Mia said, trying to look as kindly at him as she could.

Her headache arrived at full speed now. Bloody Munch. Bloody Curry.

'Such a tragedy.' Anders Finstad shifted his gaze to his hands again. 'Camilla was so special. She just was. Really.'

'Did she come here often?'

'Yes.' Finstad nodded. 'Almost every evening, in some periods. She was one of the few girls who had her own locker. Did I mention that she was very talented? When she came here the first time, she had barely ever sat on a horse. I remember—'

'A locker?' Mia interrupted.

'Yes. The keenest girls have them. They keep all their equipment here. It's more convenient that way.'

'Can I look inside?'

'Oh – of course.'

Chapter 25

Isabella Jung's dad had always told her not to judge a book by its cover, and she had tried to live by that principle, not letting her first impression of someone determine their relationship, but now she was absolutely sure: she could not stand the sight of Benedikte Riis.

They had gathered in the TV lounge while waiting to be called individually to talk to the police, and Benedikte Riis had been the first to go in; of course she had. She had demanded to be interviewed first because she *knew Camilla better than anyone, she had been her best friend, and the last person to see her alive,* something Isabella Jung was pretty sure was bullshit, because Benedikte Riis was friends with no one but herself. Isabella had never come across anyone more self-obsessed. Isabella was overcome by the urge to tell the bitch to shut up. The last few days had been hard enough for everyone as it was. Isabella Jung was tough, she had managed on her own her whole life, but some of the residents had reacted badly to their sanctuary being overrun. Police officers everywhere. And all those reporters. Before the cordons had been put up, they would appear out of nowhere, and a couple of the girls had freaked out. Fortunately, the uniformed police officers had left by now, and only plainclothes investigators remained. There was no such thing as a normal day any more. Benedikte was back holding court in the small TV lounge. 'I told them like it was,' she said. 'Camilla and I were tight, we shared everything; if *I* don't know something, then no one knows it, do you get me?'

'Know what?' Cecilie piped up.

The tiny girl from Bergen had curled up fearfully in one corner of the sofa; she was hugging a cushion and looked as if she needed something to hide behind, something to cling to.

'Hello? Know what happened? Are you a moron?'

Benedikte Riis pressed her finger against her temple, and Isabella could barely contain herself.

'And what did you tell them?' Cecilie asked.

So much had happened that Isabella had almost forgotten the note someone had pinned to her door. The white lily. She didn't know what made her think of it now.

I like you.

The drawing below it.

Her heart had skipped a beat when she saw it. A secret admirer. Who liked *her*? Could it be . . .? No. Surely not.

Somehow, Benedikte Riis's intolerable face had found its way close to hers.

'And don't you dare tell anyone either.'

Benedikte jabbed a finger right at her; for some reason, all the girls in the room were staring at her now.

'Tell them what?' Isabella said.

'Oh, Jesus, are you deaf or something?' Benedikte sighed.

Isabella resisted the urge to get up and punch the bitch right in her stupid face.

'I said, none of us can tell them – we have to promise each other, don't we?'

She looked around the room for affirmation from her audience. Even the terrified Cecilie nodded feebly behind her cushion.

'Tell them what?' Isabella asked again.

'That she used to sneak out into the woods,' Wenche, another of the girls, said with a sigh; she had sat down by the window now and had lit a cigarette, although everyone knew that smoking inside was strictly prohibited.

'At night,' Sofia added.

'I didn't know that,' Isabella said.

'No, because you're new here, and, just so you know, don't think for one minute that Paulus fancies you just because he helps you with the orchids. Paulus helps *everybody* with the orchids, doesn't he, girls?'

Benedikte Riis laughed out loud, and Wenche and Sofia joined in.

'I promise not to say anything,' Cecilie piped up, the cushion now practically covering her face.

'Good.' Benedikte nodded.

'Why can't I tell anyone?' Isabella said, feeling a surge of defiance.

'Because I say so,' Benedikte said.

'You can't tell me what to do,' Isabella Jung said, and got up from her chair.

'Don't you dare, or—'

Benedikte's outburst was interrupted when the door opened and Helene entered.

The manager seemed exhausted. Normally, she would have told Wenche off for smoking, but not today.

'Isabella?' Helene Eriksen said wearily.

'Yes?' Isabella replied, and turned around.

'Your turn. They want to talk to you now.'

Chapter 26

Mia Krüger desperately wished she had got more sleep because then she might have felt a little stronger, handled this a little more professionally. The moment Anders Finstad opened the door to the stable, she suddenly felt sixteen again.

The place reminded her of Sigrid.

Mia stopped in the doorway, unable to move.

'Oh, I forgot the locker keys. I'm so sorry,' the owner of the equestrian centre said.

'No problem.' Mia smiled.

'Do you mind waiting here? I'll be back in a sec.'

'I'm in no hurry,' Mia nodded and stepped back from the doorway as Finstad rushed back across the yard.

Twice a week. Sitting in the back of her dad's Volvo. Going to a riding school near Horten. They had watched her, the whole family, Sigrid, smiling, sitting on the black horse, her blonde hair poking out from under the helmet. The smells of the stables brought back happy memories for Mia, but for some reason they also made her feel nauseous. She could not keep it in. She leaned against a wall and just made it round the corner before it came up. She vomited what little she had in her stomach, yet still she continued to gag. She stood bent double, gasping for air.

What on earth?

Her vision blurred. She had not eaten much recently. Only drunk alcohol. Swallowed pills. Not taken care of herself.

'Are you still here?'

Mia managed to pull herself together, put on a smile and walk back around the corner.

132

'There you are,' the man said, holding up a set of keys. 'I have . . .'

'If I could just use your bathroom for a moment?' Mia mumbled, pressing her lips together.

'Of course,' Finstad said. 'It's the first right inside the front door. Please, let me show you . . .'

'I'll be OK. I'll find it on my own,' she said, walking back across the yard as fast as she could. She let herself into the small lavatory and knelt in front of the toilet bowl and hyperventilated.

Hell.

Eventually, she managed to stand up again. She rinsed her mouth, splashed water on her face and looked at her reflection in the mirror. She was deathly pale. It was rare for Mia Krüger to feel scared, but her body had reacted so strongly. The memories of Sigrid in the stable had been enough.

We ought to talk about Sigrid, don't you think?

For the first time, it crossed her mind: perhaps he was right after all. Her therapist. He had sent her a text message. *You missed your last appointment. Shall I make you another one?* But she had not replied. She was back at work. That had been her original reason for going. Not to share her private life. Mia remained in front of the mirror until she felt some kind of normality return. Might it help, opening up? About her grief. Her misery. Her losses. Her mother, her father, her grandmother. Sigrid. She found a bottle of mouthwash in the bathroom cabinet and gargled with it. No way. She looked at her reflection in the mirror again and shook her head.

No. There was no way she could pour out her soul to a shrink. She washed her face.

Like hell.

This had nothing to do with her mental health. It was just a combination of not enough sleep, too much pressure, this case, and then that idiot Curry, to top it all. She was in total control. Mia nodded to her reflection in the mirror.

Total control.

She continued to stand in front of it for a few more minutes, until the colour returned to her face, then she walked back across the yard.

'Is everything all right?' Anders Finstad asked. He looked concerned.

'Pardon?' Mia smiled, and followed him into the stable. 'Yes, of course. Which one was her locker?'

She was a police officer again.

'This one,' Finstad said. 'Would you like me to open it?'

'Well, there's not much point in just looking at the door from the outside, is there?' she joked.

Finstad smiled. Fiddled briefly with the keys on the bunch in his hand, before finding the right one, while Mia took out a pair of latex gloves from the inside pocket of her jacket.

'Can I help you with anything?' Finstad asked when he had unlocked the door for her.

She could see that he was curious about the contents of the locker.

'I'll give you a shout if I need your help.' Mia smiled, and waited until he had left the stable before she opened the door to the locker.

A red riding jacket. A pair of knee-high black boots, a beige blouse on a hanger. A small piece of paper was stuck to the inside of the locker door. A hand-written note.

I like you.

There was a drawing underneath.

A bird.

It had been at the back of her mind, though she hadn't had time to process it since bumping into Curry. Munch's words from last night. The feathers at the crime scene.

Owl feathers.

Mia took out her mobile from her jacket and rang Munch. There was no reply, so she texted him a quick message instead: *Call me now.*

I like you.

A drawing.

A bird.

An owl.

Chapter 27

It should not have come as a surprise, and yet it did: how the light in the sky refused to come out, although it was early afternoon. Holger Munch lit a cigarette and watched his cold fingers in the orange glow from the tip and, yet again, the thought came back to him, the one he had had so many times recently: that people were never meant to live up here. This far north. An historic mistake. An anomaly. The Norwegian race were descendants of people who must have taken a wrong turn somewhere in the past; why else pick this cold, this darkness, when the planet was full of sunshine and beaches, fertile lands, gardens of Eden? There was little evidence of that here, he decided, as he stood with the hood of his duffel coat up, trying to discern a pattern in the information he had gathered from the hours of interviewing the girls. So far, not one of them had given them anything on which they could build any kind of investigation. They all seemed terrified, and none of them was keen to speak to the police.

Munch tightened his duffel coat and took another drag on his cigarette as the door to the main building opened and Helene Eriksen walked down the steps towards him.

'You can smoke indoors, if you like,' she said, attempting a smile, although she clearly had to force it.

She had seemed broken the first time he had met her, and the last couple of days had not helped. That little spark of life he had seen in her eyes then was completely gone now, and Munch could not help but feel sorry for her.

'And we can get you some coffee,' she offered cautiously. 'Today has been just as long for you, as it has been for us.'

'I don't drink coffee these days,' Munch said politely, 'but a cup of tea would be nice.'

'I have tea as well,' Helene smiled, and led the way back inside, where she showed him into a small sitting room on the ground floor.

'My sanctuary,' the manager said when Munch had taken a seat. 'Sometimes it's good to have a place where you can be on your own.'

Munch put his coat over the armrest of the chair. He was growing to like this woman. She helped people. She ran a home for troubled youngsters. A good person with a big heart.

'I don't have many varieties to choose from,' she said, placing a bowl of teabags on the table in front of him.

'That's quite all right,' Munch said. 'Anything to get the cold out of my bones.'

'I couldn't agree more.'

Helene sat down in the armchair opposite him as Munch picked a random teabag and poured water from a kettle into his mug.

'Do you mind if I have one?' she said, gesturing to his cigarettes on the table.

'Of course.'

'I don't smoke, not really,' Helene said apologetically, placing a cigarette between her lips. 'I quit a long time ago, it's a filthy habit, I know, but, well . . .'

'I understand.' Munch smiled as he reached across the table and flicked his lighter for her.

Helene leaned back and blew smoke up at the ceiling. She looked as if she was mulling something over, as if she had something on her mind, something she wanted to share with him, but nothing came.

'We're almost finished,' Munch said, to reassure her. 'You'll be left in peace soon, we've got a lot done, spoken to most people on our list today.'

'Have you learned anything? Has it been useful?'

'I can't discuss the details with you. I hope you can understand that,' Munch said. 'But yes, I think we've found out what we needed to.'

'Good.' Helene smiled. 'If you need anything from me, it goes without saying that you can contact me any time. You just let me know, OK?'

'Thank you, Helene. You have been nothing but helpful. We really appreciate that.'

'That's good,' she said, taking another quick drag on her cigarette, before stubbing it out in the ashtray and turning to Munch with another smile.

'I used to smoke twenty a day, but now I can manage on just a few puffs.'

Helene Eriksen sat staring into space, and Munch was suddenly reminded of Mia's words after the first interview they had held out here.

She knows something.

He coughed lightly, stubbed out his own cigarette and got up to leave.

'Thanks for the tea, but I had better get back to work. We still have quite a few names left on the list.'

'Yes, of course,' Helene Eriksen said, walking with him out of the sitting room.

'There was just one thing,' Munch said when they were back in the corridor.

'Yes?'

'I gather from the lists of residents and staff that not everyone is here today. Am I right?'

'Yes.'

'It's just that . . .' Munch said.

'Yes?'

'There's one person I'm not sure about; he might be here, but I haven't managed to arrange an interview with him.'

'Aha. Who are you thinking of?'

'Rolf Lycke,' Munch said with a light cough.

'Rolf?' Helene Eriksen said with a frown.

'Yes? I gather he's a teacher here?'

Helene shook her head. 'No, no. He stopped working here ages ago.'

'But he used to teach here?'

'Yes, but only for a brief period. He was, well, I would say, a good teacher, of course, and I would have liked him to stay, but I don't think this was the job for him. I don't want to speak ill about my girls, but, in academic terms, the level isn't terribly high – am I allowed to say that? I think Rolf Lycke had big ambitions. If you want to talk to him, I can arrange it. I mean, I still have his number somewhere, I think. Would you like me to look for it?'

'Oh, no,' Munch said. 'I'll just stick to the lists we have here.'

'OK.' Helene nodded.

Munch's mobile began to vibrate. He had turned the ring tone off during the interviews but, as usual, he had forgotten to turn off vibrate. Anette Goli's name appeared on the display.

'Yes?' Munch said.

'I think we've got him. Have you spoken to Mia? She has been trying to get hold of you. She found something at the riding school, but it doesn't matter now . . .'

'Who?'

'We have a confession.'

'Really?'

'Yes,' Goli went on. 'He handed himself in. We have him in custody. He's down at Grønland. He has confessed to the murder.'

'I'm on my way,' Munch said. He pressed the red button, made his excuses and ran out to the black Audi outside.

Chapter 28

Munch opened the door and saw that Mia was already there, in the small room adjacent to the interview room. Anette Goli was leaning against the wall, her arms folded across her chest and a satisfied smile playing on her lips. Mia was sitting on a chair munching an apple, still wearing her leather jacket, and he could tell immediately from the look on his younger colleague's face that she was entirely unimpressed.

'What have we got?' Munch said, hanging up his coat and taking a seat on the chair in front of the one-way mirror.

'Jim Fuglesang,' Anette Goli said. 'Aged thirty-two. Lives in Røyken. Less than a forty-minute drive from Hurumlandet Nurseries. Turned up at reception just under an hour ago. Confessed to the murder of Camilla Green. He used to work for the post office. He's on disability allowance now. I don't know why, but I've asked Ludvig to look into it.'

'Why is he wearing a bicycle helmet?'

'He refuses to take it off,' Anette Goli said, shrugging her shoulders.

'It's not him,' Mia said, taking another bite from her apple.

'Why not?' Munch said.

'Oh, come on, Holger. The papers reported the murder last night. How many times have we seen this before? People who want to confess? Don't ask me why, but some people would do anything to get attention. I don't understand what we're doing here, frankly. Didn't you get my text message?'

Munch got the distinct impression that Mia was extremely put out.

'I've been conducting interviews all day,' Munch said, by way of explanation.

'The drawing at the riding school,' Mia said, never taking her eyes off the man in the white bicycle helmet.

'What drawing?' Munch said.

Mia made no reply.

'Anette?' Munch said, turning around.

The blonde police lawyer shook her head; she seemed a little annoyed at the suggestion that she had dragged Mia and Munch in here for nothing. She was holding up a file, which she had not yet shown to Mia, because she had been waiting for Munch to arrive.

'I'm not a complete idiot,' Anette said, placing two photographs on the table in front of them.

'Jim Fuglesang. Aged thirty-two. On benefits. Wears a white bicycle helmet that he refuses to take off. Turns up here. Confesses to the murder. And yes, I'm not completely wet behind the ears, I know about false confessions. I wouldn't have called you if he hadn't brought these along.'

She pointed to the two pictures she had just shown them. Unwillingly, Mia turned her attention to the photographs Anette had placed in front of them.

'Bloody hell!' Munch exclaimed.

'Exactly,' Anette Goli said triumphantly.

'What the . . .?' Mia said, turning to Anette.

'Didn't I tell you?' Anette Goli said, folding her arms across her chest.

Two photographs. Blurred, but the subjects were quite clear. There could be no doubt.

'I don't understand this,' Mia said.

'I told you we had him.' Anette Goli smiled.

'OK,' Munch said, getting up. 'Let's go and find out what this nutter has to say.'

Chapter 29

Gabriel Mørk was sitting in the incident room, watching Ludvig Grønlie put up pictures on the wall. He had not told anyone yet because he did not want to come across as a starry-eyed youngster, but the hacker had had a very exciting day at work, perhaps his best ever since starting here.

He had been out of the office. He had conducted interviews at Hurumlandet Nurseries, a job that was normally the preserve of Munch, Mia and Kim Kolsø, but the scope of the investigation, or rather the sheer number of people who needed interviewing, meant that Munch had dispatched all of them, except Ylva, who had stayed behind to hold the fort at the office, and had looked envious as they left.

Gabriel sympathized. He, too, had felt like an outsider at the start – the rest of the team shared routines and codes, references he did not understand – but it was different now. It was a little like a baptism. He smiled to himself and took a swig of his Coke as Ylva entered and pulled out a chair next to him.

'Why are you still bothering with this?' the young woman asked, nodding towards Grønlie, who had just put up a picture of one of the girls from Hurumlandet Nurseries and written her name below it.

Isabella Jung.

'Bothering with what?' Gabriel asked.

'Well, we've caught him, haven't we?'

'We don't know that for sure,' Ludvig Grønlie said, putting up another picture next to the previous one and writing another name below it.

Paulus Monsen.

'Anette seemed quite confident,' Ylva said.

'We've seen this before.' Ludvig picked up another photograph from the table in front of him.

'Seen what?'

'People claiming responsibility for murders they didn't commit,' Gabriel explained, looking quickly to the experienced investigator.

'Exactly.' Ludvig put up another picture on the wall next to the others.

Benedikte Riis.

'But she seemed so sure,' Ylva said, popping a piece of bubble gum into her mouth. 'Anette Goli, I mean.'

'Nothing would give me greater pleasure.' Ludvig smiled as he put up yet another picture, this time above all the others.

Helene Eriksen.

'So have you heard anything?' Ylva asked.

'Not yet,' Ludvig said, carrying on with what he was doing.

Cecilie Markussen.

'I hope they've got him. That we've solved this already,' the young woman said, blowing a bubble.

'I agree.' Ludvig nodded and smiled at her. 'But until we're told that's the case, I think it's important to do this. There are just so many people involved.'

He let out a sigh and studied his collage, which was almost complete.

'It's a bit of a mess,' Ylva remarked.

'Oh, do you think so?' Ludvig looked at her.

'Oh, no,' the young woman hastened to add. 'No, not your wall – I meant the whole case. Messy; so many potential suspects. It's not easy to know where to start.'

Ludvig smiled, put up the final photograph and took a step back to assess his work, checking if the display was clear enough.

'So, talk me through it,' Ylva said, studying the picture wall with interest.

'Helene Eriksen. She's the boss out there. She set the whole place up.'

Ylva nodded.

'Paulus Monsen. Helene's – well, what shall we call him? – right-hand man. Aged twenty-five. An ex-resident, but now a kind of caretaker.'

'OK.'

'Two teachers,' Ludvig continued, pointing them out. 'Karl Eriksen. Eva Dahl.'

'And what were they like?' Ylva wanted to know.

'Munch and Kim interviewed the teachers,' he said. 'So we don't know the details yet. Pity, really.'

'What is?'

'That we haven't managed to debrief and review everything as a team yet. It's a bit chaotic here, if you ask me.'

The grey-haired man took another step back and sized up the picture wall again.

'So it's just girls at the Hurumlandvet Nurseries?'

'No, I don't think that was the original intention,' Ludvig said. 'Am I right, Gabriel?'

'You are, the place is for both boys and girls. There are two dormitories, but, for some reason, they only have girls living there now. We didn't find out why, did we, Ludvig?'

He looked at Ludvig, who shook his head and scratched his neck.

'So these eight girls make up all the residents?' Ylva said, pointing to them.

Something in Gabriel's pocket buzzed. He eased out his iPhone and glanced at it quickly; he would rather hear what Ludvig had to say, but when he saw the message that had just arrived, the photographs and his colleagues in the room ceased to exist for him.

Phoenix to Electron, are you there?

It took a few seconds before he understood the importance of it.

He could not remember the last time he had heard from his old friend; he typed a quick reply.

Electron here. What's up?

The reply arrived a few seconds later.

I'm outside. It's important.

143

Outside?

Gabriel quickly texted back.

Outside where? What's important?

The reply came swiftly this time as well.

13 Mariboesgate. I have something for you. The girl with the flower in her mouth.

How on earth was Skunk connected to her?

Gabriel scrambled to his feet, mumbled an apology to his colleagues, rushed out of the room and then ran as quickly as he could down the stairs.

Chapter 30

'The tenth of October. The time is 17.05. Present in the room are the head of the homicide unit at 13 Mariboesgate, Holger Munch, and investigator Mia Krüger.'

'Please state your full name,' Mia said to the man wearing the bicycle helmet as she pointed to the tape recorder.

Mia still seemed agitated and crotchety, and Munch was tempted to tell her to calm down, but he thought better of it.

'Jim,' the man said.

'Your full name,' Mia said, pointing to the tape recorder again. The man in the white bicycle helmet looked at her.

'That is my name,' he stammered, with a quick glance at Munch.

'Your full name, including your surname.'

'Jim Fuglesang,' the man with the white bicycle helmet said, and fixed his gaze on the table.

'Are you aware that you're entitled to have a lawyer present?' Munch said, ignoring the look Mia was giving him.

'What?'

'A lawyer? Would you like to have a lawyer present?'

'The chicken wanted to jump into the basket,' the man with the bicycle helmet said.

Mia looked askance at Munch, who shrugged his shoulders.

'So you decline your right to a lawyer?'

The man across the table looked at Munch as if he did not understand what he was being asked.

'I killed her,' the man with the white bicycle helmet said, straightening up slightly.

'Who?' Mia asked, leaning forwards in her chair.

'Who?' Jim Fuglesang echoed her, looking confused.

'All right, Jim, who did you kill?'

Mia was starting to calm down now. There was something about the man sitting in front of them that told her that getting angry with him would not work. He looked as if he did not even grasp the seriousness of the situation.

'Who did you kill, Jim?' Mia said again, now in a soft tone of voice.

There was clearly no need to come across as menacing. He seemed frightened and perplexed enough as it was.

'The girl in the newspaper.'

'What girl in the newspaper, Jim?' Munch asked calmly.

'The girl on the feathers.'

'Camilla?'

It took a while before the answer came.

'Yes.' Jim Fuglesang nodded hesitantly, and went back to staring at the table.

'Did you know her?'

'Who?'

'Camilla Green.'

The man with the white bicycle helmet continued to look as if he had no idea what Munch was talking about, yet he nodded all the same.

'So you knew her?' Mia asked. 'How did you know her, Jim?'

'It was summer,' said the man opposite them. 'There was a squirrel. I like squirrels.'

Munch glanced across to Mia, who merely shook her head.

'Was it in the woods?' she asked. 'Did you happen to see Camilla in the woods?'

Jim Fuglesang smiled to himself now, as if his mind was on other matters.

'I like their tails, they are so soft and bushy, and then they do this thing with their paws. To hold the pine cones. In order to nibble them? Do you know what I mean?'

He smiled again, and then clenched his teeth.

'So you saw a squirrel in the woods? In the summer?' Munch sighed, he was starting to lose patience.

'I saw lots.' The man smiled. 'They tend to live around the tall pines down by the lake. Where the red boat is.'

'Was that where you saw her?' Mia said. 'Down by the lake?'

'Who?' Jim Fuglesang said again.

'Listen . . .' Munch sighed again but was interrupted by Mia putting her hand on his shoulder.

'You were down by the lake,' she continued. 'And you were watching the squirrels?'

'Yes, they like it there.'

'And you were on your own?'

'Yes.' Jim Fuglesang nodded. 'That's how I prefer it.'

Munch did not know where Mia was going with this, but he let her carry on nevertheless.

'So, Camilla, the girl in the newspaper, she wasn't there?'

'No, she wasn't there, only the squirrel. It looked like a female, because I thought I saw a baby squirrel as well, but that was only to begin with, because then I saw the other thing, but only when I squatted down.'

Jim Fuglesang bowed his head slightly, his eyes wandered cautiously from side to side, and then he pressed his finger against his lips.

'You need to be very quiet, or they'll run away.'

'So you were down by the lake?' Mia said with a small smile. 'Was that where you took these?'

She opened the file, picked out the two photographs Anette Goli had shown them and slid them across the table.

This time the man in the white bicycle helmet reacted; he turned his gaze away from the pictures and started staring at the wall.

'Maria Theresa,' he said, and began knocking his fist on the bicycle helmet.

'Camilla.' Munch could not take much more of this.

'Maria Theresa,' Fuglesang said again, looking as if he were about to disappear into his own world completely. 'Four white rocks by the lake. The empty house.'

'Camilla,' Munch said, louder this time.

'Fourteen minutes on a good day. Sixteen minutes back.'

'Listen,' Munch said irritably, but Mia put her hand on his shoulder again.

'We had a squirrel in the garden once,' she said gently. 'When I was a kid. We had put out sunflower seeds on the feeding tray for the birds but, when we went to look to see if any had come, we saw a squirrel instead.'

Jim Fuglesang stopped hitting his head, but he continued to stare at the wall.

'My sister and I,' Mia went on. 'We put out more seeds, and it came back. We sat by the window, hidden behind the curtains while we waited, and it turned up every day, practically at the same time. But do you know what was the hardest thing?'

'No?' Jim Fuglesang was paying attention now, and he turned to face them again.

'Whether to call it Chip or Dale.'

Munch did not know what to think, why was Mia indulging this man's madness, but he let her continue.

'My twin sister wanted Chip, but I wanted Dale.'

'Chip and Dale wrecked Donald Duck's Christmas tree.' Jim Fuglesang giggled.

'I know.' Mia smiled.

'He couldn't catch them, and that made him really cross. He had put up all those Christmas decorations, and then everything was knocked over.'

'Yes, it was, wasn't it? And we never managed to agree on a name, but we took some pictures, and I'm pleased about that.'

'Of the squirrel?' Jim asked.

'Yes.' Mia nodded. 'We put them up in our bedroom so we could look at them every night before we went to sleep.'

'Dale was fatter and funnier.' The man in the bicycle helmet smiled and looked briefly once more as if he were about to disappear into his own world, but Mia brought him back.

'You like taking pictures, don't you?'

'Yes.' Jim nodded.

'And you took these?' Mia said delicately, moving her hand slowly towards the pictures on the table in front of them.

'Yes.' The man in the bicycle helmet said, this time managing to look at them.

'Do you know what I think, Jim?'

'No?'

'Let's forget about Camilla. The girl on the feathers.'

'Really?' Fuglesang said, somewhat surprised.

'Yes, let's forget about her, she's not important,' Mia went on. 'You didn't kill Camilla, why would you? You don't even know her, and you're a nice person – you would never do anything like that, would you?'

'No, never,' Jim Fuglesang assured her.

'You didn't even know her, did you?'

'No, I've never met her.'

'You just got a little scared, didn't you? When you saw the newspapers, and no wonder. I would get scared, too, wouldn't you, Holger?'

Mia looked at Munch now with a small smile. All Holger could do was shrug.

'Yes, of course,' Munch said, and cleared his throat.

'You see, Jim. Anyone in your position would get scared, because you had these pictures, didn't you?'

'I didn't do it,' Jim said, now with tears in his eyes.

'Of course you didn't.' Mia smiled.

'I didn't kill the cat.'

'Of course you didn't kill the cat.'

'Or the dog.'

'Of course you didn't kill the dog either,' Mia went on. 'You'd never harm anyone, would you, Jim?'

'No,' Fuglesang said, wiping away a tear.

'I think you're really brave,' Mia said.

'Why?'

'Coming to us with the pictures. You're helping us. Of course you didn't do it. But we would like to know where you took them. Do you understand what I'm saying?'

'The dog and the cat?' the man with the bicycle helmet asked.

Two photographs. Almost identical. Candles set out in a penta-gram. Feather beds. The cat lay on one. The dog lay on the other. Both had been killed, and their front paws posed in the same strange position as Camilla Green's hands. One up. The other along the ani-mal's side.

'Was it near the squirrel?' Mia ventured carefully.

'There were wolves in the shop,' the man in the white bicycle helmet said; he seemed to be on the verge of leaving them behind again.

'Jim?' Mia said. 'Down by the river? By the red boat?'

Seeing the photographs appeared to have upset the man in the white bicycle helmet. He resumed knocking his helmet softly and turned his gaze back towards the wall.

'Maria Theresa,' he mumbled.

'Jim,' Mia attempted again.

'Four white rocks.'

'Jim, do you remember where you took these pictures?'

'The red boat,' Fuglesang said, now hitting his helmet harder.

'Camilla,' Munch was again losing patience.

'Was it at the same place?' Mia asked. 'Was it at the same time?'

'Maria Theresa,' the man in the white bicycle helmet chanted. 'Four white rocks by the lake. The derelict house. The chicken wanted to get into the basket.'

'Jim?' Mia tried yet again. 'Where did you take these pictures? When did you take them? Was it at the same place? Was it at the same time?'

'On Tuesdays it's better to hide in the bathroom,' the man in the white bicycle helmet said, and this time he seemed to have left them for good.

At that moment there was a knock on the door, and Anette Goli popped her head round.

Mia Krüger glared at her colleague.

'Grønlie has managed to contact someone,' Goli said, nodding to Munch. 'Please could we discuss it outside?'

Munch glanced quickly at Mia, who shook her head irritably.
'OK.'
The fat investigator got up, left the room and carefully closed
the door behind him.

Chapter 31

There were few customers at Justisen, luckily, and they managed to find a quiet table where they would not be disturbed. Munch would have preferred to sit outside, so that he could smoke, but it was just too cold.

He took off his coat and sank down opposite Mia, who already had a beer lined up and was pondering her notes, lost in thought. He ordered a Farris mineral water, and wondered if perhaps he should have debriefed the whole team before going to the pub, but there was something about these times spent together, he had always enjoyed them, Mia and him at Justisen. He had told the team to turn up for an early briefing tomorrow morning; that would have to do. Besides, everyone had had an extremely long day as it was.

'So?'

'So what?' Mia said, draining her beer without taking her eyes off her notes on the table.

'Jim Fuglesang? Not our guy. Do we agree?'

Mia shook her head; it seemed almost as if she would prefer not to talk.

'Of course not,' she then said, still not looking at him.

A patient at Dikemark Hospital. In and out. Lived alone in his cottage when not in hospital, but always with support. As usual, Ludvig Grønlie had made a few phone calls, found the right people to talk to, and although Munch had contemplated keeping Jim Fuglesang in custody overnight, he had ended up handing him over to the care of social workers, who had come to collect him.

'What's the point of these dreadful tableaux?' Mia said, looking up from her notes for the first time.

She summoned the waiter and ordered another beer and a Jägermeister, then chewed on her pen while she stared into the distance.

'I mean, I've seen a lot of weird stuff.'

'Same ritual? But with a cat? And a dog?' Munch said, looking at her.

Holger Munch was one of Norway's most skilled investigators, yet there were times where he felt himself to be a mere assistant to Mia Krüger. That his job was only to point her in the right direction. He sighed, desperate for a cigarette, and suddenly remembered he had forgotten to reply to the text Miriam had sent him earlier that day.

Need to talk to you, Dad. Quite important. Please call me?

Miriam would have to wait. Everything had been a blur since they discovered Camilla Green in the woods.

'In the same position. The same pentagram of candles. On a bed of feathers. A cat. And also a dog. But let's put that aside for now,' he said, taking another sip from the bottle.

'Eh?' Mia said. She seemed to be waking up.

'I said we'll put it aside for now,' Munch repeated.

'Why?'

'This is what we've got. Two photographs. Same type of crime scene. Candles. Feathers. Cat. Dog. Even their paws posed in the same angle as Camilla Green's hands. Am I right?'

'Yes.'

She knocked back the Jägermeister, took a swig of her beer and put her pen on the table.

'OK, what else have we got?' Munch said.

'The note I found in Camilla's locker,' Mia said. 'Did you get the picture I sent you?'

Munch nodded.

'The phrase *I like you*? An owl?'

'Or a drawing of something that looks like a bird,' Munch said. 'I couldn't quite see if it was an owl.'

'But the feathers came from an owl?'

'Yes, yes,' Munch said. 'But don't forget that Grønlie said it was just an assumption. Forensics are checking it now.'

'But even so?' Mia said, taking another gulp of her beer.

'Yes.' Munch nodded.

'So we have that as well.'

'The phone records that Gabriel got,' Munch added.

'Absolutely. The message that she was OK was sent from the Nurseries.'

'Nearby at least.'

'Same mobile mast?'

'Yes.'

'Camilla went missing. Then someone took her mobile and sent a text message saying everything was OK. Near the place from which she disappeared.'

'Unless she sent it herself,' Munch said.

'Is that what we think?'

'Oh, I don't know, I'm just trying to sum up what we have.'

'Good.' Mia nodded. 'But let's assume, just for now, that she didn't send it herself.'

'Which is highly likely.'

'It means that the person we're looking for has access to the Nurseries.'

'Or lives nearby.'

'Exactly,' Mia said.

'So that's what we've got.'

'Yes.'

Munch could see that Mia was losing herself in thought again and seized the chance to nip out for a cigarette.

There were several people outside, shivering under the patio heaters, but Munch found one he could have to himself and took his mobile out of the pocket of his duffel coat.

Need to talk to you, Dad. Quite important.

His cold fingers found Miriam's number, but his call went straight to voicemail.

Hi, this is Miriam Munch. I'm afraid I can't answer your call right now . . .

Munch tried the number again a couple of times but got voice-mail. He finished his cigarette and went back inside to Mia, who had already ordered another beer and yet another Jägermeister and was sitting with her skinny shoulders hunched up over her notes.

'So this Finstad?' Munch said to get her attention.

'What?'

'Anders Finstad? Pictures of young girls?'

'I know that you never can tell for sure,' Mia said, 'but I got the impression that he's actually a decent man. He cares deeply about the riding school, and his students. There was a lot of love there, you could almost see it in the buildings. Do you know what I'm saying?'

Munch did not, but he trusted her, although her eyes were starting to swim with the alcohol.

'So it was true, his ex-wife made it all up?'

'Like I said, what would I know, but I certainly believe that he was telling the truth.'

She drummed her fingers on the table for a little while, then tucked her long, dark hair behind her ear.

'So we can cross him off?'

'What? No, not cross him off, but he's no longer at the top of my list. Who have you got?'

Munch could feel that he was starting to tire. It had been a long day.

'Helene Eriksen?' Mia said. 'In or out?'

Munch pondered it for a moment.

'I like her, but in.'

'And that Paulus guy?'

'Definitely still on the list.' Munch nodded.

'And the girls,' Mia said, glancing quickly at her piece of paper. 'Isabella Jung? Benedikte Riis? Cecilie Markussen?'

Munch strangled a yawn.

'It's way too early to tell. If you ask me, they're all on the list. We'll have to reassess after the team briefing tomorrow.'

Mia swallowed her Jägermeister as her mobile beeped with a text message. She swore and shook her head.

'What?' Munch asked.

'Curry,' she said, and heaved a sigh.

'What is it this time?'

'He's been on a bender,' Mia said. 'Needs a place to sleep. Again.'

'Trouble in paradise?' Munch drank his glass of Farris.

'Yes, he's had another row with Sunniva,' Mia mumbled, shaking her head again. 'A big one this time.'

'I see,' Munch said.

'Sorry, didn't know how much to tell you.'

'I wasn't born yesterday. But, well . . .'

'Well, what?'

'Well, what can I say? I know you're fond of Jon, but I need people I can trust.'

'Kim is leaving. Curry doesn't turn up for work. Maybe it'll just be you and me in the end,' Mia said, and winked at him.

'That's not my biggest problem right now.' Munch got up.

'Leaving already?'

'Yes. I have to get some sleep. We'll carry on tomorrow.'

He was putting on his coat just as his mobile rang. He strangled another yawn and looked at the display. Gabriel Mørk. Munch considered ignoring it but ended up taking the call.

'Munch speaking?'

There was total silence on the other end.

'Hello?'

Still not a sound.

'Are you there, Gabriel? What's going on?'

Mia looked up from her notes.

'You have to come in,' Gabriel's voice said weakly.

'What is it? What's going on?'

'You have to come in,' Gabriel said again.

'Come where?' Munch said.

'There's something I need to show you.'

The young hacker sounded upset.

'Can't it wait until tomorrow?'

'No,' Gabriel insisted. 'Absolutely not.'

'Are you serious? Are you at the office?'

'Yes.'

'OK, I'm on my way,' Munch said, and rang off.

'What was that about?'

'Gabriel called from the office. He wants me to come over now. Do you want to come with me?'

'Of course.' Mia nodded, and finished her beer.

FOUR

Chapter 32

Sunniva Rød ran up the last few steps and hung her coat in her locker. She took out her uniform and heaved a sigh as she put it on. She had worked at the hospice for almost eight years, and, to begin with, she had found it quite appealing, the tight-fitting, old-fashioned uniform, but by now she was fed up. And not just with the uniform but also with her job.

Sunniva sighed again, and went to the staff room to make herself a cup of coffee.

Fiji.

Azure sea, palm trees and freedom.

They had been saving up for almost a year, and she had been so excited about it. All last winter, nothing but cold and darkness, no time off; they had even gone without a summer holiday and she had taken all the extra shifts she could get, but she had not minded because the following January they would be going to paradise. For a whole month.

And then the bastard had done it again. Gambled away their money. Got drunk and lost everything. Again. But this time she had had enough. She truly loved Curry, no doubt about it, but she could not live like this.

No. It was the last straw. She had thrown him out, and now she felt only relief. The flat belonged to her. Her father had given them the money some years ago when they decided to move in together. And now it was all hers. She felt free.

Sunniva took her cup of coffee from the staff room and joined her colleagues for the morning briefing. The night shift had finished, the day shift was about to take over, and everyone would be updated on the previous night's events. St Helena's Hospice was where the very old came to spend their last days, weeks or months, and it was generally an uneventful place. A doctor would visit. There might be a change of medication.

After the morning briefing she treated herself to a second cup of coffee before starting her round. She needed it. Because Torvald Sund was on her list today.

The mad vicar.

There was something about the old man and the darkness in his eyes which gave her the creeps.

Sunniva put on a smile and took his breakfast tray into his room. Luckily, the vicar was asleep, so she set it down on the bedside table. A salmon and caper sandwich. Camomile tea with honey and a glass of orange juice. They knew how to look after their patients at St Helena's.

Sunniva was about to leave when the vicar suddenly opened his eyes.

'I won't get into Heaven!' the old man exclaimed, staring at her.

'Of course you will.' She smiled.

'No. I've sinned.'

The old man looked distressed.

'Oh, God, forgive me. Oh, Father, I didn't know, I didn't know. Please let me atone for my sins.'

The man raised his scrawny arms up in the air and was practically crying out to the ceiling.

'Why does no one listen?'

According to his drugs chart, the vicar received three dosages each of 10mg of diazepam and 0.5mg of morphine every day, which were administered intravenously. Sunniva checked the IV and discovered that it was empty. The night shift had failed to top up his medication. She shook her head with mild irritation and removed the bag from the stand.

'No,' the old man protested.

Sunniva looked down at him.

'No, no,' the vicar said again, pointing a crooked finger at the bag in her hand.

It took a few seconds before she realized what he was trying to say.

'You don't want your medication?'

The old man shook his head and pointed to a book on his bed-side table.

'The Bible? Would you like me to read to you?'

The vicar shook his head and looked at her with eyes that seemed more lucid now.

Then he mumbled that he wanted her to open the cupboard in his bedside table.

She reattached the IV bag to the stand, walked around the bed, knelt down by the bedside table and opened it. There was an old newspaper inside.

'This one?'

The old man nodded. He was smiling faintly now.

'Her,' he said, pointing.

'Who?' Sunniva said.

'The children are burning,' the vicar whispered, his gaze no longer so lucid.

'Torvald?' Sunniva said, placing her hand on his forehead. It was very hot.

'Torvald?'

No response.

The old man was no longer awake; his eyelids slowly closed and the crooked finger which had pointed to the newspaper hung limply beside the bed.

Sunniva Rød put the newspaper back where she had found it, tucked the old man in, went to the drug cupboard to fetch a fresh IV bag and hooked it up to the frail, wrinkled hand. She checked that the old man was sound asleep, softly closed the door behind her and continued her morning round.

Chapter 33

Gabriel Mørk was sitting very still on his chair at the back of the incident room. He had not slept for twenty-four hours, yet he did not feel tired. He had been sick several times during the night and his stomach was completely empty, yet he was not hungry. He was in shock; he must be. The day before, when Skunk had texted him, turned up outside his office out of the blue, insisting on a meeting, Gabriel had been intrigued, of course he had, but nothing could have prepared him for this.

Munch was standing by the projector, and he looked exhausted. They had not slept either, Mia and Munch; they had been with him in the office all night. Anette Goli had turned up around 3 a.m., Curry shortly afterwards, smelling strongly of booze. The only people who had yet to see the film were Kim Kolsø, Ylva and Ludvig Grønlie.

'As you will all be aware now' – Munch coughed, and looked across at the subdued gathering – 'Gabriel was contacted last night by an old friend, called . . .'

Munch glanced quickly at Gabriel.

'Skunk,' the young man mumbled.

'An old hacker friend called Skunk, who has found a film on the Internet, on some kind of secret server. And, from what I can gather, this hacker isn't particularly keen on the police, so it's entirely thanks to Gabriel that we have got it at all.'

They turned towards him now, the others, and nodded. He thought he was going to throw up again and was embarrassed at himself. He had felt proud after the trip to Hurumlandet Nurseries, a step up the ladder, no longer the newbie, and now he was right back to where he had started, on the pavement outside six months ago. A kid, that was all he was, who had thrown up at the terrible realization of what they were dealing with. How unprofessional. He rested his hands in his lap and tried to breathe calmly.

'As you know,' Munch continued, 'Camilla Green's physical condition when she was found was much worse than when she disappeared. She was extremely thin, emaciated, she had blisters and grazing on her hands and knees, and bruises everywhere. The post mortem also showed that her stomach contents consisted exclusively of pellets, some kind of animal feed, and thanks to Gabriel, we're about to find out why.'

Gabriel saw Ylva turn to him with a mixture of curiosity and fear. The newest member of the team looked very uncomfortable. Again, he could sympathize.

'Ludvig, please would you turn out the lights?' Munch said.

Ludvig got up and flicked the switch, and the room fell quiet as Munch pressed the button and the short film clip started playing on the overhead screen in front of them.

Gabriel forced himself to watch it. Maybe he could be like Mia and Munch this time. Watch it through police eyes. Look for evidence. Not see it like a normal human being, like the first time he had watched it.

The screen was black to begin with. But then she appeared, Camilla Green. It looked like she was in a basement. And as the light slowly brightened, a big wheel emerged. It was inside something that could be a cage. For a mouse or hamster, perhaps, but everything was scaled up, designed for a human being. It might have been funny if it had not been the saddest thing Gabriel had ever seen. Camilla Green was sitting inside the wheel, and at first Gabriel had not been able to understand what was going on, but his confusion had not lasted long. When Camilla Green crawled slowly inside the big, heavy wheel, its rotation made the light come on.

She was being held prisoner.

In a basement. In a cage. With no light.

Gabriel had to look away.

As Camilla Green desperately made the big wheel turn faster and faster, the struggle evident in every movement, they could see that someone had painted some letters in white on the grey wall behind her.

The chosen one.

Camilla managed to get the wheel up to a constant speed. One hand in front of the other, as fast and as steadily as she could. The team began to exchange confused looks. Why would she try to go faster? The light had already come on. Then suddenly a hatch opened and something fell onto the floor.

Food.

That was why she ran so hard.

To eat.

Gabriel could not remember when he had returned his gaze to the screen.

Pellets.

He could hold it back no longer. He could not bear to watch another second. Gabriel ran from the room, pushed open the door to the lavatory and slumped to his knees in front of the bowl as stomach acid surged up and out through his mouth and he started sweating profusely.

'Are you all right, Gabriel?'

The young hacker was incapable of saying anything. He barely registered that the door behind him had opened and that Mia had entered.

Mia stuck a hand towel under the tap and passed it to him, then knelt down beside him while he pressed the cold flannel against his face to cool down.

'I'm all right,' he muttered gingerly.

It was not the image of himself he wanted to convey. To Mia Krüger, of all people. A rookie unable to cope with the realities of the job. But it was too late to worry about that now; the night had been far too long.

'I think you had better go home,' his colleague said amicably. 'We'll do it later.'

Gabriel wiped his forehead with the soothing towel again, not sure what she meant.

'Do what?' he asked, looking up at her.

Mia put her hand on his shoulder.

'I know it's hard, but we need to know, don't we?'

'Know what?' Gabriel said, perplexed.

'Where he got it from. Your friend. Skunk. We need to know as quickly as possible.'

'Yes,' Gabriel nodded carefully, although he knew full well that that would be impossible.

Chapter 34

Curry swallowed another mouthful of coffee as Mia returned to the incident room and sat down again.

'Everything all right?' Munch asked.

'He'll be fine,' Mia said.

'Good.' Munch looked as if he did not know what to say next.

He was still standing next to the projector, strangling a yawn and scratching his beard.

'Right,' he began, but said nothing more.

Curry felt for him. He had slept on the sofa in Mia's flat again, having first drunk nearly half a bottle of whisky. He had passed out and almost failed to hear his phone when it started ringing at three o'clock in the morning.

He was totally sober now, or at least he felt like it. A mixture of incomprehension and outrage had cast a shadow over everything else.

This is bigger than we thought it was.

What kind of sick son of a bitch would do something like this? Trap a young girl inside a cage? For months? Force her to crawl inside a big wheel to get light? To get food?

Munch continued his struggle at the front of the room to find the right words. He looked like he would give almost anything to put his head on a pillow.

Curry regarded himself as a tough guy, but he had found it hard to know what to do with himself when the film had rolled across the screen. The terrified face of Camilla Green, totally exhausted.

The poor girl.

'Any questions?' Munch said eventually. 'Before we start analysing what we have seen?'

He looked around at the group, but no one said anything.

'Mia?' he said, handing over his spot by the projector to his colleague, who did not look as if the lack of sleep troubled her in any way.

'OK,' Mia said, pressing a button. 'Some of you probably want to see the film again, and you'll be able to do that, of course – there's a copy of it on our server – but for now I think we should take the time to study the footage in detail. We have divided it into a series of stills, and we'll start by focusing on a number of things you might have missed initially, but which we think might be important. There is obviously much more going on here than we first thought. Whoever is responsible for this will not have the chance even to think about a second victim. Not on our watch.'

She was impressive like this. Curry had always respected her, of course, but he could really see it now. How she could put aside her emotions, how she played the detective; he could almost hear the cogs in her brain whirring.

'Why was Camilla Green so thin when we found her? We know that now. Why did she have blisters on her hands and bruises on her knees? We know that now. And, last, why did the post-mortem report show that her stomach contained only animal feed? We also know the answer to that. So we can cross all that off our list. And I realize that it might be difficult for you to accept that what you have just seen is real, but we must remember that it is. Camilla met a truly horrific end at the hands of some monster. The more we know, the easier it will be for us to catch this bastard – or bastards – am I right?'

Curry did not know why Mia made this speech; surely it did not need saying. But then he saw Ylva. She looked as if she might faint at any moment.

'Two facts. Number one: Camilla Green was kept prisoner in a basement. Forced to live like an animal. Possibly for months. Number two: at some point the killer, or killers, murdered her, sacrificed her in something that looks very much like a ritual.'

Mia pressed the button again, and then again, back and forth between two pictures. Camilla in the basement, and in the clearing in the woods.

'So. Question one. Motive? Is it the same motive behind both crimes?'

She looked across the table, but no one said anything, so she continued.

'Is it all part of the same crime? Camilla being held in the basement, treated like an animal. Camilla resurfacing months later, naked this time, posed in a pentagram of candles. Is it the same motive? Is there a link?'

She looked up again and took a sip from her water bottle, and it was at that moment that Curry realized why Mia did not seem as tired as Munch. She was high. Curry felt a pang of guilt. She had been so supportive, letting him crash on her sofa, and he had not meant to pry, but he had not been able to help seeing the jars in the bathroom cabinet. The pills.

'I'm not saying that there isn't,' Mia continued, nodding lightly. 'But we have to ask ourselves. Why keep her prisoner? Why pose her naked in the woods?'

'And what do you think, Mia?' Kim Kolsø said. He was the first person to open his mouth.

'I don't know,' Mia replied, then paused in thought before she continued. 'I mean, doesn't it seem odd to you? I don't see the connection myself.'

Curry could see that several of the others were starting to notice it, too. That she was not her usual self. That there was something odd about her. Curry suspected that she'd taken an upper of some kind.

'I don't see any reason for any of it,' Kim Kolsø went on. 'Why would it be two different crimes? Two different motives? Did one sick bastard find her in the basement of another sick bastard and decide he could go one better?'

'You may be right,' Mia said, thinking about it again. 'But, yes, there's just . . .'

She scratched her head and took another swig from the water bottle on the table in front of her.

'Right, great, let's leave it for now. We have a huge amount of other evidence to look at. Move on.'

Kim glanced quickly at Curry, who glanced back at him but only shrugged his shoulders slightly.

'OK,' Mia continued. 'Let's look at some physical evidence, and then at something Holger and I have discovered.'

She clicked again, several times in a row.

'First off. This wheel. I wouldn't have thought you could buy it in a shop. Did someone build it? We need to look into it.'

Another picture.

'The writing on the wall behind her. *The chosen one*. Why is Camilla the chosen one?'

Another picture.

'The footage. Yes, the footage itself. Why was she filmed? Was it for personal viewing? I mean, it was found on a server. Was it shared with anyone? Was that the reason for keeping her prisoner? To film her? And later share the film with others?'

She took another sip of water, and it was obvious now. She was talking non-stop and her eyes were the size of plates.

'That particular point, I think we'll have an answer to once Gabriel wakes up and we get hold of this . . .'

She looked across to Munch, who was so exhausted that, for the first time ever, he had not taken advantage of the pauses in her briefing to have a cigarette.

'Skunk,' he mumbled.

Mia nodded. 'There's more here, obviously, but from a purely practical point of view, I think that's the crucial stuff: where does the wheel come from? *The chosen one*? Was that her? Why? And . . .'

She got lost in her own train of thought, but Curry helped her back on track.

'The film itself.'

'Yes, that's right. Thank you, Jon. The film. Why was it made? Why was it found on a server? It seems risky, doesn't it? Sharing it?'

Mia smiled, tucked her hair behind her ear and looked across at the team again.

'Any questions? Any comments so far?'

You should have got some sleep, Mia, Curry thought, but he did not say it out loud.

Ylva cautiously raised her hand. She seemed to be bouncing back after the initial shock.

'You mentioned something you had found?'

'Yes, good,' Mia said, walking briskly up to the Mac to open a file she had prepared. 'This is a small extract from the film. It's about forty seconds into it. Try to see if you can spot it, OK?' She smiled to the team. 'Are you ready?'

Hesitant nodding all around.

Mia pressed a key on the Mac and suddenly the seventeen-year-old girl was alive on the overhead screen again. Camilla Green. She was off the wheel now and kneeling on the floor. Eager hands trying to stuff as many pellets as she could into her mouth.

Animal feed, for pity's sake.

Bastard.

'Did you see it?' Mia said eagerly, looking across at the team once more when the short clip had finished.

Curry looked around, but everyone was shaking their heads, apart from Munch, who already knew what Mia was talking about but who was trying to keep his eyes open nevertheless.

'OK,' Mia said. 'I'll play it again and, this time, try to ignore Camilla. I know it's difficult, but try to pretend she's not there. Look at the wall behind the wheel. OK?'

Mia hit the key on the Mac again, and the short footage was replayed. Curry tried to do as Mia had said, keeping his eyes away from the girl kneeling in the front, and suddenly he saw it.

'Shit!' Ylva burst out, right next to him.

'Jesus,' Kim Kolsø mumbled.

'Exactly,' Mia nodded, almost triumphantly.

'Bloody hell!' Anette Goli exclaimed.

Holger Munch rose slowly from his chair. It was clear that he was almost at the end of his strength.

'This is very good progress.' He yawned. He was so tired that he struggled to put on his coat. 'But I need a break now. We'll meet again for a team briefing this evening. Let's say six o'clock.'

Their fat boss put up the hood of his duffel coat, staggered across the room and left without closing the door behind him.

Chapter 35

Miriam Munch was weak. She had hoped that it would pass. That she would manage to stay away, but all she had done these last few days was think about him. His face. *Ziggy.* And now she was here, in some café in Grünerløkka, feeling a mixture of giddy anticipation and guilt. A secret rendezvous. A place she would not normally visit. Where no one she knew might suddenly turn up. Marion was with Grannie and Rolf again, but Miriam Munch did not feel bad about that, because her daughter loved being with Grannie. The problem was Johannes.

One morning a few days ago, she had almost blurted it out. She hated this dishonesty. This sneaking about. She had to say something. About how she felt. They had been in bed, both of them had woken up early, Marion had yet to get up, and Miriam had decided the time was now – *We need to talk* – but then his mobile had rung – the hospital, please could he come in earlier; and the moment had passed.

Miriam ordered another cup of tea and went back to her table. A quarter past. He was late. She had been embarrassingly early, eager as a schoolgirl on her first date; her skin had been tingling as she had travelled here on the tram, almost incapable of sitting still, but now that she had been here for a while she was starting to feel a little awkward. She felt as if everyone could tell from looking at her that she was waiting for someone, someone she should not be waiting for. Miriam picked up a newspaper in order to have something to do, to hide behind, and started flicking through it, initially without much interest.

The girl in the woods, of course. The paper was mostly about that. The girl they had found naked, in bizarre circumstances, a kind of ritual in the woods on the far side of Hurumlandet. Camilla, that was her name. Camilla Green. She had been living in some sort of hostel for teenagers. Miriam put the paper down again. She could not bear to think about it. It was just too awful.

That must have been why he had left Marion's birthday party early. Her father. Because they had found this girl. She started feeling guilty about him, too, all the years when she had treated him so badly. Blamed him for the divorce. A naked girl on feathers on the ground, surrounded by candles in the middle of the forest. Now she wished she had been more understanding. No wonder he had had to leave. Miriam got up and ordered a beer; she was not in the habit of drinking in the afternoon, but she needed it today to steady her nerves.

By the time he finally arrived, Miriam had managed to drink a second beer and was starting to get annoyed with him. She had even considered leaving, but her anger evaporated the moment he and his gentle smile appeared in the doorway and he sat down on a chair on the other side of the table.

'I'm sorry I'm late,' Ziggy said.

'That's all right.' Miriam smiled.

'Thank you. Again, I'm so sorry. Are we drinking beer? Would you like another one?'

Miriam wavered. Three beers this early in the afternoon? She had promised to pick Marion up after dinner, but her daughter probably would not mind another sleepover at Grannie's. And Johannes was working late – again.

'Why not?'

Ziggy went up to the counter to order.

It came over her again. Another surge of guilty conscience.

What did she really think she was doing here?

She was happy. Wasn't she?

Johannes, Marion and her. Miriam had never imagined it would be any other way. The thought had never even crossed her mind. Not until six weeks ago.

Ziggy carefully carried two beers to their table and sat down again.

'I really am very sorry for being so late. My sister called, and – family stuff, I don't want to bore you with it.'

'You're not boring me, I'd like to hear about it,' Miriam said, taking a sip of her beer.

'Really?' Ziggy said. He sounded a little surprised.

'Absolutely. We have to have something to talk about, don't we?'

She winked at him, and the young man smiled back. Ever since they met, it had been like that between them. No awkward silences. Easy.

'What?' Ziggy smiled, looking at her.

'No, nothing.' She laughed.

'Oh, go on,' the young man teased her.

'No, seriously. It was nothing. So tell me. Your sister? Has something happened? How many brothers and sisters do you have?'

He leaned back in his chair and studied her, as if he were thinking about something. Sizing her up.

'You don't know who I am, do you?' he asked.

'What do you mean? Of course I know who you are.'

'No, not like that,' Ziggy said. 'You don't know who my family is? You really don't?'

Miriam did not understand what he was talking about.

'No, you've never talked about them. It hasn't come up, I mean, we've only just . . .'

Miriam got tangled up in her own words, and she blushed.

'I didn't mean it like that.' Ziggy smiled. 'I don't know quite what we're . . . I mean, what do you want? Because I know what I want.'

'And what do you want?' Miriam said, not quite daring to look at him.

'I think you know,' he said, suddenly putting his hand on hers for a moment.

She had turned her hand to stroke his when the door behind them opened and she automatically snatched it back, though the face that appeared did not belong to anyone she knew.

'Sorry,' Ziggy said. 'I didn't mean to make you uncomfortable.'

'No, no, you're not. It's just that, well, you know how it is.'

Miriam looked at him. Ziggy nodded back to indicate that he understood completely. It was what they had talked about that night in his flat. He had already told her it would not be a problem that she had a child.

'So, your family?' Miriam said, changing the subject.

'Yes, were you serious? You really don't know who my family is?'

Miriam must have looked very confused, because the young man laughed briefly.

'You have a sister,' she said. 'That's all I know. You haven't said much else. Should I be embarrassed about something? Was I really that drunk that night? Did you tell me things I don't remember?'

He laughed again.

'Embarrassed, no, God, no, I'm just relieved. It's rare for people not to know about my family. Let's drink to that.'

Miriam was becoming genuinely intrigued. She had clearly missed something.

'You have to tell me now,' she insisted.

'It's nothing bad, I promise,' Ziggy said. 'In fact, it's quite nice not to be thought of as one of them. Like I said, I think this is a first.'

'I want to know everything about you,' Miriam said. 'To be honest, I think about you nearly all the time.'

She could not believe she had just said that. It had to be the alcohol talking. She started to blush again, but it could not be helped.

'I want to know everything about you, too.' Ziggy leaned across the table towards her. 'And I think about you, too. Perhaps I shouldn't, and I don't know what we're going to do about it, but that's the way it is.'

It was beating faster now, her heart under her jumper, as he smiled at her and gently touched her hand again.

Damn it, Miriam.

What do you think you're doing?

A secret rendezvous?

'So who is this mysterious family of yours?' she asked bashfully.

'What else do you know about me?' Ziggy smiled, leaning back in his chair.

'Your surname is Simonsen,' Miriam began.

'Ziggy Simonsen, that's me.'

The name rang a faint bell. Simonsen?

'I wasn't christened Ziggy, of course. Jon-Sigvard. That's what they called me. Sigvard had to be in there somewhere. Family tradition.'

He smiled faintly at her under his dark fringe.

'Carl-Sigvard Simonsen?'

Ziggy nodded.

'*He* is your father? The billionaire?'

'Yep.' Ziggy nodded.

'Sorry,' Miriam said with a small smile.

'Sorry? Why on earth do you think you have to apologize?' He smiled, and raised his beer to her again.

'I don't read the gossip columns,' Miriam said by way of apology. 'Or enough newspapers, unfortunately.'

'Hey, I'm pleased.' The young man smiled again. 'I could meet you as myself, and not like some . . .'

He seemed lost in his own thoughts now, as if something burdened him, and a darkness she did not recognize spread across his bright, open face.

'So, you're a rich kid?' Miriam said to lighten the mood. 'My ship has come in.'

He came back to her. He smiled once more and pinned his gorgeous blue eyes on her.

'Does that mean what I think it means?'

'What?'

'That we are doing this?'

'Doing what?' Miriam said coquettishly, though she knew only too well what Ziggy was implying.

'You and me?' he said, caressing her hand again.

This time she let her hand stay where it was. His lovely hand against hers.

'I think I need another beer,' she whispered.

Chapter 36

'Moonbeam.' The face of the man in the doorway lit up in a smile. 'I wondered when you would turn up. I had a feeling you would when I saw the picture in the newspapers. Come in, come in.'

Mia Krüger crossed the threshold and followed the thin man with the ponytail into his flat.

'No need to take off your shoes, we don't stand on ceremony here. Would you like a drink, or something stronger?'

Mia knew exactly what he was suggesting. The small flat reeked of marijuana.

'Please excuse the mess. I don't get a lot of visitors. I prefer my own company, as you know.'

'It's fine.' Mia smiled and moved a messy pile of stuff from one end of the sofa so she could sit down.

'Good, good,' the man with the ponytail said, and flopped into an armchair opposite her, still smiling. 'So I can't offer you anything?' He gestured towards the table. 'I've got some good Afghan. Straight from the grower. Banned in thirty countries, he-he. No, not really, but it's still good. Soft as butter. And some Maroc lying around here somewhere, if you fancy a calmer trip? Are you sure I can't tempt you?'

Sebastian Larsen grinned at her. She was a little surprised that he had replied to her so quickly. He did not like visitors, but, right now, he actually seemed pleased to see her.

'No, thank you. You know I don't touch that stuff,' Mia smiled, feeling it was starting to affect her now, the desire for sleep.

'It's up to you. But you don't mind if I indulge?'

'Please yourself,' Mia said with a light shrug.

Sebastian Larsen. Social anthropologist. Used to work at the University of Oslo. A brilliant mind that had quickly risen up the academic ranks, until he was thrown out for selling marijuana to the students. Mia had called on his services in previous cases, but these days senior police officers pretty much discouraged it. The force did not want to be associated with a man like Sebastian Larsen, and Mia could see why: the smell in the flat and the smile on his face was more than enough.

'It's been ages, Moonbeam. Good to see you. I thought you had forgotten all about me.'

'I've been busy,' Mia smiled, feeling the tiredness again.

Munch had given her strict instructions: *get some rest* – but she had been unable to make her body switch off. Instead, she had swallowed some pills. She had been thinking about Sebastian Larsen ever since they had found Camilla. The occult. Rituals. Mia could think of no one else who knew more about this subject than the man currently sitting in front of her.

He had his own blog these days, she believed; that was how he had managed since he got kicked out of the university. Conspiracy theories. That was pretty much all he wrote about. She looked him up every now and then. *New evidence: the Americans never landed on the moon. Area 51, witnesses say: we saw extraterrestrials.* And so on.

'You're sure?' Larsen said, taking a drag from the bong in front of him.

'No, thank you,' Mia said, shaking her head again.

'As you wish.' He smiled and filled the room with smoke as he exhaled.

He had been highly regarded at the university. Travelled the world to give lectures. Right until he had let his weakness – or perhaps his liberal attitude – become known.

'You know why I'm here?' Mia said, aware that her eyes were starting to close.

She stuffed her hand into her pocket, fidgeted with the white pills which would give her a little extra energy, but she held back. Enough now. She had to get some sleep soon.

'Of course.' Sebastian nodded, looking earnestly at her. 'In fact, I'm glad you came. I was hoping you would.'

'So what do you think?'

'About the pictures in the newspapers?'

Mia nodded.

Sebastian Larsen ran a hand over his hair, and hesitated.

'Well, what's there to say? It's not easy to draw conclusions from just one picture on the cover of a newspaper. Do you have anything else for me?'

'Possibly,' Mia said. 'But you have to give me something first.'

'So you no longer trust me, is that it?'

Mia grinned and indicated the bong on the table. 'Would you?'

Larsen giggled. 'Point taken.'

He went over to his laptop and entered the address of a newspaper website.

'This is very interesting, I have to admit,' he said, bringing up the photograph which had been in the newspapers.

The forest floor. The feathers. The five candles.

'It's a pentagram, of course, but you already know that, don't you?' Larsen looked at her.

Mia nodded.

'I haven't seen the feathers before,' he said, turning his attention back to the screen. 'But the candle formation is well known; the pentagram is used by many, it's thousands of years old – but if I'm to help you, you're going to have to give me a bit more.'

Mia could sense he was already intrigued, but she still had her doubts as to whether she should show him the photographs in her bag of Camilla Green.

'The pentagram. Let's say that it's a ritual. Who would do something like that today?' she asked.

'Where do you want me to start?'

'With what's most relevant.'

'So you have nothing more to show me?'

'If you were to name names, I mean, based only on this, then who would it be?' Mia said, ignoring his question.

Larsen typed away, brought up a new webpage. 'OTO,' he said, nodding at the screen.

'Who?'

'Ordo Templi Orientis.'

'What does that mean?'

'*Do what thou wilt shall be the whole of the law. Love is the law, love under will.* Founded in 1895, a Knights Templar order breaking with the Church. Have you heard of Aleister Crowley?'

'Yes.' Mia nodded.

'Thelemite teachings?'

'Not quite.'

'Satanism?'

'Yes, of course.'

'Many people think that Aleister Crowley was the man behind OTO, but he wasn't; Crowley didn't join until 1904, when he—'

'What did you say before that?'

'What?'

'Thelemite teaching?'

'*Do what thou wilt,*' Larsen said, turning towards her.

'What does that mean?'

'You need to bear in mind that, at that time, the Church—' Larsen began, but Mia did not have the energy for a lecture.

'The short version?'

Larsen looked at her and shook his head. 'You said you wanted to know.' He sounded a little hurt.

'Sorry, Sebastian,' she said, putting her hand on his shoulder. 'It has been a long couple of days. So this organization . . .?'

'Ordo Templi Orientis.'

'It exists here in Norway?'

'Oh, yes, alive and kicking. Has its own senate established in 2008. Lodges in most major cities; Bergen and Trondheim have figured prominently in recent years.'

'And they live according to this . . . thelemite teaching?'

'*Do what thou wilt shall be the whole of the law,*' Larsen quoted again.

'And what does that mean?'

He turned with a small smile. 'What do you think it means, Mia? *Do what you want?*'

'Enlighten me,' Mia said.

'The rights of the individual. Resistance against government control. Against the teachings of the Church. Against the conventional moral and ethical norms forced upon us.'

'Which means?'

'Oh, come on, Mia, are you even listening to me?'

Larsen looked at her and shook his head. He was right, Mia thought: he had just inhaled illegal substances from God knows where, and yet his brain was working better than hers.

She slipped her hand into her pocket again.

Another pill?

No, she had to sleep now. Her body was on the verge of giving up. She needed to rest soon.

'Of course I'm listening,' Mia mumbled, turning to the screen again. 'OTO. Satanism. Thelemite teaching. Do what you will. Alive and kicking in Norway today.'

'They keep their rituals secret, like all other sects,' Larsen said. 'I've spoken to some of them – well, former members – and it's serious stuff.'

'Like what?'

'Sexual magic. Ritual sacrifice. Break away from society. Give away your body. Give away your mind. Be free.'

'Sexual magic?'

Larsen smiled faintly now. 'Yep.'

'Which means what exactly?'

'Well, if one of the senators wants you to take off your clothes and devote yourself to thelemite teaching in front of old men wearing masks, then you do it.'

'Senators?'

'Yes, interesting, isn't it?' Larsen said. 'How all these sects, which claim to exist in order to escape the strict controls society imposes, end up being just as controlling? They promise you freedom, but there's no freedom with them. Of course there isn't.'

'And you think this looks like them?' Mia said, pointing at the screen again.

'Way too early to say,' Larsen replied. 'Do you have anything else to show me?'

'Who else have we got?'

'Take your pick,' Larsen said, bringing up another webpage on his screen.

Google Maps this time. He typed in an address and leaned back.

'What are we looking at?' Mia said.

'The Palace.'

'What do you mean?'

'The official residence of the Norwegian royal family,' Larsen said, expanding the picture a little. 'This is Parkveien. You know where Parkveien is?'

Mia looked at him with a frown. Of course she knew. It was one of the most expensive streets in Norway, in the heart of Oslo, home of the Prime Minister and several embassies.

'Where are you going with this?'

'These organizations all have their addresses on Parkveien,' Larsen said, clicking a few more times. 'I mean, right behind the Palace. The Order of Norwegian Druids.'

'Druids?'

'Yes. Address Parkveien.'

Larsen clicked again. 'The Order of the Knights Templar. Address Parkveien.'

'And all these . . . I mean . . . the pentagram?'

Mia thought she was about to pass out.

'No, I'm not saying that. It's most likely either OTO or the sect your boss belongs to.'

'Munch?'

Larsen laughed out loud. 'No, not Munch, I don't think he would feel at home there.'

'Then who?'

Larsen brought up yet another website.

'Mikkelson,' said the thin man, pointing at the screen.

'Mikkelson?'

'Yep. Rikard Mikkelson.' Larsen nodded. 'Proud member of the Norwegian Order of Freemasons.'

Mia suddenly felt a little more awake. 'Freemasons?'

'Oh, yes, they love pentagrams. They're desperate to come across as pillars of the community, God-fearing, hah . . . Did you see the video where the grandmasters of the Thirty-third Degree are dressed in gowns with their willies hanging out as they sacrifice a goat?'

'No,' Mia said, not quite sure whether to believe him now.

Was Larsen still high, or was it the academic talking?

'Mikkelson is a member. As are most of the great and the good in this country. Freemasons, Mia. Grown men who take part in rituals. They join hands. They dress up in costumes. They drink blood from silver goblets. Oh, how gullible we are. Do you really think decisions about this country are made in government meetings?'

Larsen reached out for the bong on the table and lit it again.

'Sebastian,' she said earnestly, fixing her eyes on the small, skinny man in front of her.

'Yes?' Larsen said.

'I'm about to show you something. Something I obviously should not be showing you, but I'm going to do it anyway.'

'OK.'

He seemed almost a little nervous now.

'I need you to tell me exactly what you think, OK?'

'Yes, of course.'

'I appreciate it. What you've just shown me. I'll look into it, but right now I need something specific from you, OK?'

Mia got up, went out into the passage and took the folder from her bag. She came back to the messy living room and squatted down on her haunches in front of Larsen, who was almost as excited as a little kid now. Mia opened the file, and she watched his eyes widen as she placed the photograph of Camilla Green on the table in front of him.

'Shit.'

'Yep,' Mia said. 'And let me make this absolutely clear, Sebastian, if I ever hear even a squeak about this, on your blog or anywhere else, that you have seen this picture, then I, well, I don't know . . .'

'I get it.' Larsen nodded earnestly, and she could see that he meant it.

'You see why I've come to you? It's not random, how these candles have been arranged?' Mia had seen Munch stagger out of the incident room earlier today, barely able to speak clearly, and she was starting to feel the same way.

'Oh, no, no, a pentagram is, well, for people who believe in it, it's . . .' Larsen drifted off, studying the image in front of him. 'Well, there's the standard interpretation.' Larsen cleared his throat; he was quite lucid now.

Being a specialist in theories was one thing, but being face to face with the reality, a picture of a seventeen-year-old girl naked on a bed of feathers, surrounded by a pentagram of candles, there was no doubt that he struggled to take it in.

'Let's pretend I know nothing,' Mia said. 'Teach me.'

'OK.' Larsen nodded nervously. 'The pentagram has, as you know from its name, five corners. And each one of them symbolizes something.'

'What?'

'The traditional interpretation is quite standard. Shall I take it from the top, clockwise . . .?'

Her mobile started to vibrate. Mia picked it up, struggling to focus on the name on the display. Kim Kolsø. She pressed the red button and returned the phone to her pocket.

'The soul is at the top,' Sebastian said.

'Go on,' Mia said.

'The other points are water, fire, earth, air.'

'Water, fire, earth, air?'

'Yes.'

'OK, great. Thank you, Sebastian.'

Mia took the picture from the table and was about to put it back in the file when she was stopped by a thin hand.

'But that's just – how can I put it? – the standard version. Kids' stuff. There is a deeper interpretation.'

'Go on?'

Larsen stared at the photograph again.

'Birth, virgin, mother, law, death,' he said in a low voice, not taking his eyes off the photograph.

Mia stifled a yawn.

'And look how her arms have been arranged,' he continued.

'How are they arranged, in your opinion?'

'Birth. And mother.' The skinny man nodded gravely.

Mia fumbled to get her mobile out of her pocket and call for a cab.

'Thank you, Sebastian.'

'It can't be a coincidence, can it?'

Mia smiled at him and put the photograph into her bag as she got up.

Sleep. She could not put it off any longer.

'Birth and mother,' Larsen said gravely.

'Thank you, Sebastian,' said Mia again.

She stumbled down the stairs and fell into the cab that was waiting for her.

Chapter 37

They had moved on, visiting several cafés; Marion would be spending the night with Grannie, and, as predicted, she was overjoyed about it. Miriam had not had a reply from Johannes. She had tried calling him, half hoping he would ride to her rescue, but he had not picked up his phone or replied to her text messages.

She stared into her glass, which was already empty again. Ziggy was outside, talking on his mobile. Miriam Munch could not help watching him furtively through the window as he stood there, gesturing on the pavement with a smile on his lips; just the sight of him made her warm all over. She went up to the bar and ordered another two beers as Ziggy came back through the doors.

'Another one here?' He winked. 'You don't want to escape to another bar?'

'No, do you?'

'No, it's all the same to me,' the handsome young man said with a light shrug.

'Or perhaps you need to go home?' Miriam said, carrying the beers back to the table.

Ziggy smiled. 'Definitely not. And you?'

'No,' Miriam said resolutely, clinking her glass against his.

This was a quieter bar with soft music, where the lighting was muted, with booths where they could hide away. Miriam slipped her hand across the table and felt his warm fingers mesh with hers.

'Important call?'

'Oh, it was only Jacob.'

'Jacob who?'

'You've met him,' Ziggy reminded her.

'Have I?' Miriam giggled over the rim of her beer glass.

'At Julie's party? Round glasses? Likes to look smart?'

'Oh, yes, of course.' Miriam nodded, remembering him now. The boy who had made a pathetic attempt at chatting her up until he realized that she was a mother.

'So do you think we should . . .?' he said, caressing her cheek softly.

'Yes, Jon-Sigvard. I do. I mean, if you do?'

He laughed under his fringe.

'Just as long as you don't call me Jon-Sigvard,' he said, and took a swig of his beer.

'Deal.' Miriam smiled, and laughed as well.

'It's just that . . .' Ziggy said, cupping his hands around his glass now; he continued to stare into his drink.

'It's just that what?'

'Well, what if you discover things about me that you don't like,' he said, looking up at her again.

'That's the chance we'll have to take, isn't it? You might discover things about me that you don't like, mightn't you?' She smiled at him.

'I very much doubt that.'

'You're an idiot.'

'No, I mean it,' Ziggy said, bordering on serious now.

'What do you mean?'

'I feel I'm putting you in a difficult situation. With Marion and everything . . .'

'I'm a grown woman,' Miriam said. 'Marion will be fine whatever happens.'

'Yes, but even so,' Ziggy said, wavering again.

'What?'

'What if I were to tell you that I do things that might land me in prison?'

'What do you mean?' Miriam laughed.

'That I'm a criminal?' Ziggy said.

Miriam giggled again before she realized that he was serious.

'I find that hard to believe. What do you do, rob banks?'

'No, I don't rob banks.' He winked at her. 'But . . .'

Miriam was intrigued now. She could see he wanted to tell her something.

'I mean, family life and all that, maybe my lifestyle doesn't fit in with . . . Oh, I don't know.'

He fidgeted with his glass.

Miriam waited for the alarm bells to ring; she had a sixth sense for such things, but nothing happened.

'I like you, Miriam,' he said, taking her hand again.

'I like you too, Ziggy.'

'If I tell you a secret, can you handle it?'

'I'm sure I can. Have you killed someone?'

'What? No, Christ, do you believe I'm capable of that?' Ziggy looked horrified.

'Well, I don't know,' Miriam said. 'You tell me you might go to prison, but that you're not a bank robber, what am I supposed to believe?'

Too much alcohol. She could feel it now. The words came out of her mouth without having gone through her brain.

'OK,' Ziggy said, looking as if he had finally made up his mind. 'You know the place where we met, don't you?'

'The Animal Protection League shelter,' Miriam said.

'Yes, well, for me, volunteering has never been enough.'

'What do you mean?'

'People who mistreat animals. I hate it.'

'Of course.'

'No, I don't think you quite understand, I *hate* it.'

She had never seen that expression in his eyes before.

'And that's what we're talking about? That's what makes you a "criminal"?' Miriam made quotation marks with her fingers.

'In the eyes of the law,' Ziggy said, picking up his mobile from the table, pressing some keys and sliding it across to her.

An old newspaper article: 'Animal activists raid Løken Farm.'

'That was you?' Miriam was taken aback.

Ziggy nodded.

'Løken Farm? That place out on Mysen that takes in cats and dogs and sells them on for animal testing abroad?' Miriam had followed the story closely. Quietly rooting for the animals and their saviours.

He nodded again.

'You raided the farm in the middle of the night. You saved several animals, didn't you?'

'Yes,' Ziggy said.

'And you were scared to tell me this?'

He nodded.

'You had no reason to be.' Miriam chuckled. 'Hell, I'll join you.'

'Are you serious?' Ziggy said.

'What do you think?' Miriam said. 'Those bastards? Any time.'

He was smiling broadly now.

'Was that what your call was about?'

'Which call?'

'The one you just had with . . . what's his name . . . Joakim?'

'Jacob.'

'Yes, sorry, was that what it was about?'

Ziggy nodded under his fringe.

'What are you planning?'

He glanced around quickly, a moment of paranoia, as if anyone in the dark bar would care.

'A new place,' Ziggy said, pressing a few keys on his mobile and sliding it across to her again.

Miriam was not quite sure what she was looking at.

'What's this?'

'A pharmaceutical company. Atlantis Farms.'

'Atlantis Farms? That's a terrible name.' Miriam smiled. 'Don't these companies usually sound a bit zingier? Novartis? AstraZeneca? Pfizer?'

'It's not the name of the company, just a testing station in Hurum. They experiment on all kinds of animals. But no one seems to care, it's as if someone higher up the system is, well, you can barely find the place on the map, but we've managed to . . .'

Ziggy leaned back in the booth again and suddenly seemed reticent, as if he had said too much. He took another swig of his beer and looked around the room. Miriam slid his phone back across the table.

'Yes,' she said, and now she was smiling again.

The young man looked puzzled, not sure what she meant.

'Yes,' she said again, extending her hand across the table.

'Yes to what?' Ziggy said.

'To what you asked me earlier today,' Miriam said, cautiously caressing his arm.

'Yes?'

'Yes.'

'Are you sure?'

'I am.' Miriam nodded. 'I like you.'

'I like you too,' Ziggy said, and looked down.

It took a few seconds before he spoke again.

'I don't know if this is something you're supposed to ask, but . . .'

'What is it?'

'Please may I kiss you?'

'You may.' Miriam Munch smiled again, and took a quick breath before she closed her eyes and slowly leaned forwards.

Chapter 38

Mia awoke with a start, but stayed where she was, gasping for air. It was a nightmare. It was not real. She sat up on her mattress, cradling her head in her hands, her heart pounding under her jumper. She had fallen asleep fully dressed, and had been sweating so much that her clothes were sticking to her body.

Shit.

She had truly believed it. Normally, she slept soundly. Normally, she had soothing dreams, as if there were a kind of wall inside her so that, no matter how much evil she faced when awake, goodness would take over when she put her head on the pillow and nodded off. But not this time.

Damn.

Mia got up from the bed and staggered into the bathroom; she was still wearing her leather jacket and her shoes. Splashed water on her face. The nightmare lingered, refusing to let go, so she continued to dunk her hands and face in the cold water until she calmed down, then she stumbled into the living room, where she collapsed on the sofa. Her dream had been about Sigrid. Not the beautiful dream she usually had. Her sister smiling at her, running through a field.

Come, Mia, come.

No, she had been in the basement. In the basement in Tøyen, where Sigrid had sat on a filthy mattress with a rubber strap around her arm and a syringe by her side, ready for her fix, the one which had killed her that night just over ten years ago. Mia had been there. Or so it had felt. She had been present in the same room. Seen all the rubbish around her sister, felt the stench of urine sting her nostrils; the contrast to pretty Sigrid could not have been greater. Mia had tried talking to her, but no words had come out of her mouth. She had tried to move, to come to her sister's rescue, but her body had been paralysed. Panic was what she had felt, and it lingered in her still. Mia tried to breathe more calmly, and fished her mobile out of her jacket pocket. It was almost midnight. She had missed the team briefing, but there were no calls or messages from Munch. Some from Kim Kolsø, but nothing from Holger. Strange. Why not? For a moment she wondered if she was still dreaming. The possibility that what she was experiencing now might not be real either scared her, that the shadow might be here now, the shadow she had seen on the wall behind Sigrid. She tried checking her mobile again, but it slipped between her fingers and fell on to the floor, and she was unable to bend down to retrieve it. Too frightened to look. To take her eyes off the room she was in.

The shadow on the wall.

Damn it, it had to be the pills.

She did not usually take them. When she took pills, it was always to escape. To rest. But she had fooled herself. Swallowed pills she should not have. And now they had wrecked her mind. Mia bent down to get her phone, still without taking her eyes off the wall in front of her, trembling fingers fumbling on the floor, but she could not find it.

Because she had changed her mind. Sigrid. That was what she had done. Mia had stood there, helpless in the filthy stench, and watched as her sister sank her teeth into the rubber strap. Tied it around her scrawny arm just above the elbow. She had seen her place the lump in the small spoon. The heroin. Hold the lighter underneath it until it bubbled. A ball of cotton wool and a little water; Mia did not know why, did not know enough about how junkies shoot up, but the ritual had seemed familiar, as if she had seen it before. Close-ups of bubbles in the dip of the spoon. The tip of the needle sucking the liquid into the syringe. The stench. Mia pinched her nose now; the stench was so strong that she could not shake it off. This had to be a dream, surely? Would it come here, too?

The shadow.

Mia continued to search for her mobile, still not taking her eyes off the wall opposite her, and finally she found it. She picked it up and placed it on the table in front of her. Almost too scared to look at the display. Why had Munch not called her? She moved her hand to her nose. The stench. It was still here. Excrement and rubbish. The smell of human misery. And her twin sister there, on the mattress right in front of her, and there was nothing she could do. No sounds came out of her mouth, no matter how hard she screamed; her legs refused to move across the filthy floor, no matter how desperately she tried.

Close-ups again. Fingers tapping the white skin hard in order to find a vein. Her thumb on the plunger, and then an image of the tip as a little of the heroin trickled out – not much, just enough to make sure there was no air trapped inside. Don't get air in your veins. An air bubble in the syringe can kill you. And then she saw Sigrid's lovely eyes. And her pretty lips. And her arm raising the syringe towards the blue vein, which had swelled up under the yellow rubber strap. But then, she had changed her mind.

Sigrid.

She had wanted to live.

And Sigrid had looked at her. She had looked deep into Mia's eyes. And then she had nodded to her. Smiled like she used to. Winked at her. Put down the syringe on the mattress. She had started to loosen the rubber strap around her arm when the shadow on the wall appeared. And it had looked as if Sigrid was about to stand up. Wanting to come over to her, to stroke her hair like she used to when Mia was sad. When she had hurt herself. If someone at school had been mean to her. Sigrid's hand on her hair; and Mia could feel how much she missed it, as she had stood there in her nightmare, surrounded by the stench of human degradation: Sigrid's warm, lovely hand over her hair.

It's going to be all right, Mia.

We have each other.

You and me for ever, OK?

But then Sigrid could no longer see her. Mia had tried listening to the conversation, because she could see lips moving, but her ears did not work, she could not understand what was going on, but she saw Sigrid look down at the filthy floor, nod and sit down again on the urine-stained mattress. More close-ups. The syringe was back in her hand. The tip of the needle heading for the bulging, blue vein.

The shadow on the wall.

It was the same shadow as in the basement where Camilla Green had been held prisoner.

A human being with feathers.

A feathered man.

And then the close-ups started again, with Sigrid in the centre. Her thumb on the syringe. Injecting into the vein. Her eyes, which first opened like a smile, only to close slowly until the girl Mia loved more than anything in the whole world lay lifeless on the mattress in front of her.

No.

Mia tried breathing calmly now and felt the real world slowly return around her. The unopened cardboard boxes. The kitchen counter with the leftovers of the food she had failed to eat. She carefully took her hand away from her nose, but the smell was still there, and then she realized that it was coming from her. The pills. Synthetic poison that her body did not want and was trying frantically to rid itself of in a bath of sweat; chemical smells not from the basement, but from her. Mia stood up carefully and stepped out of her foul-smelling clothes, saw her garments fall one by one until she stood naked on the floor in the cold flat. She wrapped the blanket from the sofa around her as her mobile rang, a vibrating little creature on the table in front of her.

Kim Kolsø.

Mia sat down on the sofa again, tightened the blanket around her and pressed the green button.

'Yes?'

'Mia?' Kim Kolsø said. He sounded like someone from another world.

Someone from far away.

'Are you there, Mia?'

Mia nodded.

'Hello?'

'Hi, yes, sorry, I'm here, Kim, how are things?' Mia said, pulling her legs up under the blanket.

'Did I wake you?'

'No, of course not, I was already up.'

'OK, I just thought I ought to check in. Is everything OK?'

'Yes, of course, and how about you?'

She answered on autopilot, but she could feel that her body and her brain were starting to wake up now. She was no longer in her nightmare. She was in her flat. Naked under the blanket, and with Kim Kolsø on the phone. No shadows on the walls.

'I'm good. Did Munch call you?'

'No, I haven't heard from him,' she said.

'Same here. I've tried, but I haven't managed to get hold of him. I thought it might be just as well to let him sleep. I couldn't get hold of Gabriel either, so I thought the same might apply to him. He's had a shock.'

'Yes,' Mia replied, without fully paying attention.

It grew quiet for a moment, as if Kim expected her to add something.

'So we just had a short meeting, mainly a summing-up; we wanted to wait for you, of course, but I did the best I could. Are you sure you're OK?'

'Yes, yes, everything is fine,' Mia said, getting up.

She padded across the floor, still with the blanket around her, and touched the radiators below the window. They were cold. She had remembered to pay her electricity bill, hadn't she? She turned on the radiators and staggered back to the sofa.

'Well, it's just . . .' Kim Kolsø went on. 'I think the team was a bit worried about you. You know, after we watched that video.'

The shadow on the wall.

The feathered human being.

'Well, I'm fine. So what did you talk about at the meeting?' Mia cleared her throat.

'Only about what we've got. Forensic evidence from the note you found in the equestrian centre. No other fingerprints apart from Camilla's own. Her phone records. That someone at the Nurseries must have sent the message saying she was fine.'

'Or someone nearby,' Mia said. She was awake now.

'Yes, of course, but what are the chances of that?'

'No, I know. But even so.'

'And then, new information from the post-mortem report.'

'Yes?'

'Nothing we can use, sadly. It's as we thought. She was strangled. Vik thinks it happened at the crime scene, but he can't be one hundred per cent sure.'

'So she walked into the forest of her own free will?'

'No, he didn't say that, but, yes, it's possible; or not of her own free will exactly . . .'

Mia knew what he meant. Camilla Green had walked on her own two feet through the forest. But obviously not of her own free will.

After three months in a wheel in a basement.

'Then we have some evidence that the guys from Forensics discovered out at Hurumlandet Nurseries, which I don't really know what we do with.'

'What was it?'

'They found cannabis plants in one of the greenhouses.'

'Really?' Mia said. 'How many?'

Mia had a sudden flashback to her meeting with Sebastian Larsen. In the flat that had reeked as if someone had decided to move Amsterdam to Oslo. She had not had time to process it yet. OTO, the Freemasons. The meaning behind the pentagram. She did not know how much importance to attach to it. If Larsen's mind had left this planet for good, or whether he had said something that was actually useful.

'I think they found eight.'

'So, for personal consumption?'

'I don't know.' Kim yawned.

'We can talk about it tomorrow.'

'OK.'

'Have we been asked to turn up for a specific time?'

'Like I said, I didn't manage to get hold of Holger, so I told everybody nine o'clock. Is that all right with you?'

'Yes, yes, of course,' Mia said, tightening the blanket around her naked body.

'And another thing. I paid Olga Lund another visit.'

'Olga who?'

'The old lady who lives in Hurum?'

'Of course. The woman who used TV programmes to tell her the time. Did you learn anything?'

'No, sadly, she couldn't tell us anything besides what we already knew: a white van with some sort of logo on the side, could be a flower.'

'From the Nurseries?' Mia wondered out loud, waking up a little more.

'That was my hope, too,' Kim said. 'But she said she thought it could have been an orange.'

'I think we should forget about her for now. But she was sure it was a white van?'

'Yes,' Kolsø said. 'Only the problem is, according to Ludvig, that thousands of white vans are registered in Oslo and Buskerud, so where do we start?'

'Quite,' Mia said. 'No, let's drop it. Unless we have nothing else.'

She could feel that the flat was starting to heat up now. She stretched out her legs towards the table, and yawned faintly. The chemical sleep had not helped. She needed real sleep.

'Ah, yes,' Kim said, disappearing again, as if leafing through something. 'The wig.'

The virgin in the blonde wig.

'Of course. Did we find anything on it?'

'This is a bit strange . . .' Kim said, pausing again, as if he could not quite believe the information in front of him.

'Yes?'

'No, this has to be a joke.'

'What does?'

'The wig. As far as I'm aware, a wig is something you buy from a joke shop. For a fancy-dress party, right? "I want to go as Marilyn Monroe and I need a cheap wig" – are you with me?'

Mia was even more awake now; she could hear that Kim was excited. 'But this isn't that kind of wig?'

'No,' Kim went on, and Mia imagined that he was still looking at the notes in front of him.

'This is just the preliminary report, but even so . . .'

'Yes?'

'The guy I spoke to at the lab – Tormod, or maybe he was called Torgeir, I don't really remember – he said they found genuine hair from at least twenty different women in it.'

'In the wig?'

'Yes,' Kolsø said.

'Is that very unusual?' Mia asked.

'I wouldn't know,' Kim continued. 'But, if it's very expensive, perhaps it was made to order? How many shops make something like that? Long, blonde wigs using real hair from that many women must be quite pricey, don't you think? Maybe it's something we should follow up?'

'Definitely,' Mia said, getting up from the sofa. She walked over to the radiator below the window and felt the heat against her naked body. She stood there, looking out across Bislett Stadium. Life outside. People who did not need to live like her. Who had had a beer with a friend and were now heading home to snuggle up with their loved one. A couple with their arms entwined; young people smiling, crossing the street without a care in the world. A woman in a red jacket under a street-light, the hood pulled over her head, her hands stuffed into the pockets, gazing up at a window, probably the flat above or below hers, maybe waiting for a friend to let her in. Normal people. Normal life. And she realized that she envied them. Getting up in the morning. Going to work. Returning home in the evening. Turning on the TV. Having weekends off. Making pizza.

'Are you still there?' Kim said. He had said something she had missed.

'Yes, I'm still here.'

'So what do you think?'

'Why don't we talk about it tomorrow morning?' Mia said, shuffling back to the sofa.

'Yes, sure,' Kim Kolsø said, and again she got the feeling that he was holding something back.

'Good job, Kim.'

'What? Thanks, but . . .'

He grew quiet again. It was a long time before he spoke.

'You are keeping me in the loop, aren't you?'

At first Mia did not understand his question.

'I mean, Holger and you?'

'In the loop?' Mia said. 'How?'

And out it came, the insecurity she had sensed below the surface of everything he had told her.

'Well, it's just that, Emilie and I . . .' Kim Kolsø mumbled '. . . ever since I requested a transfer . . . perhaps I feel that . . . that I am already out? That you're doing this without me?'

Mia had nothing but deep respect for Kolsø. If she had to trust someone with her life, he would definitely have been near the top of the list. She had never heard him talk like this before.

'Kim . . .?' Mia said, tightening the blanket around her once more.

'Yes?'

'Of course we're not.'

'Are you quite sure?' the normally confident man said, and again Mia was taken aback by the tone of his voice.

'Why the hell would we do that? You're the best member of the team. Of course you're in the loop, Kim,' Mia said, getting up again.

'OK, good.'

'I wouldn't have it any other way.'

'So team briefing at nine o'clock tomorrow.'

'Yep.'

'Great,' Kim said, and it sounded as if he was about to add something, but he did not. 'I'll see you then.'

'See you at nine,' Mia said, pressed the red button, put down the phone, walked into the shower and stood there with her head bowed until the hot water ran out.

Chapter 39

Helene Eriksen turned off the ignition, got out of her car and lit a cigarette. She zipped her quilted jacket right up to her neck. A meeting in a deserted road, under the cover of darkness, this late at night? She shouldn't be doing this. She took a deep drag on her cigarette, watched the red tip light up her fingers and realized that she was shivering. From cold, possibly – October had arrived and brought with it a darkness normally associated with November or December – but that was not the only reason. She pulled down her sleeves and continued to peer down the empty road after the headlights she knew would soon appear.

'Show me.'

Tongue out.

'Good girl. Next.'

It was more than thirty years ago, and still it had not lost its power over her. She continued to wake up in the middle of the night, sheets drenched in sweat from the nightmare where she was back sleeping on the old sofa again, scared of where her brother had been, scared of the consequences. The fear of being punished by the women, if she said the wrong thing. Thought the wrong thoughts. She had been seven years old then, she was over forty now, yet it had never left her.

'It's not your fault.'

They were the first words he had said to her, the psychologist. She had been eleven years old, twelve maybe, she could not remember, only that his room had smelt strange, and she had struggled to speak.

'It's not your fault, Helene. I want you to begin with that. This is what you need to tell yourself: it was not your fault. Can you do this for me? Are you able to start with that?'

Helene Eriksen climbed on to the bonnet, pulled up her legs and sat in the darkness, her eyes taking in the landscape around her. The shadows of the trees started to take on strange shapes. She tossed aside the half-finished cigarette and got back behind the wheel. It was safer inside. She stuck the key in the ignition and turned it ninety degrees so that she could switch on the heater and the radio.

'Show me.'

Tongue out.

'Good boy. Next.'

She pressed a few buttons and found a radio station she liked, music to distract her mind. She turned up the sound and sat drumming her fingers on the steering wheel, while she peered out through the windscreen for the lights that would soon show up.

'Do you think you can manage that, Helene?'

Their hair had been bleached. They had all worn the same clothes. Done everything the women told them. Always the same, day in and day out. School, yoga, housework, homework, pills, school, yoga, housework, homework, pills. Thirty years ago. How long would it retain its hold over her?

'I know it's difficult, but I'm here to help you.'

Helene Eriksen took out the packet from her pocket and lit another cigarette, although she did not really want one, rolled down the window so the smoke could escape, but closed it quickly; way too cold outside.

'What are you thinking about, Helene?'

Twelve years old in a chair in Oslo in front of a strange man with a moustache.

'It's not your fault, do you understand that, Helene?'

She took another drag on her cigarette and turned up the volume of the radio again; she liked how the music filled the car.

Bankruptcy Auction. Market garden for sale.

She had been twenty-two years old and she had done what they wanted her to do. Got an education. Made something of herself.

Location: Hurumlandet. 28 hectares of land. Three green-houses. In good condition, but in need of restoration.

She had caught the bus out there. And she had felt so certain afterwards; this was what she really wanted to do with her life.

Help others.

Helene turned off the radio, checked her watch and got out of the car again. She considered lighting another cigarette but decided there was no point, so she just stood with her hands stuffed in the pockets of her jacket, staring into the darkness.

'What are you thinking about now, Helene?'

But she had to do something. She lit another cigarette.

More than thirty years ago? Surely she should be over it by now?

Helene Eriksen took another drag on her cigarette as the lights she had been waiting for suddenly appeared and the white van pulled up and stopped right next to her.

'Hi, what's up?' the man behind the wheel said.

'Don't tell me you haven't heard?' Helene replied.

'Heard what?'

'Tell me you're joking,' Helene said, and went right up to him. She could see him mulling it over, before he spoke.

'Yes, but it has nothing to do with me.'

Helene really wanted to believe him. She would have given any-thing to be able to believe him, but she could not quite convince herself.

Her brother.

He had no clothes on.

He was completely naked, but his whole body was covered by . . . feathers?

'They're asking questions,' she said, tightening her jacket around her.

'About what?'

'About everyone, everything.'

'For Christ's sake, Helene. Do you really think I did it?'

'You were down there, weren't you? In your cottage? All summer? You weren't at home, were you? I just had to . . . ask you. I love you so much.' She smiled weakly.

Her brother smiled and stuck his hand out of the open side window.

'I love you too, Helene, but seriously? Why are we meeting in the middle of nowhere, late at night? There's no need for that.'

She felt like an idiot now. She tightened her jacket even more as her brother smiled and held her hand through the open window.

'No, I know, it's just . . . You know, the feathers and everything.'

'I finished with that a long time ago. Now go home and get some sleep, will you?'

Helene Eriksen felt his warm hand leave hers before he rolled up the window.

And then he was gone again, just as swiftly as he had appeared.

FIVE

Chapter 40

Holger Munch seemed well rested as he stood in front of the overhead screen in the incident room; he smiled as he waited for everyone to sit down. Gabriel Mørk did not feel quite so perky. For the first time since the investigation began, he had considered staying at home. Take a day off to create some distance from it all. The film he had seen had distressed him, he felt unwell; perhaps he was coming down with some kind of bug? Besides, spending a day with his girlfriend would be good, wouldn't it? Perhaps they could go shopping for baby clothes for the little boy who would soon arrive.

And yet he had gone to work, because Gabriel knew that these were all excuses. The real reason he did not feel like going in was Skunk. He knew questions would be asked. They needed to find him, and Gabriel was the obvious candidate to do that, but the truth was that the young hacker had no idea how to find his old friend.

'Right, everyone, good morning.' Munch smiled from the projector as people started to settle down. 'I'm sorry I bailed out on you last night, must be old age.'

He winked at them, and was rewarded with muted laughter from his team.

'Before I begin, does anyone have anything that I don't know about?'

Gabriel could see Ylva shift restlessly in her chair; she had been the first person to arrive at the incident room and was clearly keen to share a discovery she had made.

'I have something,' she said, smiling, not raising her hand this time.

'Go on?' Munch said.

'The tattoo.' Ylva got up to pass Munch a sheet of paper.

The young woman continued to stand up, unsure as to whether she should sit down again, while Munch assessed the paper she had given him.

'Aha, great.' He smiled. 'What are we looking at?'

Munch nodded to indicate that she could stay put in order to share this new information with the rest of the team. Gabriel could see that Ylva was a little nervous, but she was mostly proud at having spotted something; she stuffed her hand into her pocket and paused before she began speaking.

'OK, so, Camilla had this tattoo on her arm, didn't she?'

Nodding across the room.

A horse's head with the letters A and F below it.

'I stayed up last night because something about it kept bugging me. It kept going round my mind; I knew that I had seen it somewhere before, but I couldn't remember where.'

Ylva was smiling faintly now, but stared at the floor before she continued. It was clear she felt a little awkward being in front of everyone else but also that she was excited.

Munch had found the photograph of the tattoo, which formed a part of the display behind him. Camilla's arm. The horse's head. The letters A and F.

'And then I wondered, what if they're not just the letters A and F? What about this line, do you see it?'

Ylva went up to the wall and pointed at the tattoo. The team gave her all their attention now; they seemed to be finally waking up.

'What if this line isn't just a line but another letter? Can you see it?'

'An L?' Mia nodded slowly.

'Exactly.' Ylva smiled. 'What if the letters are not just A and F, but, yes, look here . . .'

She went up to the wall and pointed again. 'ALF.'

'ALF?' Curry yawned. 'The guy's name is Alf?'

Scattered laughter.

'What?' Curry said, looking around.

'Ignore him, Ylva.' Munch nodded.

'I didn't realize what it was, until I spotted the L. And it took some searching, but I found this on the Internet last night.'

She glanced across to Munch.

'I've printed out several copies. Would you like me to . . .?'

Munch smiled and nodded. Ylva went quickly back to her seat and distributed the print-outs.

'What are we looking at?' Kim Kolsø asked.

'The Animal Liberation Front,' Ylva said, now back next to Munch. 'ALF. It's their logo, or one of them, at least. The horse's head with the initials below.'

There was murmuring across the room, and the young woman beamed with pride. She glanced quickly at Munch again, who nodded for her to continue.

'The Animal Liberation Front was formed in England back in 1974 and is today active in more than forty countries. They're known for their aggressive attitude to people and companies that keep animals in captivity, especially labs that carry out animal testing. They have been called a terrorist organization on behalf of animals. They don't shy away from using vicious, sometimes illegal means to achieve their goals.'

'And we have those in Norway?' Mia asked.

'That's where it gets a bit complicated,' Ylva went on. 'In Norway, they also call themselves the Animal Liberation Front, and they were very active between 1992 and 2004, carrying out a series of raids against fur farmers, shops selling furs, and so on. They have their own website, but it hasn't been updated since 2009, so I'm not sure whether they're still active or whether they have just gone underground.'

Ylva looked at Munch again, who indicated that she could sit down.

'So our friend Camilla Green had an Animal Liberation Front tattoo on her arm.'

Munch looked down at the piece of paper Ylva had given him. and smiled at her again.

'Good work, Ylva. Really good work.'

The young woman blushed happily.

'I want you to keep working on this. See what you can find out. Can we link Camilla to them in any recent raids? Ludvig will help you with the archives and anything else you might need, OK?'

Ylva nodded at Ludvig, who smiled back.

'Good,' Munch said. 'A great start to the day.'

Gabriel expected that Munch would go outside for a cigarette now, but he did not. He turned to the projector instead, clearly keen to get on.

'We have quite a few leads now, so it's time that we prioritize them, OK?'

Nodding from the team.

'First, the evidence found at the Nurseries. Cannabis?'

He looked towards Kim Kolsø.

'Not that many plants, seven or eight maybe.'

'And do we think it's relevant to our investigation?'

Kim shrugged. 'It's too early to say, but it's worth checking out. I know it's not our department, and I can't imagine that our friends from the Drug Squad will be all that interested in such a small amount, but the way I see it, Helene Eriksen has some explaining to do.'

'If she knew about them, that is,' Munch said.

'Of course,' Kolsø said. 'But somebody out there did, and it might lead us to something.'

'Right, definitely. We'll pay them another visit. Kim, will you handle that?'

Kolsø nodded.

'Good. And while you're out there, the note with the owl drawing. It's our strongest lead so far. Find out if anyone at the Nurseries has seen it before. Did someone there write it? Does anyone there know anything about it?'

Kim Kolsø nodded again. 'I'll deal with it.'

'I'm coming with you,' Curry said.

'Good,' Munch said, clicking. The next picture appeared. 'The wig?'

'Yes,' Ludvig said, looking down at his notes. 'Quite an expensive item, genuine hair, not something you can buy just anywhere. Only a few shops in this country stock this type of thing, but there's one called . . .' He flicked through his papers. 'Ruh's Wigs, up in Frogner. I thought we might start there. If it was bought there, they might have some paperwork. If not, perhaps they can give us an idea where the killer might have got it.'

'Good,' Munch clicked again. 'And then we have these.'

Gabriel pushed back against his chair when he saw two photographs he had never seen before. He noticed that several of his colleagues reacted in the same way.

'What?' Curry said, staring at the screen.

'Anette?' Munch said, nodding to the blonde police lawyer.

'As you probably know,' Goli took over, 'a man confessed to the murder a few days ago. Jim Fuglesang, aged thirty-two, who lives not far from the place where Camilla was found. A psychiatric patient at Dikemark Hospital for several years, as we understand it. As you already know, we don't believe that he is our killer. What is interesting is that, when he turned himself in at Grønland, he had these pictures on him.'

Gabriel looked closely at them. They showed a cat and a dog. Killed and posed in the same manner as Camilla Green. On a bed of feathers. In a pentagram of candles.

'Oh my God!' Ylva exclaimed.

'What the hell is this?' Curry grunted.

Munch gave a light shrug. 'That's exactly what we don't know. What are we looking at? Any suggestions?' He looked across the room.

'Bloody hell!' Curry swore again. 'The same ritual? With two animals? What kind of sick bastard is this?'

He looked quickly towards Mia.

'Maybe he or they are practising. There's certainly an escalation but, without further information, I'm not sure we can conclude much. As Munch said, we just don't know,' replied Mia, who was unusually subdued today.

It was clear that they had been studying the pictures for a while without coming up with an explanation. Gabriel did not know why the pictures had not been shared with everyone in the team until now, but Munch and Mia usually had their reasons.

'It hasn't been possible for us to interview Jim Fuglesang because, well . . .'

He looked towards Anette Goli again.

'I spoke to a consultant at Dikemark yesterday, and he says that Fuglesang can't be disturbed under any circumstances. Clearly, it all became too much for him, and I believe he has stopped talking altogether. He is heavily medicated. I didn't get the details – doctor–patient confidentiality, and all that – but that was how I understood it.'

'But it's on our to-do list, isn't it?' Munch said.

'Obviously,' Goli nodded. 'As soon as it's feasible.'

'Where did he take these pictures? When did he take them? We need to find that out as soon as we can.'

Munch turned towards the grotesque photographs of the animals on the screen again.

'Mia?'

Mia Krüger got up from her chair now and walked up to Munch. There was something about her today, her eyes, her posture; she seemed terribly exhausted, not quite with it.

'As Holger said, we don't understand the connection yet, but there is one; there can be little doubt about that. This must relate to the murder of Camilla Green. It can't be a coincidence.'

She pointed to the pictures.

'The feathers. The candles. And, not least, the posing of the arms or, in this case, the paws, do you see? Arranged at the same angles as Camilla's. One up. And one down to the side. Twelve noon and four o'clock. But why? We don't know that yet.'

Mia looked as if she was about to add something, but changed her mind and went back to her chair. Munch looked around at the assembly again.

'Any first impressions?'

'Sick son of a bitch,' Curry growled.

'Thank you, Curry,' Holger said. 'Any other first impressions? Associations? Anything?'

No one said anything. The others seemed just as shocked as Gabriel at the photographs in front of them.

'OK, we'll leave it for now. Until we're able to interview Jim Fuglesang again, OK?'

Munch looked across to Anette Goli again, who nodded in return.

'OK,' Munch said, clicking again.

Another picture appeared on the wall, and once again Gabriel was startled, while the others stayed calm. They must have looked at this yesterday after he had had to go home. It was a still photograph from the footage.

A feather-clad figure.

A human being with feathers?

Gabriel could not help shuddering, and it came back to him. The nausea. This was no ordinary murder case. He steeled himself and noticed how everyone else around him had also grown very quiet. Munch seemed to weigh his words carefully before he spoke.

'Like I said when we saw it yesterday, we have a feeling that what we're seeing here is the killer.'

'Shit,' Curry said, shaking his head.

'I know the image is blurred,' Munch said, as he pointed, 'but it looks as if someone is sitting there.'

Gabriel could see that Munch was starting to struggle.

'Watching her,' he added quickly, then pulled himself together again. 'Camilla is a prisoner. And she has an audience. Someone who, well . . .?'

'A bird man?' Curry said. 'What is this really about? Who the hell has feathers all over their body?'

'Our thinking is that this . . . creature, is watching her. That he has her locked up in order to watch. Perhaps purely for his own enjoyment? We don't know.'

Gabriel saw Munch glance at Mia – this was her field, this was where she usually explained baffling elements like these to them – but Mia continued to sit quietly on her seat.

'OK,' Munch said, scratching his head. 'Yes, we don't understand what we're dealing with here, but we need to discuss it.'

Munch looked across to Mia again, but there was still no response.

'The owl feathers,' Ludvig Grønlie said.

'Yes,' Munch said. He seemed relieved that someone else had joined in.

'I found out something, but I don't know if it's relevant.'

Ludvig looked at his notes again.

'What is it?' Munch asked.

'It was buried in the archives, not a priority – I stumbled across it by accident, whether it's useful I don't know, but even so—'

'What did you find?'

'There was a break-in some months ago, at the Natural History Museum in Tøyen. Like I said, a minor case, but it caught my eye because there was something unusual about it.'

Everyone looked at the older investigator.

'I'm sure you all know where the museum is? It forms part of the Botanical Gardens in Tøyen. They also have a natural-history block. And on . . .'

Grønlie looked down at his notes again.

'. . . the sixth of August, they reported that someone had broken into an exhibition entitled "Native and Non-native Animals", and this was the odd bit, that was why I noticed it. They have a cabinet displaying every kind of Norwegian owl, and the items in it were the only items to be taken. I mean, it could be nothing, but it's worth checking out, isn't it?'

'Absolutely.' Munch nodded. 'Well done, Ludvig. Do we have a contact person up there?'

Grønlie looked at his notes again. 'The break-in was reported by Tor Olsen, senior curator, according to the file. I mean, Camilla was found on a bed of owl feathers. Someone stole a whole collection of Norwegian owls.'

'We need to look into that. At once.' Munch nodded again, gravely. 'Excellent work, Ludvig. Mia, please would you go up there?'

Mia Krüger looked up as if she had been interrupted from thinking about something.

'The owl feathers? The break-in at the Natural History Museum? Would you deal with that, please?'

'Yes, of course,' she said with a light cough, looking as if she did not quite know what he was talking about.

'OK,' Munch said.

Gabriel realized that it was his turn now.

'This hacker who found the film. Your old friend, Skunk, have you made any progress?'

They looked at him, all of them.

'I've tried, I have nothing yet, but I'm still trying, I . . .'

'OK, good,' Munch said. 'Carry on with that and see what you can find. We really need to talk to him. We need to know where he found it.'

'OK.' Gabriel nodded, surprised and relieved at having been let off so easily.

Munch looked back at Mia. 'Please could you and I have a chat in my office?'

'What?' Mia said, still not quite present.

'In my office? Do you have five minutes?'

Mia looked up and stared at him. 'Of course.' She coughed again.

'OK, fine,' Munch said to the rest of the team. 'If anyone discovers anything else, bring it to my attention at once. I suggest a briefing at the end of today. We'll decide the time later.'

There was nodding from the team, and Mia Krüger quietly got up from her chair and slowly followed Munch into his office.

Chapter 41

Munch closed the door after Mia, and sat down behind his desk. She slumped on the small sofa. Munch looked back at her while he wondered what to say. Mia was staring at him with a somewhat vague expression he could not interpret, as if she was not all there.

'So, what's up?' she said at length.

'Well, that was what I was going to ask you.'

'What?' Mia woke up a little at that.

Munch weighed up his words. It had been on his mind for days now. First down at Justisen, then at yesterday's briefing, and now during the morning meeting. Mikkelson had suspended her. Asked her to see a therapist in order to be declared fit for duty. To see if she was ready for this. Munch had disagreed strongly – it was typical Mikkelson – but in the last few days Munch had started to think that Mikkelson might have been right after all. Perhaps she really was not ready. It was only six months since he had found her alone on that island off the coast of Trøndelag.

And though she had never said anything to him, he had worked it out. She hadn't been there on holiday. She had gone there to escape. To kill herself. He had persuaded her to come back to Oslo with him. And now he had done it again. Brought her back to work. Perhaps he had made the wrong decision. Maybe she needed time off. She might not be ready for this.

'How are you doing, Mia? Are you well? Is everything OK?'

Mia Krüger awoke from her hibernation and fixed her eyes on him. An irritated, alert gaze this time: the Mia he knew so well.

'Tell me you're kidding?'

She knew where he was going with this, and she definitely didn't appreciate it.

'I didn't mean it like that,' Munch said, holding up his hands. 'I just want you to be well, that's all. You're my responsibility, aren't you?'

He tried a disarming smile, but she did not fall for it. She continued to study him with suspicious eyes.

'Has Mikkelson been after you?'

'What? No, no.'

'Have I done something wrong? Embarrassed the department again? Do we look bad in the papers, because we haven't solved this yet? I mean, how long is it since we found her? Six days? Christ, we've made huge progress, we have lots of leads . . .'

She leaned forward on the sofa, frustrated.

'No, no. Mikkelson hasn't said anything. No one is unhappy.'

'I should bloody well think they're not,' Mia fumed. 'Bloody Mikkelson.'

'This has nothing to do with Mikkelson.'

'So what's the problem?' Mia said, throwing up her hands.

'I'm the problem,' Munch ventured cautiously.

'What do you mean?'

'I'm worried about you.' He tried another smile.

'Worried? Jesus, Munch? Worried about what?'

'Not about the quality of your work, obviously. Christ, Mia, we can't manage without you. I'm just thinking about . . . Well, what about your health?'

'My health?' Mia said, calming a little at this. 'I'm fine – don't I look it?'

Munch did not speak his mind. Because she looked like crap.

'Of course. Honestly, can't a friend be allowed a little . . . ?'

'Meddling?' Mia smiled mischievously, returning to her old self now.

'Ha-ha,' Munch said. 'Concern. "Concern" was the word I was looking for.'

Mia smiled faintly and found a lozenge in her jacket pocket. Placed it on her tongue and looked at him with slightly friendlier eyes.

'For God's sake, Munch, you're not my mum.'

Though she seemed pleased that he had asked all the same. That he cared.

'I've been a bit tired recently, I don't mind admitting that.' She sighed. 'Haven't slept all that well. Got some stuff in my head to deal with, but nothing I can't handle, OK? I've been through worse.'

'So you don't need a day or two off?'

'You're giving me time off?' Mia chuckled. 'Get a grip, Holger, or I might start to think that you're going soft. Perhaps you're right. Maybe you are getting on a bit? Taking me off halfway through the case?'

Mia clearly found this genuinely funny. She chuckled to herself, shaking her head. Munch wasn't convinced.

'So everything is all right?'

'Of course everything is all right, Holger. Jesus, do you have these conversations with all your staff, or is it just me?' She winked and got up. 'Thank you for your interest, but I'm fine.'

'Good.' Munch nodded. 'Where do you intend to start?'

'I'll let you know what I find at the Natural History Museum,' Mia said.

'Fine,' Munch smiled. There was a knock on the door and Ludvig Grønlie popped his head round.

'I found something,' the older investigator said. 'Am I disturbing you?'

He looked at Munch, then at Mia, then back at Munch again.

'Oh no, come in. What have you got?'

Ludvig Grønlie smiled and placed a piece of paper on the desk in front of Munch.

'Another missing-persons case,' Grønlie said.

'I see?'

'From Hurumlandet Nurseries.' Munch studied the piece of paper and furrowed his brow.

'What is it?' Mia said.

'Nine years ago,' Grønlie said. 'A boy was reported missing.'

'From the Nurseries?'

'Yes. Mats Henriksen. Went for a walk in the woods, never came back.'

'Please can I see?' Mia asked, taking the paper from Holger.

'And he was never found?' Munch asked gravely, looking up at Grønlie.

'No. According to the file, the police searched for him, but not for very long.'

'Why not?' Mia was curious now.

'The boy was believed to be suicidal,' Grønlie went on. 'The case was shelved.'

'But no body?' Munch said.

'Nope. He was never found,' Ludvig said. 'Do you think there might be a connection?'

'Definitely worth checking out. Good job, Ludvig. Run his name through the system and see what it turns up.'

'OK,' Grønlie nodded, and left the office.

'This is really interesting,' Mia said, without taking her eyes off the paper in front of her.

'What are you thinking?'

'I don't know yet.'

'You know I'm only—' Munch began, but he was interrupted by the look Mia gave him.

'What? Wanting to look after me?' she said sarcastically.

'Yes.'

Mia got up from the sofa and headed for the door. 'I can take care of myself, Holger.'

'I know that. I was only trying to . . .'

He could not think how to finish his sentence, so he just stayed behind the desk with an attempt at a smile on his lips as she gave him back the piece of paper and left the office.

Chapter 42

The aroma of freshly brewed coffee and fried bacon woke Miriam Munch. She continued to lie with her head on the pillow, still half asleep, before she opened her eyes and realized that she was at home.

What day was it? Friday? Shit, what time was it? Marion needed taking to school – but then she remembered: Marion was with Grannie. Grannie would be taking her. Miriam had been out. Out with Ziggy. It had grown late. She had had too many beers. She could not quite remember how many, and the end of the evening was a bit of a blur, but at least she was home. She had made it home.

Phew.

She had not given in to temptation. It had been strong, the urge to throw caution to the wind, go back to his flat, slip under his duvet and stay there for ever, but she had held it together, thank God. Controlled herself. She remembered thinking at the bottom of one of her beers: *I have to talk to Johannes first, before I do anything else, before this goes too far. We have to talk. I have to tell him, I owe him that.* She stretched out her arms and glanced at the alarm clock on the bedside table. Quarter past eleven. She had been asleep a long time. She raised her head from the pillow but had to lie back down again. Way too many beers. Her temples were pounding. Had they finished off with a couple of tequilas? Probably.

A lovely evening. A fantastic evening, in truth. Miriam Munch had not felt this great for ages. Had she ever felt like this? So happy. So light, somehow? She could not remember. Quarter past eleven? And could she smell breakfast being cooked in the kitchen?

She crawled out of bed, went to shower and enjoyed the hot water cascading over her face and her body. Her hangovers tended to pass quickly, no matter how much she drank. Not like some of her friends, who would be bedridden for a whole day. A hot shower and something to eat and she would be right as rain. Miriam bowed her head and turned up the temperature. The shower spray massaged her neck and she felt better already. How they had envied her resilience back then, her friends. When they used to party four days out of seven, when they practically lived in bars and restaurants. A long time ago. Old Miriam. Not new Miriam. Now she was yummy-mummy Miriam with under-floor heating in the bathroom, an upmarket-gym membership and downlighters in the hallway. Miriam found a towel; right now, she was grateful for the underfloor heating. It was only October, but it felt as if it were winter already. She was cold all the time, almost to the bone; she had already started yearning for spring. She towel-dried her hair in front of the mirror, and despaired at herself, but she could see that she was smiling. She had done that a great deal recently, caught herself smiling.

Freshly brewed coffee? At quarter past eleven?

Miriam wrapped the towel around her hair, put on a bathrobe and left the bathroom. She jumped when she discovered a smiling Johannes in the kitchen, busy making breakfast. *But who else had she been expecting?* He had set the table. Juice, fresh bread, cheeses – he had even found the white tablecloth.

'Hello, darling,' he said, giving her a peck on the cheek before returning to the cooker. 'Would you like your eggs boiled or fried?'

Miriam continued to stand in her bathrobe in the middle of the floor, not knowing what to say. Why was he not at work?

'Fried, I think?' Miriam said, sensing it had come out as a question.

'You sit down, and I'll bring you some coffee. Would you like some coffee?'

'Er, yes.' Miriam nodded, still mystified, but she sat down.

Had she missed something? Forgotten something? Was it her birthday? Their anniversary? Why was he not at the hospital?

'Would you like milk?'

'Milk?'

'In your coffee?'

'Er, no,' Miriam said, still clueless as to what was going on.

Johannes smiled as he crossed the floor and put a cup of coffee in front of her on the table, gave her another kiss on the cheek and went back to the cooker.

'Late night, was it?'

'Fairly,' Miriam said cautiously, raising the cup to her lips. 'Why?'

'No reason. I was just wondering,' Johannes said, bending over the frying pan. 'I spoke to Marianne yesterday, and she said Marion was with her, that you had gone out with a girlfriend. Did you have a good time?'

'Julie.' Miriam nodded slowly, feeling a pang of guilt.

'Oh, yes, Julie from the old days? How is she?'

'All right,' Miriam said over the rim of the cup. 'You know what she's like. Boy trouble. Needed cheering up.'

'She's lucky to have you.' Johannes smiled, carried the frying pan across to the table and slid the eggs on to her plate.

'Yes,' Miriam said, totally confused.

She could not remember the last time they had had breakfast together.

'Is your mobile working?' Johannes said, sitting down.

'It's playing up,' Miriam mumbled. 'I get some messages, but not all, and I've got some missed calls as well; no idea why. Why do you ask?'

'Because I tried calling you, but you didn't pick up.'

'I didn't know,' Miriam said, feeling really guilty now.

Her headache, which the shower had managed to soothe away, started to come back.

'Perhaps there's a problem with your contract.' Johannes smiled again, pouring juice into her glass. 'Or you need an upgrade or something. I'm sure it's easily fixed.'

He sliced some cheese and put it on a bread roll in front of him.

Miriam had a sudden flashback to last night. Ziggy. His handsome eyes across the table. She had made up her mind. She wanted to live an honest life. She had to tell Johannes. But her courage was failing her now, seeing his trusting face across the table. Was it their anniversary after all, an anniversary she did not remember? But they had met in the summer. They had agreed that they were an item, posted it on Facebook like two teenagers, *in a relationship*, on 8 August – that was their anniversary, wasn't it? It had to be something else.

'Oh, I almost forgot,' Johannes got up.

He stood with his hands behind his back, like he used to do in the old days when he had bought her a present. *Would you like the left or the right hand?*

'Is it my birthday?' Miriam smiled.

'No, but I can still buy you a present, can't I?'

'You got me a present?'

'Yes.' Johannes nodded. 'Would you like the left or the right hand?'

'Left,' Miriam said.

'Here you go,' Johannes said, putting a box on the table in front of her.

'Why aren't you at work?'

'Aren't you going to open it?'

'Yes, of course, I was just wondering. Why aren't you at the hospital?'

'I have good news,' Johannes said, sitting down again.

'Go on then, tell me.'

'Open your present first.' Johannes laughed.

Miriam slowly unwrapped the gift, desperately trying not to give in to her guilty conscience. She opened the box inside the wrapping paper.

'Wow,' she smiled, still somewhat confused. 'Thank you.'

'A fitness watch. It tells you how far you have run. Your pulse rate. For when you work out.'

'Great. That's . . . brilliant.'

'It's something you wanted, isn't it?'

'Absolutely. Thank you, Johannes, that's really nice of you.'

It sounded strange, the voice coming from her mouth. As if it were not hers but someone else's. When did their relationship turn into this? Johannes and her? Had it always been like this? Had she never been herself?

That voice was so different to the one that had spoken last night.

So you're in?

Of course I'm in.

Are you sure?

God, what do you think? I want to rescue innocent animals from the lab.

That's wonderful. We're meeting tomorrow night. Will you be there?

Of course I'll be there.

'So why aren't you at work?' Miriam cleared her throat, trying to hide behind the rim of her coffee cup.

'Like I said, I have good news.'

'That's great.'

'I've been chosen to go to Sydney. The medical conference, you know?' Johannes beamed with pride. His eyes were practically shining.

'Wow, that's . . . amazing.'

'Yes, isn't it? Sunde's name had been put forward, but, well, I don't wish to speak ill of a colleague, but they picked me instead. You know what this means, don't you?' Johannes's eyes were still shining.

'Of course.'

'That I'm likely to make consultant in a few years. You didn't see that coming, did you?'

'No,' Miriam said. 'Or I mean, yes . . . Congratulations, Johannes.'

She was at a total loss for words.

'Thank you. But I had to ask you first – I can't just disappear like that! Leave you to look after Marion and everything, that wouldn't be fair.'

'What do you mean?'

'The plane leaves this Monday. The seminar lasts two weeks and – I'm really sorry to give you so little notice, but how about it? The conference? Do you mind if I go? Is it all right with you?'

And then it dawned on her. What all this was really about. The tablecloth. The unexpected present. It wasn't her birthday or their anniversary. He was about to go abroad on short notice, and he felt bad about it.

'Will you manage? Will you be OK?'

'You're going to Australia on Monday, and you plan to be away for two weeks?'

'Sydney.' Johannes grinned.

'Yes, of course it's OK,' Miriam said.

'Will you really be able to manage? With Marion, I mean?'

'Oh, for goodness' sake, of course I will. I can always call Mum. It's not a problem.'

'Thank you, Miriam,' Johannes said, taking her hand.

For the first time in their relationship, Miriam found him being so close to her a little uncomfortable.

'Aren't you going to try it on?'

'What?'

'The watch?'

'Er, yes, of course.' Miriam strapped the blue fitness watch around her wrist.

'It suits you.'

'Do you think so?'

'Definitely.'

He squeezed her hand, and Miriam tentatively squeezed his back.

'I think we ought to celebrate, don't you? The hospital has given me the weekend off. Perhaps Marion could stay with your mum and Rolf one more night? We could go out for dinner or something?'

'Tonight?'

Will you be there?

Of course, I'll be there.

'That would have been wonderful.' Miriam coughed, reclaiming her hand and picking up her coffee cup. 'But I promised Julie.'

'Again? Tonight?'

'Yes.' She nodded. 'It was stupid, but she's not feeling too good. The truth is, she's quite upset.'

'OK.'

'But how about tomorrow?'

'Tomorrow would be just as good,' Johannes said, getting up. 'I'm going to call Dad.'

'I'm sure he'll be delighted.' Miriam smiled, hiding behind her coffee again while Johannes took out his mobile.

Chapter 43

One of the police officers was quite fit, Benedikte Riis had to admit.

Kim, that was his name; smooth, dark hair falling to the left, quite cute. Not a patch on Paulus, obviously, and yet she could not help feeling flustered, as Helene asked everyone to settle down. The handsome police officer wanted to make an announcement about a piece of paper, a childish drawing, scribbles and a picture of an owl.

'Please, everyone, be quiet. This is important,' Helene said to them again.

'So, if any of you have seen this note before, or something that looks like it, you must tell us at once,' the police officer stated, also for the second time, as he circulated copies of the drawing around the tables.

'Those of us who are here will make sure that anyone who isn't will get to see it as well, won't we?'

Helene smiled and nodded at the class, but Benedikte Riis's mind was already on other things.

A drawing found in Camilla Green's locker.

Whatever.

She felt a little sick at the thought.

Camilla Green.

Everything had been great until the day *she* turned up, with her silvery laughter and her sparkling eyes. Benedikte had felt it at once; she could tell from the way he acted around her. Paulus. That he liked her. Not that he and Benedikte had ever had sex, let alone kissed, but she had sensed that there was something between them. That he preferred her to the others. He certainly paid her more attention. And although, deep down, she had known that it would never, ever happen, she had not been able to stop herself from hoping that one day he would see it. That she loved him, and that the two of them were meant for each other.

Paulus and Benedikte.

She had carved their names into her desk in her room. Inside a heart. Covered it so no one would see. And every time she trailed her fingers over their names, she had felt that they were destined to be together.

And it had almost been real, it really had; he had shown her his hideaway in the woods, he had shown her the place where he would never bring any of the others; they had hung out together until the day *she* turned up.

Camilla Green.

Benedikte had scarcely been able to hide her jealousy when she realized how obsessed Paulus had become with her. How he showed her around. His arm on her back. His smile, his handsome brown eyes looking at the new girl in a way he had never looked at Benedikte.

She was glad that Camilla was gone.

It might be horrible to think such thoughts, but she did. She was glad Camilla was no longer around. All she did was ruin things. Because she did not love Paulus, not like Benedikte did. Camilla was just attention-seeking. The way she tossed her hair. Made eyes at him in the dining hall. That was not true love; it was not the kind of love Paulus and she shared. Benedikte had known it right from day one, when he helped Camilla get her suitcase out of the taxi. Welcomed her. Shown her to her room. She did not want to call her a *slut*, no, but ever since Camilla Green arrived, things between Paulus and her had not been the same.

She had to protect him; that was her role, because he did not know what was good for him. Like that business with the plants in the furthest greenhouse. The cannabis plants. Had he shown them to any of the other girls? No, he hadn't. Only to her.

I want to show you something, but you can't tell anyone.

Because she was the one he really wanted.

Paulus and Benedikte.

Her fingers touching the heart on her desk every evening before she kissed it good night.

'So, girls, we're going to help the police with this note, aren't we? It's important.'

She looked across the room, and then they were back outside, going their separate ways. Benedikte pulled up the hood of her puffa jacket; she could see her cloudy breath in the cold air.

Something was out of kilter with the world. This cold in October. It was not supposed to be like this. Perhaps it was a sign. That things were not as they should be. That someone had to do something. And now something had happened, hadn't it? Camilla was gone. Perhaps Paulus would realize it now? The early frost? That he had made the wrong choice?

She had to see him right away; she could feel it. They had a lot to talk about. The others had been looking for him when the police turned up with that note, but they had not found him.

But she knew where he was.

Of course she did.

Benedikte Riis knew everything there was to know about Paulus. She would often follow him. Spy on him. It was better this way. That he did not always know. He needed someone to look after him.

The hideout at the far end of the Nurseries. Right up against the neighbouring fence. It was his den. It was where he would hang out. Not many people knew about it, but she did. Because he had taken her there. Shown her how to roll a joint. She had done it many times before, but she had pretended not to know because she liked it, him showing her how.

And they had smoked pot together, giggling at everything, and since that evening it had almost become a habit; Friday or Saturday evening, the two of them out there, laughing together. Right up until *she* turned up.

Camilla Green.

Sometimes Benedikte would stand outside. Below the window. Without them knowing. Listen to them whispering and laughing together inside.

'Paulus?'

Benedikte knocked, but there was no reply.

'Paulus?'

She knocked again, pushed open the small door and cautiously entered the shed.

Chapter 44

Tor Olsen, senior curator at the Natural History Museum, was a man in his fifties who looked a little like Albert Einstein, with a mess of white hair standing up on all sides.

'Finally, there you are,' Tor Olsen said, showing Mia Krüger into his office. 'About time, I must say. Coffee, tea, or do we get straight down to business?'

It was clear that the curator took this very seriously. The break-in at the museum. The missing owls. A dozen patrol cars with flashing blue lights and screaming sirens ought to have turned up ages ago. Mia was bemused but made sure to hide it. She was used to it now. It was not an uncommon reaction when the public first encountered crime. They expected the police to respond immediately. Crack the case, like they did on TV. It was sweet, really, this naivety, but, sadly, very far from the truth. About 130,000 break-ins were reported in Norway last year. Of those, 120,000 had been shelved. Shameful, really. And Mia doubted that already scarce police resources would be made available to solve the theft of some stuffed owls. Thirty-three murders. Twenty-three solved. No cases abandoned. She much preferred this statistic. But break-ins? No, nothing to boast about there. Not her problem, either. She had enough on her plate as it was.

'Happy to get straight down to it.' Mia nodded.

'Is it just you?' the absent-minded man said, looking around.

'Excuse me?'

'You're here on your own? Where are the others?'

Mia concealed another smile.

'You do realize that we have a unique collection here, don't you? More than two million species from across the world. Mammals, birds, fish, insects, reptiles, molluscs, intestinal worms?'

'Intestinal worms?'

Olsen looked at her over his glasses. 'Invertebrates? Single-celled and multicellular organisms?'

The senior curator shook his head and heaved a sigh. He had already decided that the police had not entrusted an investigation of this magnitude to the right person.

'But only the owls were stolen?' Mia said.

'Only?' Olsen said, staring at her. 'Every type of Norwegian owl gathered in one place may not seem like a lot to you – after all, we only have ten species – but even so, have you any idea how much work I've invested in this?'

'I understand.' Mia nodded gravely. 'Ten species in Norway? Owls?'

'There is the European pygmy owl, the boreal owl, the short-eared owl, the northern hawk-owl, two types of Eurasian owls, the tawny owl, the great grey owl, the Ural owl, the snowy owl – and the barn owl makes eleven; we have had several sightings of it, but it doesn't nest in Norway.'

'Good heavens. And where were they exhibited?'

'In our permanent collection. "Native and Non-native Animals". We rarely make changes to it but, one day, I had this idea. Owls. Norwegian owls. An exciting bird. A mysterious bird. Young people would appreciate it. Increase our visitor numbers? Do you follow?'

Mia struggled to keep a straight face. She very much doubted that the youth of today would be tempted to look up from their screens to see a unique collection of Norwegian owls displayed at the Natural History Museum.

'I do. Good idea. Great thought.'

'Thank you.' Olsen smiled. 'I imagine you would like to inspect the crime scene? And perhaps you would also like to see our collection now that you're here, anyway?'

'Sure,' said Mia, following him out of the office.

'We call the first display "Under the Sea",' Olsen said when they reached the start of the exhibition. 'As you can see, we have sea scorpions, snake pipefish, mackerel, herring, school sharks . . .'

Mia began to suspect that this was a complete waste of time. She was still exhausted after visiting Sebastian Larsen, and she had yet to process the information the social anthropologist had given her. Sects. Orders. Senators and high priests. A kind of darkness she could not comprehend. Here in Norway? She found it hard to believe.

'We call the second display "Mountain Birds",' Olsen continued, but Mia was barely listening now. 'As you can see, there is the European shag, the common murre, the razor-billed auk . . .'

She could not shake off the feeling that there was a golden nugget somewhere among all the things that Larsen had told her.

OTO. Thelemite teaching. *Do what thou wilt shall be the law.* Nonsense, most likely. A bunch of harmless idiots, at best. But combined with Camilla in the pentagram of candles and the horrific video they had discovered?

'And the fifth display . . .' Olsen went on, but Mia had reached her limit. It was a waste of time.

'And where is the bird display?' she said.

'Oh, that's empty now,' the curator said. 'We exhibit reindeer in its place. Would you like to—'

'No, I think I'll stop here.' Mia smiled.

Tor Olsen looked surprised.

'I mean, if there's nothing to see, then I'd better leave.'

'So soon?'

'I've learned a lot. You've been a great help.'

'Very well, then,' the curator said.

On her way out, Mia glanced up and spotted a camera in a corner. 'You film all the visitors?'

'Yes, but only during opening hours, sadly.'

'And the break-in happened at night?'

'Yes, I told you when I reported it. Haven't you read the report? I turned up for work, like I always do, at a quarter past seven, and when I—'

'Of course. I'm just double-checking,' Mia said. 'So no pictures?'

'No, sadly not,' the curator said, and let her out of the exhibition.

'Do you get many visitors?'

'I wouldn't say many – mainly school groups – most people come for the Botanical Gardens. That's unique, and sometimes they pop in here as well.'

'School groups, did you say?' Mia said, interested now. 'Do you have a list of such visits?'

'Yes, we do,' Olsen nodded. 'But Ruth keeps it.'

The Botanical Gardens. Hurumlandet Nurseries. Plants. Flowers. It was a shot in the dark, but it was worth a try.

'And Ruth isn't here now?'

'No, Ruth has gone to Gran Canaria. She has rheumatism and gets the trips paid for by the state. The warm weather is good for her joints, you know.'

'Please would you ask Ruth to send me a list of schools that visited the museum in the time leading up to the break-in? When she comes back?'

Mia found her card in her inside pocket, and gave it to him.

'She'll be back on Tuesday. And yes, of course I will,' the senior curator said, looking at her card.

When he had read it, his eyes widened. 'Homicide unit? But . . .?'

'I'll expect to hear from you or Ruth, OK?' She smiled.

The man with the white hair nodded cautiously, now seeing her in a completely different light. Mia felt his eyes follow her all the way down the stairs and out of the gate.

What a waste of time.

She should have spent the day doing something more productive. She looked at her phone. Almost three o'clock. She had managed a few hours' kip after the strange conversation in Munch's office. She had left feeling really pissed off but was starting to see that he might have a point. She got into the car as her phone started ringing.

'Yes, Mia here?'

'It's Holger.'

She could hear it in his voice. That something had happened.

'Any news?'

'Most certainly,' Munch said hastily. 'Kim and Curry had a breakthrough at the Nurseries. Paulus Monsen and one of the girls out there, Benedikte Riis.'

'What about them?'

Munch disappeared for a moment. Mia could hear that something was going on in the background.

'They're bringing them down to Grønland to be interviewed. We'll take it from there.'

'Grønland?'

'Yes.'

'I'm on my way,' Mia said quickly, and stuck the key in the ignition.

Chapter 45

Mia closed the door softly behind her and went into the small room where Curry was sitting on a chair watching Munch and Kim Kolsø, who had already sat down in the interview room with Paulus Monsen on the other side of the table. The young man with the dark curls looked stressed, his eyes flitting from side to side.

'What's happening?' she asked, sitting down on the chair next to Curry.

'Do you want the short or the long version?' he said.

'Short, please,' Mia said, without taking her eyes off the people on the other side of the window.

'We were about to leave when that boy stormed across the yard with the girl chasing after him. He seemed hacked off about something, and she looked as if she had been crying, red-eyed and all upset . . .'

'This is starting to sound like the long version.' Mia smiled.

'Ha-ha,' Curry said.

He looked better than the last time she had seen him. As if the quarrel with Sunniva had been resolved and he was starting to think like a police officer again.

'And then?'

'Paulus admitted growing cannabis in the greenhouse and being in a relationship with Camilla Green.'

'Really?'

'Yep.'

'And why didn't he tell us earlier? How did he explain that?'

'She was under sixteen when it started,' Curry said. 'Nice guy, eh?'

He leaned closer to the glass as if to scrutinize the young man.

'Chats up minors, persuades them to come with him to his hideaway, where he gets them high on dope before taking advantage of them.'

'Hideaway?'

'He had a kind of love nest on the far side of the estate.'

'And have we had a look at it?'

'Forensics are there now.' Curry nodded, leaning back again.

'I didn't know what to say,' said the young man in the interview room.

Mia turned down the volume in order to hear the rest of Curry's update.

'And what about the girl? Benedikte?'

'She's in interview room B.'

'Has anyone talked to her yet?'

Curry shook his head.

'And what's her part in all this? Why did you bring her in?'

Mia found a lozenge in her jacket pocket and looked at Paulus, who was sitting very still now.

'They're blaming each other,' Curry said.

'For the murder?' Mia was taken aback.

Curry nodded. 'A crime of passion. Some kind of love triangle. The two of them had a fight right in front of us. We had to handcuff them. Since then neither of them has said very much.'

'So what's the plan?'

'The plan?' Curry said.

'Yes. What are we thinking now? What has Munch said?'

'Not a lot so far,' Curry said with a shrug. 'Him first. Then her. Then back to him, I think.'

'He's not interviewing them at the same time?'

'No. Munch thought the girl should be left to stew on her own for a while. Waiting always scares them.'

'That's true,' Mia said, she rose from the chair, went out into the corridor and knocked on the door to the interview room.

Kim Kolsø opened the door for her.

'Time to swap?' Mia offered.

'OK.' Kolsø nodded, letting her in.

'The time is 16.05,' Munch said into the tape recorder. 'Investigator Kim Kolsø has left the room. Mia Krüger has arrived.'

Mia hung her leather jacket on the back of the chair and sat down.

'Hi, Paulus. Mia Krüger,' Mia said, extending her hand across the table.

The young man glanced after Kim, who had just left the room, then looked nervously at Mia before tentatively shaking her hand.

'Paulus Monsen.'

'I've heard a lot about you. People say you're a nice guy. Very competent, everybody at the Nurseries sings your praises . . .'

'Really?' the young man said. He sounded a little confused.

'You're skilful.' Mia smiled. 'Good at your job. Must be nice to hear. That everyone thinks so highly of you.'

'Er, yes, thank you,' Paulus said, glancing nervously at Munch, who clearly had not been quite as friendly.

'And just so you know it, the dope, the plants, we don't really care about them – it's not our business, OK? A bit of cannabis, a few plants – so what? That could happen to anyone.'

Mia was aware of a stony stare from Munch, but ignored it.

'All right?' She smiled at the young man, who continued to look puzzled.

He glanced quickly at Munch again, but it was clear he was more comfortable looking at her.

'It was just a few plants,' he said in a low voice.

'Like I said, forget about it. Seriously, it's nothing.'

Mia could see him dropping his guard now. The young man leaned back in his chair slightly, and raked his hands through his curls.

'It was just for personal consumption. I wasn't going to sell it or anything, if that's what you're thinking.'

'Exactly. Don't give it another thought.'

Munch was about to open his mouth, but Mia nudged him under the table.

'But what is a little more serious . . .' Mia said, pretending to mull it over.

She could sense that the young man on the chair had started to get nervous again.

'What?' he said.

'Well, it's Benedikte. She . . .' Mia said at length, letting the remark linger in the air.

'What did Benedikte say?' the young man demanded to know.

Mia gave a light shrug and raised her eyebrows.

'That bitch!' Paulus suddenly burst out. 'Is she saying that I killed Camilla?' His eyes were flashing now. 'She's lying,' Paulus said desperately, getting up from the chair. 'You have to believe me.'

'Sit down,' Munch ordered him.

The young man continued to stand. He looked imploringly at them both.

'Sit down,' Munch ordered him again.

Paulus sat down and buried his head in his hands. 'You have to believe me, Benedikte is out of her mind, bonkers, I'm going to . . .'

'Kill her, too?' Munch said calmly.

'What?' He looked up at them, wide-eyed.

'Are you going to kill Benedikte, like you killed Camilla?'

'What? No, for God's sake. I didn't kill Camilla, I keep telling you!'

'I thought you had confessed,' Munch went on. 'I thought that was why you're here?'

'Confessed? No, I've only confessed to growing the plants.' He looked at Mia again, hoping she would come to his rescue, but Mia said nothing, she just let Munch carry on.

'So you started a relationship with Camilla Green when she was under the age of consent. You drugged her in your hideout and had sex with her. Is that what happened?'

'No,' Paulus said, fixing his eyes on the table again.

'So you weren't in a relationship with Camilla?' Mia said amicably. 'You weren't a couple?'

'Yes, but . . .'

'But what?'

'It wasn't like he said.' He nodded towards Munch. 'He made it sound really ugly.'

Mia cut in. 'So how was it, then? Between Camilla and you?'

'It was . . . beautiful,' Paulus ventured.

'You were fond of her?'

'I loved her,' the young man said, and Mia could see that he was struggling to keep the tears at bay now.

'And she loved you, too?'

The young man seemed as if he needed time to think before he replied. As if he did not know the answer.

'I think so,' he said, after a while.

'But . . .?'

'But she . . . Camilla was special. She wanted to live her own life. She was a totally free spirit, if you know what I mean?'

Paulus looked up again but avoided making eye contact with Munch; he looked only at Mia now, with almost pleading eyes.

'Please believe me: I didn't kill her. I would never do anything to hurt Camilla. I loved her. I would have done anything for her.'

'But she didn't want you and so you just took what you wanted anyway,' Munch asserted crudely.

Mia glared at Munch and shook her head in despair. Mia Krüger had nothing but respect for her boss but, at times, he could be rather too simplistic.

'No,' Paulus said, retreating into himself again.

Mia glowered at Munch, who merely shrugged his shoulders.

'You mentioned something to my colleagues,' she said cautiously, 'which I've been wondering about.'

'What?' Paulus said, not looking at her.

'As far as I can gather, you accused Benedikte of having killed Camilla, is that right?'

There was a short silence before the young man replied. 'It was just something I said in the heat of the moment. I was angry.'

'With Benedikte?'

'Yes.'

'Why?'

'She came down to my hideaway,' the young man said, raising his gaze again. 'Started babbling about how we were meant for each other, how great it was that Camilla was gone, so now she and I could finally be together, and that was why she had sent the message.'

'What message?' Munch asked.

'Eh?' Paulus said. He did not seem to be completely there.

'What message?' Munch asked again.

'The one from Camilla's mobile.'

'Benedikte had Camilla's mobile?'

Mia glanced quickly at Munch, who returned her look of surprise.

'She found it in Camilla's room after she disappeared,' Paulus went on. He was clearly exhausted now.

'I want to be quite clear about this,' Munch said. 'Which text message are we talking about?'

Paulus ran his hand across his forehead. 'She sent a message to Helene saying everything was all right.'

'From Camilla's mobile?'

Paulus nodded quietly.

'And that's when I lost my cool. I didn't mean to accuse Benedikte of having killed her. I'm sorry I said it. She may be crazy, but she would never do anything like that.'

'Did she say anything about why she sent the text message?' Mia wanted to know.

'So no one would look for her.'

'Because if Camilla was gone for good, the two of you could finally be together?'

'Something like that,' the young man mumbled, looking like he found talking difficult now.

'Let's take a break,' Munch said, looking at Mia, who nodded back. 'Are you hungry, Paulus? Would you like something to eat or drink?'

The boy with the curls gave a light shrug and replied without looking at them.

'A burger, perhaps. And a Coke. I haven't been eating much recently . . .'

They could see that he could barely manage it now, to hold back the tears.

'The time is 16.32. Interview with Paulus Monsen terminated,' Munch said, turning off the tape recorder.

Chapter 46

Miriam Munch was standing in the street outside the red-brick apartment block, having second thoughts. She had been so sure. What she had felt the night before, she had never experienced anything like it, but after brunch with Johannes other thoughts started sneaking into her mind. She was not worried about Johannes, no; she was thinking about Marion. Poor little Marion, how would she take it? After all, she had done nothing wrong. Why should a lovely little six-year-old girl have to go through this, her whole world falling apart, because her mother was in love with another man?

Miriam glanced at the watch Johannes had given her, and felt guilty again. Johannes had made such an effort, taken time off work, cooked them a lovely brunch, suggested that they go out for dinner, bought her a present. Yes, he had had an agenda because he wanted to go to Sydney, but so what? She glanced quickly up at the building again, at the flat where she had spent the night not that long ago.

Eight o'clock. That was the time it started. The meeting. Atlantis Farms. A laboratory in Hurum that used animals for illegal experiments. She still had time to change her mind. She had not signed her life away. She could go back on the tram. Ride it all the way home. Put on a dress. Go out for dinner with Johannes after all – no, he had volunteered for a night shift now. She could take the car. Pick Marion up. Watch a film or something. *Snow White*. Or *Sleeping Beauty*. One of those princess films six-year-old girls could not get enough of. She could almost feel Marion's warm body under the blanket on the sofa. Little fingers in a bowl of popcorn. Eager, naive blue eyes fixed on the screen.

'Don't eat the apple, it's been poisoned!'

Miriam smiled to herself and found a cigarette in her coat pocket. She lit it and tightened the scarf around her neck.

A raid?

Years ago, she would not have thought twice about it. Never wondered whether taking part was wise. Miriam Munch hated injustice. Vile people in positions of power who exploited others, be it people or animals, to increase their profits. She had loved her time with Amnesty International. Getting up in the morning, feeling that what she did had some kind of value, that she could make a difference. But then, at the age of nineteen she had had Marion, and she had worried about her ability to handle mother-hood, fearing that she might not be good enough, and so she had devoted all her time to the little girl.

Sod it.

There had to be limits.

Atlantis Farms. Helpless animals trapped in cages, subjected to pain every day, only so that people who already had far too much money could have more.

She wanted to take part.

Miriam threw the cigarette on the ground and quickly marched up the stairs to the second-floor flat.

'Hi.' Ziggy smiled as he opened the door. 'I was starting to think you weren't coming.'

'Am I too late?' Miriam said, hanging up her coat and scarf on a peg in the hallway.

'Oh no.' Ziggy showed her into the living room. 'We started at seven, not that it matters.'

'I thought you said eight?' Miriam said.

'Doesn't matter.' Ziggy winked and introduced her to the small group in the living room.

'Everyone, for those of you who haven't met her before, this is Miriam Munch. She'll be coming with us on Tuesday. I know that some of you might think it strange to include a newcomer, but I can assure you that Miriam is one of us, and we need all the help we can get, don't we?'

'Hi,' Miriam said.

'Hi.'

'Welcome.'

'Nice to meet you.'

'Hi, Miriam,' Julie said, getting up to hug her and pass her a glass of wine. 'It's so cool that you decided to join us.'

'Looking forward to it,' Miriam said, finding a seat next to her friend on the floor.

'I'm the one who suggested her, so you know that she's all right.'

It was the young man with the round glasses from the kitchen. He smiled at her, a little embarrassed, a kind of apology perhaps for having tried to chat her up, not knowing who she was.

'That's not entirely true now, Jacob, is it?' Ziggy said.

'Of course it is. I said, she's the daughter of Holger Munch himself, we need to get her to join us, get inside information and all that.'

'Yes, all right, Jacob, Miriam joining us is entirely down to you. Thank you so much,' Ziggy said.

'My pleasure, my pleasure.' Jacob bowed lightly in front of them all.

'But seriously, it's not going to be a problem, is it?' A young man in an Icelandic sweater was leaning against the window, his arms folded across his chest, his face grave. Miriam had seen him at Julie's party, but she could not remember his name.

'What is?' Ziggy said.

'That she's related to a police officer?'

'No, no,' Ziggy began. 'She is—'

'Thank you, Ziggy, but I can defend myself,' Miriam said, suddenly finding herself standing in the middle of the room with everyone's eyes on her. It was not something she had planned, but she was buoyed up with a sense of purpose.

'Yes, erm.' She smiled, regretting it a little, but there was no way back, so she took a deep breath and soldiered on. 'So my name is Miriam. Hello, everyone.'

'Hello, Miriam.'

'Welcome.'

The faces around her continued to smile, except for the man in the Icelandic sweater by the window, whose eyes were still dark and whose arms remained folded across his chest.

'I don't know if any of you used to hang out at Blitz, but that was where I started, back when I was fifteen. I've marched against racism and Nazism, I used to belong to Amnesty, today I volunteer for the Animal Protection League. I've been chained to the railings in front of the Storting, I've been kicked in the head by a police horse and got fifteen stitches as a result. I've promoted women's rights, and yes, to be honest, I don't know a lot about what you're about to do – what *we're* about to do – but trapping animals in cages, whatever the reason, makes me so mad that . . .'

Miriam ran out of steam, and continued to stand, not knowing what to say.

'There was no need for you to do that, Miriam. We trust you,' Ziggy said. 'But thank you all the same.'

'I recommended her, so she's already accepted, am I right?' Jacob piped up.

Miriam sat down again, a little uncomfortable with her overly dramatic performance.

Ziggy clapped his hands and gazed around the small group. 'Any questions before we move on?'

Chapter 47

'What do you think?' Munch said.

He had just carried a beer and a Farris mineral water gingerly across the floor in Justisen, and set down the beer on the table in front of her.

'About keeping them overnight, you mean?'

'Yes.'

Mia took a leisurely swig of her beer, in a half-hearted attempt to hide her thirst in front of Munch.

She had not taken any pills for almost twenty-four hours and she could feel that she needed it now, the alcohol, to calm her nerves.

'It's unnecessary.'

'So you don't think that one of them did it?'

'No,' Mia said. 'Do you?'

'It's just possible.'

'What is?'

'That we're making this more complicated than it really is,' Munch said, putting his coat on an adjacent chair.

'In what way?'

'OK, let's ignore how she was killed and look at motives instead.'

Mia took another unhurried swig of her beer. 'Benedikte was jealous?'

'Yes.' Munch nodded. 'And a bit highly strung, didn't you think so?'

'I did. But if she wanted to get rid of Camilla, why leave her body where we would find it?'

'Fair point, but even so?'

'She doesn't seem the type. Way too sensitive. Flaky. This is much more calculated. More planned. Crimes of passion rarely are.'

She took another swig of her beer. Twenty-four hours without any medication; she was starting to suffer withdrawal symptoms.

'But they can be, can't they?' Munch argued.

Mia looked at him and wondered why he insisted on keeping this option open: that Benedikte Riis or Paulus Monsen was the person they were looking for. To her it was blindingly obvious that neither of them was the killer. They were just two young people who had got themselves caught in a harmless love triangle. She had not needed to spend long in the interview room before reaching that conclusion, but Munch did not seem to want to let his suspicions go.

'Yes, sure, but I just don't see it. And his motive? Sex with a minor? A few cannabis plants in the greenhouse? So what's your theory?'

'They might be in it together,' Munch suggested, taking a sip of his Farris.

'Do you want to know what I think?' Mia said, now knocking her beer back.

'Yes.'

'That they told us the truth. Benedikte Riis was obsessed with Paulus. I can see why to some extent: he's a good-looking, char-ismatic young man. Camilla arrives, and Paulus takes a fancy to her. They fall in love. They start a relationship. Then Camilla goes missing. Benedikte finds her mobile, sends a text message saying she is fine so nobody will look for her. Then she can have lover boy all to herself.'

'Just like they told us then?' Munch said.

'I think so.' Mia summoned the waiter and pointed at her empty glass.

'So why are we still talking about it?' Munch wanted to know.

Mia smiled faintly. 'You're the one who keeps talking about it, not me.'

'So you think we should release them tonight?'

'It might be worth having another go. Something useful might turn up tomorrow, though I very much doubt it.'

Mia smiled politely to the waiter who brought her another beer.

'So you think Benedikte threw the mobile in a bin afterwards and that we won't ever find it?'

Mia nodded and raised the glass to her lips. She had made up her mind now: no more pills, even though she knew it was going to be hard. She would miss the haziness they gave her and their ability to suppress the images in her head.

The naked, twisted body on the heather.

The shadow on the wall.

The nightmare which had made her lose her grip on reality for a moment.

I think it's your job that's making you ill.

This evil.

This darkness.

Thank God, she could feel the beer kicking in now.

'And nothing from the Natural History Museum?' Munch said, taking another sip of his Farris.

'Waste of time,' Mia said. 'How about Ludvig? The wig? The specialist shop?'

'No luck there either.' Munch sighed. 'It wasn't bought from them, but I believe there's another shop which he'll try tomorrow.'

'OK.'

'So what do we think? If the two people we've currently got locked up didn't do it, who did?'

'Helene Eriksen. The two teachers. One of the seven other girls.'

'Anders Finstad has been crossed off the list?'

'The way I see it, yes.'

'So it's someone from the Nurseries?'

'What do you think?'

Munch let out a sigh and fell silent for a moment. And Mia realized why he was still considering the possibility that Paulus and Benedikte might have done it. Because they had no other potential suspects. So much information, so much evidence, and yet they were fumbling about in the dark, and Munch hated it.

'Still nothing from the crime scene?' Mia asked.

Munch shook his head in despair. 'No footprints. No DNA from Camilla's body.'

'She wasn't pregnant, was she?'

'What? No, not according to Vik, why?' Munch looked at her with interest.

'The pentagram,' Mia said. 'I've been looking into it. Its symbolism.'

'And?'

'I mean, there has to be a reason why she was posed like that. Unless someone is trying to mislead us?'

'Absolutely,' Munch said. 'And what did you find? Is this about pregnancy?'

'Not exactly, but, yes, you remember how her arms had been arranged?'

'I do.'

'Pointing at two candles in the pentagram?'

'Yes?'

'They're significant,' Mia continued. 'The five points represent spirit, water, fire, earth and air.'

'Right,' Munch said. 'But what do they have to do with pregnancy?'

'There's another level of symbolism.'

Mia could see that she was losing him now.

'Go on?'

'The deeper symbolism shows that her arms were pointing at something else. Mother. And birth.'

'Right,' Munch said, frowning. 'But she wasn't pregnant?'

'No, but I still think it could be relevant. I need time to look into it. See if I can find something we can use, something which ties in with everything else we have. I thought I might shut myself away, explore it.'

'Do whatever you need, as long as you leave your mobile on,' Munch said, and put on his duffel coat. 'I need some sleep now. I still have a faint hope we might get more out of the two of them tomorrow. Do you want to share a cab?'

Mia could see from his expression that this was not a question. He was being Daddy Holger now. Who wanted to make sure that she got home to bed in time.

'Yes, that would be great.' Mia smiled, feigning a yawn before getting up and putting on her leather jacket.

Chapter 48

Mia Krüger waited until the rear lights on the taxi had disappeared before pulling her woolly hat further down over her ears and heading towards Hegdehaugsveien. The thought of her cold, sparsely furnished flat held little appeal. She would not be able to sleep. Besides, she wanted another drink. She needed to lose herself.

Friday night in the city of Oslo. She tightened her jacket around her and walked through the streets with her head down, lacking the energy to make eye contact with the people she passed, the normal world she would never be allowed to join. People who went to work Monday to Friday and partied at the weekend. She nodded briefly to the bouncer. The pub was busy, but the table in the far corner where she liked to hide was free. How very convenient. She ordered a Guinness and a Jägermeister and slid down on the red sofa. Everyone else was there with someone. She was in the corner alone. Apart from this world. Smiling faces with glasses in both hands, out with friends, with other people, while she sat alone in the corner, feeling a kind of responsibility for them all.

Get a grip.

Mia knocked back the Jägermeister, washed it down with a swig of her Guinness and shook her head.

Are you feeling sorry for yourself?

No, she really had to get her act together. This was not like her. She took out the notepad and pen from her bag and placed them on the table in front of her. Who was she? She was Mia Krüger, wasn't she? Was she going to just sit here, wallowing in self-pity? Hell, no. There had to be limits. Mia opened her notepad, took the cap off the pen and found a blank page. The psychologist. It was his fault.

I think your job is making you ill.

Total bullshit. She regretted it now, agreeing to have therapy. Letting some idiot into her head, making her think that it was true, that she needed fixing. She had kept him at arm's length, really she had. In every session. Said yes and no where she was supposed to, and yet he had got under her skin.

The idea there was something wrong with her.

Screw that. She made up her mind at that moment, helped along by the warmth of the alcohol, that they could think whatever the hell they liked. Mikkelson, Mattias Wang, even Munch; she knew exactly the kind of person she was, and she was just fine.

They had undermined her. Tiny, whispering voices coming at her from all sides, but now she was drawing a line. She waved over the waiter and pointed to her empty shot glass, and soon afterwards another Jägermeister appeared on her table. What the hell did they know about what it was like to be her? More text messages from her therapist. *Shall I make you another appointment? I think that would be a good idea.* Munch's eyes across the table. *I think you need to rest.*

Tossers.

Mia smiled to herself, drank a mouthful of Guinness and put pen to paper.

Blank sheets.

Important. Look at everything afresh.

Strong. She felt strong again. Whether or not it was the alcohol talking made no difference right now. She emptied her Guinness, waved another round over to the table and ignored the commotion in the pub with a smile on her lips. Her pen flew across the paper.

Camilla. The chosen one. Mother. Birth. Seventeen years old. Ditzy. Unconventional. Feathers. Owl? Death? Strangled. Why strangled? Why something around her neck? Breathing? Air. Breath is life? Her arms. In the forest? Why wasn't she dressed?

Mia knocked back a big swig of the dark beer without taking any notice of what was happening around her. She wrote *ritual* over her last notes and moved the pen to the opposite page of the notepad, wrote *basement* at the top, drained her shot glass quickly and put pen to paper again.

Dark. Darkness. Animals? What is it about animals? Why are you an animal? Food. Animal feed. Why are you not allowed to eat, Camilla? Who is watching you? Why is he watching you? And why are you not wearing the wig when you are running on the wheel? When he is looking at you? Why is he looking at you? Because it is you without the wig? Why are you yourself in the basement? But not when you're lying in the forest?

Mia ordered another round, although she had yet to finish her Guinness. She emptied her glass, just in time for the next round to arrive, raised the small shot glass to her lips and leaned back slightly in the red sofa in order to glance at her notes.

She was on to something.

She was livid that she had allowed them to mess with her mind. She would never let it happen again.

She was definitely on to something.

Mia popped the pen in her mouth. *One: as you lie before us, new, different. In the forest. On the feathers. Protected? New born? Two: when you're an animal in the cage, when you run on the wheel, when you have to perform. Do you have to perform, Camilla? Do you have to show what you can do?*

Mia turned the page and let the pen race across the next blank sheet.

Mother? Did you want to become a mother, Camilla? Did you want a child? The chosen one. Why were you the chosen one? Were you going to be the mother? Of the child?

Mia became aware of someone standing by her table, the waiter probably, and tried to wave him away, she had plenty in her glasses, but the person refused to move.

'Mia Krüger?' the figure said, and though Mia would rather be left alone, she looked up reluctantly from her notes.

'Yes?'

A young man was standing in front of her. He wore a black suit and a freshly ironed white shirt but had a beanie pulled over his head.

'I'm busy,' Mia said.

The young man took off the beanie and bushy hair appeared, black on both sides with a white stripe down the middle.

Mia could feel her irritation build. She was on to something. The answer was somewhere on the papers in front of her.

'I'm Skunk,' the young man introduced himself.

'What?'

'My name is Skunk,' the young man said again, smiling crookedly at her. 'Are you still busy?'

Chapter 49

Sunniva Rød had worked the afternoon shift and was more exhausted than usual. She had slept badly, tossing and turning in her bed, dreaming bizarre dreams. She wondered what could have prompted them. Was it because he had stopped calling? At first he had rung her all the time, endless calls and lots of messages, then a complete stop. Nothing. Had something happened to Curry? Had he been in an accident? Perhaps she ought to ring round to check? She let out a sigh and entered the last room she needed to check before she could finish for the day. Torvald Sund, the mad vicar. She would usually pause outside his door, bracing herself before going inside, but she was too tired today; she did not have the energy. She just wanted to go home and get some sleep.

She entered the room and was a little startled when she saw him sitting up, eyes wide open and a smile playing on his lips. As if he had been waiting for her to arrive.

'I'm going to die soon,' the vicar announced.

'Don't talk like that, Torvald,' Sunniva said, walking over to his bedside table to clear away the lunch that her colleagues had brought him but which he had not touched.

'Aren't you hungry? Don't you want something to eat?' Sunniva said.

'I won't need food in Heaven,' the vicar continued to smile, still not taking his eyes off her. He made her feel uneasy.

'Don't say such things,' Sunniva said. 'You have many good days left.'

'I'm going to die soon,' the vicar said again, more insistent this time. 'But I don't mind because I will get into Heaven after all. God has told me that I can atone for my sins.'

Sunniva began to clear away the food.

I won't go to Heaven.

I have sinned.

Why hadn't Curry called? Had something happened?

She picked up the tray from the bedside table and made to leave.

'No, listen to me,' the vicar insisted.

Sunniva's gaze was imploring now. She was so tired.

'I have to clear this away, Torvald,' she said, forcing a smile. 'And then my shift is over. But the others will be here soon, so it's going to be OK.'

'No,' the old man said loudly, raising a crooked finger. 'It has to be you.'

Sunniva was startled, and she stopped in the middle of the floor with the tray in her hands.

The mad vicar.

No. She just wanted to go home.

'Please,' he said in a feeble voice as she reached the door. 'I didn't mean to shout, God forgive me, but this is the way it must happen. You're the messenger.'

Sunniva turned and looked at him. He was staring at her, pleading. He had folded his hands.

'Please?'

'Listen to what?' Sunniva sighed.

'Thank you so much,' the old man said, when he saw Sunniva put down the tray on the table by the door and come back to his bedside. 'We both thank you, God and I. The messenger.'

He raised his hands towards the heavens and murmured something.

'Why am I the messenger, Torvald?' Sunniva said. 'And what's the message? And who is it for?'

The vicar smiled at her again. 'At first it made no sense to me, but then I found out who you are.'

'Who I am? But you know who I am, Torvald. We've known each other for ages.'

'Oh, no, no,' the old man said with a light cough. 'Not until I heard the other nurses talk.'

'What do you mean?'

'Oh, you know, they whisper and gossip when they change my bed. They don't think Torvald has ears, they think he's not even human, just someone waiting to die: no, he won't know that we're talking about Sunniva.'

'What?' Sunniva was confused. 'What do they say about me?'

Suddenly she was intrigued by what the old man had to say.

'And that was when I realized that you were the messenger,' the old man said happily, then he looked as if he had been distracted by something.

'What do they say about me?' Sunniva said, bringing him back.

'Oh, nothing to worry about. Only that you and the policeman are no longer getting married. That he drinks and gambles away your money.'

'What the f—' Sunniva burst out, but stopped herself. She worked in the one place in Norway where swearing could lead to dismissal.

'How dare they—'

'Hush, hush, my friend, it's all for the best.'

'How can that be . . .?'

'So it's true? He's a police officer?'

'Yes, sort of.' Sunniva nodded.

'Oh, God, thank you. Now I will go to Heaven.' The old man smiled, and clapped his wrinkly hands.

'Torvald, I don't know if—' Sunniva sighed, but he interrupted her.

'A great sin can only be redeemed through a great good deed.'

'I don't know . . .'

'So says the Scripture, and that is the word of God,' the vicar went on, taking no notice of her.

Sunniva had a feeling he was heading into madness again, and yet there was something in his eyes that told her that today was different. She had never seen him this alert before.

'So I'm the messenger,' she said. 'What did you want to tell me?'

'You've seen the papers?' the old man said, still lucid.

'What do you mean?'

'The sacrificial lamb in the circle of sin?'

Sunniva had to think hard before she realized what he was referring to. The young girl found murdered in the forest on the far side of Hurumlandet. The papers had written about little else recently. Naked. Strangled. In some kind of ritual. Even thinking about it sent shivers down her spine.

'What about her?' Sunniva said, still intrigued.

'I know who it was.'

'Who the girl was?'

'No,' he said, exasperated at her inability to follow his train of thought.

'Then who?'

'God's will.' The vicar nodded, content again.

'Torvald, what are you talking about?' Sunniva said.

The old man folded his hands across his chest and closed his eyes for a moment as if he were having a conversation with someone inside his head; then he opened them again and looked right at her.

'I know who killed her.'

Chapter 50

The man who had sat down at her table had intelligent eyes; he seemed calm and self-assured, yet Mia Krüger was not sure what to make of him. He wore a white shirt and a black suit that made him look like a businessman, but his crazy hair, black on the sides with a broad, white stripe down the middle, seemed to contradict the look. She saw how he had earned his nickname, Skunk.

Normally, she was good at this, reading people, but this young man exuded something she had never come across before. He was dressed up for the occasion like an actor. As if he wanted to be special and had put on these clothes in order to stand out from the crowd. She soon realized how wrong she was.

He could not have cared less about his appearance. He could look any way he wanted to, because he did not care what other people thought. He was himself, and if anyone had a problem with that, well, they could go to hell. Skunk raised the beer glass to his lips and smiled at her across the rim. Perhaps it was the alcohol, but for the first time in as long as Mia could remember, she had a feeling that here was a man she might actually, yes . . .

She did not finish the thought but emptied her own beer, put on her police face again and put the notebook and pen to one side.

'So you're not busy?'

He might be a bit cocky, but Mia did not mind.

'I am, actually,' she said.

'I don't usually do this,' Skunk said, taking his eyes off her for the first time, and staring out of the window.

'Do what?'

'Talk to the police,' he smiled, looking at her again.

'No, we get that,' Mia said. 'Gabriel made it quite clear.'

'Gabriel, yes.' Skunk sighed, raising his glass again. 'He went over to the dark side . . .'

'According to him, you're the one who went over to the dark side,' she said as the waiter placed fresh drinks on the white tablecloth between them.

'He said that?' Skunk said.

'I thought you were the villain? And that Gabriel is the one helping us?'

'That depends on how you look at it.'

'Of course.' Mia smiled, taking a sip of her Guinness.

'I don't normally do this.'

Skunk took off his jacket and hung it carefully on the back of the chair.

'So you say. Why are you here, then?'

'Let's call it conscience. Or, more accurately, curiosity.'

'Curiosity?'

Skunk smiled. 'You're exactly how I imagined you.'

'And how is that?'

Her head was starting to spin now. Mia had had quite a lot to drink, but she tried to stay in control.

'Why don't we stop pussyfooting around and get straight to the point?'

Skunk looked at her, and again Mia had the feeling that, if she had not been working, if the young man who had turned up out of the blue had not been absolutely crucial to the case she was investigating, then she might . . .

She dropped the thought.

'Absolutely.' Mia nodded.

'Two things,' he said, taking another sip of his beer.

'Yes?'

'One,' he said, looking at her, 'the location of the server.'

'Where you found the film?'

'Yes, but first you need to accept the following,' Skunk said. 'You know nothing and can do nothing.'

'Me?'

'I'm not saying this in order to patronize you, but this is technical. I know that you're the best in your field, but let us say for a moment that I'm the best in mine, OK?'

'Gabriel is very good,' Mia said.

Skunk smiled. 'Yes, Gabriel is good, but he's way too nice. Do you know what a white hacker is?'

'No,' Mia said.

'OK. Then you probably won't know what a black hacker is?'

Mia shook her head again.

'OK,' Skunk said, draining his glass and looking at her. 'How about another round?'

Mia nodded, and Skunk summoned the waiter.

'OK, so where did you find the film? Where was the server?' she asked.

'I can't say for sure,' Skunk said, emptying his shot glass.

'Why not?'

'Because they always hide them. How technical are you?'

'What do you mean?'

'How much do you know about computers?'

Mia decided to stop drinking.

'OK, let's pretend I know nothing. How would you explain it to me?'

'The server where I found the film,' Skunk said, taking another sip of his beer, 'let's say it was in Russia.'

'OK?'

'But it wasn't,' the young man with the stripy hair smiled again, and she could see now that he was a little tipsy.

'Do you know anything about mirrors? About ghost IP addresses?'

'Nothing.' Mia smiled now, focusing on her pen and notepad.

'You can hide servers.'

'So you don't know where you found it?'

'Yes and no,' he said, taking another sip of his beer. 'No matter how hard they try to hide them, they leave behind traces, and what little I've found in Norway came from a house in St Hanshaugen.'

'This server was there, in St Hanshaugen? That was where you found the film?'

Mia left her drinks untouched on the table.

'Ullevålsveien number 61. I've checked it out. It used to be a bookshop.'

'A bookshop?'

'Second-hand.'

'But now?' Mia prompted him.

'Yes, exactly, it *used* to be, but there's nothing there now.'

'You've checked?'

'Yes, they used to sell antiquarian books. Old books. Books on the occult, as far as I could gather. You know, Satanists, that kind of stuff?'

He smiled archly across his beer glass.

'But it has closed? There is nothing there now?'

'Nothing at all.' Skunk nodded slowly. 'But . . .'

'Yes?'

'The evidence wasn't clear. It could just be yet another decoy.'

'OK,' Mia said. 'And the second thing?'

'What?'

'You said there were two things, one and two?'

Skunk put down his glass on the white tablecloth. 'Yes. And that's the worst part.'

Mia did not know what to think. Skunk seemed quite drunk, although he had only had a couple of drinks.

'What is?'

'You've seen the film, right?' he said, leaning across the table towards her. 'Have you – I mean, the police – found out what it's really about?'

'What do you mean, what the film is really about?'

'You haven't, have you?'

'I don't know. What if we haven't?'

The waiter came over to them again. It was last orders, but Mia waved him away.

'The film – the girl in the wheel – have you seen it?'

Her image of the hacker with the stripy hair on the other side of the table was starting to swim, and Mia was glad she had stopped drinking.

'Of course. So what's the second thing?' Mia said as the lights in the bar were turned on around them.

'What?' Skunk said, his eyes glassy now.

'Number two?' Mia prompted him. 'If the server was number one, then what's number two?'

Skunk put down his empty glass on the white tablecloth in front of her.

'It's not a film,' he said with swimming eyes.

'What do you mean?'

'It's not a film,' Skunk said again, looking at her.

'Of course it's a film.'

'No. It's an extract from a live feed.'

'What?'

'A live feed. It's live.'

'What are you saying?'

Skunk raised his gaze from the table and looked at her gravely. 'They streamed her on the Internet. Exhibited her.'

'What?' Mia exclaimed, as the waiter came over and told them it was closing time, that they had to leave.

'It's live,' Skunk said again. 'Someone filmed her over a period of time, streaming her live on the Net, probably making money in the process.'

'But how?' Mia asked, as the bouncer made his way towards them.

'Time to go home,' the bouncer announced with a smile.

'How will I find you?' Mia said when they were out on the cold pavement in Hegdehaugsveien.

The young hacker put on his jacket and pulled his beanie over his ears as a vacant taxi pulled up in the street in front of them.

'You won't,' Skunk said, and winked at her.

'Yes, but . . .?'

'Tøyen,' the hacker said to the cab driver before getting into the back and shutting the car door behind him.

Chapter 51

Hugo Lang, a sixty-two-year-old investment banker, stepped down from his private jet at Zurich Airport and into the white Bentley waiting to take him home. The drive to his palatial home on the shore of Lake Pfäffikersee took just over twenty minutes, and he did not exchange one word with the driver. The ageing Swiss never spoke to the staff.

Calling Hugo Lang a banker was possibly an exaggeration, because all his wealth was inherited and he had never done a day's work in his life. His father, the steel magnate Ernst Lang, had died seven years earlier; he had been one of Europe's most successful businessmen, and his son might have been expected to carry on the business, but Hugo had sold all the companies he had inherited. He had kept the chateau in Switzerland, an estate on Bermuda, flats in New York, Paris, London and Hong Kong, but, otherwise, the one-hundred-year-old family business, LangKrupp, and all its subsidiaries were sold to new owners. Those who had been left nothing – uncles, aunts and other peripheral family members – had done what they could to stop him; the media had been full of accounts of horrified relatives going through the courts to prevent the sale – but he had pushed through with it all the same. Hugo Lang did not care what other people thought.

He let his driver open the door for him, and entered the chateau without looking at the staff taking his jacket and hat. He had more important things to think about, and today felt like a big day.

Hugo Lang had always been a collector, but it was not until his father died and left him all his money that he was finally in a position to buy anything he liked. His father had been a miser, but that no longer mattered. His mother had died when he was fourteen, but Hugo had never missed her. Ernst Lang had died from leukaemia, and been on his deathbed at the chateau for a long time; a new wing had been built purely for him, practically a small hospital, and Hugo had visited from time to time, not because he wanted to or in any way felt sorry for the old man, merely to ensure that the old fool did not suddenly get it into his head to leave his money to someone else.

Following the death of his father, he had got rid of everything that reminded him of his parents. Photographs, clothing, portraits on the wall. He saw no reason to keep them; he needed space for his collections.

He kept his car collection in several garages in the courtyard. He had lost count of how many he had, and he rarely drove them, but he liked owning them, touching them, looking at them, knowing that they were his. His collection included a Hennessey Venom GT, a Porsche 918 Spyder, a Ferrari F12 Berlinetta, an Aston Martin Vanquish, a Mercedes CL65 AMG Coupe, and usually this would be his first activity after a trip abroad, inspecting his garages, running his hand over some of the cars, but not today.

Today he had more important things on his mind.

He went straight to his study, sat down in the deep office chair, turned on his computer and felt his heart pound under his shirt. This was a rare occurrence. Hugo Lang never got very excited about anything. When he made a new acquisition, he would occasionally feel a brief flutter of excitement. Like the time he had bought what had then been the world's most expensive stamp, an 1885 Swedish yellow three-shilling stamp, the only one of its kind in the whole world. He had bid on it in secret, and bought it for just under twenty-three million Swiss francs, and at the time he had felt a kind of quiver in his body, but it had quickly passed. He had bought expensive wine the next day, a case of Domaine Leroy Musigny Grand Cru in order to revive the feeling, but it had made no noticeable difference.

But this. This was like nothing he had ever known.

He had never felt such pleasure. Maybe when he saw the sums in his bank accounts after all the companies had been sold, but no, not even that could compare to this.

Hugo Lang got up, made the long walk across the Italian marble floor to make sure that the door was locked, then sat down in front of his computer again. His fingers trembled as he typed the secret Internet address on the keyboard.

It was more than one week since the Norwegian girl in the wheel had disappeared from his screen, and he was missing her already. He had had his bed moved into his study, had all his meals served in here, so that they could be together all the time. At night when he could not sleep, he might walk up to her and touch the screen. It was so good to have her so near, but now she was gone, and he had not been himself since.

Hugo Lang had seen such things before. If you had money and you knew where to go, there was always something to watch, but it was rarely real. He could smell a fake from miles away, but this?

No, this was real.

He had found the advert a few months earlier in the darkest part of the Internet, and what he had liked about it was its exclusivity.

Five highest bidders only.

Only five people. Hugo Lang did not like sharing, and he would have liked to have had her all to himself, but five was not bad, four others he could cope with, as long as he did not know who they were, which of course he did not; nor did they know his identity.

She was gone now, and he missed her, but today a new girl would be chosen, and the sixty-two-year-old's fingers were shaking so badly he could barely hit the right keys on the keyboard. He leaned back in the big leather chair with a smile on his lips, feeling his heart beat even faster as the webpage opened on the large screen on the wall in front of him.

An almost black page, a short text in English.

Who do you want?

Who will be the chosen one?

And two photographs below. Two Norwegian girls.

271

He was so excited he could barely sit still in his chair. His forehead was clammy with sweat and he kept having to wipe his glasses on his shirt in order to be able to read the names below the photographs.

Two Norwegian girls. One blonde. The other dark.

Isabella Jung.

Miriam Munch.

He had missed her so much, but soon there would be a new one. One of these two girls, and Hugo Lang decided that he already liked them both.

Hugo Lang thought about it for a moment before he clicked on one picture, closed the webpage, got up from his chair and went to his bedroom to change for dinner.

SIX

Chapter 52

Mia Krüger pulled up in front of the white cottage with a feeling that something was wrong. The unexpected meeting last night. This hacker, Skunk, who, according to Gabriel, hated the police, had suddenly appeared out of nowhere. Even charmed her. But on her way home and, later, on the sofa with her notes, she had started to question his motives. Why had he appeared in the first place? How had he found her? What did they really know about this young man? Skunk? They did not even know his real name. He had discovered this film. By accident? On some mysterious server? Which now for some reason was suddenly gone? She shook her head at herself and found her mobile in her pocket.

'Ludvig Grønlie.'

'Yes, hi, it's Mia.'

'Hi, Mia, where are you?'

Mia looked at the white cottage in front of her. The back of beyond would be the kindest way to describe it; she had spent so long finding the place that it had started to grow dark. She had been on the verge of giving up when she finally spotted the small access road, which had been so well hidden it was tempting to think someone had done it on purpose.

'In the countryside,' Mia said.

'Where?'

'I'm just checking something. Would you do me a favour?'

'Of course,' Ludvig said. 'What do you need?'

'I need some information about an address.'

'Sure. Which one?'

'Ullevålsveien number 61.'

'Right, what do you want to know?'

'Everything you can find.'

'OK?' Grønlie hesitated. 'It would be a bit easier if I knew what I was looking for?'

'Sorry. The address only cropped up yesterday. I'm mostly interested in anything about a bookshop selling old books on the ground floor of the building.'

'An antiquarian bookshop?'

'Exactly.' Mia rang off, put her phone in her pocket and got out of the car.

The small white cottage stood facing her. There was a red out-house on one side of the yard. Otherwise, just forest. Dense trees covered in hoar frost. And not a sound to be heard anywhere. Who could live in a place like this? There was *nothing* here. Mia wondered if she should ring the doorbell, although she knew there would be no one at home.

Jim Fuglesang.

The man with the white bicycle helmet.

This was where he lived. In the small white cottage surrounded by tall trees in the middle of nowhere; Mia thought it looked like something out of a horror film.

Claustrophobic.

It was deserted.

Not a sound.

A man with mental-health issues. Who had been readmitted to Dikemark Hospital. Impossible to interview. When they had first spoken to him, she had not believed that he was the man they were looking for. An impromptu confession, a mentally unstable person who thought that he had committed a murder. Nothing they could take seriously, of course, so they had released him immediately and she had dismissed him from her mind, but now she was having second thoughts. What would she have done if she had been the killer? If she wanted to avoid capture, how would she have done it, if not this way? Who would suspect an idiot in a white bicycle helmet who pretends that he doesn't know what he is talking about? And Skunk was similar. Who would suspect a young hacker who loathes the police but then suddenly turns up to help them because his 'conscience' tells him he must?

A sick bastard.

Mia looked for the doorbell but found none so she knocked on the door instead. No one at home. As she had expected. Jim Fuglesang was drugged up to the eyeballs at Dikemark, probably still wearing his bicycle helmet, but even so she raised her fist and knocked on the white door a second time.

Who would want to live out here?

What kind of person would choose to live like this?

Mia stuffed her hands into the pockets of her leather jacket, waited a few minutes until she had established that no one was coming, then calmly walked around the house, across the frosty grass, and stepped up on the veranda on the other side.

It did not take her long to open the door. She slipped softly inside and uttered a faint *Hello, is anyone here?*, but there was no reply. Well, at least that part was true. Jim Fuglesang really must be locked up at Dikemark. She had the whole house to herself. Entering without a warrant was illegal, of course, but Mia Krüger had stopped caring about such formalities a long time ago. Munch obviously had to follow the rules, apply for search warrants, which, given the hopeless bureaucracy in which they were mired, always took days, or it did when they had no specific grounds; they might have in this case, but she did not have the patience to wait. Mia walked across the living-room floor and found a light switch on a wall.

The room that appeared was pretty much as she had expected. Tidy. Clean. Clearly the home of a single man. It did not take Mia long to find what she was looking for. She quickly located the photo albums, neatly lined up in the bookcase facing her and, as she had also hoped, in meticulous chronological order.

'Do you like taking pictures?'

'Yes.'

You did not need to be the sharpest knife in the drawer to have noticed it. The glue marks on the back of the pictures. Old, brittle glue. The pictures used to be in an album. Cheap, brown plastic albums were lined up on the bottom shelf. The first was labelled 1989, the last 2012. She felt a twinge of compassion as she took out the first few albums, sat down on the beige sofa and started flicking through them. Not a single human being featured in any of them. The pictures showed trees, squirrels, steps, a feeding table. All dated and with a caption. *A nice budgie*, 21 February 1994. *The birch leaves are out*, 5 May 1998. She started turning the pages more quickly because she knew exactly what she was looking for, and it was easy to find: Blank spaces. Pages in the books where the pictures used to be. She soon found them. *The dead cat*, 4 April 2006. *The poor dog*, 8 August 2007. Six years ago. Five years ago. That long? With a one-year interval? Why would they . . .?

Her train of thought was interrupted when the darkness that had now settled across the yard outside suddenly lit up briefly, only to grow dark again. She had not heard the car arrive, but there could be no doubt.

There was someone outside.

Mia reacted quickly; she returned the albums to the shelf, slipped out through the veranda door and hid behind the corner of the house, her lips pressed shut, so that her breathing would not give her away.

How quiet it was out here.

She could hear her own heartbeat.

She could hear her own breathing.

Who would want to live so far away from everyone?

And then a sudden thought:

Why the hell had she not brought a gun?

She was banned, of course, from carrying a weapon. That applied to all members of Oslo's police force. Officers were only allowed to carry a weapon if they were part of an armed response unit or had special permission. Mia had always preferred Glocks and had tried several models: the Glock 17, which was the standard model, but she also had a Glock 26, which was lighter and easier to conceal on her body. It was little comfort now. She could kick herself for not thinking to bring one.

A car in the yard.

She heard someone get out of the vehicle, followed by a knock on the door. First once, then twice. A visitor. Jim Fuglesang had a visitor. She took a deep breath, rounded the corner. Her police instinct took over and she scanned the area. There was a man on the steps, he weighed approximately eighty kilos and wore a coat; there was a white van parked in the yard, two seats in the front, no one in the passenger seat; a quick look in every direction, no other movement; the man on the steps appeared to be alone and was almost as startled at seeing her as she was at seeing him.

'Who are you?' the man stuttered.

'Hi, I'm sorry,' Mia said, put on a smile and walked towards him. 'Mia Krüger, Oslo Police. I'm looking for Jim Fuglesang. Does he live here?'

'Er, yes,' the man with the beard said.

'It doesn't look as if he's in,' Mia said, still smiling.

'Er, no,' the man said. 'Police? Has Jim done something wrong?'

'No, no, it's just a routine visit. And you are?'

The man on the steps still looked shocked at meeting anyone out here.

'Henrik,' he said. 'I, well . . .'

He gestured towards his van, and she saw it now, the logo on the side.

Hurumlandet Supermarket.

'I deliver his shopping, but I hadn't heard from him for a few days so I thought he might not have been able to leave the house, and I . . .'

'Do you know him well?'

'No, I wouldn't say that,' the man replied. 'But he has been a customer for years. He's a bit – well, at times he needs help.'

Mia had another quick look around. There was hardly any light left. Bloody autumn. She had not come here solely to check the albums; she had another reason which was just as important. She had hoped to try to find the path leading to the lake where Fuglesang had taken the pictures.

'Doesn't look like he's in,' Mia said with a light shrug.

'He's not in any trouble, is he?'

'No, it was about a . . . traffic incident in the area, a collision. We're just checking to see if anyone saw anything.'

'Oh dear,' the man said, and walked down the steps with a worried look on his face. 'A collision? Was anyone hurt?'

'No,' Mia said, looking around irritably again.

The light had disappeared suddenly. As if someone had turned off a switch.

Shit.

'Is there anything I can do?' the man offered. 'I mean, I know everyone around here. Where did it happen?'

'Is that your shop?' Mia said, pointing at the name on the van.

'Yes,' the man said.

'Henrik, did you say your name was?'

'Yes, Henrik Eriksen, I—'

'I'll call you if I have any questions, OK?' She put the smile back on.

'Yes, of course. Would you like my number?'

'I can find it, if I need it,' Mia said, and got back in her car.

She turned the car around in the small yard and drove down the narrow road.

Bloody darkness.

She would have to come back some other time. She had reached the main road when her mobile rang.

'Yes?'

'It's Ludvig.'

'Yes?'

'You wanted to know about that address?'

'What did you find?'

'Not very much. The building is mainly flats, but there are businesses on the ground floor.'

Finally, a streetlight appeared at the side of the road, and Mia relaxed. She was back in civilization.

'Any second-hand bookshops?'

'No, not as far as I can see.'

Crap.

The creepy feeling came back. Last night's unexpected meeting. Out of the blue. He had tricked her. The hacker. Skunk.

Bastard.

'Thank you, Ludvig,' Mia said, and drove back to Oslo.

Chapter 53

Isabella Jung was sitting on her bed in her room, still wearing her coat, feeling her heart beat faster under her jumper. Someone had slipped another note under her door. Same writing as before.

Please would you meet me? In secret.

Just you and me?

She was back from visiting her dad in his new council flat in Fredrikstad. It was a long time since she had last seen him, and she had been excited about going, but their time together had not turned out the way she had hoped. He had not said very much. She had almost got the impression that she was in the way. It was nice to be back at the Nurseries.

Isabella smiled and trailed her finger slowly across the white paper.

Please would you meet me?

Of course she would.

She had guessed that it was from him when she got the first note. The one that had been pinned to her door. It must be Paulus. She had seen it in his eyes the first time he showed her the orchids. And she could not remember if she had looked at him the same way but, later, whenever she had the chance, she had made sure to do so.

She understood that it had to be a secret. She had yet to turn sixteen, that was the reason. She was too young. A minor. Illicit love – only that made it more tantalizing.

Isabella Jung was only fifteen years old, but she felt she had been a grown-up ever since she was little. She did not give a toss about age. What was age, anyway? It was just a number. But she understood him, of course she did. He was over twenty. He would lose his job; he might even go to prison, for all she knew. So she had kept it a secret.

Just as he had. They had never touched. Not even hugged. Only exchanged looks. Him looking at her and her looking back at him.

But then, finally, the note:

I like you.

And now this other one:

Please would you meet me? In secret.

Just you and me?

Isabella cherished the words, but she was confused. She had barely returned to the Nurseries before the rumours had reached her. The police had taken away Paulus and Benedikte Riis. They had had a row outside, the police had handcuffed them, and no one had heard from them since. A worried Isabella had gone to see Helene, but she had been turned away at the door.

'I'm a bit busy right now, please come back later.'

'But I just—?'

'Later, Isabella, OK?'

It was obviously to do with Camilla Green – all the girls agreed on that – but no one knew what was really going on. Some said they had heard Benedikte accuse Paulus of killing Camilla. All lies, of course. Everyone knew what Benedikte Riis was like. A liar. She would say anything to get attention. Of course Paulus had not done anything.

There was a sudden knock on her door, and Cecilie popped her head round.

'Are you asleep?' the skinny girl whispered.

'No, no, come in.' Isabella smiled and quickly stuffed the note under her pillow.

'Have you heard any more?' Cecilie asked, sitting down on the bed next to her.

'No, nothing, I've only just got back. You?'

'People are saying all sorts of things,' Cecilie said miserably, and now Isabella could see that her friend had been crying.

'Don't listen to them,' Isabella said, putting her arms around the trembling girl.

'Some say Benedikte murdered Camilla,' Cecilie said. 'Others that Paulus did it. Oh my God, what if it's true?'

Isabella sympathized; nothing felt safe now. She could feel it, too. The reporters. The police. The serenity and security out here had been destroyed.

'It's obviously not true.' Isabella smiled.

'You don't think so?' Cecilie mumbled, looking at her with her trusting eyes.

They were the same age, but sometimes Isabella felt like Cecilie was only little. Cecilie had had a bad start. Bad people. Wicked people. Isabella had heard the gruesome details, but she could not bear to think about them now. Instead, she tried to think happy thoughts.

Please would you meet me? In secret.

Of course she would meet Paulus. She knew about that place of his. His secret place. The hideout on the far side of the estate. She also knew about his plants, but she had not told anyone.

'Paulus hasn't killed anyone,' Isabella asserted.

'What about Benedikte?'

'Definitely not. She's horrible, but she's also as thick as two short planks. She couldn't have pulled it off, even if she had wanted to, could she?'

Isabella saw that Cecilie was starting to smile now.

'She is, isn't she? As thick as two short planks?'

'Yes.' Isabella smiled again.

'Do you remember when we visited the Natural History Museum and she asked why they didn't have any monkeys?'

Isabella giggled.

'And why all the animals were standing so still?'

Cecilie was grinning now.

'She thought we were at the zoo.' Isabella howled with laughter.

Cecilie joined in. 'How stupid can you get?'

'Really stupid.'

'I hate bad people,' Cecilie said suddenly, and curled up to Isabella again.

'I'll look after you. You don't have to be scared,' Isabella said, stroking the girl's hair again.

Suddenly the door was opened and a breathless Synne appeared.

'They're back.'

'Who?'

'Paulus and Benedikte. They're back. They've just arrived. In a police car. They went straight to Helene's office.'

He was back.

Isabella's heart skipped a beat.

Please would you meet me? In secret.

Just you and me?

She smiled.

Of course I will.

Chapter 54

Holger Munch hung up his duffel coat in the hallway, took off his shoes, went to the bathroom and opened the medicine cabinet. He found some painkillers, popped two in his mouth and washed them down with water before going to the living room, not knowing quite what to do with himself.

He had been so tired that he had gone straight to bed after meeting Mia at Justisen, but he had been unable to sleep. Tossing and turning under his duvet, he had got up again and wandered aimlessly around the flat, before finally getting dressed and going for a walk.

The headache had come without warning. There was a throbbing in his temples and behind his eyes. As if someone had slammed a bat into the back of his head, he had started to see stars and had a metallic taste in his mouth. *A migraine?*

Holger Munch was perfectly aware that he was far from being the healthiest man on the planet, but his head had never troubled him before. It was almost three o'clock. In the morning. Why? He felt no tiredness now. Just this constant headache. He waited for the pills to kick in. Was he getting old? He was what – fifty-four, fifty-five, in a few days? – surely that was no age? Or was it? He shuffled into the kitchen, turned on the kettle and opened the door to the fridge. Food. Food had never been a problem for the fat investigator but, as he stood there, staring into the fridge, for once he could not see a single item he fancied. He took a mug from the cupboard above the sink, waited for the kettle to boil, then carried his mug of tea into the living room, where he stopped in front of the CD shelf.

Something tasty to eat. Music in the background while he channel-hopped with the volume on mute. That was his usual routine. Clear his mind, switch off from the day that was nearly over; a form of meditation. A good meal, music, images from across the world flickering on the screen in the background – but now he could find nothing he wanted to listen to either. Munch sat down on the sofa and sipped his tea as the pain in his head slowly dissipated. It was pitch black outside the windows. The world was asleep, but he was unable to wind down. Suddenly, the flat felt gloomy. He had done his best, made a home for himself in Theresesgate. A yucca palm in a corner. Pictures of Miriam and Marion above the sofa. This CD rack, which covered most of the wall behind the television. He had been kidding himself, pretending to himself that this was a home, but it was not. No matter how he looked at it. Storage, that was all it was. Somewhere to be.

While he waited for . . .

Munch did not complete the thought but went to the bathroom and took another two painkillers. Pretended not to see the wedding ring he had taken off and left in there. He went back to the kitchen and opened the fridge, still without appetite. Went back to the CDs in vain.

He was heading back to the sofa when his doorbell rang. He stopped for a moment before he understood the noise. He so rarely had visitors the sound was almost unknown to him. And in the middle of the night? It had to be a mistake. Someone had pressed the wrong button on their way home after a night out, but then the bell rang again. And again.

Now irritated, Munch went over to the intercom.

'Hello?'

'Hi, Holger, it's Mia.'

'What?'

'It's Mia. Please can I come up?'

It returned instantly. The feeling that someone was bashing a nail into his temple.

'Holger, are you there?'

He had to steel himself in order to answer.

'Do you know what time it is? What's happened?'

Mia outside his door. That was a first.

'Skunk,' Mia said, a grating voice at the end of the intercom. 'The hacker.'

'What?' Holger said, leaning against the wall.

'I think we're being played. Please can I come up?'

'It's the middle of the night,' Munch objected, pressing his hand against his forehead.

'I know, but we need to talk,' Mia insisted. 'Are you going to let me in or what?' she said, far below, in the street.

'Yes, of course,' Munch said, and managed to pull himself together enough to press the button that unlocked the front door.

Chapter 55

The little boy lay under the duvet, looking at the calendar on the wall next to his bed. He was so excited his whole body was taut. The big day. The one they had been looking forward to for so long. His mum had talked about it ever since . . . he tried counting, but he did not have enough fingers . . . well, certainly since the summer, probably before that. The big day. When everything would happen. OK, so he did not know exactly what would happen, but it was terribly important, and bigger than the sun or the moon, and the birth of the Earth. He pulled his thin duvet closely around his neck and looked at the calendar again. Although his mum had told him to go to sleep, it was quite impossible. December 1999. That was what it said. That was the year now. 1999. But that was not the exciting bit, the exciting bit was the page behind December 1999, the one he was not allowed to see until the clock struck twelve. He had sneaked a peek anyway; he couldn't help himself. January 2000. Imagine that? The year 2000? The boy smiled to himself and could feel his toes curl up at the far end of the bed, like they always did when he was as happy as he was now; he could feel it all the way through his body, right up to his ears, which tended to get very hot, and that was good, because the small room was cold in December. Very cold. And they could only afford to buy logs for the wood-burning stove in the living room. Stoves were expensive. As was wood. He would usually go to sleep in his clothes and a woolly hat, but he could feel them all the same, his toes, how they curled up inside his socks.

The big day. A new millennium. Fancy that. That just one day could be so important? That just a few minutes on the clock could make such a difference? The hands would go tick-tock and, hey presto! the hands would take away everything that was wicked, and the big day would arrive, the one they had been looking forward to. He tried counting again, but he still did not have enough fingers, nor was it easy to find all of them inside his mittens.

The little boy had a clock on his wall, but it did not show the right time because the batteries had stopped working some time ago, and new ones were expensive; the hands were stuck on a quarter past five all the time. He could not trust it, so he had tried counting ever since his mum had told him to go to bed. The clock in the living room had shown five minutes past eight, and he had counted the seconds like this: *one thousand and one, one thousand and two, one thousand and three*; but after one thousand five hundred and something, his head had started to spin, so it was better to wait in his bed until his mum came to tell him that it had arrived.

The big day.

He still did not know what would happen, but he knew the evil spirits would disappear somehow, and he hoped his mum would be happier. He thought that she would be, because she had been looking forward to this for a long time.

The little boy pulled his woolly hat further down over his ears and tried to keep warm under the flimsy duvet.

'The basement is too big,' his mum would often say, whenever he asked why the house was always so cold.

'Your dad wasn't quite right in the head, but he knew about building houses. He knew what was coming, that we would need a place to hide when it blows up, when the world goes under, but he made it too big, there should have been more house and less basement, because it gets cold underground, and then the cold seeps up through the floorboards, do you understand?'

He did not understand much of what his mum said when she talked about his dad, because he had never met him, but he would nod anyway, because she did not like him asking too many questions. He knew that his dad was a real person because he had built the house. He had never actually seen him with his own eyes, but his mum could not build anything, so it had to be true. Sometimes he would imagine that his dad was like Pippi Longstocking's pirate dad. That he was a very good dad, but that he had to be away a lot of the time, that he might turn up one day, a cheerful man with a big, bushy beard. He had never said anything to his mum – he had barely said it out loud to himself – but he had often wondered if the big day might be about that. That his dad might be the surprise. That his dad would burst through the door with golden treasures, lift up his mum and whirl her around, and he would bring them presents from every corner of the world, and one of them would be a wood-burning stove just for him, so he would never be cold again in his little room that never seemed to heat up, especially not in December.

He had given a lot of thought to what the big day would bring. He had made a list. He had not shown it to his mum; he kept it under his pillow. Now there were seven things on it: seven things he hoped might happen on the big day.

He wondered whether to take it out now and look at it again, but his mum had told him to go to bed, lie still and not come out, although the clock in the living room had shown only 8.05.

THE BIG DAY.

He had written it in capital letters across the top of the paper. He had taught himself to write, and he was proud of that. Also counting. Telling the time. The alphabet. All by himself, and that was good because, like Pippi, he did not go to school. To begin with he had not understood the writing he saw everywhere. On the back of the cornflakes box, on the tube of toothpaste, on the side of milk cartons, inside the three books he had in his room; at first they were just weird squiggles, small drawings, but one day when his mum was out of the house, it had come to him. He did not know how it had happened, but it had to do with the words which came out of his mum's mouth and the words he used to reply, which at first he had thought just existed in the air, but then he had made the connection that they were the same words written on the things he was looking at.

Good night.

Milk.

January.

Soap.

You can win.

You can win a trip to Disneyland.

And he had used a pen to write down the words on a piece of paper, and the discovery had been almost as exciting as lying under the duvet, waiting for the big day. How the words in his mouth and the letters he saw everywhere could be written down on paper with just a small pen.

The little boy got up now, left his bed in order to move about a bit, get his circulation going, because, even fully dressed he was freezing cold under the flimsy duvet and, when he breathed, cloudy puffs came out of his mouth.

His dad had built the house, but the boy could not help thinking that, though his dad was good at construction and they did indeed need somewhere to hide when the world fell apart, his mum still had a point. The basement was too big. It made no difference that he wore his clothes to bed, his room was still freezing cold, and for a moment he wondered if it might be all right to go back to the living room, where the stove was, but he decided against it. If he had learned anything, then it was that it was terribly important not to make his mum angry.

The little boy went over to his wardrobe and found another jumper. A Norwegian knitted sweater. It was the finest one he owned, and he wore it only on birthdays or when he was allowed to leave the house, but he put it on nevertheless, on top of all his other clothes, and crept back under the duvet. He glanced up at the calendar again: 1999, a bad year; he could not wait until he could turn the page.

January 2000.

A new millennium.

He was not naughty, certainly not. He always did as he was told, and his mum had only said that he had to go to bed, not that he could not look at his list.

The little boy pulled off his mittens, found his torch, took out the list he had hidden under his pillow, and smiled.

THE BIG DAY

My wish list:

1. Mum will be happy.
2. Dad comes back and makes the basement smaller.
3. I am allowed to leave the house.
4. I stop pulling Mum's hair when I brush it.
5. I am allowed to go to school.
6. I can tell Mum that I know the alphabet, the numbers, and that I can read and write without her getting angry.
7. I get a friend.

The wind came suddenly, knocking on the walls, refusing to go away. It continued through the thin windows; it breathed icy air across his face, on to the small patch of skin that was exposed between his woolly hat and the edge of his duvet.

Yet again he considered getting up and going to the living room, but he did not, because his mum had told him not to.

His mum.

The little boy had no other people around him – he never had had – he had only ever had his mum.

When she left the house, he would be home alone. Sometimes it would be days before she returned, but it did not matter. She was everything to him.

He would brush her pretty, blonde hair in front of the stove. Help her sponge and soap those parts of her body she could not easily wash herself. The little boy smiled now.

The big day.

And without knowing it, he had closed his eyes so tightly that he disappeared from the cold room and into his dreams, and when he woke up again, he knew it, even though the clock on his wall still showed quarter past five.

It was no longer 1999.

It was the year 2000.

The big day.

It had to be. Only she had forgotten to wake him up. He flung aside his duvet and ran from the cold bedroom. Grinning from ear to ear, he marched through the living room towards her bedroom. Silly Mummy. He opened the door to her bedroom and stopped in his tracks.

A rope was hanging from a roof rafter.

From the rope, which was tight around her neck, hung a naked body with long blonde hair, immobile limbs and a blue face. Her eyes were wide open, and her mouth did not look as if it could speak.

The little boy pulled a chair out on to the floor, sat down, looked expectantly at the naked body hanging from the roof and smiled to himself.

And waited patiently for her to wake up.

Chapter 56

His pounding headache was starting to ease off at last. Munch strangled a small yawn as he placed a mug of tea for Mia on the table.

'Is that the best you can do?' she said, scowling at the mug.

'What do you mean?'

'Don't you have anything stronger?'

'It's the middle of the night, Mia. Can't we do this tomorrow?'

'No, it's important.' Mia was slurring her words, and Munch realized that she was quite drunk already, yet eager and alert in her own way.

His colleague had not bothered taking off her shoes or her jacket; she had just plonked down on his sofa, looking at him with this glow in her eyes he had seen many times before. She had made a breakthrough. It had always been a mystery to him how Mia did it, but he had learned to trust this expression.

'I don't drink, Mia, you know that.' Munch yawned.

'I know, but come on?' Mia smiled, nodding in the direction of a shelf below all the CDs.

Joke presents from his team. Every birthday. Let's give the tee-totaller something expensive he will never be able to drink. There were eight unopened bottles of whisky whose labels meant nothing to him, nor did he care to find out.

'Help yourself,' Munch said, shaking his head as Mia got up from the sofa, fetched one of the bottles and opened it.

'Do you have a glass?'

Munch went into the kitchen, grabbed a glass from a cupboard and caught sight of a smiling face on a picture on the fridge door, then he remembered.

Miriam had called him.

And he had forgotten to call her back, in the midst of every-thing. Shit. He had made up his mind to be more available to his family. He carried the glass into the living room, where he realized that Mia had been talking the whole time.

What's wrong with my head?

'He came to me,' Mia said, filling her glass.

'Who?'

'Skunk. He tracked me down at Lorry.'

'Skunk?' Munch was surprised.

'Totally out of the blue.' Mia smiled, taking a sip of her drink.

Munch nodded again.

'Impossible to find.' Mia smiled. 'Impossible to contact.'

Munch let her carry on talking.

'A live feed. That was what he said.'

'What?'

'The film we got. Of Camilla in the wheel. It wasn't just a recording; he said it was a live feed.'

'A feed?'

Munch began to wake up.

'Yes.' Mia nodded impatiently. 'He said they had been filming her. Broadcasting her. For months.'

'Oh my God,' Munch said, with a feeling of revulsion.

'Yes, sick or what?'

'That's dreadful . . .'

'But that wasn't what I wanted to tell you,' Mia said, refilling her glass.

So she had been to Lorry, she had not gone home, and she had clearly had a fair amount to drink. She raised the glass to her lips again and pretty much drained it before she went on.

'Mia, I—'

'No, no, listen to me,' she said passionately. 'How would you know? That it's not a recording. That it's a live feed. Unless you . . .' She grinned and looked at him again, almost coherent despite being so drunk.

'Were a part of it?'

'Exactly,' Mia said.

'Damn.'

'Yep.'

'He just turned up?'

'Yes. Out of nowhere.'

'And you think his conscience is troubling him? That he's our guy?'

'Yes.' Mia nodded vehemently.

Suddenly Munch felt wide awake.

'So what do we do?' Mia asked.

'We find him. Interview him. See if we have grounds for charging him.'

'No, not him.'

'What do you mean?'

'What do we do about Gabriel?' Mia said.

'Come again?'

'The two of them are close.'

'So you think Gabriel knows more than he's telling us?'

Mia shrugged. 'Don't you think it's odd that Gabriel hasn't told us who Skunk is and where we can find him?'

'Mia . . .'

'No, listen to me, please. A video suddenly pops up. Out of nowhere. And Gabriel – well, how long have we known him, really? Six months?'

'Mia, you're not suggesting that—'

'No, I'm serious, Holger, I'm on to something.' Mia cut him off. She drained her glass, and refilled it – again.

'Yes, but—'

'No, listen to me, Holger. Skunk knows something. I think he knows a great deal. And if Skunk knows something, I think maybe Gabriel knows it, too. We have to ask him, but it has to be done sensitively, that's why I had to talk to you right away. Do you get it now?'

Munch nodded pensively. 'It would be better for you to do it,' he said at length.

'Do what?'

'Talk to Gabriel. Tomorrow. He likes you. Get him to tell you what he knows.'

It started to sneak up on him again. The taste of metal in his mouth. The feeling of someone banging a nail into his head.

'OK,' Mia said, emptying her glass.

'But not in front of the others, promise?'

'No, of course not.'

'We have a team briefing at 10 a.m. Perhaps you could do it afterwards?'

'OK.' Mia nodded, getting up.

'So you think it's him?' Munch said when they were back in the hallway. 'Skunk?'

'Yes. It feels like it, there's definitely something there.'

'All right, but be nice to Gabriel,' Munch said, opening the door for her.

'Of course,' Mia said.

And disappeared down the stairs with a smile on her lips.

Chapter 57

Gabriel could feel that something was amiss, and his suspicion was confirmed when Mia asked him to come to her office right after the meeting.

'What's going on?' Gabriel said baffled, when Mia asked him to close the door behind him.

Mia looked at him with an expression he had not seen before, distrustful and intrigued at the same time, her head slightly tilted, almost as if she were trying to read his mind.

'What's going on?' Gabriel said again. He pulled out a chair and sat down.

'I need to ask you something,' Mia said. 'And you need to be totally honest with me.'

'Honest with you?' Gabriel smiled. 'Why wouldn't I be?'

Mia found a lozenge in her pocket and placed it on her tongue, still not taking her eyes off him.

'Skunk,' Mia said.

'Yes? What about him?' Gabriel said with a light shrug.

'How close are you, really?'

The knot in Gabriel's stomach tightened. 'What do you mean?' he said.

'What I asked you,' Mia said, still fixing her eyes on him.

Suddenly their conversation felt like an interrogation, and Gabriel did not like it.

'We used to be good friends,' he said.

'How good?'

'Very good friends. Where are you going with this?'

'But not any more?'

'No, not any more.' Gabriel sighed. 'What is this, Mia, are you accusing me of something?'

'I don't know,' Mia said, tilting her head again. 'Do we have something to accuse you of?'

We?

Gabriel began to get annoyed. They had been talking about him behind his back, Munch and her; possibly some of the others.

'I honestly don't know where he is,' Gabriel said, flinging out his arms. 'Now that might make me an idiot, but I don't understand why you would want to accuse me of anything.'

'So you haven't seen him for a long time?'

'Not for years,' Gabriel said, shaking his head. 'Not until he suddenly got in touch.'

'So you're not friends any more?'

'No.'

'What happened?'

Gabriel had had enough. He was already exhausted. He had slept badly; he was unable to get the images out of his head, no matter how hard he tried. The emaciated girl on her knees on the floor. The writing on the wall behind her. The feather-clad shadow. Just thinking about it made him shake.

'Listen,' he said, in a voice which came out much angrier than he had intended. 'I know I'm new here, that I'm not as good as the others, but I do my best, and if I had known where he was, I would have told you. Don't you think I've looked for him? Don't you realize that? Did you really think I wouldn't? But I've had no response, and do you know why? Because Skunk doesn't want to be found. Because . . .'

He stopped. He had to calm himself down, his blood was starting to boil.

'Because?' Mia said.

'Well, what do you think?' he asked her.

'Because he gets up to things which can't bear the light of day.'

'Exactly,' Gabriel said, flinging out his arms again. 'And now what? You all think I'm a part of it? Is that it? Screw you, Mia, I'm not putting up with this. I've worked like a maniac ever since—'

Mia raised her hand and interrupted him before he had time to say anything else.

'Sorry, Gabriel,' she said, and her gaze softened. 'But I had to be sure.'

'Be sure of what?' Gabriel snapped at her.

'I'm sorry,' she said again.

Mia got up from her chair and perched on the edge of her desk in front of him.

'Is that what you've been thinking? *All* of you? Is that what you've been talking about? How Gabriel and Skunk are in it together? That the old hackers are running a business on the side? Locking up girls in basements? Seriously, Mia? You make me sick.'

Gabriel was so angry now that he could barely control his temper. He had not seen this coming. How could they think that of him? Had she any idea how proud he was of being a part of this team?

'Gabriel,' Mia said.

She moved nearer to him, and put her hand on his shoulder. He wondered if she was closing in for a hug. She looked genuinely sorry.

'There are times when I'm not as tactful as I ought to be,' she said, not taking her hand off his shoulder. 'I – well, I forget to think before I speak. Please forgive me. It's not that I thought you were involved, but . . .'

'But what?'

'Sometimes if you like someone, then you protect them, don't you?'

'And you thought I might be protecting Skunk?'

'Something like that, yes.' Mia nodded. She sounded contrite.

'Number one,' Gabriel said, 'I'm sure Skunk can manage just fine on his own. Number two, we're no longer friends. Number three, even if we had still been friends, if I thought that he was involved in something that we – yes, I say *we* because I'm a part of this team, although it's clear that you don't think so – something that *we* were working on, I would never have held anything back.

Is that what you really think of me, Mia? And here was I thinking that we were—'

'Gabriel,' Mia said, looking truly sorry now. 'Of course you're a part of the team. Everyone likes you, and thinks you're doing a fantastic job, I mean, you've only been here six months and we can't manage without you, OK? Please believe that's how we see it.'

'Well, clearly it's not.'

'OK, please bear with me for a moment.'

'Go on?'

'A film appears right out of the blue. A hacker just *happens* to have found it. On a server he can't point us to. He gives it to an old colleague who works for the police. This colleague doesn't know *how to contact him*. I mean, if you were me? You would look into this? Wouldn't you?'

Gabriel mulled it over, and conceded that she did have a point.

'So?' Mia said, smiling at him. 'Are we good now? Interview over? Everything is all right? And you understand why? So we're done?'

'OK.' Gabriel nodded, smiling a little. 'So who have you been talking to?'

'About what?'

'About this? Your suspicion that I wasn't telling the truth?'

'Only Munch,' Mia said. 'And he thought I was wrong, just so you know.'

'Really?'

'I forget to think before I speak sometimes, and everybody here likes you. Have I done enough grovelling?'

'Yeah, all right,' Gabriel said.

'Great.' Mia smiled. 'Now I want to talk to you about the real reason I asked you in here. He tracked me down.'

'Who?'

'Skunk.'

'You're kidding? No. He hates the police.'

'I'm not joking,' Mia said. 'I was in the pub, and suddenly he just appeared.'

'That doesn't make any sense.' Gabriel sounded puzzled.

'No, it's weird, isn't it?'

'Totally.'

'That's what I thought. And he said some things which only you can help me with. Can we take a look at it?'

'Sure.' Gabriel nodded.

Chapter 58

It was much warmer here, in the new bed they had let him sleep in. He had been here for some days now, and still he did not know where he was, or who these people were, but they had told him that he was safe, and that he did not need to be scared any longer.

The little boy did not understand them, but they had given him food, and he was pleased about that, because he had not eaten for a long time.

The strange faces seemed nice, but they were also quite stupid. For example, they did not realize that the walls in their house were very thin and that he could hear them talking about him once he had gone to bed. His mum had always said that he should be wary of people, that they could not be trusted. He could see now that she had been right. Because these strangers said one thing to him when he was in the room and another when they were on the other side of the wall.

This is insane.

She has kept him a prisoner in that cabin for ten years.

He has never met other children.

Christ Almighty.

He sat underneath her for over a week.

Starving.

He tried to understand what they were talking about; he was no fool, they were clearly talking about him, but he could not grasp the full implications. Nor could he understand why his mum was not here. They had taken her down from the roof beam, the people who had turned up, and he had been looking forward to seeing her again, but she didn't seem ready, or maybe he was meant to wait for her here in this house with the strangers who could not be trusted. They were stupid, but their food was good. And the rooms were warm. And he was especially excited about the books. They had lots and lots of books.

They said that he had to talk to a man with a thin moustache who had a job as something called a psychologist. The man with the thin moustache said that he was allowed to eat the sweets in the bowl on the table between them, probably to trick him, like people did, but he ate them anyway, because they tasted nice, and he nodded in all the right places, while the man talked.

The man told him about something called death. That his mum was gone, and that she would never come back. To begin with, he did not believe him, of course, but as time passed, he began to think that maybe there was a grain of truth in it after all. Because no matter how long he waited and how much he hoped that she would be there when he opened his eyes under the duvet in the morning, she did not come. So this *death* place must exist after all, and his mum clearly intended to spend some time there. He did not know for how long, nor did he ask because, every time he opened his mouth, whether it was to the women who brought his food, or the psychologist man with the sweets, they would look at him strangely.

As if he were stupid.

They never said so outright, but he could see it in their eyes. So he stopped asking questions. He learned to nod instead. He smiled and he nodded, and they liked that. And the walls in the house were very thin, but because he became very good at not telling anyone how he felt, the words on the other side of the wall began to change when they discussed him.

He's doing incredibly well.

What a relief.

What a nightmare, can you imagine? All alone with a crazy mother in a cabin for ten years?

But now he's doing so well.

Have you noticed how clever he is? How much reading he's doing?

Did you hear what Nils said?

No, what did he say?

About the laptop?
What about it?
At first he didn't know what it was.
Really?
I mean, he has never seen one before, but now he uses it all the time. Nils said he has never seen anybody pick up something that quickly.

By now he had been there for a year. He had read all the books in the house several times, including the books the people told him were just for grown-ups.

Don't say mean things about my mum.

Once or twice, whatever was inside him had almost slipped out and made them take back the bad things they had said about his mum, but he had managed to control himself. He became very good at it. They never noticed.

Oh, he's so cute.

Yes, isn't he?

The voices through the wall. And that was how he wanted it. He did not like the words he had overheard the first nights. They had made him shiver under the duvet, even though he was quite warm.

But being here was nice in some ways.

Mostly because of the books.

And the other children.

Not to begin with. The children's faces had been strange, like those of the grown-ups, but once he had worked out how to copy them, learned not to be himself but merely smile and never show them how he felt on the inside, things had improved.

Still, it was the laptop that fascinated him more than anything.

It was a man called Nils who had first shown it to him. The small plastic rectangle which opened to reveal a whole new world.

'Have you really never seen a laptop before?'

And the little boy had felt it then, how the rage inside him nearly came out, but he had managed to keep his face clear of expression.

You would not believe the head on that boy.

Amazing, isn't it? Growing up in those circumstances, and doing as well as he is.

No, I mean it. He's like Beethoven.

I don't follow?

The moment Beethoven saw a piano, he knew what to do with it.

What?

Some people have to learn, but Beethoven, he just looked at it, sat down and started playing. He knew immediately what to do.

What are you talking about, Nils?

That boy had never seen a computer in all his life. But the moment he sat down in front of it, it was as if he just instinctively knew how it worked.

I'm so glad he's doing so well.

No, you don't understand. This boy is exceptional.

Two years passed. He grew used to all the different flavours of sweets. And although the children would come and go, he enjoyed being with them. Death was clearly an important person who was looking after his mum until she was ready to come back. In time he began to feel that this place was almost his home. It was nothing like life with his mum, obviously, but it was all right. The voices behind the wall now said only nice things about him. The children in the school playground were happy to play football with him or climb on the climbing frame. He was content to wait here. For death to finish with his mum. He slept better at nights. He felt happy every time he woke up.

Right until the day when a car pulled into the yard outside the house and one of the women who looked after him came over to him.

'I want you to meet someone.'

'Yes?' he had replied with his smiling face.

'You're going to get a new home.'

He struggled to make sense of the words.

'Hello,' said a woman with blonde hair who had emerged from the unfamiliar car.

'Hello,' he said, holding out his hand and bowing like he had been taught he should.

'My name is Helene,' the smiling woman said. 'Helene Eriksen.'

'Why don't we all go inside and get to know each other?' said the woman who looked after him.

So that is what they had done, gone inside, and there were crusty rolls on a plate on the table and red squash for him to drink, and then the face of the new woman had grown serious and she had put her hand on his shoulder.

'We're so happy about it, we really are. That you are going to be a part of our family now.'

The boy did not understand what was happening, and the thing inside him bared its teeth, but he had managed to smile at her all the same, with that face he had learned to show the outside world.

Chapter 59

Mia Krüger carried her coffee cup back to the table and picked up a newspaper along the way. She flicked through it, but the articles depressed her, so she put it down and focused on something positive. The taste of her cortado. And the fact that she had struck gold with her first attempt. She was always reluctant to call other departments for help, but the investigator from Kripos had been more than willing.

Police clueless.

Who killed Camilla Green?

She got this feeling every time she flicked through the tabloids, that it was a kind of battle. The police versus the killer. It was childish. Firstly, if the police did not catch the killer immediately, they were vilified. Secondly – and this was possibly her pet hate – this adulation of criminals. No matter how dreadful their crimes, endless column inches were devoted to them. Mia took another sip of her coffee and started to think that Munch might have a point after all: he despised reporters. She had never really minded them before. Even when they had hounded her back when she shot Markus Skog and she had been forced to hide out in a hotel in Majorstuen. Idiots, did they not see they were part of the problem? That there were people out there who would do anything for their fifteen minutes of fame?

Mark Chapman, who had shot John Lennon.

Just to get his name in the papers.

John Hinckley, who had shot Ronald Reagan in an attempt to impress the actress Jodie Foster.

Were reporters really that ignorant about recent history? Did they not realize the part they played?

Ritual murder unsolved.

Police outwitted.

She tried not to read the headlines, but it was hard not to. She had put down her newspaper, but people around her were still holding theirs up, normal people out for lunch, with an unswerving belief that the media told the truth.

Mia had never seen him before, but he was not difficult to spot; he might as well have worn a sign as he came through the doors and scouted for her across the room.

Kripos.

Cybercrime Unit.

The man in the suit nodded when he saw her, made a beeline for her table, and they shook hands.

'Robert Larsen,' he introduced himself, and sat down.

'Mia Krüger.'

'How nice to finally meet you.' The man smiled. 'And how convenient that you called today, of all days.'

'Why?'

'Kristian Karlsen,' Larsen said with another small smile.

'You mean Skunk?'

'Yes, Skunk,' the Kripos investigator said, then summoned the waiter and pointed to Mia's cup to indicate that he wanted the same.

He took a file from his briefcase and placed it on the table in front of her.

'I must admit that I was surprised to get your call. We've had him on our radar for a while, but I didn't know that it was that serious.'

'What do you mean?'

'Murder,' Larsen said. 'I mean, we have a lot on him, but nothing that points in that direction.'

'Like I said on the phone, we don't know very much yet,' Mia said. 'But we thought it was worth checking out.'

'I get it.' The Kripos investigator smiled and winked at her. 'Top secret, eh?'

Mia did not like much about this man, but she decided not to let on. 'So what have you got?'

'Kristian Karlsen.' Larsen cleared his throat and opened the file in front of him. 'A black hacker. You're familiar with the term?'

Mia nodded. Skunk had used the term himself, so she had looked it up. There were different types of hackers. She believed that Gabriel was a white hacker. One of the good guys.

'And you have heard of the group Anonymous? Lulz-Sec?'

'I've heard about Anonymous,' Mia said.

'They're becoming quite the celebrities these days,' Larsen said, as the waiter brought his coffee. 'They came from a place called 4chan/b/. Have you heard of that?'

'Definitely not.' Mia smiled, sensing this was the way forward with him. Feign ignorance, even though Gabriel had explained some of it to her. The man opposite her seemed to enjoy showing off, and all she cared about was the contents of the folder on the table.

'The long or the short version?' Larsen asked her.

'Short version, please.'

'OK. The website 4chan. Nothing but a bunch of young idiots, really. Misfits. Right up until they realized how many they were.'

Larsen took a sip of his coffee.

'I see,' Mia said.

'Yes, I'm talking about people who don't fit in,' he explained. 'Who now hold the power. I mean, these guys, teenagers, they might be only fourteen or fifteen years old, but they can bring society to a halt if they want to.'

'How?'

'Air traffic, streetlights, banks, water supply – seriously, everything is computerized now; nothing is written down on paper these days. Do you follow?'

'Oh, I see.' Mia nodded.

'DDOS,' Larsen said.

'What?'

The man in the suit smiled. 'A DDOS attack? Do you know what that is?'

'No idea.'

The suit from Kripos grinned again. He seemed enormously pleased with his opportunity to hold forth.

'Basically, it's what happens when hackers send an extreme number of requests to a website, so many that, ultimately, it can't cope with them and it crashes. They've done this with big companies, who have been forced to take down their websites temporarily.'

'I understand,' Mia said and glanced at the file on the table in front of her. 'But what does that have to do with Skunk?'

'We believe that Kristian Karlsen is one of the people here in Norway who was behind these attacks. And the FBI has asked us to make sure that he's punished for it.'

'Do you have any actual evidence?'

'About what?'

'That Skunk was a part of this?'

'We're almost one hundred per cent sure,' Larsen said, taking another sip of his coffee.

'That means no.'

'Oh no, we're just biding our time.' The man in the suit winked at her.

'What do you mean?'

'What you have to realize is that these people are incredibly good at hiding. Online, I mean.'

'But you already know where he is?'

'In real life?'

'Yes.'

'Of course. We have had him under surveillance for a long time.'

'So you know where Skunk lives?'

'We would be pretty rubbish at our job if we didn't, don't you think?'

'Any chance that I, well, that I might be . . .'

Mia had not even completed her sentence before Larsen took a sheet of paper from his file and pushed it across to her.

'That's where he is?' Mia said, staring incredulously at the address in front of her.

The man in the suit nodded.

'You owe me one.' Larsen raised the coffee cup to his lips and winked at her again.

'Definitely,' Mia said, and forced a smile. 'Thank you.'

'Any time. You'll keep me posted?'

'Absolutely. Again, thank you.' Mia smiled, emptied her coffee cup, left the café as quickly as she could, found her mobile and rang Munch.

Chapter 60

Miriam Munch was in the car on her way back from Gardermoen Airport with Marion in the rear. She had felt guilty and dishonest, but it had gone better than expected, mainly because they had been late. Johannes had practically had to run through Security, so there had been no time for long goodbyes.

'Don't get eaten by a shark,' Marion had said, giving her dad a big hug.

'I promise.' Johannes smiled, and just had time to give Miriam a quick kiss.

They had waved him through and, a moment later, Marion had seemed a little sad at him leaving, but, sitting in the car now, she seemed to have bounced back. Mostly because Miriam had broken one of her rules and allowed the little girl to watch a movie on her iPad in the car.

She could still change her mind, she could; she did not have to see Ziggy again, she could drop out of the raid tomorrow night; but though she had a choice, she knew that it was already too late. She had not spoken to Johannes; it would have wrecked his trip and she did not want to spoil it for him, but when he came back, she would tell him.

It would be a relief in so many ways. Honesty. Not having to sneak around any more. She glanced up at the rear-view mirror and saw her pretty daughter laugh at something on the screen, and she felt another pang of guilt, but ignored it.

Marion was going to be fine.

Miriam was absolutely sure of it.

'Am I going to Grannie's?' the little girl said, as she saw that they had pulled up outside the white house in Røa.

'Yes.' Miriam nodded, getting out of the car and waving to her mother, who was already on the doorstep waiting for them.

'Yeeees!' Marion exclaimed, and could barely sit still long enough to get out of her seatbelt.

'Did it go OK?' Marianne Munch asked, taking the overnight bag from Miriam.

'Yes, we were a bit late setting off, but we got there in time.'

'Grannie, please can I watch TV?' Marion said, running straight inside the house without waiting for a reply.

'So, until Wednesday?' her mother said, looking at Miriam.

'Yes, do you mind?'

'Of course not.'

'I'm only glad you can help Julie,' her mother said, and again Miriam felt a little guilty, but lying was her only option; she could not tell her mother what she was really doing.

An illegal raid.

Don't tell anyone.

A little white lie.

'But apart from that, is she OK? I haven't seen her for ages.'

'Yes, but you know what she's like. Terribly sensitive. Boy trouble, that's all. It'll pass.'

'Yes, I know, it's not easy, but I'm glad that she has you,' her mother said, stroking her cheek lightly. 'Do you want to say bye to Mummy?' she called out down the hallway, and Marion came running and gave her a quick hug.

'I'll see you on Wednesday.' Miriam smiled and headed back to the car.

'Give my love to Julie.' Her mother waved and went back inside the white house.

Chapter 61

Mia Krüger had a horrible feeling that she had made a huge mistake as she stood next to Munch behind the window to the interview room. The young hacker with the black-and-white hair sat very still. He looked at them. Although he could not see them, he knew that they were there, and he had sat like this without saying anything at all ever since they brought him in, more than twenty-four hours ago.

'Still nothing?' Anette Goli said, joining them.

'No.' Mia heaved a sigh.

'He keeps saying the same thing?'

'Exactly the same thing every time,' Munch said, scratching his beard.

'He still doesn't want a lawyer?'

'No, he says he doesn't need one,' Mia said, looking back at the young man, who continued to sit very still, his eyes fixed on them.

'Well, he's right about that,' Goli said, and took a seat.

'Nothing from his computers?' Munch asked.

'No,' Anette said. 'I've just spoken to one of our technicians, and they can't find anything. He seemed almost impressed.'

'In what way?' Mia asked.

'There's nothing there,' Goli said, throwing up her hands.

'There must have been something?' Munch insisted.

'No,' Goli said, shaking her head. 'All gone. Completely blank.'

'What do you mean?'

'There's *nothing* there. And I don't mean there was nothing incriminating. They were quite simply blank.'

'How odd,' Munch said.

'I took the liberty of asking Gabriel how that was possible. I hope that was all right. He didn't seem to be in the best of moods – has something happened?'

'My fault,' Mia said. 'I was too hard on him. I have apologized. I'm hoping it'll pass.'

'Right,' Anette said. 'You accused him of being an accomplice because he knows Skunk, but didn't know where he was. Is that what you're saying?'

Mia could hear the sarcasm but ignored it; she had too many other things on her mind.

'I'll make it up to Gabriel. Like I said, I've already apologized.'

'Good,' Anette said and exhaled. 'Because it's a little far-fetched, isn't it?'

Mia could feel that the police lawyer was looking at Munch.

'What is?' Mia said, mildly irritated.

'Why is he really here?' She nodded towards the young hacker, who had yet to move.

'He brought us the film,' Munch said.

'In order to help us?'

'Possibly,' Munch said. 'But—'

'So what did Gabriel say?' Mia interrupted.

'About what?'

'About there being nothing on the computers we found at Skunk's place.'

'Pretty much the same reaction as the other technician I spoke to,' Anette said. 'He was impressed.'

'Can anyone explain to me what's going on?' Munch asked, turning to them. 'I know I'm from a different age, and I'm sorry if I need to be spoon-fed, but why was there nothing on his computers? And why do IT guys find this so impressive?'

The fat investigator looked at them both now, and it was clear that he had not understood a word of their conversation.

'It's impressive because they are nerds,' Mia said, without taking her eyes off the room next door. 'Skunk was clearly prepared. In case someone raided his bunker, like we did, he had set up a system that would delete everything.'

SAMUEL BJORK

'And that's impressive because . . .?' Munch asked, still looking quizzical.

'Because it's not easy,' Anette said.

'OK,' Munch said. 'So what have we got? What's next?'

'We have nothing,' Anette Goli said. 'All we have is a theory.' She looked somewhat uneasily at Mia now. 'And the fact that he brought us the film.'

'And that means what?' Munch said.

'What do you mean?' Goli said.

'I mean, how long can we keep him? Where do we go from here?'

'There's no doubt that he knows his rights.' Goli said with a sigh, glancing at the young hacker. 'If I've understood you correctly, he has stated only his name, his date of birth and his address.'

Mia nodded.

'Several times.' Munch sighed now.

'And, as you know, that's all he is required to do under the law,' the police lawyer continued. 'This young man knows exactly where we are. After four hours, we need to charge him, then we have twenty-four hours to bring him before a judge to apply for him to be remanded in custody—'

'We know how to do our job.' Mia cut her off, somewhat impatiently.

'As we arrested him on a Sunday,' Anette Goli said, ignoring her, 'which is not a working day, we could have kept him longer, if we had charged him, which we didn't do yesterday because, well, because all we can charge him with is helping us and, the last time I checked, that wasn't a crime. Right now, we're the ones breaking the law. With every passing minute.'

Anette tapped her wrist in order to emphasize her point, and Mia felt even more irritated, but she knew perfectly well that Goli was right.

'So, we're not going to charge him?'

Munch looked at Mia.

'We have nothing to charge him with,' Anette said.

'Perverting the course of justice?' Mia suggested.

318

'How?'

'He said he found the film on a server in a second-hand book-shop in Ullevålsveien, which Grønlie checked, and it doesn't exist.'

'And when did the suspect make this false statement?'

Goli had put on her lawyer voice now.

'You already know that,' Mia said. 'At the pub.'

'So the suspect was in a state of intoxication when he spoke to you? When he spoke to a police officer, who was also under the influence of alcohol? Without a lawyer present? I would also like to point out, Your Honour, that the accused is a teetotaller, and normally doesn't drink alcohol and, that night, my client—'

'All right, all right,' Munch said, holding up his hands.

'We have nothing,' Goli reiterated.

'What did you just say?' Mia asked.

'We can't charge him with anything,' Anette said again.

'No, not that. He doesn't drink alcohol – how do you know that?'

'Gabriel told me.'

'But why . . .?' Mia stared at the young hacker. 'He felt bad about something,' she mumbled.

'What?' Munch said.

'If he doesn't drink? Why track me down? Why drink that night? He must have felt guilty.'

'We have to release him,' the police lawyer urged them. 'This is nonsense. He is just here because Mia had a *hunch*. I mean, ser-iously. I know you're brilliant, Mia, but hello? Holger? Keeping him here is illegal. If he wants to sue us, he has grounds.'

'What did Kripos say?' Munch wanted to know.

'They haven't got anything either.' Anette sighed. 'He's on their list, that's all. I mean, if they had been able to arrest him for something, they would have done so a long time ago.'

'You're sure of that? That he doesn't usually drink?' Mia said, without looking at Anette.

'Gabriel told me,' Goli said. 'Why would he lie?' She looked towards Munch again, and threw up her hands. 'I mean, for God's sake, the boy came to us with a film he had found, he helped our investigation, he's been sitting in there for far too long, we have nothing to charge him with. Kripos has nothing on him. The boy is clean.'

'Give me five minutes,' Mia said.

'Holger?' Anette appealed to him. 'We have no grounds on which to . . .'

Mia never heard the end of the sentence, because she had already left. She opened the door to the room, where Skunk was sitting with his hands in his lap, his back just as straight as when they brought him in.

'Hi,' Mia said, sitting down on the chair opposite him.

Skunk looked at her.

'Aren't you going to turn on the recorder? The time is 18.05. Interview resumed. Present in the room is Mia Krüger—'

'No,' Mia said, folding her arms on the table and resting her head on them.

'My name is Kristian Karlsen,' the young hacker reeled off. 'I was born on 5 April 1989. My current address is—'

'Yes, Skunk, you've told us. We get it. You know how this works, your rights and all that.'

Mia leaned back in the chair and looked at him. The hacker with the black-and-white hair met her gaze, and still he did not move.

'Listen . . .'

'My name is Kristian Karlsen—' he began again, but Mia cut him off.

'OK, Skunk, my mistake. OK? My mistake.'

The hacker continued to sit very still, and Mia did not say anything either. She had a feeling about something here, but she could not identify what it was.

He had come to her.

Found her at Lorry.

He had drunk alcohol. Although he usually didn't drink.

'It doesn't count unless you turn on the tape recorder,' Skunk said. 'Unless the people next door are recording it, but that's no use, because, as far as I'm aware, the person being interviewed—'

'OK, Skunk,' Mia interrupted him again, putting her hand to her head. 'We're not going to charge you. We have nothing to charge you with. According to my colleague in there' – she gestured to the window behind her – 'you're a hero. You helped our investigation, gave us information we would never have found without you, OK?'

The young man in front of her continued to sit very still, not taking his eyes off her.

'My mistake, OK, Skunk? Can we leave it at that?'

'My name is Kristian Karlsen—'

Mia cut him off again.

'I've already said that I made a mistake. I'm sorry, OK? Sometimes – well, quite often, this doesn't work.' Mia pressed her finger against her temple, and smiled faintly. 'Today, I've already managed to make a young man I really like, a colleague who is incredibly dedicated and hard-working, feel like a piece of crap, and yes, again it was my fault, but I just . . .' Mia fell quiet again.

'You need to turn on the recorder,' Skunk said.

'This is what I've been thinking,' Mia said. 'And you don't need to say anything. But bear with me here. Can you do that?'

Skunk stared at her, still without moving a muscle.

'This is my life, OK, can I tell you a bit about that?' Mia said. 'We find a naked girl in the woods. She has been killed. Someone strangled her. Someone placed her on a bed of feathers. In a penta-gram of candles. A human being. A young woman. Her whole life in front of her. And it haunts me. I can't sleep. Do you understand, Skunk? This is my life. This is my job. Making sure that the sick son of a bitch who thinks he can take a pretty young girl like her, do what he likes to her and get away with it, gets his just punishment. That's how I feel from the moment I wake up in the morning till I go to bed at night. Do you understand?'

Mia could almost hear what Munch must be thinking through the wall behind her now, and she expected him to intervene at any moment, but she no longer cared. Even if they could not charge Skunk with anything. Even if the law was on his side. There was something he was not telling them.

321

Mia looked up at the young hacker again, and she could see that the stony expression he had worn for the last twenty-four hours was starting to soften.

'You have to turn on the recorder, if . . .' Skunk said, but he did not finish his sentence.

'OK,' Mia continued. 'I don't think you did it. We can't charge you with anything, and the lads from IT think you're one hell of a guy because you managed to wipe your computers when they tried to look at them – not that I give a toss about that. Congratulations to you: you're the greatest hacker in the world, or whatever you want to be. I really don't care.'

The young man in front of her sat very still.

'This is what I'm thinking,' Mia went on. 'You had nothing to do with this. You would never do anything like this, hurt anyone like that. Of course you wouldn't.'

Skunk still said nothing.

'But,' Mia said, 'I think you feel guilty about something. That was why you came to see me. I wondered about it down at Lorry, why a young man like you got so drunk in such a short time, and now I've learned that you don't usually drink. So there's my theory.'

The hacker in front of her kept his mouth closed, but the expression in his eyes had changed.

'So you came to me,' Mia continued, 'and at first I couldn't work out how you found me, but then I realized how simple it was. Everyone in my unit has mobiles with GPS and all that – it was easy for you to hack our system and track us all – but then why drink yourself into a stupor if you had something important to tell me?'

The young man kept his silence.

'What I think is this,' Mia went on. 'You found this film and it made you feel just as sick as we did when we saw it. But then . . .'

She paused and looked at him, and she could see that his eyes were not as hard as they had been.

'But then you realized that you were somehow involved. I'm not saying that you're an accomplice. Or that you knew that you were being paid to make something which would be used to commit a crime. And I don't know what the hell they're called, or what the difference is – JavaScript, Flash programming; Christ, I can barely work my own email – but you do, don't you? You're the best. Our engineers are singing your praises, you're that brilliant. Some time ago, someone – and I bet you don't even know their name – paid you to create something. Devise a program, write machine code that would enable them to transmit a live feed globally in that part of the Internet I know nothing about. And that was what you had worked out. That, though you didn't know it, you had been party to a serious crime. So you got drunk, something you never do, and came to me. You who hate the authorities. It would never cross your mind to help the police. Yet you found me, and you were going to tell me, weren't you? That you had made something for an anonymous client? You had been paid, but the client had used you. And that's why you came. Am I close, Skunk? Is that why you tracked me down?'

The young man with the black-and-white hair looked at her with an expression in his eyes she could not quite fathom.

'My name is Kristian Karlsen,' Skunk said, fixing his gaze on the table. 'My date of birth is 5 April 1989. My current address is—'

The door behind him opened, and Munch entered the interview room.

'You're free to go. We won't be charging you with anything, and I'm sorry that we kept you here longer than we should have. If you can help us in any other way, we would be very grateful. You know where to find us.'

Mia saw the young hacker get up and head for the door. As he left the room, he stopped for a moment and looked at her and, for a fraction of a second, she thought he might say something, but then he closed his mouth and was gone.

'Mia?' Munch said, looking at her. 'A word?'

Mia Krüger got slowly up from the chair and followed her boss out of the interview room.

SEVEN

Chapter 62

Mia got into her car as soon as she woke up, but day did not break until she reached the cemetery. She should have been at the briefing meeting, but had asked for time off, and Munch had been happy to give her that. She had asked only for a few hours, but Munch had made it very clear that she could take as long as she needed. Her behaviour yesterday had only reinforced her indulgent boss's opinion that she was not well. That she should not have been back at work.

Mia got out of her car, fetched the flowers from the back and walked slowly towards the graves. She tended to her grandmother's grave first. Then her parents'. She saved the biggest bouquet for last, and stood in front of the grey stone with the same deep grief she always had out here.

Sigrid Krüger
Sister, friend and daughter.
Born 11 November 1979. Died 18 April 2002.

It had been more than ten years, but it still weighed so heavily on her that she did not want to live. People said that the pain of grief would pass, diminish. That time was a great healer. But not for her. Mia Krüger felt the loss of her sister just as strongly now as the day her body was discovered in that filthy basement in Tøyen.

Mia removed the flowers that had been killed by the frost and placed the new bouquet in a pot in front of the gravestone. She knelt down to clear away twigs and leaves, and the grass felt cold to the touch. Winter had come far too early, and it would only get worse. And darker. Like her thoughts. Perhaps they were better off without her. The team. After all, she had made up her mind, hadn't she? To leave all this behind?

She felt barely human, anyway, so why not just let go? Her body and her mind were running on artificial stimulants: alcohol, pills; she had opened the pill jar again last night and let the little white friends lull her to sleep; she had been exhausted after the interview. Her body was full of sharp thorns. Anette Goli had patronized her and shaken her head – *I think you need to go back to your therapist* – even Holger had mumbled into his beard and left her standing alone in the corridor.

Yes, sure. You can have some time off, Mia.

Take all the time you need.

So she had imploded. At home in her empty flat. Given up trying to act like a normal human being. Be positive. Quit the pills. Hell, no. She had been tempted to end it right there and then, but she had not had enough pills. She had swallowed most of them that afternoon when Holger had unexpectedly knocked on her door, and she had not got round to getting more. She had enough to knock herself out, make the thorns in her body stop hurting her; she had curled up in a blanket on the balcony and let the city lights dance in front of her eyes until they finally grew so blurry that she did not know whether or not she was dreaming. She had staggered inside, huddled under the blanket, her cheeks red, cold on the outside but warm on the inside, and her final thought before she disappeared was:

I'm coming, Sigrid.

And yet she had woken up after all, in a dark and lonely room, and she could not stand it any longer. No more loneliness. She wanted to be with them. This was where she belonged.

Mia got up and looked at the grave in front of her. She would lie next to her sister. She smiled faintly; it was a thought that had not occurred to her before, but it soothed her. Her parents were in the same grave, of course. What a dimwit she had been. She should be lying next to Sigrid. It was how it ought to be.

Sigrid and Mia Krüger

Snow White and Sleeping Beauty

Born 11 November 1979.
Together for ever.
'What medication are you currently on?'

Her therapist. Mattias Wang. One of his many questions she had no interest in answering.

'There are new drugs that I think might help you feel a bit better. If you decide to pursue that option, I mean?'

She had no interest in feeling better. Did they not get it? Why was that so hard to understand? She wanted to disappear, that was her goal. And she had already made up her mind. Leave the world behind. She had found the perfect spot. Hitra. An island in the sea, where the sky looked as if it carried on for ever. Then Munch had turned up and brought her back. And she had solved the case. But still she was not free. She had been suspended, but she had clung to a belief that her colleagues were her new family, and that, if only she could get back to work, then everything would be all right. Only it wasn't.

It was clear now, wasn't it?

Not just to her, but to everyone else.

The look Anette had given her. Munch's eyes as he told her she could take as much time off as she needed.

Mia pulled her woolly hat further down over her ears and stood in front of the grave with a sense of serenity she had not experienced for a long time.

Come, Mia, come.

Home. A kind of home. It was becoming increasingly clear to her now, as she stood facing the frost-covered stone. End this. She had tried, but she was clearly no longer up to the job. She had lost her touch. Her ability to help. To enter the minds of these sick people. She had been suspended. Only to suffer on her own every night in a cold flat in a cold city; she did not need that any more. They could manage without her.

Take as long as you need.

Would they miss her? Yes, perhaps, but so what? What good would it do? Would solving this case help? There would always be new cases. They had fetched her from peaceful Hitra in order to help them, and she had done that. Only it had not been the end of it, had it? There were fresh cruelties. Mia Krüger made her living from her mind, delving into this darkness that had always been a part of her.

Mia muttered curses under her breath. She detested the feeling that had come over her. This weakness. It was not like her. She had made a mistake with the hacker. Skunk. She had looked like an idiot in front of the others.

Sigrid and Mia Krüger
Born 11 November 1979.

A new gravestone. She would need to organize that. To be sure to get the wording right.

Together for ever.

She had organized all three gravestones. Four funerals. Her whole family, everyone she loved, she had arranged them all. She knew exactly who to call to get the stone she wanted.

Mia took her mobile out of her pocket with cold, stiff fingers, just as it started ringing with a number she did not recognize, and she answered out of habit: 'Yes?'

An unfamiliar voice on the other end, and Mia had to concentrate to make out what the caller was saying. It was an elderly woman.

'My name is Ruth Lie,' the woman's voice said. 'Am I speaking to Mia Krüger?'

'Yes?'

'I work at the Natural History Museum in Tøyen,' the voice said. 'I gather you wanted me to call you?'

'Ruth who?' Mia said, regretting taking the call.

'Lie,' the voice continued. 'The Natural History Museum. Olsen, our senior curator, gave me your card. I believe you had some questions about a school visit?'

Her brain slowly went into action and, finally, it came back: Tor Olsen's secretary. Up at the Botanical Gardens.

'Yes, of course, hello,' Mia said. 'How can I help you?'

'We have it,' said Ruth Lie, who sounded brighter than her boss.

'Have what?' Mia said.

'Am I speaking to the right person?' said the voice on the phone. 'Mia Krüger?'

She left the phone for a moment, as if she wanted to double-check the business card Mia had left with the curator.

'Yes, that's me.' Mia cleared her throat.

'You're looking for a list of all the schools who have visited us recently?'

'Yes, that's it,' Mia said, pulling herself together.

'I have it here in front of me,' the voice continued. 'Are you interested in anyone in particular?'

'Hurumlandet Nurseries,' Mia said, starting to get a grip.

'Ah, you mean Helene,' the woman chirped.

'Have they visited you?'

'Oh, yes, they come here every year. They're not like most schools, are they, but she does a great job, and I always enjoy their visits. You know, the young people there, everything they have been through, and what she has achieved. I'm so happy every time she calls.'

'So they've been?'

'Oh, yes, every summer,' Ruth Lie said. 'Our gardens – well, you've been here?'

'Yes, I've been there. So when did they last visit?'

'The third of August,' the woman on the phone said. 'Every year. Always early August. Olsen said you were asking about CCTV recordings? It's about the break-in, isn't it?'

'Yes,' Mia said. 'The stolen owls.'

'I'm so glad that someone cares,' the voice on the phone went on. 'You know what the police are like. Break-ins and burglaries, it's almost as if people can get away with anything these days.'

'I do understand,' Mia said, managing to follow the conversation now. 'So? What do you have?'

'Footage of everyone who visits the museum. No night-time recordings – our budget won't stretch to that – but we have footage of everyone who visits during opening hours.'

'Including the group from Hurumlandet?'

'Of course,' the voice on the phone said. 'Do you think it might have been one of them?'

'What?'

331

There was a pause, as if the voice on the phone still did not quite believe she was speaking to the right person.

'Someone from Helene's group? Who stole the owls?'

'We don't know that yet,' Mia said, pulling herself together again.

'I really hope not, but – who knows? They're not regular students, are they?'

'No,' Mia mumbled.

'So do you want me to send it to you?'

Mia Krüger had a strong urge to just hang up. The real world in her ear. They could all go to hell. She had made up her mind, yet they had talked her into coming back. She had done what she was supposed to. Talked to a therapist, trying to become normal not for her personal benefit, but so that they could use her for their own ends.

'Hello?' the voice on the phone said again.

'It would be great if you could send it over,' Mia said. 'But don't send it to me. Please would you email it to my colleague, Ludvig Grønlie?'

'Of course,' Ruth Lie said. 'Do you have his email address?'

Mia found Grønlie's details on her mobile and gave them to the woman on the other end.

'Great. I'll send it as soon as I've spoken to our technician, who has the footage.'

'Good.' Mia nodded. 'Thank you so much.'

'Happy to help,' the voice on the phone said, and disappeared.

Mia looked at her phone and decided to turn it off. There was no need to have it switched on any more. No need to be in contact with the rest of the world. She was done with it. So done with it.

Together for ever.

She pressed her finger against the top of her mobile, intending to keep it there – one final push and it would go black – when it started ringing again.

She stared at the display.

Curry.

Mia pressed *ignore*, but to no avail; his name reappeared a few seconds later.

'Yes?' She sighed as she answered her phone.

'Where are you?' Curry asked. He sounded excited and breathless, almost as if he had run a marathon.

'Åsgårdstrand,' Mia said absent-mindedly.

'Why weren't you at the briefing?'

Mia said nothing. Curry just carried on.

'I've just had a call from Sunniva. You have to come in.'

Mia shook her head. Curry and Sunniva. Trouble in paradise. Mia no longer cared.

'Listen—' she began, but he refused to shut up.

'No, it's not what you're thinking,' Curry said, as if he could read her mind. 'She has been calling me for days, only I didn't pick up, because I . . .'

Two crows were sitting in a tree. Mia watched them while Curry's voice droned on in her ear. They looked peaceful as they sat there. Two birds in a tree in a cemetery. Soon there would be two girls sharing the grave below them. She smiled faintly to herself as the crows took off and flew towards the pale October sun.

'What?' she exclaimed, as Curry's news slowly sank in.

'I know,' Curry enthused. 'Sounds insane, doesn't it, but I believe her, there's no reason for her to lie. I know her, she would never—'

'Tell me again,' Mia interrupted him, feeling herself slowly wake up.

'A vicar, a patient at the hospice, who knew them when they were little,' Curry panted, far away. 'Helene Eriksen. She has a brother.'

He was rambling now. He could barely get the words out in the right order.

'He wanted to confess his sins. He's dying, I think. Something about him not going to Heaven unless he put things right.'

'Helene Eriksen has a brother who is dying?'

'No, not him, the vicar. Listen, why don't you just come over? They're waiting for us upstairs, and I don't want to meet her on my own, you know . . . Something about a sect in Australia. And him taking money. He wants to atone for his sins.'

'Curry,' Mia said, trying to calm her colleague down, but he refused to be placated.

'He came home sick.'

'The vicar?'

'No, the brother. Sick in the head.'

'Curry.'

'They're waiting for us now, they've asked us to come—'

'Curry,' Mia said, sternly now, and finally managed to shut the bulldog up.

'Yes?'

'Haven't we had enough of this by now?'

'What?' Curry was confused.

'Random people confessing to killing her?'

'What do you mean?'

Mia heaved a sigh. She regretted taking the call. Not turning off her mobile.

'Fuglesang with his bicycle helmet. God knows how many others have called. I don't know why, but, in cases like these, some people are overcome with an urge to confess their sins. You know that, don't you? And this time – who did you say he was? A vicar on his deathbed? I mean, give me a—'

'He knew stuff,' Curry went on, but Mia could feel she was already drifting away again.

No. Enough. No more.

'I believe they were given money,' Curry said, refusing to give up. 'When they came home. Some form of compensation. Helene Eriksen opened the Nurseries. And her brother bought a grocery shop when he had recovered.'

Mia was only half listening. The crows had disappeared, and the cemetery lay completely silent around her.

'Talk to Munch.' She sighed.

'He's in a bloody awful mood. Have the two of you had a row?'

'Listen, Curry,' Mia began, but she did not have the energy to go on.

'It sounds legit,' Curry said, refusing to back down. 'Sunniva called and talked for ten minutes without a break. I mean, the fact that she even called me . . .'

Something else popped up in her head as Curry continued rambling into her ear.

'What did you say?' Mia said, now fully engaged.

'That we have to check it out—'

'No, not that. Helene Eriksen. She has a brother?'

'Yes, he runs a shop in the area, but I . . .'

Jim Fuglesang.

'I mean, why else would she call me, you know she doesn't want to talk to me, so . . .'

The white van in the yard.

'Anyway, it's worth checking out this vicar. I mean, it's not as if we have a lot else to . . .'

His eyes over the beard.

In the middle of nowhere.

Delivering groceries.

Outside the cottage which had given her the creeps.

'Find Munch,' she said quickly, and started running down the gravel path.

The logo on the side of the van.

Hurumlandet Supermarket.

'Eh?' Curry said.

'Get hold of Holger. Tell him to meet us there.'

'You think there might be something in it?'

Mia fumbled for her keys in her pocket. 'Where does she work?'

'St Helena's Hospice, it's a private hospital up at—'

'Text me the address,' Mia said, getting into the car.

'What do you mean? Are you coming in?'

'I'm on my way. Get hold of Munch. Now.'

Mia rang off, stuck the key in the ignition and heard the wheels spin on the gravel as she stamped on the accelerator and saw the cemetery disappear in her rear-view mirror.

Chapter 63

Isabella Jung sat in her bedroom with butterflies in her tummy. It was not yet time, but it soon would be. Soon it would happen. She had dressed up. She was not wearing her ripped jeans; today, she was wearing a dress, she had put on make-up, spent hours in front of the mirror – not that it mattered, perhaps, how she looked, but, she had decided to dress up all the same. Do her hair. She smiled as she twirled around.

Please would you meet me? In secret.

Just you and me?

Four o'clock behind the hideout.

Are you my chosen one?

The fifteen-year-old girl could barely believe her luck. It was almost like a dream, all of it. All these years. First in Hammerfest with her mum. Then with all these strange families where she did not belong. The tiny voice at the back of her head that kept saying to her:

One day.

One fine day, Isabella.

Everything will turn out all right.

Only it had not seemed like it. She had been angry with the voice many times. It had lied to her, tricked her, said things to make her feel better, and she had almost given up hope at the eating-disorder clinic in Ullevål, when she had found the knife in the kitchen and cut into her head. Afterwards they had called her crazy, but she was not, she had only tried to cut it out, make it go away. This stupid voice that had promised her so much but only ever lied to her and deceived her, and yet it had turned out to be truthful after all. She had apologized to it, the voice, some days after arriving at

Hurumlandet Nurseries. Because it had been right. Not immediately, but over time. The peace and the security. Her very own room. The flowers. Helene, who made her feel good about herself. As if she were worth something. She had apologized many times in her bed at night.

Sorry, you were right.

And the voice had forgiven her.

Never mind, and it's going to get even better for you.

And now she realized what it had meant. She got up and admired herself in the mirror once more. Smiled at herself and ran her hands across the white dress.

Four o'clock behind the hideout.

Her cheeks were tingling now. She sat down on the bed, only to get straight up again. Two hours to go. Dear God, how would she cope? How slowly the hands moved. Way too slowly. She paced restlessly up and down the floor a couple of times, not knowing what to do with herself.

You'll be fine, the voice said. *It's only two hours.*

Isabella Jung nodded in response, and calmly sat down on her bed again, regretting not listening to it all the time, like she ought to have done.

It would be all right.

Everything would be just fine.

She closed her eyes, and tried imagining what it would be like.

Behind the hideout.

In just a few hours.

The fifteen-year-old rested her head on the pillow, and she smiled as she curled up very carefully so the white dress would not get creased.

Chapter 64

Munch took another deep drag on his cigarette; he was finding it hard to think straight. The headache. The nail going into his brain. He had swallowed painkillers throughout the day, but it refused to shift. Yesterday had been bad enough, with Mia's performance in the interview room, and Anette Goli, who had been after him about all the rules they had broken, bringing in and keeping Skunk purely on a hunch of Mia's. He had seen it in Anette's eyes. The accusations.

He was a crap boss.

He pulled the hood of his duffel coat over his head and lit another cigarette with the tip from the first as he felt another dart of pain to his temple; he was forced to close his eyes and breathe deeply while he waited for it to subside. What the hell was this? He knew he was not the fittest person on the planet, but he had never felt pain like this before. Well, once before, but that was more than fifteen years ago. When he had lost his father. The days leading up to it. An articulated lorry on the other side of the road, and an intoxicated driver. The same nail into his brain, a physical manifestation that something terrible was about to happen. He did not believe in omens, though, obviously.

Munch closed his eyes until the pain began to fade away, and took a fresh drag on his cigarette as Mia emerged from the imposing front door of the grand building. A private hospital for the rich, some of whom clearly thought that there was a world after this one and that they had the right to make up any stories they liked, as long it enabled them to meet their fictitious creator with a clean slate.

'Are you all right?' Mia asked, tightening her jacket around her.
'Eh? Yes, yes.'

Mia had a smile on her lips and could barely stand still. 'So?'

'So what?' Munch grunted. 'Was he telling the truth?'

There had been no need to ask.

It was clear that Mia, in contrast to Munch, was absolutely convinced that the story they had heard was true.

Mia pulled her woolly hat further down her ears and looked anxiously at him.

'Are you really OK?'

'What? Yes, of course.' The fat investigator nodded, and chucked his cigarette on the ground.

It started to ease off. The pain from the nail in his brain. He found another cigarette, lit it and snapped out of the dark place he had been in his mind. The articulated lorry on the wrong side of the road. The look in Anette Goli's eyes in the corridor last night.

'So what are we waiting for?'

'You really believe him?'

'Why wouldn't we?'

'I don't want to play devil's advocate here.' Munch sighed. 'But it's a bit far-fetched, isn't it?'

'Oh, Holger, don't go all negative on me. I thought that was my job?'

Munch took another drag on his cigarette and smiled.

'A couple visit a vicar in the early 1970s in order to get married. Only they can't because she already has children, and he's the heir to a shipping empire, and his father doesn't want impure blood in the family.'

'Yes.' Mia nodded.

'So they send the children to Australia and get married.'

'That's right.'

'Seriously, Mia? The mother then dies in a mysterious car accident. The vicar is paid off to keep his mouth shut. Years later, the children are brought back, and this millionaire—'

'Billionaire,' Mia corrected him. 'Carl-Sigvard Simonsen.'

'OK.' Munch sighed again. 'This billionaire gives them money as compensation for their suffering? The girl buys a place where she can help other children who have had a rough childhood, just like she has. The boy buys a grocery shop? I mean, pull the other one, Mia!'

'Why not?'

'This is just another Fuglesang.'

'For God's sake, Holger.'

'Did you see him? That vicar has practically left this world already. He went to cloud cuckoo land a long time ago. We should drop this. Follow other leads.'

'Like what?' Mia demanded.

He could see that she was annoyed with him now.

'The wig,' Munch said. 'This hacker, Skunk. I don't agree with Anette. I think there might still be something there. The film. It must have come from somewhere. The tattoo. The Animal Liberation Front. This is a dead end, Mia, I mean it.'

'I've seen him,' Mia said, looking sternly at him.

'Who?'

'The brother?'

'Yes, but . . .'

'I met him. Out at Jim Fuglesang's place.'

'The bicycle-helmet guy?'

Mia nodded.

'I thought he was being pumped full of drugs at Dikemark?'

'Yes, but I went to his house anyway.'

'When?'

'Doesn't matter when,' Mia snapped. 'But he was there.'

'Who?'

Munch threw his cigarette on the ground, and was about to light yet another one when the front door opened and Curry popped his head out.

'He's awake again. Singing like a canary. I think you need to hear this.'

Munch looked at Mia. 'No, let's call it a day,' he said.

'For Christ's sake,' Mia said, despairing now.

'No,' Munch insisted, taking out his cigarettes again. 'We'll work with what we have. Team briefing at six this evening. This is a wild-goose chase.'

'Come on,' Curry urged them from the doorway. 'You've got to listen to this.'

'No,' Munch said, finding his car keys in his pocket.

'He says the brother liked dressing up as an owl,' Curry persisted.

Munch stopped in his tracks and saw Mia look at him.

'Feathers on his body. I mean, why the hell would he say that if he's just talking nonsense?'

'Holger?' Mia said.

Munch looked at her, put his car keys back in his pocket and quickly followed her up the steps.

Chapter 65

Isabella Jung was glad she had put on a warm jumper, because it was freezing cold behind the hideout. She had put on tights under her dress as well. Not so flattering, perhaps, but autumn had suddenly turned into winter, and shivering as she sat here was not a good look.

Four o'clock behind the hideout.

But it was five now, and there was still no sign of him. She pulled her sleeves over her hands, wishing she had brought a woolly hat. Normally, she didn't care about such things, how her hair looked, but it had seemed important today, so she had left her hat behind in her bedroom.

One hour late.

Not very nice. Not very gentlemanly. She started to think about her dad to pass the time. She had had an email from him not long ago. He had been to the Mediterranean. She knew what kind of trip it would have been. They would have gone there to drink; they did that sometimes, he and his friends. They'd buy plane tickets to Spain when one of them got their benefits, or won something on the horses, and they would stay down there until they had drunk up all the money. Drinking abroad was cheaper. She had learned that as a child.

During the short periods she had been allowed to live with him in Fredrikstad, she would often listen to him and his mates through the wall. They rarely argued, they would just sit and chat as they drank; at times they played music, sometimes cards. Occasionally she would hear a glass fall to the floor, or someone stumble in the passage on the way to the loo, but they never bothered her. He had been very careful with that. Anyone who went into Isabella's room was never allowed back in the house. Every morning she would tidy up, unless someone was sleeping in the living room on the sofa or on the floor; then she would stay in her room, or perhaps go outside and just wander around. But if no one was there, she would tidy up, make it nice for Dad when he woke up. It was important to be a gentleman. They talked a lot about that, through the wall. Open doors for ladies. Be polite. Be on time. Things like that.

This one was not very punctual.

At seven o'clock, she gave up. It was simply too cold. Her ears were bright red and she could barely bend her fingers. She was also starting to get cross. Why would he write that he wanted to meet her in secret and then not turn up? She knew he was at the Nurseries. She had seen him there.

The more she thought about it, the angrier she grew.

She got up from the tree stump where she had been sitting and marched resolutely through the woods. It was pitch black now, and starting to get a bit scary, but she would soon see the light from the yard ahead of her and then she would feel much safer.

She was going to confront him.

Isabella Jung might be only fifteen years old, but she had guts; she was tougher than most boys she had met. No, his behaviour was unacceptable. She would not allow herself to be treated like this.

Isabella had just reached the light from the lamp in the yard when she saw Paulus come running from the main building.

Perfect timing.

The young man with the dark curls was putting on a puffa jacket and heading in her direction.

'Where were you?' Isabella demanded to know, stopping him.

'What?' Paulus was confused.

'Why didn't you turn up?'

'Eh?' Paulus shook his head. 'I don't have time for this,' he said, trying to get past her, but she prevented him.

'What do you think you're doing, Isabella?'

'This,' Isabella said, taking the note from her pocket.

Please would you meet me? In secret.

Just you and me?

Four o'clock behind the hideout.

Are you my chosen one?

'Why didn't you turn up? Were you ever going to turn up? Or were you just having me on? Are you that kind of guy?'

'What?' Paulus said, looking even more confused.

'You didn't write this?' Isabella said, shoving the note right into his face while grabbing his puffa jacket.

'No!' Paulus declared. 'Absolutely not. What kind of guy do you think I am?'

The truth dawned on her as he stared back at her. It was not from him. She had been set up. She could feel her face grow hot, her cheeks reddening, and she quickly let go of his jacket.

'Sorry,' she said. 'I just—'

'Listen, I really don't have time for this,' Paulus said, looking as if he neither understood nor cared what she was talking about.

'Has something happened?' Isabella said.

'They've arrested Helene.'

'What!'

'And Henrik, her brother.'

'What? Why?'

'For the murder of Camilla Green,' he stuttered, looking gravely at her.

'But . . .'

'Sorry, I really have to go,' Paulus muttered, then he rushed off.

Leaving the fifteen-year-old girl all alone in the yard.

Chapter 66

Helene Eriksen was ashen-faced and so nervous that she jumped when Mia and Munch entered the small interview room.

'He hasn't done anything. You have to believe me,' she implored them, and got up from her chair.

'Hello, Helene,' Mia said. 'You should probably sit down again. We're going to be here for a while.'

'But I . . . Please, believe me. Holger?'

The normally confident manager of Hurumlandet Nurseries was a shadow of her former self. She looked almost beseechingly at Munch before slumping back in her chair and covering her face with her hands.

'It doesn't look good for either of you,' Munch said, sitting down next to Mia.

'Me?' Helene sounded frightened. 'But I haven't done anything.'

'But you think he might have?' Mia said.

'What? No, Henrik hasn't done anything either. Dear God, he's as gentle as a lamb, he would never hurt anyone. I don't care what people have been telling you, you must believe me.'

'And what have they been telling us?' Mia said calmly.

She looked at Munch, and down at the tape recorder on the side of the table, but Munch shook his head discreetly.

'Where is Henrik?' Helene asked desperately.

'Your brother is next door, waiting for his lawyer.'

'He doesn't need a lawyer,' Helene said. 'He hasn't done anything wrong, I keep telling you.'

'He definitely needs a lawyer,' Munch went on coolly. 'We have advised him to get one because, in a few hours, he'll be charged with the murder of Camilla Green. He'll be brought before a judge in order to be remanded in custody overnight.'

Helene looked at Munch again, then swiftly down at the tape recorder, but Munch shook his head again.

'No, no, no. Please believe me. He hasn't done anything.' Helene Eriksen was on the verge of tears now. 'I don't care what people might have told you. You *have* to listen to me, I'm begging you. Besides, he wasn't at home. He was—'

'And what do you think people have told us?' Mia cut her off.

The blonde woman paused, then she continued. 'The business about the feathers,' she said in a low voice. 'People can be so mean. They gossip. Why can't they just mind their own business. It makes me so mad that—'

'You could kill someone?'

'What?' Helene Eriksen said, looking at Mia. 'No, of course not. I was just—'

'Were you there? Or did you just help him cover it up?' Munch said.

'What?'

'After all, he is your brother,' Mia said. 'I mean, it's understandable. You're very close, aren't you? After everything you have been through?'

'No, when did you . . .?' Helene Eriksen stuttered. 'Of course I didn't help him.'

'So he acted alone?'

'No, Henrik hasn't done anything. Why won't you listen to me?'

'But you knew that he – well, how can I put it? – liked dressing up as a bird?'

'But that was years ago. I hate small towns, nothing but curtain twitchers. Sometimes—'

'So he has stopped?'

'Stopped what?'

'Dressing up as a bird?' Mia continued.

'Yes, for God's sake, I just told you—'

'How long ago?'

'Years, I mean, it hasn't happened since—'

'So you admit that he liked dressing up as a bird?' Munch said.

'Yes, but that was in the past. I just told you.'

Munch was aware that Mia's eyes were starting to sparkle again.

'Was this before or after you were brought back from Australia?'

Helene Eriksen grew quiet now, as if she had to travel back in her mind to a time she would rather forget.

'Not immediately after we came back,' she said quietly. 'He needed help, don't you understand? They had hurt him. It wasn't his fault. It doesn't make him a killer. Those psychos down there kept us imprisoned. They made us believe all sorts of things, punished us for the slightest offence. I'm proud of him, I am, let me tell you that.'

Helene Eriksen straightened up a little in her chair and, for a moment, they could see something of the woman they had first met at the Nurseries.

'After everything he has been through, he has done incredibly well. I'm proud of him. Not many people would survive something like that. He's the best person I know. I would do anything for him.'

'And indeed, you did,' Mia said.

'What?'

'When did you realize that he had killed Camilla?' Munch said.

'What?' Helene stammered. 'Haven't you been listening to a word I've said?'

'No, Holger,' Mia said, looking at Munch. 'That wasn't the question you were supposed to ask.'

'Oh?' Munch said, looking back at Mia Krüger rather than Helene Eriksen.

'You were supposed to ask when she began *suspecting* that her brother had done it,' Mia said.

'Right, sorry, my mistake.' Munch smiled, turning to Helene Eriksen again. 'When did you begin to suspect that Henrik had killed Camilla Green?'

'I don't know,' the blonde woman said, drumming her fingers nervously on the table. 'Are you asking about the first time, when I thought that perhaps—'

'When Henrik's name first came to mind, yes.' Munch nodded cautiously.

'It was that picture in the papers, of course. When I saw that the forest floor was covered in feathers,' Helene Eriksen said tentatively, glancing quickly up at them both. 'Well, you know. Where Camilla had been lying.'

'Because he didn't stop it immediately? I mean, after you came back from Australia?' Mia said in a friendly voice.

'What do you mean?'

'Dressing up as a bird,' Munch said.

Helene Eriksen glared at them.

'You don't recover from something like that overnight. Have you any idea how we were treated? What Henrik was subjected to? They locked him in a beaten-earth cellar. Not just once, several times. We were treated like lab rats. I mean, for God's sake, I was nearly three years old. Henrik was nearly five. When we were sent there. Do you know what we had to suffer? We thought it was how the world really was, do you understand? Is it any wonder he got ill? That he found a place inside his mind where he could escape?'

'So he carried on doing it?' Munch asked.

'Yes, and what of it? I'm incredibly proud of him. He has done so well for himself.'

'That's all very touching,' Mia Krüger said, taking out the envelope she had kept in the inside pocket of her leather jacket. 'And, under normal circumstances, I would feel very sorry for both of you.'

The dark-haired investigator opened the envelope and placed the photograph on the table in front of Helene Eriksen.

Camilla Green.

Naked on the forest floor.

With terrified, open eyes.

Mia looked at Munch again, who nodded to indicate that she should turn on the recorder.

'The time is 18.25. Present in the room is the head of the investigative unit at 13 Mariboesgate, Holger Munch, homicide investigator Mia Krüger and . . .'

Helene Eriksen's face had been almost white when they entered, but it drained of any remaining colour when she saw the photograph Mia had just placed in front of her.

'Your name, date of birth and your current address,' Mia said, pointing to the tape recorder.

Several seconds passed, and Mia had to repeat her request before the Nurseries manager was able to open her mouth.

'Helene Eriksen. 25 July 1969. Hurumlandet Nurseries, 3482 Tofte.'

The words came out slowly between the white lips, while her eyes were still unable to tear themselves away from the horrific photograph.

'You're entitled to have a lawyer present,' Mia continued. 'And if you can't afford legal advice, you'll be allocated a lawyer—'

She was interrupted by a knock on the door; Anette Goli popped her head round and nodded to Munch to indicate that he should join her outside.

'What is it?' he asked when he had closed the door behind him.

'We have a problem,' Anette Goli said. 'His lawyer is here.'

'And?'

'He was out of the country.'

'What!'

Munch frowned.

'Henrik Eriksen. He was out of the country.'

'Out of the country?' Munch echoed.

'He has a farmhouse in Italy,' Goli said. 'Spends every summer there.'

'I don't follow.'

'Henrik Eriksen. He wasn't in Norway when Camilla was murdered.'

'But that's impossible!' Munch exclaimed.

'So what do we do?' the police lawyer wanted to know.

'You and Kim,' Munch said, having considered his options.

'Seriously?'

'Standard interview. Get as much out of him as you can in, say, twenty minutes, and then we'll meet back out here.'

'OK.' Anette Goli nodded briefly as Munch opened the door and went back into the interview room.

Chapter 67

Gabriel Mørk was sitting in his office in Mariboesgate, unable to decide what kind of mood he was in. How had they even considered that he might have been involved in this?

'Gabriel?' said a voice by the door, interrupting his train of thought.

'Yes?'

'Can you spare a few minutes?' It was Ludvig Grønlie. 'I could do with a fresh pair of eyes.'

'Sure,' the young hacker said, and followed the older police officer down the corridor and into his office.

The offices were practically deserted now, had been so all day. The only other staff member left was Ylva, who was chewing gum in front of her screen. Everyone else was down at Grønland.

'What is it?' Gabriel asked, and took up position behind Grønlie's chair as Grønlie sat down.

'This film I've got,' Ludvig said.

'Right.'

'From the Natural History Museum. Did you know about that?'

'About what?' Gabriel said.

'Evidently not.' Grønlie smiled.

The older investigator double-clicked on an icon on his desktop and a black-and-white film appeared on his screen.

The film showed a group of people entering something that could be a gallery or a museum.

'What are we looking at?'

'The Botanical Gardens in Tøyen. Hurumlandet Nurseries' school trip. To the Natural History Museum.'

'Go on?' Gabriel said.

The video was jerky and blurred. Clearly, surveillance-camera footage. A group of people were met by a man with fluffy white hair and shown up some steps.

'So far so good,' Ludvig said, clicking further on.

Gabriel peered at the screen.

'Then suddenly, what do you think? Take a look at this.'

Grønlie turned to Gabriel as the group on the film entered a room with animals in different display cabinets.

'Bit odd, isn't it?'

'What is?' Gabriel said.

'Let's go back a bit,' Ludvig said, moving the cursor on the screen. 'Here,' he said, pressing the stop button. 'Do you see it now?'

Gabriel looked at the image but shook his head. 'What are you talking about?'

'Let's print it out,' the older investigator said, pressing a key on the keyboard.

Gabriel followed Grønlie into the incident room via the printer.

Ludvig put up the picture he had just printed out next to the others already hanging there. 'Pretty much everyone is on the CCTV photo, am I right?' He turned to Gabriel while he pointed at the print-out.

'Helene Eriksen. Paulus Monsen. Isabella Jung.'

Mørk followed Ludvig's finger across the picture and nodded.

'So who is this?'

Ludvig indicated a face on the picture. A face Gabriel did not recognize. A young man in a shirt, with round glasses, who, in contrast to the rest of the group, did not look at the animals on display but had his eyes fixed firmly at the camera.

'I don't think he's on our list,' Gabriel said.

'Well, that's odd,' Grønlie said.

'Look, we have everyone here, don't we? The teachers, Helene Eriksen, Monsen, the girls – but this lad?'

Gabriel looked up at the picture gallery which Ludvig had made earlier of all the residents, all the teachers, but he could not see this new face anywhere.

'And why is he looking straight at the camera?'

'That *is* weird,' Gabriel said.

'Yes, isn't it? A school trip? Everyone is looking at the animals, no matter how bored they might be, but this guy is looking at the camera as if he—'

'Is checking out where it is,' Gabriel said.

'Now, I might just be suspicious by nature, so that was why I needed a fresh pair of eyes. Does this help us?'

Gabriel continued to study the new picture on the wall. The eyes behind the glasses, looking up at him, almost surprised, while the attention of the rest of the group was directed at whatever the white-haired guy was pointing at.

'Wow,' he said, not taking his eyes off the young man in the shirt.

'He's not on our wall, is he? I mean, you can't see him, can you?'

Again Grønlie gestured towards the photographs showing every face at Hurumlandet Nurseries.

'Definitely not.'

'So I'm not losing my marbles? Starting to miss things?' Ludvig smiled at him.

'Why on earth is he looking at the camera?' Gabriel asked.

'Because he wants to know where it is.'

'Definitely,' Gabriel said, and continued to stare, almost mesmerized, at the unfamiliar face that was looking back at him.

A young man in a white shirt with round glasses.

'I'm calling Mia,' Grønlie said, running back to his office to fetch his phone.

Chapter 68

The little boy thought the new place was weird, and it took time before he grew used to it, but it got better over time. They did not have quite so many books here, but the walls were thicker, so he couldn't hear people talking about him at night, and the lady who was in charge was also quite nice. Helene. She did not look at him strangely, like people had done in the other places. She treated him like just another young person living here, because there were no small children in this home, not that it mattered. He preferred his own company anyway.

There were seven teenagers, but only one boy, Mats, and he really liked Mats. Mats reminded him a little of his mum, always talking about the terrible state of the world, and how sick people were in their heads. Mats also liked putting on make-up, not quite like Mum: he put black around his eyes, and he painted his nails with black nail polish. Mats liked everything black. He only ever wore black clothes and had posters on his walls of people playing in bands; they, too, were dressed in black, with white make-up on their faces, and bracelets with spikes. Metal. That was their music. The young boy did not say very much; he would mostly listen while Mats played music in his bedroom while he lectured him. There were many different types of metal. There was speed metal, death metal and, Mats's personal favourite, black metal. He did not think much of the music – too much howling – but he liked the stories, especially the ones about black metal. About bands sacrificing goats and having naked people crucified on stage, and lyrics about Satan and death.

When the boy had been there about a year, he felt almost at home. It was not like living with his mum, of course not, yet this place was better than the other one. They had greenhouses and he learned how to look after plants and flowers, and he liked the lessons, too; although he was younger than the other students, he was the cleverest and his teachers would often take him aside after class.

Have you finished this already?

I think we're going to have to get you some new books.

He liked all the subjects: English, Norwegian, maths, geography; every time he opened a new book it was like encountering a new world, and he could not get enough of it. The boy was especially fond of Rolf, one of the teachers there, the one who praised him the most. Rolf gave him assignments none of the other children got. He would smile broadly every time he completed them. It was Rolf who made sure he got his own laptop – not everyone had one – and for a while he could barely sleep. It was almost as if he did not need sleep, because there was so much to learn. He liked staying up all night surrounded by books and with his laptop, and he could hardly wait until he was given another assignment.

But, mostly, he liked spending time with Mats. He tried keeping clear of the girls as best he could. He was sure they were exactly like his mum had warned him girls were, smiling on the outside but dishonest and rotten on the inside, so it was best to keep his distance. Mats did not like girls either. In fact, Mats liked nothing except for metal. He loathed books, unless they were about rituals and blood and Satan and how to bring people back from the dead.

'Helene is a moron,' Mats had said to him one evening in his bedroom, but the boy thought differently.

He regarded Helene as one of the nicest people he had met since he was taken away from his mum, but he said nothing. He did not want to fall out with Mats, in case Mats would not let him come to his room again.

'But her brother, he's cool.'

'Henrik? The one with the shop?'

'Yes.' Mats had smiled.

'Why is he cool?'

'Did you know that they used to belong to a sect?'

'No,' the boy said, not entirely sure he knew what a sect was, but Mats continued to smile, so it was probably a good thing.

'In Australia,' Mats went on. 'When they were kids. A sect called The Family. They experimented on the kids. Made them think that a woman called Ann was their mum. They had to wear the same clothes and have their hair the same way. They were stuffed full of drugs – Anatensol, Haloperidol, Tofranil. Even LSD. Imagine that? Kids getting high on LSD while being locked in small, dark rooms all on their own.'

The boy, who was now becoming a teenager, did not know what those names meant, but Mats was an expert on medication; he had to take pills every day, though he did not always do so, so there was no doubt that he knew what he was talking about.

'They totally freaked out. It messed with their heads.' Mats smiled. 'Especially the brother, Henrik. He believed he was an owl.'

'An owl?'

'The bird of death.'

The boy was spellbound as Mats spoke.

About how Henrik, the brother with the shop, who seemed like a normal person, used to glue feathers to his body and perform rituals in a hideout by the fence, killing birds in order to make people come back from the dead.

'It's a long time ago, but I'm telling you it's the truth. I hear he's normal now, but for a while he was completely wacko. Just like you.'

'Like me?'

He had not understood what Mats had said.

'Yeah, like you. I mean, hello? Locked up with your mum in that house your whole life, never seeing other people? Living with a crazy bitch like her? We're so alike, you and I. You may look like a dimwit, but in your mind you're a real sicko, and I like that. Screw normality. An owl, I mean . . . He glued feathers to his body – how cool is that?'

The boy had not felt much when Mats took him out on the moors and showed him how to make people come back from the dead. They had taken a small bird from its nest and Mats had strangled it with a shoelace. Then they had placed it in a penta-gram of candles while Mats read aloud strange words from one of his books.

He had not felt very much afterwards either.

When he had killed Mats.

With a knife he had stolen from the kitchen. His reaction was more one of curiosity, the way the black kohl eyes stared up at him as the blood spilled across the dark ground.

Mats had tried to speak, but he had not been able to, just his big eyes staring up at the boy until he finally stopped moving.

'We don't talk about Mum like that.'

No emotion. Just vague curiosity. The air had stopped coming out of Mats's mouth. His eyes did not close, although he was no longer alive. Death. A bit of a let-down, really.

He didn't like to look at the bird, though.

He had carried it carefully through the woods after rolling Mats into a bog and watching as the body disappeared into the black soil, and then he had buried the bird in a beautiful place with flowers and sunlight spilling through the trees. He had made a cru-cifix from sticks – not an upside-down one, like those he had seen on the posters in Mats's bedroom, but an ordinary crucifix like the ones you saw in cemeteries – and, later that night, as he crawled under his duvet, he had felt the weight of disappointment. Because it had not worked.

He had had the same feeling a few years later.

He was in his mid-teens by then, and his teachers still praised him. Rolf was no longer there, but there were others, and they also gave him books the other teenagers could not read. He had got himself a moped and was able to drive himself anywhere he wanted to go. He had driven back to the house, of course. Back to his mum. The house had been smelly, the windows broken, and animals seemed to have been living there, so he had started to tidy up. When he was not in the classroom, or tending to the plants, he would get on his moped and, after several months, the house was starting to look nice again.

Same feeling. The bird must have been too small an animal, so he chose a cat the next time. He copied what Mats had done with the candles and the words, but still she had not come back. Then he tried with a dog but that had not worked either.

The owl. The bird of death.

He had bought glue from a shop and stolen feathers from a nearby farm where the Nurseries normally bought their eggs, from the cages where the laying hens lived. He had smeared himself with the glue, stuck the feathers on to his skin, arranged the dog's paws the way Mats had said they needed to be, at certain points in the pentagram based on sketches in his books, but it had not worked either.

That night, after the dog, he had not felt well. He had lain in his bed, unable to sleep. The dog had had nice eyes. Just like the cat. The boy continued to stare at the ceiling, and then he made up his mind. Animals – it was not their fault. His mum had been right. People were rotten. But not animals. They just lived in nature. You had to take care of animals. They had never hurt anyone.

It would have to be a person.

In order for it to work.

A dead ringer.

For his mum.

Chapter 69

Miriam Munch was standing in the street below their apartment in Oscarsgate in Frogner, realizing that she no longer knew who she was. Once, she had been a rebellious teenager with no money in the bank who had protested with her friends and clashed with police officers on horseback. These days, she lived with a doctor in an apartment in the smartest part of Oslo, whose entrance had a CCTV camera, the balcony a view of the German Embassy, and she had enough money to buy whatever she wanted. She puffed nervously on her cigarette, feeling butterflies in her tummy.

She was dressed in black. There was a balaclava in her ruck-sack. Alive. That was what she felt. Alive and part of something important. It had been a long time. Life in comfortable Frogner was certainly easy, knowing that Marion could play safely without finding used needles in the playground or be mugged on her way to school, but what about her?

What about Miriam?

She had not felt this amazing for a long time.

Miriam decided against lighting another cigarette and scouted for the car that would soon be there.

A convincing cover story?

Yes.

She had already spoken to Julie.

A break-up with some guy.

Needing a shoulder to cry on.

No problem.

Miriam decided to light another cigarette after all and had almost finished smoking it when the car she had been expecting came round the corner and pulled up in front of her. She threw aside the cigarette and smiled as she got in.

'Everything OK?' Jacob asked.

'Sure,' Miriam said. 'Where's Ziggy?'

'He got a lift with Geir. They left fifteen minutes ago.'

'Right.' Miriam nodded.

'So we're definitely doing this? Are you sure?'

'I can't wait.' She smiled and put on her seatbelt as the young man with the round glasses put the car in gear, drove down Uranienborgveien and headed for Hurumlandet.

Chapter 70

Mia Krüger put the white plastic cup into the slot, pressed the button and watched as something that was supposed to be coffee poured out of the ancient machine. It would have to do. She carried the hot plastic cup down the corridor and into the small room where Anette Goli and Kim were sitting with Munch, who was looking unusually gloomy.

'OK?' Munch said. 'Anette?'

Mia raised the cup to her lips, only to put it straight back down on the table again. The coffee tasted even worse than it looked.

'As I was saying,' Goli said, looking across to Kim Kolsø.

'Henrik Eriksen, he wasn't here,' Kim Kolsø said.

'What!' Mia exclaimed.

'Last summer. When the girl disappeared,' Kolsø explained.

Mia looked at Munch.

'He has a house in Tuscany,' Anette Goli went on. 'Goes there for three months every summer. He wasn't in Norway.'

Mia looked at Munch again, and he gave a light shrug.

'So we have nothing on him,' Kim said. 'He wasn't here. When it happened. I think—'

'But, for Pete's sake,' Mia burst out. 'The man glues feathers all over his body, he thinks he's a bird . . .'

She glanced at Munch, who merely shrugged again and pressed his hand against his temple.

'His lawyer says,' Goli continued, 'that he can produce witnesses who will confirm that he was in Italy all summer.'

'No way,' Mia said.

'He wasn't in the country. We have nothing on him.'

'But Helene Eriksen has already confirmed it? I mean, the feathers. The sect they belonged to? That he was sick in the head. Wanted to be an owl. Come on, people, I don't understand what we're—'

'He wasn't in Norway,' Anette repeated.

'Tuscany,' Kim Kolsø added.

'Well, he could just have flown back, couldn't he?'

'No, sorry,' Anette said. 'He was abroad the whole time.'

'How do we know that?' Mia challenged her.

Anette slid a piece of paper towards Munch.

The fat investigator looked at it and nodded.

'What?' Mia said.

'His phone records.' Munch sighed, pushing the paper back across the table.

'He didn't do it,' Kim Kolsø said.

'But seriously, Holger,' Mia said, ignoring the piece of paper they had now pushed towards her. 'The feathers? An owl? She admitted it!'

Munch was standing with his hands pressed against his temples now, not saying anything.

'That he was sick in the head? Come on, Holger?'

'Are you sure?' Munch said after a pause.

'One hundred per cent,' Goli replied.

'He wasn't here,' Kim insisted.

Mia felt crushed with disappointment. The phone in her pocket vibrated, as it had done a hundred times in the last hour. She took out her mobile and looked at it.

'So what do we do? Do we have to let them go?'

A long list of calls from Ludvig Grønlie. And an MMS with a picture.

Why don't you pick up your phone?

Who is this young man?

Watch his expression.

Looking at the camera.

'Yes, we have no choice,' Anette Goli said. 'We thought we might be able to keep Helene Eriksen, because she, well, *thought* that her brother might have done it, but how long do you think that will stand up?'

'OK.' Munch nodded. 'We'll release them.'

A photograph of a school group. A place Mia had visited. The Natural History Museum. Everyone looking at the guide, some animals in a display cabinet. Except for one person. A young man with round spectacles and wearing a white shirt. With curious eyes. Directed at the surveillance camera.

'So is that it?' Munch said.

'We can keep them overnight, if we like,' Goli said.

'I need a few minutes with Helene Eriksen,' Mia said.

'Why?' Munch wanted to know.

'I want to know who this is.'

She slid her mobile across to Munch, who narrowed his eyes and clutched his head again.

'What am I looking at?' he asked.

'A CCTV photo from the Natural History Museum.'

'OK,' Munch said. 'We'll keep them overnight.'

'Holger?' Anette Goli said. 'Are you all right?'

'What? Yes, yes, of course. I just need . . . A glass of water would be good,' Munch mumbled, and left the room.

The three investigators looked at each other.

'Is he ill?' Anette asked.

Kim Kolsø shrugged as Mia went out into the corridor and back to the interview room where Helene Eriksen sat slumped over the table with her head resting on her hands.

'Who is this?' Mia said, placing her mobile on the table in front of her.

'What?' Helene mumbled.

'This young man,' Mia said, pointing to the picture Ludvig had sent her.

Helene Eriksen seemed completely distracted, as if she had no idea what Mia had just asked.

'Who?'

'This boy? In the picture? Who is he?'

Helene Eriksen slowly picked up the mobile and sat staring at it, perplexed, as if she did not know why she was here.

'You went on a school trip, didn't you? To the Natural History Museum? In August?'

'How did you get this?' Helene said.

'You were there?'

'Yes? Why?'

'Who is the young man?'

Helene frowned and looked up at Mia, then back down at the picture.

'Do you mean Jacob?'

'His name is Jacob?' Mia said.

'Yes,' Helene nodded. 'But . . .?'

'Why did he go on the trip? He's not a resident, is he? And he doesn't work there either?'

'No – or, yes . . .'

'Why was his name not on the lists we were given?'

'What do you mean?'

'You were supposed to send us lists of all the residents and staff, only this boy didn't appear in either of them.'

'Jacob used to live with us,' Helene Eriksen said slowly, looking down at the picture again. 'But that was many years ago.'

'And yet he was on the school trip?'

'Yes, yes. He often visits us. Jacob was our youngest ever resident, and one of those who lived with us the longest. He's practically family. He often stops by, and we're all pleased to see him. He helps us with our computers – he doesn't want any money for it, so he's not an employee, but . . .'

'Computers? He's good with them?'

'Jacob? I should say so.' Helene Eriksen was starting to smile. 'He's a genius. A child prodigy. Incredible, really, given everything he has been through.'

'What's his full name?' Mia said, trying not to show Helene Eriksen how keen she was to know it.

'Jacob Marstrander.' Helene said, seeming confused. 'Surely you don't think that . . . ?'

Chapter 71

There was something attractive about the lights along the E18. Miriam did not quite know why, but she had always liked them; a childhood memory, she supposed, from the back of the family Volvo on the way to visit her grandparents. The warm glow from the lamps. Wheels against tarmac. Soft voices from the front. Her parents. The way they would flirt with each other with the radio in the background, always after a mild quarrel: she wanted jazz, he wanted classical. How safe she had felt in those days.

'More coffee?' Jacob said, pushing his round glasses up his nose.

'I still have some left, so no, not just now.' Miriam smiled, taking another sip from the metal cup. They had to stay awake, after all; this could take all night.

'I brought two Thermos flasks.'

He turned up the heating a little inside the car.

It was cold outside. Practically winter. But Miriam still felt warm. She leaned back against the headrest and looked up at the lights again. The naivety she had had as a child almost made her smile now; how innocent and pretty everything had been. Her mother's hands softly stroking her father's hair. The way he had smiled at her. Time without end. Childhood was like that. Every single moment would last for ever. She emptied the coffee cup and smiled to herself, a little sleepy now; with every streetlight they passed she got flashbacks to the lovely trips of the past. She had given it a great deal of thought recently, what she had been like as a teenager. She couldn't wait to grow up. Now, she realized how good her life had been back then. She smiled, and poured herself another cup of coffee from the Thermos.

'Odd, isn't it?' Jacob said.

'What is?' Miriam said, her eyes starting to close.

'Sometimes you can plan too much, and then it turns out there had been no need.'

The young man with the round glasses smiled as he looked at her, but his face was a little odd; it was almost as if Miriam could not focus on it properly.

'Do you know what I mean?'

'No, not really,' Miriam said, taking another sip of coffee.

She needed to stay alert, clear-headed. It could take time. They might have to be there all night, and she was already starting to nod off. Not good. She drank more coffee as Jacob turned to her and smiled again.

'Take the coffee, for example,' Jacob said. 'I packed Coke, Farris and bottled water, in case you didn't want coffee.'

Miriam didn't know what he was talking about. She leaned back and looked up at the lights again. They seemed even warmer and more yellow than she remembered them. Billie Holiday. Her mother always loved her singing. Miriam smiled to herself and suddenly had to concentrate to keep hold of her cup, which seemed to be slipping out between her fingers.

'But you said yes to coffee immediately, so the others were wasted.' Jacob chuckled softly, and shook his head. 'I could have spent that time doing other things, don't you see?'

Miriam looked drowsily in his direction, but his face was no longer there.

'How long until . . . we . . . get there?' she mumbled. 'Until we join . . . the others?'

It took her for ever to utter the last sentence.

'Oh, they'll have to manage without us.'

'What . . . do you mean?'

'We have more important things to do, don't we?'

The young man with the round glasses turned and smiled at her again.

But Miriam did not see it.

She was already asleep.

EIGHT

Chapter 72

Hugo Lang from Switzerland felt almost like a little kid. He was tingling all over with excitement. He had not felt anything this strongly since he saw the last girl on the screen.

The two of them together. The young woman in the basement and him. Two lonely people who had found one another. He had never felt such contentment. They were meant to be together. He had stroked her hair when she was asleep. He had smiled when she ran on the wheel – she was so good at it, making the food drop out of the dispenser – then suddenly she was gone, and his longing had been like a bottomless pit.

But now she was back. Not the same woman – well, almost the same – yet he liked her already, perhaps even more than her predecessor.

Hugo Lang smiled, and moved his chair closer to the big screen. *Miriam Munch.*

That was a strange name, had been his first reaction, but then he felt bad because the name made no difference, she was his friend, held captive just for his sake, so that he could be with her. So that they could be together – *together*. The first day, she had got on his nerves because she had done nothing. She had just sat there. Fingers trembling at the end of her thin hands, hugging her pretty body. Eyes that hardly ever closed; confused, terrified eyes that did not understand where she was. And she had cried. Tears down her pretty, white cheeks. And then this desperate banging on the door or the windows, or whatever they were, and he had not liked it. He had been in his dressing gown, there was a log fire burning in the fireplace, he had a small glass of cognac – it was unnecessary, it really was: why could they not enjoy this moment together? But in the end she had come round, and now everything was fine.

Hugo Lang smiled and trailed his hand over her cheek on the screen. He had been fond of her predecessor. But already now, after only two days, he was starting to feel that he liked this one better. Funny, really.

She had been a bad girl on the first day.

She had not understood it. How things were done. But then he had come into the cage, and after that she had done what she was told.

Run on the wheel.

Eat the food that comes out of the hole.

Hugo Lang took another sip of his cognac, and moved his leather chair even closer. Placed his hand on the screen and stroked her hair gently before pressing his lips against the screen to kiss her.

Nothing naughty, or intrusive, no, no.

Just a little peck on the cheek.

He leaned back in his chair, raised his glass in a toast and smiled to himself.

Chapter 73

Holger Munch washed down the painkillers with water from the tap and wheezed as he looked at his reflection in the mirror above the sink.

What the hell?

He splashed cold water on his face, but the pain still refused to ease. Perhaps his doctor had been right, after all. Unhealthy. Exercise more. Smoke less. Was that why he felt so bad?

The fat investigator wiped his face with the sleeve of his jumper and continued to breathe slowly in and out while he waited for the pills to work. They were taking a five-minute break in their briefing. The others were waiting for him. On edge. They all had been since this latest name had appeared.

Jacob Marstrander.

Munch had had his doubts to begin with; there had been so many false starts in this investigation, so many suspects already, but now he was sure: this was the man they were looking for.

The only problem was that Jacob Marstrander would appear to have vanished into thin air. It had been two days now, and still nothing. They had turned over his flat in Ullevålsveien, but to no avail. They had raided his office, a small one-person operation, JM Consult, but found nothing which could tell them anything about his whereabouts.

A sick bastard.

Munch stuck his head under the tap and drank more water, finally feeling the painkillers taking effect. He took a last look in the mirror, ran his hand across his face, plastered on a smile and walked calmly back into the incident room.

'OK, where were we?' he said, taking up his position by the screen. 'Ludvig?'

'Still nothing from any of the airports,' Grønlie said. 'Of course, he could have tried to get away by train, or in a car, but we have no records of anyone by that name crossing the border.'

'So he's still in Norway?'

'We don't know,' Kim Kolsø said. 'But we have alerted Interpol.'

'Good.' Munch nodded.

'And Marstrander's photograph?'

'Was distributed this morning to all the newspapers – that was what you wanted, wasn't it?' Anette Goli said.

'We all agreed, didn't we?' Munch said.

'No, not all of us,' Curry grunted.

'Leave it, please, Curry. No more.' Goli sighed.

'What?'

'We did agree,' Ludvig Grønlie interjected.

'It's stupid, that's all I'm saying,' Curry grunted again. 'It happens every time. Once you put a picture in the media, the phones won't stop ringing with calls from well-meaning idiots who think they have seen someone suspicious lurking around their garage. I mean—'

'The last time I checked, I was in charge of this unit,' Munch said sternly. 'And I gave the order to release his picture today, didn't I?'

'I know,' Curry went on. 'I just—'

'It's already on the Internet,' Ylva said, holding up her mobile.

'Good. Let's hope it pays off.'

Munch's head throbbed. He took a sip of water from the bottle on the table. 'OK, anything else?' He looked around the room. 'Where is Mia?' he said with a frown.

'I got a text message. She had something to do. She'll be here later,' Grønlie said.

'Like what?'

'She didn't say.'

'All right.' Munch sounded irritated, and had to take a moment before he continued. 'It has been two days, and no one has seen neither hide nor hair of Jacob Marstrander. That's just not good enough, people. Someone must know something. He must have been seen somewhere. Was his car registered leaving the capital?'

'There's nothing from any of the toll roads,' Kim said.

'What about his phone?'

'According to Telenor, it was last used at his home address on Friday,' Gabriel Mørk said. 'Since then, not a squeak.'

'And the computer we found in his office?'

'Completely blank,' Gabriel said.

'Seriously, guys?' Munch sighed. 'Nothing?'

'Do you want us to interview the residents at the Nurseries again?' Kim Kolsø wanted to know. 'I know we were there yesterday, but some of the girls could be hiding something?'

'It's worth a try,' Munch said. 'Will you do it?'

Kim nodded.

'That leaflet we found,' Ylva ventured cautiously.

'Yes?'

'*Stop Løken Farm*. The Animal Protection League.'

'Yes? Any luck?'

'Nothing so far, but there's something a bit odd . . .'

Munch grew impatient as his headache returned with a vengeance. 'Check it again,' he said abruptly. 'Check for any links to – what were they called again?'

'The Animal Liberation Front.'

'Yes. Good. Try again. See if we can rustle up something there. Three days, people, this isn't good enough.'

Munch took another sip of water from the bottle as his mobile vibrated on the table in front of him.

Marianne?

Munch made his excuses and quickly went out onto the balcony.

'Hello?'

'Holger?'

He could tell from her voice. Even after all these years.

That something was wrong.

'Are you there, Holger?' Her voice was trembling.

'Yes, I'm here, Marianne. What's the matter?'

He found a cigarette in his jacket pocket.

'Have you heard from Miriam?'

'What, no? Not for a few days, why?'

It grew quiet on the other end.

'It's just that . . .'

'What's the matter?' Munch said again, lighting his cigarette.

'She was supposed to pick Marion up last night, but I can't get hold of her.'

'What do you mean?'

'I've been looking after Marion . . .'

'Is Miriam away?'

'I'm not sure,' Marianne went on. 'I mean, I don't want to cause trouble, but I didn't know who else to call.'

'Of course you should call me,' Munch said.

'You don't mind?'

'Of course not, Marianne. I'm sure it's nothing,' Munch tried. 'You know what Miriam can be like—'

'She's not fifteen any more, Holger,' Marianne cut him off. 'I'm worried. She was supposed to be here last night. She lied to me, Holger.'

'What do you mean?'

'She said she was helping Julie with something, but I've called Julie, and yes, it took a little time, but it turns out it was more than that.'

'More than what?'

'A raid.'

'What are you talking about?'

'An illegal raid. She wasn't helping Julie, she just used her as an excuse.'

Munch was struggling to keep up.

'What raid is this, Marianne?'

'It took time, but I made Julie tell me in the end. She has gone back to protesting again.'

'Miriam?'

'Are you even listening to me, Holger?' Her voice was shrill now, and Munch finally was fully alert. His headache was gone.

'Calm down, Marianne,' Munch said, taking another drag on his cigarette. 'I'm sure there's nothing to worry about. We've seen this before, haven't we? It's just like her. Rebellious. You know what Miriam is like, she always has to—'

'Christ, Holger, she's missing! Are you even listening to what I'm saying?'

'Of course I'm listening to you. She joined in with a raid? What raid?'

'Animal Protection League,' Marianne said. 'Some place out in Hurum. Only she was supposed to be back last night.'

'Start from the beginning. Where was she going?'

'Julie said that something went wrong,' Marianne explained. 'So it was called off. The raid. They had agreed in advance that they would go into hiding for three days, should anything go wrong.'

'So she's in hiding?' Munch said, somewhat confused.

'No, Holger. The guy who gave Miriam a lift is the one whose picture is all over the Internet.'

'Who is?'

'The man you're looking for. From the other case.'

Far away, on the other end of the line, Marianne sounded as if her strength was running out. 'I'm scared, Holger,' Marianne whispered.

'Are you talking about Jacob Marstrander?'

'Yes,' Marianne whispered.

What the hell?

'When did you talk to Julie?'

It was impossible.

'Two minutes ago. Just now.'

How could . . .? How did . . .?

'And Julie is sure that Miriam got into his car?'

'Julie told me about him. She was scared. She thinks something must have happened. None of the others can contact him either.'

This isn't happening.

'Is Julie at home now?'

Keep your voice steady. Don't make Marianne more worried than she already is.

'Yes, in Møllergata. Do you remember where she lives?'
Miriam.
'Yes, yes, of course I remember.'
Animal Protection League.
'So will you talk to her?'
No.
'Of course, Marianne. I'm going to hang up now, so I can call her, OK? I'll talk to you very soon.'
This isn't happening.
Munch rang off and ran back to the incident room, where he was met by gawping faces.
'Curry. Kim. You're coming with me!' Munch shouted.
Two shocked faces looked back at him.
'OK?'
'The rest of you, I need everything we have about an attempt to free some animals, a raid that was allegedly planned to take place in Hurum a few days ago by the Animal Protection League. I need everything you can find. Start with Julie Vik. She's our way in. I need that information now. Yesterday.'
'What are we—' Ludvig Grønlie began, but Munch was already out of the door.

Chapter 74

Miriam Munch woke up freezing cold. She tried to make herself as tiny as possible, curling up in a foetal position, tightening the small blanket around her shivering body. She had finally managed to fall asleep, exhausted, having crawled on her hands and knees for hours, but the hunger and the cold that slipped in through the cracks in the walls had roused her from her sleep and brought her back to this nightmare. She was still in shock. She had sat in the car. Going down the E18. She had been thinking about her parents. She had been a child again. Drowsy and warm. The contrast to the room she was now in could not be greater.

A joke. That had been her first thought when the initial shock had abated. *Where was she?* An icy floor. A dark basement. *Who was messing with her?* She had not even realized the seriousness of her situation when the squeaky door had opened and the feathered creature had entered. She had thought it must be a dream. *I'm still asleep.* The terror had not come until later. To begin with, she had looked around with curiosity. Someone had built a strange room underground. She had felt very small in this dream. Like Alice in Wonderland. She had turned into a small animal. There was a big wheel in which she could run. A bottle of water on the wall with a spout from which she could drink.

No no no.

She was bound to wake up soon.

This isn't happening.

Perhaps she should try thinking positive thoughts?

Please, God.

Marion. Perhaps she should try thinking about Marion?

Help me.

Perhaps that would help her wake up?

Please.

Somebody.

Help me.

Miriam Munch narrowed her eyes and tried to keep her hunger at bay. And the nausea. She had thrown up in a corner after going on the big wheel. Her palms and knees were smarting, but she had made up her mind not to cry any more. She had tried chewing the brown pellets that had come out of the wall and which were supposed to be food. She had swallowed some, but they had come straight back up again. She refused to do this. *If only it hadn't been so cold.*

Miriam carefully moved into a sitting position. She made an attempt to stand up, and slowly got to her feet, crouching at first, then she slapped her shoulders a couple of times and began bending her stiff, aching legs to get her circulation going again.

Oh, God, she was so hungry.

Miriam could see cloudy breath coming out of her mouth as she tried blowing a little warmth on to her cold fingers.

Please, God.

She was bound to wake up soon.

Help me.

Mum. Marion. Dad.

Somebody.

Please.

Miriam jumped as the door opened and the feathered creature appeared in the doorway.

'Jacob,' she pleaded, retreating in terror to a corner of the room.

'You're not very nice,' the feather-clad young man said, aiming a pistol at her.

'Jacob, I . . .' Miriam tried again, but her voice failed her. All that came out from between her lips was a murmur which was swallowed up by the cold room.

'Shut up,' the feather-clad creature ordered her. 'Why aren't you doing anything? I've already explained to you how everything works here. And still you won't do it. You were nice for a little while, but now you don't seem to understand. Do I have to explain everything to you again?'

The young man in the feathers took a step towards her and pointed the gun at her face.

'No, please,' she stuttered, holding up her hands in front of her.

'Are you stupid or something?'

His eyes were black. He shook his head as his feathered hand tightened its hold on the gun.

'Is that why you could do it for a while, but not any more? Because you're stupid?'

'No,' she stuttered.

'It must be why, because it's not difficult. Do you think it's difficult?'

'No, no,' Miriam stammered.

'Or perhaps you think someone is on their way to save you? Maybe some of your boyfriends?'

He was grinning at her now. Glistening white teeth in the middle of his feathered face.

'Or Daddy? Your daddy in the police? Do you think he'll come to your rescue? Save his little girl?'

Miriam Munch was shaking now.

'No one is coming,' the feather-clad figure in front of her continued. 'They may be smart, but I'm much smarter. They'll never find you.'

He grinned again, chuckling across the barrel of the gun.

'I could just shoot you on the spot, but that wouldn't be any fun for the audience, would it?'

Miriam had no idea what audience he was referring to.

'This is my show. I thought of everything. Clever, don't you think? It's about being creative, putting on a decent show, something unique, something the punters are willing to pay for.'

Miriam still had no idea what he was talking about.

'You're lucky, you really are.' The feathered young man smiled, a taut smile beneath cold, soulless eyes. 'Very lucky, in fact,' he continued. 'You're a star now. People have paid millions of kroner to watch you perform. And you weren't even the chosen one.'

The young man in front of her scratched his head with the gun and chuckled to himself.

'Can you believe it? You weren't even the chosen one – the other girl got three votes. They prefer the young ones, you see, but it's *my* show. I invented it. The wheel. The writing on the wall. So *I* get to decide. I chose you because I like you. You're special. Your daddy is a policeman. Wasn't that nice of me? Not to pick the other girl, although they voted for her?'

Miriam nodded cautiously. 'Jacob . . .' she began tentatively. She felt as if she had sandpaper in her mouth.

'No, no, no,' the man with the cold eyes said, aiming the gun at her again. 'We don't talk. We just listen.'

Miriam closed her mouth and stared at the floor.

'This is the last time I'm coming down,' the young man said. 'Now, you'll do as you're told; if not, I'll have to fetch the other girl after all. It's important to give the public what they've paid for, don't you think?'

'Yes,' Miriam mumbled, without looking up.

'Do you want me to shoot you now, or will you do as you've been told?'

'I'll do it now,' Miriam whispered.

The young man with the feathers looked for a moment as if considering whether she would keep her promise, then he lowered his gun and bared his white teeth again.

'Good.'

He chortled to himself before closing the heavy door, leaving her alone in the cold, dark room.

Chapter 75

Mia could not say where the hunch had come from, but there had been something odd about the white cottage in the middle of nowhere. Ever since her previous trip out here, she had felt it beckoning her. Jim Fuglesang's house. All alone, surrounded by nothing. Frozen trees. Silence. Not the kind of silence that made her feel serene, like the peace on Hitra. Being by the sea. The cries of seagulls. This was different. Another kind of silence which made her sharpen her senses. She looked around warily as she walked from the car and up towards the white cottage. She was armed this time, and it made her more confident. She had felt naked the last time, a little frightened, and that was out of character. When she got back, she had not been able to work out what had triggered this reaction, and it had intrigued her; she knew that she had to go back, but with everything else that was going on, she had only made time for it now. Perhaps it was still not a priority, but a few hours could not hurt, and she wanted to get it done while it was still daylight.

Mia was walking towards the cottage but stopped and changed her mind; instead, she chose a small footpath leading down towards the woods. She had already been inside the house. It was not there. Whatever she was looking for.

Fourteen minutes on a good day.

Jim Fuglesang had taken pictures many years ago. Glued them into an album. A cat. And a dog. Posed in a pentagram of candles, on feather beds.

And yes, Mia was not like most people; she could not articulate her strange fascination with this place in the back of beyond, but

381

it was there, and it made it simpler for her. She could set aside her feelings. Whether or not she could explain them was irrelevant. Because Jim Fuglesang had taken pictures of crime scenes involving animals, and they were directly linked to the murder of Camilla Green. And those pictures had been taken somewhere nearby.

Sixteen minutes back.

She had formed an impression of the landscape on her last visit. There was only one road to the house, and then a path that led down towards the forest. He could have taken the pictures elsewhere, of course. Anywhere, in fact; but it was less likely. *Fourteen minutes on a good day, sixteen minutes back*. Mia was convinced that this description must fit a place familiar to the man in the white bicycle helmet. *On a good day*. He was used to the route. Back. Back had to mean home, didn't it? Fourteen minutes one way. Two minutes more the other. So downhill there. Uphill home. Mia pulled her woolly hat further down over her ears, convinced that this footpath must have been the one Fuglesang had talked about.

A path leading to a lake.

Damn it, why was she so jittery?

She was normally never scared of anything.

Four white rocks.

Mia nearly jumped when she reached a clearing among the trees and saw them at the edge of a dark lake. Four white stones, neatly positioned in front of something which might once have been a jetty, and her heart beat even faster when she saw the boat which had once been new but now lay rotting, partly submerged at the edge of the lake.

A red, wooden dinghy. With white letters at the top by the rotting gunwale.

Maria Theresa.

Mia Krüger looked up and spotted a small building a few hundred metres away. On the far side of the lake. A small house. Grey, as if all colour had been erased from its walls, its windows boarded up, uninhabited, abandoned, but even so . . .

Mia fumbled to get her mobile out of the pocket of her leather jacket.

There was smoke rising from the chimney.

Fourteen minutes on a good day.

Sixteen minutes back.

Four white rocks.

Maria Theresa.

Bingo.

Mia found Munch's number on her mobile with trembling fingers, but the small gadget refused to obey her.

No signal.

Shit.

She tried again, waving the phone in the air, walking up and down, away from the lake, then down towards the old jetty again. Still no signal. Mia muttered curses under her breath, put the phone back in her pocket, stopped and assessed the landscape, before deciding on the path to the left around the dark lake.

The abandoned house had grey, wooden walls.

Smoke rising from the chimney.

Trees refusing to let her pass.

The path ending.

Uneven terrain.

She took out her mobile again.

Still no signal.

Branches swiping her face.

Shit shit shit.

Her heart was pounding under her jacket when Mia reached the abandoned house on the far side of the lake.

Boarded-up windows.

Shut.

An old, green Volvo.

Mia crept across the small yard and peered carefully through the windows of the car. A Thermos flask. Cans of fizzy pop. A black bag. Mia carefully opened the car door, climbed across to the passenger seat. A handbag containing Kleenex, lipstick, and a purse with a driver's licence.

Mia nearly had a heart attack when she saw the face staring back at her from the driver's licence.

Miriam?

What the hell was she doing here?

Chapter 76

Miriam Munch was kneeling on the unforgiving basement floor, trying to chew the small, hard chunks that had come out of the hole in the wall. Animal feed. She had vowed never to put these vile pellets in her mouth again, but she could hold out no longer. She was so hungry. Her body was screaming for nourishment. She had almost fainted inside the big wheel, where she had to crawl on all fours to make it go round. She had blisters on the palms of her hands, and bleeding cuts to her knees. She could not go on. She needed something in her stomach, or she would die. That was how she felt. *She was going to die in this icy basement.*

Unless she had something to eat soon.

She picked up half a dozen pellets from the floor and placed them on her tongue. Tried hard not to think about what they were made of, crushed them with her teeth, pretending everything was fine. She stuck her head under the spout of the big water bottle and swallowed as best she could, and this time the pellets did not come back up. Thank God.

She put more on her tongue and repeated the process, chewing as best she could while trying to distract her mind, then drinking from the water bottle and swallowing them.

Help me.

Miriam tightened the blanket around her, and closed her eyes. She disappeared into her mind. This was not real. She was not here. She was somewhere else. She was at home. At the breakfast table. Marion had just woken up. She could smell freshly brewed coffee. Marion was sleepy. She did not want to take off her PJs. She just wanted to sit on her mum's lap. In Miriam's fantasy, there were no insects. No bugs crawling across the concrete floor. No icy gusts of a far too early winter coming through the cracks in the floorboards. There was underfloor heating. Marion wanted her hair in a ponytail. Johannes smiled at both of them. He did not have to go anywhere. Not to Australia. It was just the three of them. They were spending the whole day together. It was a day off. They were going to watch a movie and eat popcorn.

Why doesn't anyone come?

Help me.

Please.

Miriam had barely registered the door opening before the feather-clad young man appeared in front of her with his gun raised and something in his other hand.

'There has been a change of plan.'

'What?' Miriam mumbled, refusing to let the warmth from her kitchen at home disappear from her mind's eye.

'Get up,' the man said, giving her a kick to rouse her.

She slowly sat up, tightening the blanket around her more.

'There has been a change of plan,' the young man with the dark eyes repeated. 'I knew I should have gone with the other one. You're no good, and now everything is ruined.'

Miriam slowly opened her eyes and looked at him. An outstretched arm holding the gun, and something being waved in the air. A blonde wig.

'But there's still time for this,' the man with the black eyes told her. 'Try this on.'

Miriam did not know what he meant.

'Put it on, I want to see how it looks.'

'Jacob, please,' Miriam pleaded, but she did not even know if the words had passed her lips.

'Put it on,' the man sneered, thrusting the wig at her. 'I underestimated them. A photograph? Me? Can you imagine how they found that?'

'What are you talking about?' Miriam murmured, still not knowing if the words had left her lips.

'Put it on,' the feather-clad creature ordered her again.

She nodded cautiously and slipped the wig slowly over her head. The young man looked at her sideways.

'You look like her.' He smiled. 'That's good. Then it wasn't a waste after all.'

Miriam tried saying something, but she was unable to.

'Don't you worry about me,' the man said. 'I'll be fine. I admit it's a little early – after all, they've paid for three months – but that's not a problem as long as we get to do what we have to, don't you agree?'

'What . . . are you going to do to me?' Miriam stuttered, and this time she must have spoken out loud, because the feather-clad young man reacted and looked at her curiously.

'I'm going to kill you. What did you think I was going to do?'

Miriam was dumbstruck.

'I was going to wait but now that they've put my picture on the Internet, it's better that we get it done as quickly as possible, before anyone gets here.' The young man with the feathers smiled faintly. 'Come on.'

And he stroked her wig carefully. 'I've made everything ready outside.'

Chapter 77

Mia Krüger eased her way out of the Volvo and produced her gun from its arm holster. Fortunately, she had come prepared this time. She had driven out here on a hunch. Jim Fuglesang's house. The photographs. His rambling during the interview. Four white rocks. A red boat. An abandoned house across a dark lake. Jacob Marstrander's hiding place. How could it be otherwise. It had to be the place. But . . .

Miriam?

What was she doing here?

Miriam Munch?

With Jacob Marstrander?

What the hell was going on?

Mia crouched, making herself as small as possible, and moved along the side of the car, never taking her eyes off the door of the dilapidated house in front of her.

Smoke rising from the chimney. But still no sign of life inside. Mia stayed low while looking for somewhere she could get a mobile signal. A small hill. Anything. She pulled her phone out of her pocket, gripping her Glock firmly in the other hand, but nothing.

No signal.

Again she cursed all those mobile-phone providers' advertisements that filled the airwaves with their claims about unbeatable coverage. Scantily clad girls on mountain tops, smiling boys waterskiing off shore – where was the signal when she bloody needed it? She held up her phone again, but still nothing.

Damn.

She spotted an elevation not far away and quietly made her way up it, still not taking her eyes off the door to the old house.

A few more steps, and then her iPhone finally flashed. Coverage. No – signal lost again. Yes, there it was. No, crap . . .

She pressed Munch's number.

No.

Ludvig's.

Damn.

Then, suddenly, she got through.

'Grønlie speaking.'

'It's Mia,' Mia whispered. 'Can you hear me?'

'Hello?' Ludvig Grønlie said, far away.

'Can you hear me?' Mia said, as loud as she dared.

'Mia? Is that you? Are you there? Holger is—'

'Forget Holger,' Mia whispered hoarsely as Grønlie disappeared again. 'I've found Marstrander. And, for some reason, Miriam is here. You have to—'

'Hello?' Grønlie said again.

'Can you hear what I'm saying, Ludvig?'

'Are you there, Mia?'

'Yes, I bloody well am. GPS me, for Christ's sake, track my phone. I've found him. Marstrander. I'm sure of it. And for some reason—'

'Mia? I'm losing you,' Grønlie said, far away again.

'Just GPS me, Ludvig. Did you hear that? Find me. I've—'

'Hello?'

'Ludvig?'

'Are you there, Mia?

Mia swore loudly and so failed to hear the frozen heather crack behind her.

'Did you get that, Ludvig?'

'Hello, Mia . . .?'

'Find me, Ludvig. GPS me,' Mia said desperately, and managed to turn just as the feathered hand swiped through the air towards her face.

She raised her hands instinctively to protect herself. Against whatever was coming. A shadow of something. Metal against her cold fingers desperately trying to shield her head.

'Mia?'

Her phone was no longer in her hand. There was the swooshing sound of an object hurtling through the air towards her once again, with even greater force this time; she could just about make out a sneer in the shadows as her hand yielded, metal against skin and bone.

Cold.

She heard the sound.

There was someone down in the yard.

Of her fingers breaking.

Miriam.

Before the pain came.

With her hands tied.

Blood running from her temple, over her eyes, into her mouth.

Blindfolded. Wearing a blonde wig.

Her phone lay in the heather somewhere, still talking, still calling her name.

'Mia, are you there?'

Don't be scared, Miriam.

The heavy metal swiped through the air again.

I'll take care of you.

For the third time.

It'll be all right, Miriam.

But then.

For the fourth time.

She was no longer able to stay awake.

Chapter 78

A constant stream of tears was flowing down the young woman's face and Holger Munch had no idea how to make her stop crying.

Shut up.

More than anything, this was what he wanted to say.

Shut up, for God's sake, and tell me what happened.

'Julie,' Munch said calmly, smiling at the young woman. 'It's fine. Just calm down. We'll find them very soon.'

'But I didn't know,' the young woman sobbed.

'Of course, you didn't, Julie. It's not your fault, but it's important that you tell us everything you do know, OK? So if you're able, if you can manage it, do you think you can . . .? Please try to remember anything that might help us.'

Curry and Kim Kolsø looked like two question marks at the back of the room, but they wisely said nothing.

'It went wrong,' Julie sobbed, finally producing something reminiscent of a complete sentence.

'What went wrong?' Munch said, patting her hand gently.

'The entire raid,' Julie said, looking properly at him for the first time since they had arrived at her flat in Møllergata.

'So Miriam was with you?'

'What?'

'At the animal raid? She took part?'

'Yes,' the young woman nodded, glancing furtively at the two investigators leaning against the wall behind him.

'Why?' Munch said, but realized instantly that it was the wrong question.

'What do you mean?' Julie said.

'Jacob Marstrander,' Munch said in a soothing voice, patting her hand again. 'All I'm asking is how you know each other. How does Miriam know this Jacob?'

'I'm not sure what you mean?' Julie said, wiping a tear from her cheek.

'I'm just wondering,' Munch said, as patiently as he could manage, 'because I've never heard him mentioned – well, as one of her friends – and I . . .'

'Ziggy,' Julie said tentatively.

'Ziggy?' Munch asked.

'Ziggy Simonsen. Do you know him?'

'No.'

'He was the one who said that . . . well . . . he's a friend of Jacob's. You know who Ziggy is, don't you? Or maybe she hasn't said anything?'

Julie Vik looked at him now, and hesitated.

'Yes, yes . . .' Munch said.

'You don't know, do you?'

'Yes, yes, I . . .'

'She said she was going to tell you,' Julie said, wiping her face on the sleeve of her jumper. 'Did she not tell you?'

Munch glanced quickly over his shoulder at Curry and Kim Kolsø, who nodded.

A new name.

Ziggy Simonsen.

Curry took out his mobile and left the room.

'What was she going to tell me?' Munch ventured carefully, stroking the young woman's arm.

The tears had stopped now, and she looked at him almost with interest.

'About her and Ziggy?' Julie said. 'She hasn't told you?'

'No,' Munch said softly as his mobile started ringing in his pocket.

'Then I don't think I should say anything either,' the young woman said, looking down again.

'Julie,' Munch urged her.

His phone rang again.

'I don't know,' Julie said, the tears starting to flow again.

'Tell me what you know,' Munch said, more firmly than he had intended. 'Jacob and Miriam know one another. And both of them are missing. You can understand that this is important information for us, can't you?'

Another ring tone, no longer from his pocket but elsewhere in the room.

'Yes, but I . . .' The young woman looked up at him.

'Holger,' Kim said behind him, but Munch waved him away.

'Miriam and Jacob. Do you know where they are?'

'Holger,' Kim said again, but Munch ignored him.

'I just—'

'Munch,' Kim said, putting his hand on his shoulder this time.

'What?' Munch hissed irritably, as Kim Kolsø handed him his phone.

'Holger?'

Ludvig Grønlie's voice in his ear suddenly.

'What?' Munch grunted.

'Mia,' Ludvig said.

'What about her?'

'She's found them.'

'What?'

'Miriam. And Marstrander.'

'What are you saying . . .?'

'We know where they are.'

'Who?'

'Holger? Do you understand what I'm saying? We've found them.'

Munch shot to his feet. 'How?'

'Mia's mobile. She called me and asked me to GPS her; she saw them, she's found them. Holger. We have them. We have a specific location. Hurum. That's where they are, Holger. We've found them.'

'Get me a helicopter,' Munch said, already heading for the door.

'What?' Grønlie said.

'We're on our way. Get me a fucking helicopter. NOW! We'll be there in three minutes.'

Chapter 79

The pain in her hand was almost unbearable. She didn't know how long she had been unconscious.

Mia Krüger opened her eyes and staggered to her feet; she instinctively held her left arm close to her chest and tried to work out where she was. The cold. The frosty ground. Her body protested, but she forced herself upright nevertheless. Stood swaying with her head bowed while reality slowly came back to her.

Miriam.

Mia had followed Jim Fuglesang's cryptic references. The photographs. The four white stones. The red boat. Found the derelict house. And she had not realized what she had stumbled across until it was too late. Jacob Marstrander. And Miriam had been there? No mobile coverage. Too irritated by that to be careful. He had attacked from behind. Invisible blows to her head. Thank God she had managed to raise her arm.

Damn.

Mia took a step forwards but quickly learned that she was not in control. Her head tried to tell her something, but her body refused to listen. She tripped, landed on the frozen heather and felt fresh pain shoot through her. He had broken her hand. She was unable to move her arm. And her eye – she could not see out of her left eye because of the blood. She could taste blood.

Amateur.

Slowly, she got to her feet again and stood dazed and confused on the barren ground in an attempt to pull herself together.

Her gun?

Mia was on the verge of blacking out, but she was starting to remember now. The blows to her head. She had managed to protect her head with her left hand, which was why it no longer worked.

She took a few faltering steps, not knowing in which direction to move. The Glock? Had he taken her gun?

Miriam.

He had abducted her. The feather-clad young man.

What the . . .?

She tripped again, fell face first into the heather, but managed yet again to get back on her feet. She stuffed her left hand inside her jacket. *All her fingers broken.* It had shielded her against the blows. It was the reason she was still alive. How long had she been unconscious?

Mia slipped her right hand inside the lining of her trousers and pressed her eyes shut in an attempt to clear the blood. Left, no. But her right one, yes, she could see now. She knew where she was. Her Glock 17. He had taken it, he must have done, because she could not see it anywhere – but then her mood improved when she felt the metal of a barrel tucked into the waistband of her trousers.

The small one. Her Glock 26. She had been in the middle of nowhere before, she had felt vulnerable then and there was no way on earth she had been going to allow that to happen again, so she had brought two weapons this time. Mia pulled out the gun, and finally got a vague sense of where she was. The house. The car. A path leading further into the forest.

Jacob Marstrander.

Mia tucked her left hand further inside the leather jacket, suppressing the pain, and started walking in the direction she guessed they would have taken.

What the hell was Miriam doing out here?

The grey, derelict house.

The door was now wide open.

So, not inside.

The path leading to the lake.

Back to Fuglesang's house.

No.

The path.

Mia flicked off the safety catch on the Glock and gripped the gun hard, as her legs finally obeyed her brain and allowed her to walk towards the forest clearing behind the house, where the two of them were likely to have headed.

How long had she been unconscious?

A few hundred metres further on she resisted a sudden urge to throw up. Everything inside her wanted out. She had to lean against a tree.

The right way, Mia.

Just do it.

She managed to hold it in and staggered on, getting steadier with each step. They had to still be there, somewhere in the forest, his body covered in feathers, Miriam blindfolded and with her hands tied. Mia was holding the Glock in front of her, forcing her feet to carry her forward when, suddenly, she spotted them.

The clearing in between the trees.

Miriam kneeling.

In front of something . . .?

Mia could not see clearly, and yet she knew what it was.

A place of sacrifice.

Candles in a pentagram. Feathers on the ground.

No.

Mia quickly looked about her, realizing she could go no further. He would see her if she continued straight on. She made a quick decision, veered from the path and stayed close to the trees on the edge of the clearing.

An open space.

He was doing something.

She had no clothes on.

There was something around her neck.

Miriam was kneeling in the clearing, naked, with her hands tied.

Mia moved carefully between the trees to get a better look. She raised her Glock, but her hand was trembling. The barrel was pointing just as much at Miriam as at the animal in the feathers.

Shit.

What was he doing now?

She crept a little closer.

The clearing was not large. Mia looked around, finally got her brain to work enough to give her the full picture. There was the path on which she had arrived. A semicircle of trees behind which she was now hiding. On the horizon behind Miriam – Mia had to blink in order to make the perspective work –

A sheer drop.

He had built a place of sacrifice in a clearing, right on the edge of a precipice.

No.

Mia crept softly between the trees. At last, her body seemed to respond fully to her brain. Her left eye was glued shut with what she took to be blood from her head wound, but it made no difference now, because she was able to move again. Her body and her brain were working together. She made her way through the heather, each step taking her closer, as the feather-clad young man stood up, walked behind Miriam and grabbed hold of something.

Shit.

He had put a rope around her neck.

Strangled and posed in a pentagram of candles.

Mia edged her way closer. It was now or never; he would kill Miriam unless she did something. She raised the Glock up to her eye again but was still unable to see what she was aiming at.

Then, suddenly, there was a noise from the sky. The young man instinctively looked up at the clouds, a stunned expression on his face.

A chopping sound.

A helicopter.

So they had got her message after all.

They had found her.

But then.

Mia Krüger would play this movie back in her head every night in the weeks that followed.

Sweat on her pillow.

Waking with a scream.

Slow motion.

The feather-clad young man gazing in wonder at the sky, at the noise that drowned out the quiet forest. Distracted, his hands fell to his sides.

Miriam kneeling there.

Naked.

A helicopter.

The sound of rescue.

The sound of freedom.

And then she started running.

Mia raised her Glock and leapt out into the clearing.

No, no.

'Miriam!'

The man startled at the sudden change – the helicopter in the sky, Mia charging at him, her gun suddenly appearing in his hands, the Glock he had taken from her – trying to take it all in.

'Miriam!'

The film continued.

Hands tied, naked legs running, towards the sound of freedom, towards the edge of the precipice.

No, Miriam, no!

She could see the helicopter now. The young man aimed the gun at Mia, but she took no notice of the bullets slamming around her feet. She discovered a strength she did not know she possessed.

'Miriam!'

Mia raised the gun up to her right eye as she ran into the clearing. She heard the sound of the rotor blades as the mechanical animal hovered at the edge of the void.

And then she was gone.

Miriam did not even feel it.

Over the edge.

The feather-clad young man. Eyes that did not understand what was happening, as Mia finally found him in her sights and emptied the magazine into him.

'Miriam!'

White fingers letting go of the gun he was holding as he slumped to his knees on to the cold ground.

She could not see Munch's eyes, but she could sense them, the white in them, as he watched his naked daughter fall through the air.

Mia saw her last three shots find their target.

An expression in his eyes she could not quite place.

Skin behind quivering feathers.

And then he was gone.

She was barely conscious when she reached the edge of the precipice and saw the twisted, white, naked body at the bottom.

Miriam.

Mia sank to her knees, about to pass out. The gun slipped from her hands.

No.

Please.

The sound of the helicopter faded away.

And then.

Miriam.

She was no longer there.

NINE

Chapter 80

The snow came almost as if the church bells had announced it. It was the twenty-second of December, and the newspapers had written about little else for days. No white Christmas this year? But then it came, big, light flakes falling in time with the heavy toll of the funeral bells in Gamle Aker church. A funeral so near to Christmas. Mia Krüger could hardly have felt worse as she tightened her jacket around her and hurried between the gravestones towards the big church door.

They were all here. Kim. Curry. Mikkelson. Anette. Ludvig Grønlie. Dark suits. Dark coats. Dark faces. Bowed heads, small nods. She could not see Munch anywhere. He must be inside already. After all, he had been closest. He had arranged everything. The coffin. The flowers. *RIP. A last farewell from friends and colleagues.* Mia had not spoken to Munch for almost two months, but she presumed that he had made the arrangements, and as the rusty red church door opened and the mourners slowly started filing into the church, she had it confirmed. She could see his back at the front, his head bowed, right next to the white coffin covered in flowers.

The ceremony was simple, but moving. Mia had never been religious. She could not understand why anyone might need to believe in anything outside themselves, why they would come together in an old building, sit on uncomfortable seats, while a vicar spoke about how God took care of his own and welcomed everyone to His Kingdom, yet, during the short ceremony, she could not help but be moved by the beauty of the ritual. United in grief. A last farewell.

Organ music. A few words from the vicar. A eulogy from Munch, who seemed upset but looked better than she had feared.

It could have been so much worse.

She caught herself thinking this as the coffin was carried out of the church. Six men as pallbearers, Munch and Mikkelson among them.

It could have been Miriam.

She felt a little heartless as the coffin was lowered into the ground. A small gathering, mostly old colleagues, the odd face she did not recognize, but not many; he had been like that, Per Lindkvist: it was the life he had chosen. Investigator first, human being second. Seventy-five years; almost like a father to Munch. A good police officer who had sacrificed everything for the job and had found it hard to adjust to retirement, but at least he had lived the life he wanted.

It could have been much worse.

Handshakes and nods as the crowd slowly dispersed. There would be a reception later, beers and some singing at Justisen, like Lindkvist would have wanted, but Mia did not have the energy to join in.

She had known him, but not well.

A legendary police officer.

A good friend to older members of the unit.

But she was not up to it. She just wanted to go home. It was three days before Christmas. She would try to survive, try to get through it. She was here to pay her respects, but she had an ulterior motive.

Talk to Holger.

Her boss had asked for privacy after what had happened to Miriam two months earlier, and Mia, along with everyone else, had obviously respected that.

She stepped aside and did not go up to him until he was standing alone under a snow-covered tree near the coffin they had just accompanied to its final resting place.

'Hello, Holger,' she said cautiously, keeping her distance, a physical gesture as if to ask whether it would be OK if they had a few words.

'Hello, Mia.' Munch smiled, a little wearily, nodding to indicate that her presence was welcome.

'How are things?' The words coming out of her mouth felt strange, but she did not know what else to say.

'Better.'

'And Miriam?' Mia ventured tentatively.

Munch disappeared for a moment, heavy lids above red skin.

'She'll make it, but they can't say much else.'

'About what?'

Munch thought about it before he opened his mouth again.

'She can't walk yet, and they don't know if she ever will. But she has started to speak, a few words. And she recognized me yesterday.'

'Well, that's good,' Mia said, not sure if it was the right thing to say.

'Yes, isn't it?'

A period of silence followed. Delicate snowflakes fell around them.

'We've been working with Interpol, and they have caught all five of them,' Mia said. 'Everyone who bought access to the live feed. One French national. One wealthy Swiss. It ended up being a high-profile case. I don't know if you saw it – it was on CNN, prime-time in the USA. We caught everyone involved.'

'Did you now? Well, that's good,' Munch said, without appearing to have heard her.

'And Simonsen, the billionaire,' Mia went on, not sure if she should. 'I interviewed him, too. The old case from Sandefjord. When they sent the children – Helene Eriksen and her brother – to Australia. It turned out the vicar was telling the truth. Their mother seems to have been ill – mental-health issues. It was she who persuaded Simonsen to send the children away; she only wanted him for his money, you see. She died in an accident, and

I've checked with Sandefjord police, but they didn't have much about it, other than . . .'

Munch was not looking at her now. He let the cigarette burn between his fingers without smoking it, his gaze turned only inwards.

'Well, according to Simonsen, when he found out that the children weren't safe, that they had been sent to live with this sect, then he helped them with money. The Nurseries for her, a shop for him, so – well, at least the two of them were telling the truth . . .'

Munch looked down between his fingers and saw that the cigarette had burned itself out. He threw it away, fumbled in his duffel-coat pocket and placed a new cigarette between his lips.

'We won't know for a long time,' Munch said. 'But Marianne and I are hoping for the best. That's all we can do.'

He was smiling at her now, with eyes that were not quite present.

'If she can walk again?'

'I have faith. That's important, don't you think?' Munch turned to her. 'Thinking positively, I mean?'

'Of course.' Mia nodded, feeling queasy now.

'I have faith,' Munch said again.

'Let me know if there's anything I can do,' Mia said, tightening her jacket around her. 'And give her my love. Tell her that I'll be happy to visit.'

It took a few seconds. The lighter approached the tip of the cigarette without them meeting. Big fingers hanging in the air.

'I will. That's kind, Mia. Thank you for coming.'

She felt in need of a hug, but there was only a clumsy handshake for goodbye. In any case, he was no longer here. Mia pulled her hat down over her ears, tightened her jacket even more and ignored the looks she got on her way to the church gate. She had no intention of staying here a moment longer. She found the road leading to Bislett as the snow started to fall more densely.

Three days until Christmas. She had promised herself to try, but now she did not know if she could manage it. Christmas Eve. In a cold flat. Alone. Yet again. But she could not disappear. Miriam was in a bed up at Ullevål Hospital. Unable to move. Barely able to speak. She could not do that to Munch. Kill herself. Not now.

Mia crossed the street, shielding her face against the snow falling heavily now: a white Oslo, a Christmas everyone would love. With heavy footsteps, she walked down Sofiesgate and found the keys in her pocket.

Mia barely noticed her, the woman in the red puffa jacket on her doorstep, looking as if she had been standing there for a long time, just waiting for Mia to turn up, eager hands attaching something to the door handle, before she disappeared down the steps.

And was lost in the snow.

Samuel Bjork is the pen name of Norwegian novelist, playwright and singer/songwriter Frode Sander Øien. *The Owl Always Hunts at Night* is the second in his Munch and Krüger series, *I'm Travelling Alone* was the first. Both have been bestsellers across Scandinavia and the rest of Europe.